Including stories by

ROBERT SHECKLEY
DANIEL GALOUYE
LEIGH BRACKETT
RAY BRADBURY
JACK VANCE
A. E. VAN VOGT
RANDALL GARRETT
ISAAC ASIMOV

Edited by Brian W. Aldiss

Space Opera

Science Fiction from the Golden Age

Futura Publications Limited

A Futura Book

First published in Great Britain in 1974
by Weidenfeld and Nicolson
First Futura Publications edition 1974
Introduction and original material
Copyright © Brian W. Aldiss 1974

ISBN 0 8600 7058 1
Printed in Great Britain by
C. Nicholls & Company Ltd.
The Philips Park Press
Manchester.

Futura Publications Limited,
49 Poland Street,
LONDON WIA 2LG

ACKNOWLEDGEMENTS

Grateful acknowledgement is made for the use of the following material:

'Zirn Left Unguarded', by Robert Sheckley, copyright © 1972 by Robert Sheckley, reprinted by permission of A. D. Peters and Company and Harold Matson Company, Inc.

'Tonight The Sky Will Fall', by Daniel Galouye, copyright 1953 by Daniel Galouye, reprinted by permission of E. J. Carnell Literary Agency.

'The Star Of Life', by Edmond Hamilton, copyright 1947 by Edmond Hamilton, reprinted by permission of the author and the author's agents, Scott Meredith Literary Agency, Inc.

'After Ixmal', by Jeff Sutton, copyright © 1962 by Jeff Sutton, reprinted by permission of the author.

'Sea Change', by Thomas N. Scortia, copyright 1956 by Thomas N. Scortia, reprinted by permission of the author.

'Breaking Point', by James Gunn, copyright 1953 by James Gunn, reprinted by permission of the author and the author's agent, Robert P. Mills, Ltd.

'Sword of Rhiannon', by Leigh Brackett, copyright 1953 by Leigh Brackett, reprinted by permission of the author.

'All Summer In A Day', by Ray Bradbury, copyright 1954 by Fantasy House, Inc., reprinted by permission of Harold Matson Company, Inc.

'The Mitr', by Jack Vance, copyright 1953 by Jack Vance, reprinted by permission of the author.

'The Paradox Men', by Charles Harness, copyright 1949 by Charles Harness, reprinted by permission of the author and the author's agents, Scott Meredith Literary Agency, Inc.

'The Storm', by A. E. van Vogt, copyright 1943 by A. E. van Vogt, reprinted by permission of E. J. Carnell Literary Agency and Forrest J. Ackerman.

'Time Fuze', by Randall Garrett, copyright 1954 by Randall Garrett, reprinted by permission of the author and the author's agents, Scott Meredith Literary Agency, Inc.

'The Last Question', by Isaac Asimov, copyright © 1956 by Isaac Asimov, reprinted by permission of the author.

CONTENTS

Here is a quotation from one of the stories in this volume. You will come on the story by and by; meanwhile, read this . . .

A great glare lit the sky. Through the trees she saw the skyfish thunder up – higher, higher, higher. It vanished through the overcast.

There was silence along the beach: only the endless mutter of the surf.

She walked down to the water's edge, where the tide was coming in. The overcast was greying with evening.

She looked for many minutes into the sky, listening.

No sound. The damp wind blew in her face, ruffling her hair.

The style of the writing, indeed the mood expressed, is staunchly traditional. The rough farewell it depicts is, in its essence, probably a part of every human's experience since Neanderthal days. But this passage describes a spaceship leaving an alien female on a far distant planet. Only in this century has it become possible for writers to write such a scene in such a setting.

Last century, the imagination was presented with hitherto unknown places to explore.

The utilisation of steam power in the late eighteenth century engendered a growing demand for coal. The excavation of coal naturally brought carboniferous rocks to the attention of geologists.

Below the coal-bearing rocks lay other rock – red in colour and in striking contrast to the black and grey seams above. The red rock was an estimated 10,000 feet thick, and so represented a considerable period of Earth history (just as time is money, so time becomes rock).

The red rock was named the Old Red Sandstone. In it reposed fossils of what we now call the Devonian age. A considerable number of those fossils was discovered by a

7

Scot named Hugh Miller; he was one of the first among many who, by devoted work, opened up new vistas of geological time.

Gradually, the world of the past was extended, as parts of the puzzle were put together. It became populated with an extraordinary range of extinct plants and creatures, with other continents and climates. And what might otherwise have been a series of random finds received powerful intellectual cohesion from the theories of Darwin and Wallace. Above all – we are apt to forget the fact nowadays – those theories gave a *continuity* to the unrolling panorama of the past, and obliterated the old catastrophe hypotheses which had prevailed and rendered meaningless the tale of prehistory.

Directly you have seized on the principle of continuity, reinforced by a dynamic theory like evolution, it makes intellectual sense to extend the patterns of the past into the future. It is only at this stage, when Change supplants Chance, that the future can be invented; and it is no coincidence that the stage is marked by items as diverse as the growth of vast prudential and insurance companies (who can suddenly count on customers capable of planning ahead) and by the publication of H. G. Wells's novel, *The Time Machine*, which translates the message of the distant past into the distant future.

Since then, our present moment had been still further expanded in both directions. The extent of space available to the human imagination, like the extent of time, has also increased enormously since the days when Galileo Galilei looked through a telescope and found that Jupiter had four satellites and Leuwenhoek looked through his microscope and discovered his "little animals". Our imaginations have a tremendous sphere of space/time in which to wander.

It is a curious thing how marginal is the literary response to this vastly increased field of operations. Writers as diverse as Proust, Joyce, Nabokov and Durrell have conducted introverted experiments with time structure, but direct responses to the expanding imaginative universe are limited to a few works (among the most successful, I would place Thomas Hardy's *The Dynasts*, with its blindly omnipotent Immanent Will evolving towards consciousness, Olaf

8

Stapledon's *Star Maker*, and perhaps George Bernard Shaw's plays such as *Man and Superman* and *Back to Methuselah*).

The most enthusiastic response to the new expanses has come from a field of literature known as science fiction. However naively and crudely – and at times it is neither naive nor crude – science fiction does seek to explore and humanise limits which would otherwise exist only tenuously as mathematical concepts. In this way, science fiction is itself part of the opening-up operation of science. The science fiction writers who have achieved most acclaim and respect have been those who took the Word into the Unknown, among them Arthur C. Clarke, Ray Bradbury, and Kurt Vonnegut Jnr.

Science fiction is a big muscular horny creature, with a mass of bristling antennae and proprioceptors on its skull. It has a small sister, a gentle creature with red lips and a dash of stardust in her hair. Her name is Space Opera. This volume is dedicated to her.

Science fiction is for real. Space opera is for fun. Generally.

What space opera does is take a few light years and a pinch of reality and inflate thoroughly with melodrama, dreams, and a seasoning of screwy ideas.

Even in the period when magazine science fiction was a despised genre, existing without the aid of outside critics and chroniclers, it contained within it a renegade sub-genre: space opera. Space opera was heady, escapist stuff, charging on without overmuch regard for logic or literacy, while often throwing off great images, excitements, and aspirations. Nowadays – rather like grand opera – it is considered to be in decline, and is in the hands of imitators, or else has evolved into sword-and-sorcery.

Since science fiction is undergoing a massive critical reappraisal, it seems time for a fresh look at space opera. The rewards are many. There is, for instance, the pleasure of being able to rattle round the solar system and beyond without the aid of NASA, often in spaceships as big as cathedrals. About some of the more hectic examples lingers an aroma of high camp. Nostalgia aside, the stories are one of the repositories of narrative art; furthermore, they say a great deal about fundamental hopes and fears when confronted by the unknowns of distant frontiers, in a tradition stretching back at least as far as *The Odyssey*. They are, in their way, abstracts of the same impulses that lie behind traditional fairy tales.

I resist the temptation to define space opera. I had enough trouble defining the term "science fiction" when writing my history of sf, *Billion Year Spree*. The term is both vague and inspired, and must have been coined with affection and some scorn, analogously with soap opera and horse opera. And, analagously with opera itself, space opera has certain conventions which are essential to it, which are, in a way, its *raison d'être*; one may either like or dislike those conventions, but they cannot be altered except at expense to the whole. Ideally, the Earth must be in peril, there must be a quest and a man to match the mighty hour. That man must confront aliens and exotic creatures. Space must flow past the ports like wine from a pitcher. Blood must run down the palace steps, and ships launch out into the louring dark. There must be a woman fairer than the skies and a villain darker than a Black Hole. And all must come right in the end.

This is not a serious anthology. It and succeeding volumes burst with voluptuous vacuum. They have been put together to amuse. And the current success of reprintings of old sf swashbuckle by such originators as Edgar Rice Burroughs and E. E. "Doc" Smith shows how many people now turn eagerly to the artful comfort of this kind of writing. Here is the menace of many kinds of galactic awfulness, of science and genetics running amok; here too are the gorgeous princesses, the desperate quests, doomed worlds, sundry exotic creatures, deadly weapons, and the snicker of sword-blades – all of which can be defended down to the last "Aaarrrgh!" Here is the future in space, seen mistily through the eyes of yesterday.

My search has been, in the main, for stories which will be unfamiliar to most readers. Too many science fiction anthologies today are content to include stories which have already been reprinted many times. My principle has been to search out old and often scarce sources, and to choose authors who, in many cases, should be better known than they are, although I have been unable to resist my Bradburys, van Vogts, Asimovs and Sheckleys. Sources range from the year 1900 to last year.

Each story is preceded by a blurb. In order to sustain the atmosphere, I have used the original blurbs wherever possible, reprinted from the magazine in which the story first appeared.

Brian W. Aldiss

Heath House
Southmoor
September 1973

SECTION I

IS EVERYTHING AN ILLUSION . . . ?

13

Listen to this: it describes what space opera is all about!

"At night, when human discords and harmonies are hushed, in a general sense, for the greater part of twelve hours, there is nothing to moderate the blow with which the infinitely great, the stellar universe, strikes down upon the infinitely little, the mind of the beholder; and this was the case now. Having got closer to immensity than their fellow creatures, they saw at once its beauty and its frightfulness. They more and more felt the contrast between their own tiny magnitudes and those among which they had recklessly plunged, till they were oppressed with the presence of a vastness they could not cope with as an idea, and which hung about them like a nightmare."

Beauty and frightfulness, vastness and nightmare . . . All essential ingredients of space opera. The quotation, in fact, comes from *Two on a Tower*, a novel by one of the great Victorian novelists, Thomas Hardy. Hardy says of his novel that it was "the outcome of a wish to set the emotional history of two infinitesimal lives against the stupendous background of the stellar universe". A similar impulse must have moved many writers of space opera.

But there is another fundamental element in space opera, and that is escapism. Whatever else it may or may not be, it does not take place in the here-and-now, but rather in one of the wild blue yonders of space, time, and eternity.

Essentially, space opera was born of the pulp magazines, flourished there, and died there. It is still being written, but in the main by authors who owe their inspiration and impetus to the pulps. I have avoided those authors – they can speak for themselves – and have based this anthology on vanished stories archaeologised from vanished magazines – another form of escapism, possibly.

Almost the only exception to this self-made rule lies in the story which opens this first section, "Zirn Left Unguarded . . ." This recent loving parody by Robert Sheckley epitomises the tenor and content of space opera. Here are the strange races, here the moods of bitter-sweet regret. Sheckley puts us in the right humour to suffer all that is to follow.

And what follows in this first section is intended to underline further the outstanding characteristics of the genre.

After the most recent piece of writing in the book comes the oldest. George Griffith's "Honeymoon in Space" was published serially in *Pearson's Magazine* in the year 1900. The Earl of Redgrave, Rollo Lenox Smeaton Aubrey, has married the charming American lady, Lilla Zaidie; they honeymoon round the solar system in the *Astronef*, which utilises an anti-gravitational force and is stoked by an old Yorkshire engineer called Murgatroyd. Here is an account of their landing on Venus, the Love-Star, and how "Home, Sweet Home" came to be sung there. Things on Venus were never to be so peaceful again.

Without wasting further time, Donald Wandrei takes us out to the true domain of space opera, far beyond the bounds of the solar system, far beyond the present day, with all its minor hopes and fears. I came across this story as a small boy, when I was given – it was one of those volumes which, like the *Complete Short Stories of Saki*, made *All the Difference – Modern Tales of Horror*, selected by Dashiell Hammett, a splendid collection. *The hope of the universe had lain with the Red Brain . . .* It is just the thing one wants to hear while being persecuted by parents, schoolmasters, and elder brothers.

In one of the longest contributions, Daniel Galouye reminds us that space opera does not necessarily have to be set in another galaxy – provided that it includes a menace bigger than any galaxy.

"*That thing – that intellect within you – is the only thing that really exists. Nothing else exists. Not even space. Not even time. Not even matter. Only that intellect – that intangible, bodiless power of reasoning is real! That and that alone is the universe – the entire universe! . . .*"

Come in Bishop Berkeley, all is forgiven!

16

Galouye begins with a superbly paranoid situation, and concludes with thumping melodrama. "Tonight the Sky Must Fall" is, incidentally, one of this author's early stories; he has since written several successful novels, among them two pictures of nightmare universes, *Dark Universe*, and *Counterfeit World*. In those novels, as in this long story, he leaves us with the disturbing thought which seems to hang also in the air of the burning Jenghik Palace in Sheckley's tale: Is everything an illusion? There is a noble tradition of great and epical adventure in science fiction. Beginning, perhaps, with Edgar Rice Burroughs, it continues through the wide screen space opera epics of E. E. Smith, PhD., on through Jack Williamson, and even the young John W. Campbell, Jr. Lately it has been christened "sword and sorcery", but this is just the most recent protean form the the continuing epic tradition has taken. I record this all historically because here, that exceedingly fine writer and wielder of a mordant typewriter, Robert Sheckley, has finished off the up until now endless saga, written *finis* to those mighty tomes, killed the entire literature dead. Read on – if you dare!

ZIRN LEFT UNGUARDED, THE JENGHIK PALACE IN FLAMES, JON WESTERLEY DEAD

by Robert Sheckley

The bulletin came through blurred with fear. "Somebody is dancing on our graves," said Charleroi. His gaze lifted to include the entire Earth. "This will make a fine mausoleum."

"Your words are strange," she said. "Yet there is that in your manner which I find pleasing . . . Come closer, stranger, and explain yourself."

I stepped back and withdrew my sword from its scabbard. Beside me, I heard a metallic hiss; Ocpetis Marn had drawn his sword, too, and now he stood with me, back to back, as the Megenth horde approached.

"Now shall we sell our lives dearly, Jon Westerley," said Ocpetis Marn in the peculiar guttural hiss of the Mnerian race.

"Indeed we shall," I replied. "And there will be some more than one widow to dance the Passagekeen before this day is through."

He nodded. "And some disconsolate fathers will make the lonely sacrifice to the God of Deteriorations."

We smiled at each other's staunch words. Yet it was no laughing matter. The Megenth bucks advanced slowly, implacably, across the green and purple moss-sward. They had drawn their *raftii* – those long, curved, double-pointed dirks that had struck terror in the innermost recesses of the civilized galaxy. We waited.

The first blade crossed mine. I parried and thrust, catching the big fellow full in the throat. He reeled back, and I set myself for my next antagonist.

Two of them came at me this time. I could hear the sharp intake of Ocpetis's breath as he hacked and hewed with his sword. The situation was utterly hopeless.

I thought of the unprecedented combination of circumstances that had brought me to this situation. I thought of the Cities of the Terran Plurality, whose very existence depended upon the foredoomed outcome of this present

18

impasse. I thought of autumn in Carcassone, hazy mornings in Saskatoon, steel-coloured rain falling on the Black Hills. Was all this to pass? Surely not. And yet – why not?

We said to the computer: "These are the factors, this is our predicament. Do us the favour of solving our problem and saving our lives and the lives of all Earth."

The computer computed. It said: "The problem cannot be solved."

"Then how are we to go about saving Earth from destruction?"

"You don't," the computer told us.

We left sadly. But then Jenkins said, "What the hell – that was only one computer's opinion."

That cheered us up. We held our heads high. We decided to take further consultations.

The gypsy turned the card. It came up Final Judgement. We left sadly. Then Myers said, "What the hell – that's only one gypsy's opinion."

That cheered us up. We held our heads high. We decided to take further consultations.

You said it yourself: " 'A bright blossom of blood on his forehead.' You looked at me with strange eyes. Must I love you?"

It all began so suddenly. The reptilian forces of Megenth, long quiescent, suddenly began to expand due to the serum given them by Charles Engstrom, the power-crazed telepath. Jon Westerley was hastily recalled from his secret mission to Angos II. Westerley had the supreme misfortune of materializing within a ring of Black Force, due to the inadvertent treachery of Ocpetis Marn, his faithful Mnerian companion, who had, unknown to Westerley, been trapped in the Hall of Floating Mirrors, and his mind taken over by the renegade Santhis, leader of the Entropy Guild. That was the end for Westerley, and the beginning of the end for us.

The old man was in a stupor. I unstrapped him from the smouldering control chair and caught the characteristic

19

sweet-salty-sour odour of manginee – that insidious narcotic grown only in the caverns of Ingidor – whose influence had subverted our guardposts along the Wall Star Belt.

I shook him roughly. "Preston!" I cried. "For the sake of Earth, for Magda, for everything you hold dear – tell me what happened."

His eyes rolled. His mouth twitched. With vast effort he said, "Zirn! Zirn is lost, is lost, is lost!"

His head lolled forward. Death rearranged his face.

Zirn lost! My brain worked furiously. That meant that the High Star Pass was open, the negative accumulators no longer functioning, the drone soldiers overwhelmed. Zirn was a wound through which our life-blood would pour. But surely there was a way out?

President Edgars looked at the cerulean telephone. He had been warned never to use it except in the direst emergency, and perhaps not even then. But surely the present situation justified? . . . He lifted the telephone.

"Paradise Reception, Miss Ophelia speaking."

"This is President Edgars of Earth. I must speak to God immediately."

"God is out of his office just now and cannot be reached. May I be of service?"

"Well, you see," Edgars said, "I have this really bad emergency on my hands. I mean, it looks like the end of everything."

"Everything?" Miss Ophelia asked.

"Well, not *literally* everything. But it does mean the destruction of us. Of Earth and all that. If you could just bring this to God's attention – "

"Since God is omniscient, I'm sure he knows all about it."

"I'm sure he does. But I thought that if I could just speak to him personally – "

"I'm afraid that is not possible at this time. But you could leave a message. God is very good and very fair, and I'm sure he will consider your problem and do what is right and godly. He's wonderful, you know. I love God."

"We all do," Edgars said sadly.

"Is there anything else?"

20

"No. Yes! May I speak with Mr. Joseph J. Edgars, please?"

"Who is that?"

"My father. He died ten years ago."

"I'm sorry, sir. That is not permitted."

"Can you at least tell me if he's up there with you people?"

"Sorry, we are not allowed to give out that information."

"Well, can you tell me if *anybody* is up there? I mean, is there really an afterlife? Or is it maybe only you and God up there? Or maybe only you?"

"For information concerning the afterlife," Miss Ophelia said, "kindly contact your nearest priest, minister, rabbi, mullah, or anyone else on the accredited list of God representatives. Thank you for calling."

There was a sweet tinkle of chimes. Then the line went dead.

"What did the Big Fellow say?" asked General Muller.

"All I got was double-talk from his secretary."

"Personally, I don't believe in superstitions like God," General Muller said. "Even if they happen to be true, I find it healthier not to believe. Shall we get on with it?"

They got on with it.

Testimony of the robot who might have been Dr. Zach:

"My true identity is a mystery to me, and one which, under the circumstances, I do not expect to be resolved. But I was at the Jenghik Palace. I saw the Megenth warriors swarm over the crimson balustrades, overturn the candelabra, smash, kill, destroy. The governor died with a sword in his hand. The Terran Guard made their last stand in the Dolorous Keep, and perished to a man after mighty blows given and received. The ladies of the court defended themselves with daggers so small as to appear symbolic. They were granted quick passage. I saw the great fire consume the bronze eagles of Earth. The subject peoples had long fled. I watched the Jenghik Palace – that great pile, marking the furthest extent of Earth's suzerainty, topple soundlessly into the dust from which it sprung. And I knew then that all was lost, and that the fate of Terra – of which planet I consider myself a loyal son, despite the fact that I was

21

(presumably) crafted rather than created, produced rather than born – the fate of divine Terra, I say, was to be annihilated utterly, until not even the ghost of a memory remained.

"You said it yourself: 'A star exploded in his eye.' This last day I must love you. The rumours are heavy tonight, and the sky is red. I love it when you turn your head just so. Perhaps it is true that we are chaff between the iron jaws of life and death. Still, I prefer to keep time by my own watch. So I fly in the face of the evidence. I fly with you.

"It is the end, I love you, it is the end."

THE END

Theirs was the perfect marriage, so it was natural to spend their honeymoon on the Love Planet. Then they heard the rustle of angelic wings...

HONEYMOON IN SPACE

by George Griffith

While Zaidie was talking the *Astronef* was sweeping swiftly down towards the surface of Venus, through scenery of whose almost inconceivable magnificence no human words could convey any adequate idea. Underneath the cloud-veil the air was absolutely clear and transparent, clearer, indeed, than terrestrial air at the highest elevations reached by mountain-climbers, and, moreover, it seemed to be endowed with a strange, luminous quality, which made objects, no matter how distant, stand out with almost startling distinctness.

The rivers and lakes and seas which spread out beneath them, seemed never to have been ruffled by blast of storm or breath of wind, and their surfaces shone with a soft, silvery light, which seemed to come from below rather than from above.

"If this isn't heaven it must be the half-way house," said Redgrave, with what was, perhaps under the circumstances, a pardonable irreverence. "Still, after all, we don't know what the inhabitants may be like, so I think we'd better close the doors, and drop on the top of that mountain-spur running out between the two rivers into the bay. Do you notice how curious the water looks after the Earth seas; bright silver, instead of blue and green?"

"Oh, it's just lovely," said Zaidie. "Let's go down and have a walk. There's nothing to be afraid of. You'll never make me believe that a world like this can be inhabited by anything dangerous."

"Perhaps, but we mustn't forget what happened on Mars, *Madonna mia*. Still, there's one thing, we haven't been tackled by any aerial fleets yet."

"I don't think the people here want air-ships. They can fly themselves. Look! there are a lot of them coming to meet us. That was a rather wicked remark of yours, Lenox.

23

about the half-way house to heaven; but those certainly do look something like angels."

As Zaidie said this, after a somewhat lengthy pause, during which the *Astronef* had descended to within a few hundred feet of the mountain-spur, she handed her field-glasses to her husband, and pointed downwards towards an island which lay a couple of miles or so off the end of the spur.

He put the glasses to his eyes, and took a long look through them. Moving them slowly up and down, and from side to side, he saw hundreds of winged figures rising from the island and floating towards them.

"You were right, dear," he said, without taking the glass from his eyes, "and so was I. If those aren't angels, they're certainly something like men, and, I suppose, women too who can fly. We may as well stop here and wait for them. I wonder what sort of an animal they take the *Astronef* for."

He sent a message down the tube to Murgatroyd and gave a turn and a half to the steering-wheel. The propellers slowed down and the *Astronef* dropped with a hardly-perceptible shock in the midst of a little plateau covered with a thick, soft moss of a pale yellowish green, and fringed by a belt of trees which seemed to be over three hundred feet high, and whose foliage was a deep golden bronze.

They had scarcely landed before the flying figures re-appeared over the tree tops and swept downwards in long spiral curves towards the *Astronef*.

"If they're not angels, they're very like them," said Zaidie, putting down her glasses.

"There's one thing, they fly a lot better than the old masters' angels or Doré's could have done, because they have tails – or at least something that seems to serve the same purpose, and yet they haven't got feathers."

"Yes, they have, at least round the edges of their wings or whatever they are, and they've got clothes, too, silk tunics or something of that sort – and there are men and women."

"You're quite right, those fringes down their legs are feathers, and that's how they can fly. They seem to have four arms."

The flying figures which came hovering near to the *Astronef*, without evincing any apparent sign of fear, were

24

the strangest that human eyes had looked upon. In some respects they had a sufficient resemblance for them to be taken for winged men and women, while in another they bore a decided resemblance to birds. Their bodies and limbs were human in shape, but of slenderer and lighter build; and from the shoulder-blades and muscles of the back there sprang a second pair of arms arching up above their heads. Between these and the lower arms, and continued from them down the side to the ankles, there appeared to be a flexible membrane covered with a light feathery down, pure white on the inside, but on the back a brilliant golden yellow, deepening to bronze towards the edges, round which ran a deep feathery fringe.

The body was covered in front and down the back between the wings with a sort of divided tunic of a light, silken-looking material, which must have been clothing, since there were many different colours all more or less of different hue among them. Below this and attached to the inner sides of the leg from the knee downward, was another membrane which reached down to the heels, and it was this which Redgrave somewhat flippantly alluded to as a tail. Its obvious purpose was to maintain the longitudinal balance when flying.

In stature the inhabitants of the Love-Star varied from about five feet six to five feet, but both the taller and the shorter of them were all of nearly the same size, from which it was easy to conclude that this difference in stature was on Venus as well as on the Earth, one of the broad distinctions between the sexes.

They flew round the *Astronef* with an exquisite ease and grace which made Zaidie exclaim:

"Now, why weren't we made like that on Earth?"

To which Redgrave, after a look at the barometer, replied:

"Partly, I suppose, because we weren't built that way, and partly because we don't live in an atmosphere about two and a half times as dense as ours."

Then several of the winged figures alighted on the mossy covering of the plain and walked towards the vessel.

"Why, they walk just like us, only much more prettily!" said Zaidie. "And look what funny little faces they've got!

25

Half bird, half human, and soft, downy feathers instead of hair. I wonder whether they talk or sing. I wish you'd open the doors again, Lenox. I'm sure they can't possibly mean us any harm; they are far too pretty for that. What lovely soft eyes they have, and what a thousand pities it is we shan't be able to understand them."

They had left the conning-tower, and both his lordship and Murgatroyd were throwing open the sliding-doors and, to Zaidie's considerable displeasure, getting the deck Maxims ready for action in case they should be required. As soon as the doors were open Zaidie's judgment of the inhabitants of Venus was entirely justified.

Without the slightest sign of fear, but with very evident astonishment in their round golden-yellow eyes, they came walking close up to the sides of the *Astronef*. Some of them stroked her smooth, shining sides with their little hands, which Zaidie now found had only three fingers and a thumb. Many ages before they might have been birds' claws, but now they were soft and pink and plump, utterly strange to manual work as it is understood upon Earth.

"Just fancy getting Maxim guns ready to shoot those delightful things," said Zaidie, almost indignantly, as she went towards the doorway from which the gangway ladder ran down to the soft, mossy turf. "Why, not one of them has got a weapon of any sort; and just listen," she went on, stopping in the opening of the doorway, "have you ever heard music like that on Earth? I haven't. I suppose it's the way they talk. I'd give a good deal to be able to understand them. But still, it's very lovely, isn't it?"

"Ay, like the voices of syrens," said Murgatroyd, speaking for the first time since the *Astronef* had landed; for this big, grizzled, taciturn Yorkshireman, who looked upon the whole cruise through Space as a mad and almost impious adventure, which nothing but his hereditary loyalty to his master's name and family could have persuaded him to share in, had grown more and more silent as the millions of miles between the *Astronef* and his native Yorkshire village had multiplied day by day.

"Syrens – and why not, Andrew?" laughed Redgrave. "At any rate, I don't think they look likely to lure us and the *Astronef* to destruction." Then he went on: "Yes, Zaidie, I never heard anything like that before. Unearthly, of course it is, but then we're not on Earth. Now, Zaidie, they seem to talk in song-language. You did pretty well on Mars with your American, suppose we go out and show them that you can speak the song-language, too."

"What do you mean?" she said; "sing them something?"

"Yes," he replied; "they'll try to talk to you in song, and you won't be able to understand them; at least, not as far as words and sentences go. But music is the universal language on Earth, and there's no reason why it shouldn't be the same through the Solar System. Come along, tune up, little woman!"

They went together down the gangway stairs, he dressed in an ordinary suit of grey, English tweed, with a golf cap on the back of his head, and she in the last and daintiest of costumes which the art of Paris and London and New York had produced before the *Astronef* soared up from far-off Washington.

The moment that she set foot on the golden-yellow sward she was surrounded by a swarm of the winged, and yet strangely human creatures. Those nearest to her came and touched her hands and face, and stroked the folds of her dress. Others looked into her violet-blue eyes, and others put out their queer little hands and stroked her hair.

This and her clothing seemed to be the most wonderful experience for them, saving always the fact that she had only two arms and no wings. Redgrave kept close beside her until he was satisfied that these exquisite inhabitants of the new-found fairy-land were innocent of any intention of harm, and when he saw two of the winged daughters of the Love-Star put up their hands and touch the thick coils of her hair, he said:

"Take those pins and things out and let it down. They seem to think that your hair's part of your head. It's the first chance you've had to work a miracle, so you may as well do it. Show them the most beautiful thing they've ever seen."

"What babies you men can be when you get sentimental!" laughed Zaidie, as she put her hands up to her head. "How do you know that this may not be ugly in their eyes?"

"Quite impossible!" he replied. "They're a great deal too pretty themselves to think *you* ugly. Let it down!"

While he was speaking Zaidie had taken off a Spanish mantilla which she had thrown over her head as she came out, and which the ladies of Venus seemed to think was part of her hair. Then she took out the comb and one or two hairpins which kept the coils in position, deftly caught the ends, and then, after a few rapid movements of her fingers, she shook her head, and the wondering crowd about her saw, what seemed to them a shimmering veil, half gold, half silver, in the soft reflected light from the cloud-veil, fall down from her head over her shoulders.

They crowded still more closely round her, but so quietly and so gently that she felt nothing more than the touch of wondering hands on her arms, and dress, and hair. As Redgrave said afterwards, he was "absolutely out of it." They seemed to imagine him to be a kind of uncouth monster, possibly the slave of this radiant being which had come so strangely from somewhere beyond the cloud-veil. They looked at him with their golden-yellow eyes wide open, and some of them came up rather timidly and touched his clothes, which they seemed to think were his skin.

Then one or two, more daring, put their little hands up to his face and touched his moustache, and all of them, while both examinations were going on, kept up a running conversation of cooing and singing which evidently conveyed their ideas from one to the other on the subject of this most marvellous visit of these two strange beings with neither wings nor feathers, but who, most undoubtedly, had other means of flying, since it was quite certain that they had come from another world.

Their ordinary speech was a low crooning note, like the language in which doves converse, mingled with a twittering current of undertone. But every moment it rose into higher notes, evidently expressing wonder or admiration, or both.

"You were right about the universal language," said Redgrave, when he had submitted to the stroking process for a few moments. "These people talk in music, and, as far as I can see or hear, their opinion of us, or, at least, of you, is distinctly flattering. I don't know what they take *me* for, and I don't care, but as we'd better make friends with them suppose you sing them 'Home, Sweet Home', or the 'Swanee River'. I shouldn't wonder if they consider our talking voices most horrible discords, so you might as well give them something different."

While he was speaking the sounds about them suddenly hushed, and, as Redgrave said afterwards, it was something like the silence that follows a cannon shot. Then, in the midst of the hush, Zaidie put her hands behind her, looked up towards the luminous silver surface which formed the only visible sky of Venus, and began to sing "The Swanee River".

The clear, sweet notes rang up through the midst of a sudden silence. The sons and daughters of the Love-Star instantly ceased their own soft musical conversation, and Zaidie sang the old plantation song through for the first time that a human voice had sung it to ears other than human.

As the last note thrilled sweetly from her lips she looked round at the crowd of queer half-human shapes about her, and something in their unlikeness to her own kind brought back to her mind the familiar scenes which lay so far away, so many millions of miles across the dark and silent Ocean of Space.

Other winged figures, attracted by the sound of her singing, had crossed the trees, and these, during the silence which came after the singing of the song, were swiftly followed by others, until there were nearly a thousand of them gathered about the side of the *Astronef*.

There was no crowding or jostling among them. Each one treated every other with the most perfect gentleness and courtesy. No such thing as enmity or ill-feeling seemed to exist among them, and, in perfect silence, they waited for Zaidie to continue what they thought was her long speech of greeting. The temper of the throng somehow coincided exactly with the mood which her own memories had brought to her, and the next moment she sent the first line of "Home, Sweet Home" soaring up to the cloud-veiled sky.

As the notes rang up into the still, soft air, a deeper hush fell on the listening throng. Heads were bowed with a gesture almost of adoration, and many of those standing nearest to her bent their bodies forward, and expanded their wings, bringing them together over their breasts with a motion which, as they afterwards learnt, was intended to convey the

29

idea of wonder and admiration, mingled with something like a sentiment of worship.

Zaidie sang the sweet old song through from end to end, forgetting for the time being everything but the home she had left behind her on the banks of the Hudson. As the last notes left her lips, she turned round to Redgrave and looked at him with eyes dim with the first tears that had filled them since her father's death, and said, as he caught hold of her outstretched hand:

"I believe they've understood every word of it."

"Or, at any rate, every note. You may be quite certain of that," he replied. "If you had done that on Mars it might have been even more effective than the Maxim."

"For goodness sake don't talk about things like that in a heaven like this! Oh, listen! They've got the tune already!"

It was true! The dwellers of the Love-Star, whose speech was song, had instantly recognised the sweetness of the sweetest of all earthly songs. They had, of course, no idea of the meaning of the words; but the music spoke to them and told them that this fair visitant from another world could speak the same speech as theirs. Every note and cadence was repeated with absolute fidelity, and so the speech, common to the two far-distant worlds, became a link connecting this wandering son and daughter of the Earth with the sons and daughters of the Love-Star.

The throng fell back a little and two figures, apparently male and female, came to Zaidie and held out their right hands and began addressing her in perfectly harmonised song, which, though utterly unintelligible to her in the sense of speech, expressed sentiments which could not possibly be mistaken, as there was a faint suggestion of the old English song running through the little song-speech that they made, and both Zaidie and her husband rightly concluded that it was intended to convey a welcome to the strangers from beyond the cloud-veil.

THE END

Close at hand lay the heat death of the universe. Could cold intellect stay it, or –

THE RED BRAIN

by Donald Wandrei

One by one the pale stars in the sky overhead had twinkled fainter and gone out. One by one those flaming lights had dimmed and darkened. One by one they had vanished forever, and in their places had come patches of ink that blotted out immense areas of a sky once luminous with stars.

Years had passed; centuries had fled backward; the accumulating thousands had turned into millions, and they, too, had faded into the oblivion of eternity. The earth had disappeared. The sun had cooled and hardened, and had dissolved into the dust of its grave. The solar system and innumerable other systems had broken up and vanished, and their fragments had swelled the clouds of dust which were engulfing the entire universe. In the billions of years which had passed, sweeping everything on toward the gathering doom, the huge bodies, once countless, that had dotted the sky and hurtled through unmeasurable immensities of Space had lessened in number and disintegrated until the black pall of the sky was broken only at rare intervals by dim spots of light – light ever growing paler and darker.

No one knew when the dust had begun to gather, but far back in the forgotten dawn of time the dead worlds had vanished, unremembered and unmourned.

Those were the nuclei of the dust. Those were the progenitors of the universal dissolution which now approached its completion. Those were the stars which had first burned out, died, and wasted away in myriads of atoms. Those were the mushroom growths which had first passed into nothingness in a puff of dust.

Slowly the faint wisps had gathered into clouds, the clouds into seas, and the seas into monstrous oceans of gently heaving dust, dust that drifted from dead and dying worlds, from interstellar collisions of plunging stars, from rushing

31

meteors and streaming comets which flamed from the void and hurtled into the abyss.

The dust had spread and spread. The dim luminosity of the heavens had become fainter as great blots of black appeared far in the outer depths of Space. In all the millions and billions and trillions of years that had fled into the past, the cosmic dust had been gathering, and the starry horde had been dwindling. There was a time when the universe consisted of hundreds of millions of stars, planets, and suns; but they were ephemeral as life or dreams, and they faded and vanished, one by one.

The smaller worlds were obliterated first, then the larger, and so in ever-ascending steps to the unchecked giants which roared their fury and blazed their whiteness through the conquering dust and the realms of night. Never did the Cosmic Dust cease its hellish and relentless war on the universe; it choked the little aerolites; it swallowed the helpless satellites; it swirled around the leaping comets that rocketed from one black end of the universe to the other, flaming their trailing splendour, tearing paths of wild adventure through horizonless infinitudes the dust already ruled; it clawed at the planets and sucked their very being; it washed, hateful and brooding, about the monarchs and plucked at their lands and deserts.

Thicker, thicker, always thicker grew the Cosmic Dust until the giants no longer could watch each other's gyres far across the void. Instead, they thundered through the waste. lonely, despairing, and lost. In solitary grandeur they burned their brilliant beauty. In solitary defeat and death they disappeared.

Of all the stars in all the countless host that once had spotted the heavens, there remained only Antares. Antares, immensest of the stars, alone was left, the last body in the universe, inhabited by the last race ever to have consciousness, ever to live. That race, in hopeless compassion, had watched the darkening skies and had counted with miserly care the stars which resisted. Every one that twinkled out wrenched their hearts; everyone that ceased to struggle and was swallowed by the tides of dust added a new strain to the national anthem, that indescribable melody, that infinitely sombre paean of doom which tolled a solemn harmony in every heart of the dying race. The dwellers had built a great crystal dome around their world in order to keep out the dust and to keep in the atmosphere, and under this dome the watchers kept their silent sentinel. The shadows had swept in faster and faster from the farther realms of darkness, engulfing more rapidly the last of the stars. The astronomers' task had become easier, but the saddest on Antares: that of watching Death and Oblivion spread a pall of blackness over all that was, all that would be.

The last star, Mira, second only to Antares, had shone frostily pale, twinkled more darkly – and vanished. There was nothing in all Space except an illimitable expanse of dust that stretched on and on in every direction; only this, and Antares. No longer did the astronomers watch the heavens to glimpse again that dying star before it succumbed. No longer did they scan the upper reaches – everywhere swirled the dust, enshrouding Space with a choking blackness. Once there had been sown through the abyss a multitude of morbidly beautiful stars, whitely shining, wan – now there was none. Once there had been light in the sky – now there was none. Once there had been a dim phosphorescence in the vault – now it was a heavy-hanging pall of ebony, a rayless realm of gloom, a smothering thing of blackness eternal and infinite.

"We meet again in this Hall of the Mist, not in the hope that a remedy has been found, but that we find how best it is fitting that we die. We meet, not in the vain hope that we may control the dust, but in the hope that we may triumph even as we are obliterated. We cannot win the struggle, save in meeting our death heroically."

The speaker paused. All around him towered a hall of Space rampant. Far above spread a vague roof whose flowing sides melted into the lost and dreamy distances, a roof supported by unseen walls and by the mighty pillars which rolled upward at long intervals from the smoothly marbled floor. A faint haze seemed always to be hanging in the air because of the measureless lengths of that architectural colossus. Dim in the distance, the speaker reclined on a metal dais raised above the sea of beings in front of him. But he was not, in reality, a speaker, nor was he a being such as those which had inhabited the world called Earth.

Evolution, because of the unusual conditions on Antares, had proceeded along lines utterly different from those followed on the various bodies which had dotted the heavens when the deep was sprinkled with stars in the years now gone. Antares was the hugest sun that had leaped from the primeval chaos. When it cooled, it cooled far more slowly than the others, and when life once began it was assured of an existence not of thousands, not of millions, but of billions of years.

That life, when it began, had passed from the simple forms to the age of land juggernauts, and so by steps on and on up the scale. The civilizations of other worlds had reached their apex and the worlds themselves become cold and lifeless at the time when the mighty civilization of Antares was beginning. The star had then passed through a period of warfare until such terrific and fearful scourges of destruction were produced that in the Two Days War seven billion of the eight and one-half billion inhabitants were slaughtered. Those two days of carnage ended war for eons.

From then on, the golden age began. The minds of the people of Antares became bigger and bigger, their bodies proportionately smaller, until the cycle eventually was completed. Every being in front of the speaker was a monstrous heap of black viscidity, each mass an enormous brain, a sexless thing that lived for Thought. Long ago it had been discovered that life could be created artificially in tissue formed in the laboratories of the chemists. Sex was thus destroyed, and the inhabitants no longer spent their time in taking care of families. Nearly all the countless hours that were saved were put into scientific advance, with the result that the star leaped forward in an age of progress never paralleled.

The beings, rapidly becoming Brains, found that by the extermination of the parasites and bacteria on Antares, by changing their own organic structure, and by *willing* to live, they approached immortality. They discovered the secrets of Time and Space; they knew the extent of the universe, and how Space in its farther reaches became self-annihilating They knew that life was self-created and controlled its own period of duration. They knew that when a life, tired of existence, killed itself, it was dead forever; it could not live again, for death was the final chemical change of life.

These were the shapes that spread in the vast sea before the speaker. They were shapes because they could assume any form they wished. Their all-powerful minds had complete control of that which was themselves. When the Brains were desirous of travelling, they relaxed from their usual semi-rigidity and flowed from place to place like a stream of ink rushing down a hill; when they were tired, they flattened into disks; when expounding their thoughts, they became towering pillars of rigid ooze; and when lost in abstraction, or in a pleasurable contemplation of the unbounded worlds created in their minds, within which they often wandered, they resembled huge, dormant balls.

From the speaker himself had come no sound although he had imparted his thoughts to his sentient assembly. The thoughts of the Brains, when their minds permitted, emanated to those about them instantly, like electric waves. Antares was a world of unbroken silence.

The Great Brain's thoughts continued to flow out. "Long ago, the approaching doom became known to us all. We could do nothing. It does not matter greatly, of course, for existence is a useless thing which benefits no one. But nevertheless, at that meeting in an unremembered year, we asked those who were willing to try to think of some possible way of saving our own star, at least, if not the others. There was no reward offered, for there was no reward adequate. All that the Brain would receive would be glory as one of the greatest which has ever been produced. The rest of us, too, would receive only the effects of that glory in the knowledge that we had conquered Fate, hitherto, and still, considered inexorable; we would derive pleasure only from the fact that we, self-creating and all but supreme, had made ourselves supreme by conquering the most powerful menace which has ever attacked life, time, and the universe: the Cosmic Dust.

"Our most intelligent Brains have been thinking on this one subject for untold millions of years. They have excluded from their thoughts everything except the question: How can the dust be checked? They have produced innumerable plans which have been tested thoroughly. All have failed. We have hurled into the void uncontrollable

35

bolts of lightning, interplanetary sheets of flame, in the hope that we might fuse masses of the dust into new, incandescent worlds. We have anchored huge magnets throughout Space, hoping to attract the dust, which is faintly magnetic, and thus to solidify it or clear much of it from the waste. We have caused fearful disturbances by exploding our most powerful compounds in the realms about us, hoping to set the dust so violently in motion that the chaos would become tempestuous with the storms of creation. With our rays of annihilation, we have blasted billion-mile paths through the ceaselessly surging dust. We have destroyed the life on Betelgeuse and rooted there titanic developers of vacua, sprawling, whirring machines to suck the dust from Space and heap it up on that star. We have liberated enormous quantities of gas, lit them, and sent the hot and furious fires madly flashing through the affrighted dust. In our desperation, we have even asked for the aid of the Ether-Eaters. Yes, we have in finality exercised our Will-Power to sweep back the rolling billows! In vain! What has been accomplished? The dust has retreated for a moment, has paused – and has welled onward. It has returned silently triumphant, and it has again hung its pall of blackness over a fear-haunted, nightmare-ridden Space."

Swelling in soundless sorrow through the Hall of the Mist rose the racing thoughts of the Great Brain. "Our chemists with a bitter doggedness never before displayed have devoted their time to the production of Super-Brains, in the hope of making one which could defeat the Cosmic Dust. They have changed the chemicals used in our genesis; they have experimented with moulds and forms; they have tried every resource. With what result? There have come forth raging monstrosities, mad abominations, satanic horrors and ravenous foul things howling wildly the nameless and indescribable phantoms that thronged their minds. We have killed them in order to save ourselves. And the Dust has pushed onward! We have appealed to every living Brain to help us. We appealed, in the forgotten, dream-veiled centuries, for aid in any form. From time to time we have been offered plans, which for a while have made terrific inroads on the Dust, but plans which have always failed.

"The triumph of the Cosmic Dust has almost come. There is so little time left us that our efforts now must inevitably be futile. But today, in the hope that some Brain, either of the old ones or of the gigantic new ones, has discovered a possibility not yet tried, we have called this conference, the first in more than twelve thousand years."

The tense, alert silence of the hall relaxed and became soft when the thoughts of the Great Brain had stopped flowing. The electric waves which had filled the vast Hall of the Mist sank, and for a long time a strange tranquillity brooded there. But the mass was never still; the sea in front of the dais rippled and billowed from time to time as waves of thought passed through it. Yet no Brain offered to speak, and the seething expanse, as the minutes crept by, again became quiet.

In a thin column on the dais, rising high into the air, swayed the Great Brain; again and again it swept its glance around the hall, peering among the rolling, heaving shapes in the hope of finding somewhere in those thousands one which could offer a suggestion. But the minutes passed, and time lengthened, with no response; and the sadness of the fixed and changeless end crept across the last race. And the Brains, wrapped in their meditation, saw the Dust pushing at the glass shell of Antares with triumphant mockery.

The Great Brain had expected no reply, since for centuries it had been considered futile to combat the Dust; and so, when its expectation, though not its wish, was fulfilled, it relaxed and dropped, the signal that the meeting was over.

But the motion had scarcely been completed, when from deep within the centre of the sea there came a violent heave; in a moment, a section collected itself and rushed together; like a waterspout it swished upward and went streaming toward the roof until it swayed thin and tenuous as a column of smoke, the top of the Brain peering down from the dimness of the upper hall.

"I have found an infallible plan! The Red Brain has conquered the Cosmic Dust!"

A terrific tenseness leaped upon the Brains, numbed by the cry that wavered in silence down the Hall of the Mist into the empty and dreamless tomb of the farther marble. The Great Brain, hardly relaxed, rose again. And with a curious whirling motion the assembled horde suddenly revolved. Immediately, the Red Brain hung upward from the middle of a sea which had become an amphitheatre in arrangement, all Brains looking toward the centre. A suppressed expectancy and hope electrified the air.

The Red Brain was one of the later creations of the chemists, and had come forth during the experiments to produce more perfect Brains. Previously, they had all been black; but, perhaps because of impurities in the chemicals, this one had evolved in an extremely dark, dull-red colour. It was regarded with wonder by its companions, and more so when they found that many of its thoughts could not be grasped by them. What it allowed the others to know of what passed within it was to a large extent incomprehensible. No one knew how to judge the Red Brain, but much had been expected from it.

Thus, when the Red Brain sent forth its announcement, the others formed a huge circle around, their minds passive and open for the explanation. Thus they lay, silent, while awaiting the discovery. And thus they reclined, completely unprepared for what followed.

For, as the Red Brain hung in the air, it began a slow but restless swaying; and as it swayed, its thoughts poured out in a rhythmic chant. High above them it towered, a smooth, slender column, whose lofty end was moving ever faster and faster while nervous shudders rippled up and down its length. And the alien chant became stronger, stronger, until it changed into a wild and dithyrambic paean to the beauty of the past, to the glory of the present, to the splendour of the future. And the lay became a moaning praise, an exaltation; a strain of furious joy ran through it, a repetition of, "The Red Brain has conquered the Dust. Others have failed, but he has not. Play the national anthem in honour of the Red Brain, for he has triumphed. Place him at your head, for he has conquered the Dust. Exalt him who has proved himself the greatest of all. Worship him who is greater than Antares, greater than the Cosmic Dust, greater than the Universe."

Abruptly it stopped. The puzzled Brains looked up. The Red Brain had ceased its nodding motion for a moment, and had closed its thoughts to them. But along its entire length it began a gyratory spinning, until it whirled at an incredible speed. Something antagonistic suddenly emanated from it. And before the Brains could grasp the situation, before they could protect themselves by closing their minds, the will-impulses of the Red Brain, laden with hatred and death, were throbbing about them and entering their open minds. Like a whirlwind spun the Red Brain, hurtling forth its hate. Like half-inflated balloons the other Brains had lain around it; like cooling glass bubbles they tautened for a second; and like pricked balloons, as their thoughts and thus their lives were annihilated, since Thought was Life, they flattened, instantaneously, dissolving into pools of evanescent slime. By tens and by hundreds they sank, destroyed by the sweeping, unchecked thoughts of the Red Brain which filled the hall; by groups, by sections, by paths around the whole circle fell the doomed Brains in that single moment of carelessness, while pools of thick ink collected, flowed together, crept onward, and became rivers of pitch rushing down the marble floor with a soft, silken swish.

The hope of the universe had lain with the Red Brain.

And the Red Brain was mad.

THE END

I think, therefore I am . . . but suppose I don't think? Am I *not*? And what about you *and it*?

TONIGHT THE SKY WILL FALL

by Daniel F. Galouye

"I'm being followed," Tarl Brent said suddenly as he guided the girl safely to the kerb. "I'm certain, Maud," he insisted. "I wouldn't say it if I didn't know for sure."

The girl frowned until a honking horn quieted, then she drew closer to his side on the crowded sidewalk.

"Fiddlesticks!" she said, pursing her lips. "*You* being followed! That's ridiculous!"

But he quickened their pace through the noonday crowd and glanced to the left, focusing his eyes on a mirrored store column that permitted a reflected view of the area to his rear.

"Why should anyone want to follow you?" Maud glanced around uncertainly.

"I'd bet the week's payroll," he replied, ignoring the question and continuing to stare into the mirror, "that it's that man in the brown hat and pinstripe suit . . . Wait!" He tightened his grip on the girl's arm. "Don't turn around now!"

They had passed the front of the store and the advantage of the reflecting surface was no longer his. "We'll find out in a minute," he said.

The girl laughed chidingly, "I'd still be interested in knowing why you believe someone is trailing you."

"You've been my secretary long enough," he reminded her, "to know something about me. My being shadowed is just another one of the personal mysteries I've got to solve."

"Mysteries?" Maud cocked an eyebrow.

"That's right – mysteries. All the 'whys' I've got to find answers for . . . You know yourself, Maud, that only three years ago I was nothing. And look where I am now – close to my first million."

"But – there's no mystery about that. You got your start in business after you inherited a hundred thousand dollars from . . ."

"From a relative I never knew," he completed the sentence. "I still seriously doubt that any such person existed."

They waited at the next traffic intersection until the light changed. He looked over his shoulder again. Then they crossed the street.

"And you can't say I achieved success because of a preponderance of brains," he offered. "You know as well as I how much luck had to do with everything . . . I would have dropped over fifty thousand on the market just last week if our brokers hadn't made an error in jotting down instructions."

"Nice error," the girl laughed. "Brought you a profit of thirty thousand, didn't it? Why worry about anything like that, though? I wouldn't give it a thought, as long as the luck doesn't start getting *bad*."

Sidestepping an elderly woman, Tarl steered his secretary diagonally across the sidewalk toward the table-studded and umbrellaed patio of a restaurant.

"But, Maud," he protested, "every darn thing that's happened to me in the past three years *has* been luck. It's . . ."

He released the girl's arm, giving her a gentle shove in the direction of the entrance to the Patio. "Go in," he whispered, "and grab a table."

"Tarl!" Maud exclaimed. "What are you going to do?"

"I'm going to collar that guy who's been following us and find out what this is all about!" He turned abruptly and left.

"Wait!" she shouted, but he disappeared in a group of shoppers.

He strode only a short distance and spotted the man again. An expression of surprise spread over the latter's face. Tarl almost had his hand on the man's shoulder when a spectacled, elderly man, carrying several packages, emerged from a doorway. Tarl and the older man collided and crashed to the sidewalk. The third man wheeled hastily and dashed around the corner.

Leaping to his feet, Tarl felt the spectacled man on the sidewalk grasp his trouser cuff.

"You might at least help me up after knocking me down, young fellow!" the elderly gentleman said angrily, maintaining a surprisingly strong grip on Tarl's trousers.

Tarl looked down at the man, cast a futile glance in the direction of the corner and sighed. "It's too late now."

"What's that you said?"

41

"Oh, never mind, grandpa." Tarl helped the other to his feet.

Maud was still disturbed when he returned to the patio. "What happened?" she asked.

"He got away." He sat down beside her. "I'm sure of it, Maud. That man *was* following me."

The girl laughed and picked up a newspaper a former diner had left on a chair. "Here's something more interesting to talk about. It says here that: 'Physicists Establish New Speed of Light' . . ."

"Why do you suppose someone is so vitally interested in what I'm doing?" Tarl pinched his chin and stared into space.

" 'At least three renowned United States physicists,' " she continued reading from the paper, " 'today confirmed Dr. Randel Steffington's new estimate of the speed of light, which the Washington scientist established in his laboratory yesterday.

" 'The three scientists, at the conclusion of separate experiments, agreed light travels at one hundred and two thousand, three hundred and one and one-tenth miles per second, some eighty-four thousand miles a second slower than was previously supposed . . .' "

He laughed suddenly. "Okay, you win."

A waiter appeared and took their orders. Minutes passed as he sat in silence, his secretary studying the lines in his face.

"Look, Tarl," she said finally. "If you're going to brood, I won't try to keep you from discussing the matter . . . Let's have it."

His eyes grew thoughtful. "I'm not just imagining there's something mysterious going on." He crossed his arms and leaned on the table. "I began to suspect it when I was travelling to New York after I'd been informed of the inheritance. I had no money and was hopping rails on the way over . . . Almost didn't get here. There was that little whistle stop incident, where the train pulled on a siding and I got in an argument with a couple of drunks in the rail-yard.

"It wouldn't have taken them a minute to take care of me with those broken beer bottles. They were closing in, swinging, when three other bums appeared from around a boxcar.

I didn't have to strike a blow. Those three laid the others out cold. But I didn't get a chance to thank them; they disappeared too fast.

"Ever since then, things have happened that way ... Always somebody appearing from nowhere to hold on to my arm when it looked like I might step into a stream of traffic ... If I go out on the yacht and the water gets a little choppy, boats spring up from nowhere ...

"But all the unrelated incidents didn't make sense until I started putting them together a few weeks ago. Now I see they all fit into a pattern – of someone or some group trying their best to protect me in every conceivable way. Physically, economically, any way you can think of ...

"Know what made me realize that, Maud?" he asked suddenly.

The girl shook her head.

"You remember it. The papers carried it last month."

"Oh, you mean the hold up?"

"That's right ... It was in front of my home. My chauffeur and I got out of the car at the same time. This guy appeared from behind the hedge and pulled a revolver. Before he got through saying 'This is a stick-up', guns started firing all around the place ...

"Police counted twenty-six slugs in his body. Who fired those shots? Why, if for no other reason than to protect me? Why couldn't the men be found?"

Tarl's chair jarred lightly as it was struck by a chair from the table behind him. The man sitting in the chair had risen abruptly and disappeared into the restaurant proper.

Another man took his place. Maud's eyes met the newcomer's momentarily. Then she returned her attention to Tarl.

In an unpretentious building halfway across town, an office telephone rang on the fifth floor. A gaunt, middle-aged man with a dispassionate face answered the ring.

"Yes?"

"Headquarters?"

"Yes, this is headquarters ... Chief Director speaking."

"M-3 reporting."

"You've been properly relieved?"

"Of course . . . But, let's sidetrack formalities, T.J. This is serious . . . He is even more suspicious than he was yesterday. Charles, his chauffeur, and his secretary . . ."

"Never mention any member of the project by name or relationship," T.J. admonished curtly.

"Well, S-14 and B-1 were right when they reported that he showed an increasing tendency to question the work of headquarters' agents as being natural occurrences. I gather he's completely aware of the fact he is under constant surveillance. It seems he tried to run down . . ."

"Yes, we know. T-22 reported five minutes ago. The attempt was unsuccessful, thanks to F-5's quick thinking."

M-3 spoke rapidly, unhesitatingly. A telephone-wire recorder hooked to the line imprinted the agent's words on tape for the file. His words constituted an account of Tarl's conversation at the patio table.

T.J. interrupted him only once – when he mentioned the secretary's quoting from the newspaper. "Did he react at the mention of the speed of light ?"

"No. But I think B-1 ought to be cautioned further against the use of trigger language – if, as you say, there's a possibility of responsive action."

"She will be reminded," T.J. assured.

"Shall I take my post again ?" M-3 inquired.

"Of course not! You know you can have no more than one assignment a month."

"Then I'm through for the day ?"

"Through for as long as it takes you to get back here and get your nose in the files for the next thirty days."

T.J. leaned back in his chair. He pressed several buttons on the table. Three men entered the room a moment later. They took chairs around the table.

After staring at each in turn T.J. announced, "It's getting worse!"

The three looked worried. One of them asked, "What can we do, T.J.?"

"I don't know." The Chief Director toyed with a pencil. "But there'll be a directors' meeting this afternoon." He looked at his watch – "Within the next hour."

"Chances are," another said, "we've been too vigilant. We're defeating our own purpose, T.J., if we let him find out.

His suspicions might bring out just what we had hoped to suppress!"

"You think that announcement yesterday by Steffington might have triggered?" the agent on T.J.'s right asked nervously.

"No," the Chief Director assured. "We had a check on that just a few minutes ago. At least, there are no *apparent* conscious response to the 'light speed' stimulus ... As a matter of fact, there wasn't any conscious reaction to any of the scientific announcements during the past three years. It's a good thing his mind – his conscious, rather – isn't inclined toward any of the sciences."

The third man at the table mopped his brow erratically with a handkerchief.

"It'd be all over," he said, "if he ever found out he's responsible for all those startling iconoclastic discoveries ..."

T.J. cut him short. "Don't forget – he's responsible for all but the first, even though he doesn't know it. *We* are responsible for the initial one – indirectly. Of course, he caused it, but it was our prompting that was indirectly to blame."

The fourth man, who hadn't spoken until then, said hesitatingly, "I wonder whether everything would have been all right if we just hadn't tried to verify the supposition – if we'd just taken it for granted that what we suspected was true and hadn't tried to experiment by triggering the initial response?"

T.J. held up a hand protestingly. "Well, that's all in the past now. Too late to do anything. It's true – it was our test that resulted in the 'unexplained' disappearance of the planet Mercury. We know the planet didn't fall into the Sun while at apogee. We know it was just dematerialised ... But, we learned beyond a doubt what was lurking in the back of Brent's subconscious."

The agent opposite T.J. began perspiring again. "If only we had left him alone! If only we hadn't doped him and allowed Mendel to ..."

"Dr. Mendel," T.J. interrupted, "is the best psychiatrist in the world. The test stimulus was administered perfectly. Brent was in one of the most complete somnambulistic states I've ever seen. The suggestion reached his subconscious – beyond his subconscious," T.J. shuddered, "and

45

elicited the proving response. Post-hypnotic suggestions worked smoothly, judging from all reports we received. Brent never even remembered the incidents leading to his doping. I don't think anyone else besides Mendel . . ."

"Am I being discussed?" A bass voice sounded from the direction of the open door. A tall, sharp-featured man stood there.

"Ah! Dr. Mendel!" T.J. rose, crossed to the door and accompanied the doctor to a chair at the table.

"We're calling a directors' meeting," T.J. said, after Mendel had made himself comfortable.

"Then you think the situation is that serious?"

"Brent is becoming increasingly suspicious." T.J. drummed his fingers on the table-top. "We were just discussing the possibility of something having gone wrong."

"I was saying," the man on the director's right said, "that something *must* have been miscalculated . . . unprovoked responses have cropped up almost periodically since we started this project – *expressly to prevent such responses!* True, we had hoped there would be only the initial response. But others followed. And now they're getting closer together . . . I tell you, that *thing* is stirring! What about the disappearance of the common cold a year ago – ?"

"Why, that was . . ." T.J. broke in.

"And there's the matter of the newly established distance of the Earth from the Sun." The agent ignored the interruption. "And the unanticipated discovery of three elements that defy assignment to the periodic table. The disproof of Avogardo's Hypothesis . . . That's too many milestones at once. I tell you the *thing* is stirring!"

"If it's stirring to the extent that it can't be stopped and lulled back into inactivity, then there isn't very much we can do, is there?" T.J. patted his hand lightly on the table.

The other three men twisted their heads slowly, staring at one another.

Dr. Mendel rose, walked to the window and stared pensively into the busy street below.

"Gentlemen," he said, "have you ever relaxed long enough to consider the tremendous unlimited power we are toying with? If it could only be harnessed . . . Imagine

46

having all the energy that ever existed in the universe at your disposal!''

The doctor turned slowly and faced the men at the desk. His eyes, however, were not focussed on anything in the room. His voice was muted: "If there were only some way that power could be controlled – turned free under control for utilisation ... why, nothing would be impossible – *nothing*!'' He raised his voice alarmingly.

T.J. cleared his throat. "I would shudder even to think along those lines,'' he said reprovingly. "The fate of humanity depends on our being able to imprison that power so it can be applied in no other way than a natural one.''

"But, T.J.,'' Dr. Mendel turned to the Director. "The power is already being released. A planet's gone. An entire universe of micro-organisms responsible for a disease has been snuffed out. Another manifestation occurs, and we find that astronomers have been all wet for the past two hundred years – that the Earth is actually closer to the Sun; that the Sun's heat isn't as intense as we thought it was ... I am convinced there'll be other manifestations. Perhaps we should abandon our present course. Maybe we should arouse *it* to consciousness and attempt communication ...''

"No, Mendel.'' T.J. shook his head dourly. "That is our last recourse ... Anyway, I believe there is still hope for our original plan of action. We must allay Brent's suspicions. Have our agents relax their vigilance a bit. And I have another plan ...''

The four men stared at him, waiting.

"... We've overlooked one main factor until now ... we have made no concerted effort to introduce affection into his environment. Brent is still sentimentally unattached.''

"But,'' Mendel frowned, "I thought Maud, I mean B-1 ...''

"No, there's nothing there.'' T.J. shook his head. "If anything had developed between them it would have been accidental – not planned. I believe that if we find a personality that appeals to him and a physical type that will attract him, then his conscious and subconscious will become preoccupied again – perhaps lulling into complete lethargy the *thing* ...''

T.J. rose from his swivel chair. The three visiting directors

47

accepted the move as signifying the conference's end and left the room. T.J. turned to Mendel.

"At any rate, we'll thrash it all out within the next two hours. In the meantime, we'll put as many workers as we can spare on the files, digging out anything that might throw light on his preferences in women."

A jostling crowd hurried along the sidewalk in the descending darkness. Tarl, his topcoat thrown over an arm. stood impatiently behind the glass doors of his office building's lobby, waiting for his chauffeur.

A flash of chrome and black metal rolled into place in front of the building. Charles' angular, stout and friendly face framed itself in the window on the right of the automobile. He reached over the seat and released the latch on the rear door.

Tarl, pulling his hat brim lower and striding out of the building, collided with a girl who had been walking at a brisk pace. The force of the blow drew a sharp cry from her lips and she clutched at Tarl's overcoat as she sprawled on the sidewalk. He managed to keep his balance. Her small, inverted ice-cream cone-shaped hat was knocked to one side and dangled precariously over her brow, concealing one eye. Tufts of lustrous red hair fell to the shoulders of her trim suit and blended with the peach complexion of her cheeks.

The girl's full skirt had been swept upward as she fell. Its hem lay neatly across her legs, midway between knees and hips, revealing firm shapely calves and thighs. She sat there a moment, surprised – a startled expression on her attractive face.

"Whew!" she exclaimed, arranging her hat as Tarl helped her to her feet. "That was some blow!"

"I'm awfully sorry," he said earnestly. "I don't . . ."

"Oh, don't apologise," she smiled. "It was probably all my fault."

Traces of a frown appeared on his forehead, as he suddenly considered mentally the coincidental aspect of this and the other accident earlier in the day.

The girl seemed to be studying his face, as though looking for something. After a few seconds' silence, she looked away

48

with embarrassment. The alarm bell rang in Tarl's mind.

He took his hands from her arms and she stepped toward the doorway to escape the surrounding crowd. The girl faltered and almost fell. He caught her arm a second time.

"I – I – " The girl reached down and placed a hand around her ankle. "I think I might have twisted it." A moment's silence. "I don't know if I can make it home . . ."

Again the cloud of misgiving floated into his mind. This girl seemed to be anxious to further the accidental relationship.

"I could send you home in a cab," he suggested, breaking the silence.

The girl glanced momentarily at the automobile parked at the kerb. Tarl's eyebrows tensed as he interpreted her glance to betray the fact that she knew, without being so informed, he had a car and chauffeur waiting.

"Let's go," he said, taking her elbow and acting on an impulse. "We'll get a cab and see that you get home all right."

"My name's Leila Smithers," she frowned, as she limped across the sidewalk with him. "What's yours?"

"Tarl," he said, hailing a cab. "Tarl Brent."

"I live at 8642 Chestnut," she threw over her shoulder as she climbed into the vehicle.

In timed movements, Tarl thrust a bill into the hand of the driver, slammed the door behind the girl and told the cabbie, "You heard the address, get going!"

The vehicle moved off in the stream of traffic.

Even as the cab vanished he regretted his action. If the feeling he had was correct, he should have held on to her, played the game to learn all he wanted to know.

As he climbed into the front seat of his own car, he could detect signs of a headache. He hoped it wouldn't be too bad this time – wouldn't last as long as previous ones had . . .

"That was some beauty, boss," Charles observed as he pointed the car into the traffic. "Boy, I sure wish I could bump into something like that."

"Should've told me sooner, Charlie; I'd have held on to her for you." He managed a smile despite the throbbing sensation at the base of his skull.

"Yeah." Charles shook his head again and whistled. "She was some beauty!"

"So were the other two," Tarl said musingly.

"What other two?"

"Well, Charlie, I'll tell you all about it," he sighed, relaxing. "Miss redhead wasn't the only one I 'bumped' into today. She was just one of three gorgeous girls. One of the others was a blonde; one was a brunette. All meetings were accidental. All the girls were eager to become acquainted."

He turned to his chauffeur. "What do you make of that?"

"If it's like you said, I'd say you could fall in and come out smelling like a rose."

Tarl laughed. "You don't get the point . . . Three women. The three most beautiful I've ever seen. Meeting all of them, not in the same year, or the same month – but in the space of just one day. Doesn't that seem unusual to you?"

"Aw, boss," Charles remonstrated, "you're not gonna start kicking about your luck again, are you?"

"Well, Charlie, you can't say . . ."

"For cripes sakes, boss! Why don't you just relax and enjoy it? If you got three beautiful women who wanna make friends with you, why don't you let 'em? Hell, *I* wouldn't have any objections to *that*!"

"I wouldn't either, Charlie, if I knew why . . . why there should be so many of them at one time."

Tarl was silent a while. Charles broke the silence. "Ever have a girl, boss?"

"Of course I've had a girl. Just because I don't seem to be too interested in them now doesn't mean I wasn't at one time."

"Oh, ho!" Charles' head twisted in his employer's direction. "So that's it. Tell me, boss, what was she like? What happened?"

"Well – she was nice. Not beautiful. Not plain, either . . . attractive."

He fell silent again. But Charles didn't interrupt his thoughts.

"Guess I would have married her," Tarl resumed, "but she saw what was coming. She saw my growing affinity for alcohol. And she decided she didn't care to have anything more to do with me. Maybe she was selfish about it. Maybe

50

she thought she could jolt me out of the rut I was getting in ... but it didn't work. I kept on drinking. Before I knew it, she had left town. Came here. Right now she's probably somewhere in this city."

"What was her name?"

"Marcella – Marcella Boyland."

"Lived close to you?"

"In the rooming house across the street."

"I'd like to see this gal. You say ..."

"I have a picture of her." Tarl took out his wallet, fished in it several seconds and withdrew a small photograph. He handed it to Charles and replaced the wallet. The chauffeur snapped on the ceiling light and divided his attention between driving and the snapshot.

"Say!" Charles exclaimed. "She ain't bad at all! Of course, nothing like the redhead ... But she's all right!"

Charles handed the picture back to him and he placed it in his side coat pocket.

The brakes were applied suddenly and Tarl was jolted forward. A late-model sedan had stopped abruptly at the intersection ahead when the driver had a green light. The chauffeur hadn't been able to brake the car fast enough and their heavier automobile nudged the rear of the other car.

Tarl knew that not much damage could have been done. But the kerb side door of the front car was opening.

It wasn't an irate man, however, who got out of the car. He knew, when he saw the nicely shaped ankle and calf stretch out beneath the opened door to the street, that it was another young woman.

"Wasn't my fault." Charles turned to his employer. "It was his."

"Not *his*, Charlie," Tarl corrected. "Not his ... It's a woman. Another Venus. See for yourself."

The two men stepped to the street. The woman, who was not more than twenty-one, stormed up and placed her hands on her hips, fire flashing from her eyes.

"I suppose you have an excuse," she fumed, glancing first at Charles, then fastening her stare on Tarl.

"Excuse, lady!" It was Charles who exploded. "You shouldn't have stopped like you did."

51

The girl gasped. "You saw me put my hand out!" She stomped her small foot on the asphalt roadway.

"If there are any damages," Tarl stepped between the pair, "I'll see that a settlement is made – by noon tomorrow, at the latest."

The girl appeared to be pacified somewhat, but her breasts continued to rise and fall rapidly under the tight-fitting sweater. The vivacious, peppery type, Tarl guessed. It was more than suspicion that told him she was putting on an act. He was dead certain of it!

"Where do you live?" he smiled, trying to play it the way he thought she would want him to.

"You're not going to send a lawyer to deal with me?" Fire lit up her eyes again.

"I intend to see that your car is taken care of immediately," he smiled. "And, if you have no objections, I'll take you home."

The girl's face relaxed. He reached for her arm. But instead of taking her by the elbow, he grimaced in pain and staggered. Charles grabbed his arm and supported him.

"It's that pain in the head again," Tarl muttered. "Give me a hand back in the car. I'll be all right."

Then he went limp in Charles' arms . . .

The girl's face screwed into a puzzled mask.

"He's fainted," Charles explained, placing his employer in the car. Onlookers were not close enough to hear the conversation.

"Well, for God's sake, get him to a doctor!" The girl wrung her hands desperately. "Do something!"

"He'll be all right. Headquarters knows about his condition. He's under Mendel's care. You'd better report back and tell them to send Mendel to the residence right away . . . I'm taking him there now."

The girl retreated to her car. Charles leaned into the limousine and patted Tarl's wrists. His head rolling slowly, Tarl regained consciousness.

"You'll be okay, boss," Charles assured. "I'm taking you home. I've already called Dr. Mendel and told him to meet us there."

Tarl's head ached dully and throbbed against the pillow.

52

Reflected in the mirror across the bedroom was Dr. Mendel's stoic face. The psychiatrist, his back to Tarl, was filling a syringe and carefully noting the volume of liquid that was being drawn into the chamber of the instrument.

"This is going to put you into a deep sleep for the rest of the night." Mendel turned suddenly to the bed, holding the needle point upright. "I'll stay here tonight and we'll see whether you feel any better in the morning."

The psychiatrist continued talking reassuringly as he thrust the needle into the flesh of Tarl's arm. "Of course, you realise you'll have to have complete rest after this. You should be confined to bed for at least two days – remain away from the office several weeks."

The burning liquid coursed into his bloodstream and its effect was almost immediate. His vision of the room became blurred and his eyelids grew heavy.

But in the waning moments of awareness, he felt his head throbbing furiously. He laboured under the sensation that something that was a part of him – yet alien to him – was rumbling inwardly, attempting to snap its shackles and escape.

"Can you still hear me, Brent?" came the voice of Dr. Mendel – thinly, distant. Then consciousness left completely . . .

The psychiatrist sat on the edge of the bed, peering into Tarl's face. With a thumb, he elevated each of the closed eyelids. Satisfied with the appearance of Tarl's eyes, he took off his coat and threw it across a chair. Mendel's features showed an expectant half-smile.

He grasped the sheets and blankets, pulling them roughly to the foot of the bed. Twisting Tarl's body around, he tossed the limp legs over the edge of the mattress. Then he took Tarl by the shoulders and elevated him to a sitting position.

Eyes still closed, Tarl swayed once. Mendel steadied him. Then he remained motionless, seated upright on the edge of the bed.

Brushing hair from his forehead, the psychiatrist knelt before Tarl.

"I am . . ." Mendel said proddingly, grasping Tarl by the arms. The intonation was expectant – coaxing.

"I am ..." the doctor repeated louder, tightening his grip on the other's forearms.

Tarl's face twitched and his mouth opened and closed. The skin around his eyes grew taut, but the eyelids did not rise. His appearance was trance-like.

"I am ... Tarl Brent," he said finally.

"But," Mendel moved his face closer, until his almost panting breath was blowing against Tarl's cheek. "But I am more than Tarl Brent. I am. . . ."

A shudder ran through Tarl's form and the skin on his face became moist. But he remained silent, his lips now parted.

"*I am more than Tarl Brent!*" Mendel repeated, his voice raised in volume and pitch as sudden anger flared in his eyes. "I am ..."

Tarl was silent. Mendel waited, anticipation drawing his teeth together in a tight grip.

Suddenly a violent shiver ran through Tarl's body and he shouted hoarsely. There were more screams, but the eyes remained closed.

Mendel clamped a hand over the quivering lips and shook Tarl's body viciously. "Shut up, you idiot!" Mendel shouted. "Damn you, shut up!"

The spasmodic motion that wracked Tarl's throat disappeared and Mendel released him. But tremors continued to race through his body.

An expression of disgust on his face, Mendel drew his right hand back and struck Tarl across the cheek. The imprint of the knuckles etched in red on the pale skin. But even the violence of the blow did not arouse the man from his deep hypnosis.

The psychiatrist pushed Tarl back harshly on the bed. Clasping his hands behind his back, Mendel walked aimlessly around the room, his lips curled in a sneer.

"It's got to happen! It's got to happen!" he muttered absently. "I can't be wrong ... There'll be a time when it'll awaken fully!"

His pacing slowed to a restless stroll and he clenched and relaxed his fists rhythmically.

"The power!" he whispered. "The immense power! If I can only bring about the awakening at the right time! Transferring it from him to me shouldn't be too hard. But

Brent will have to be killed at the right moment ... The stakes are high – it's everything for me, or the end of everything, and everybody, even myself!''

Mendel stood suddenly at the side of the bed.

"I am Tarl Brent," he said aloud, waiting for the unconscious man to repeat the phrase.

Tarl stirred. "I am Tarl Brent," he repeated with difficulty.

"And I will retain no memory that I might have acquired from the time of the injection until my awakening."

"And I will retain no memory ..." Tarl whispered.

"The headache was the worst yet." S-14 shook his head dejectedly.

"You waited until Dr. Mendel arrived before you left, I hope." The Chief Director looked up suddenly at the agent, still in his chauffeur's uniform.

"Mendel was already there. I wouldn't have been stupid enough to leave him alone."

"And you say you have her picture with you?"

"Here it is." S-14 reached into his breast pocket. "I lifted it from Brent's clothes on the way home."

Charles handed the photograph over the table. The seven other directors strained their necks.

"That was good work," the Chief Director smiled approval. He pressed a button near his elbow. An elderly woman entered and stood by his side.

"This is her picture," he said. "We also know she lived in Broadview six years ago; her name is Marcella Boyland. She may be in this city now."

"I recognise her from the files," the woman said curtly. "I'm sure you'll find ample information on her. She's a subject."

"We ought to have enough information on her!" T.J. retorted. "It cost more than two million to collect all that material – data on everyone he's ever come in contact with and summarised notes on all his ancestors as far back as records go."

The woman took the photograph from T.J.'s outstretched hand and strode through the door she had entered.

Ten minutes later she re-entered the room. Two men

followed. Each carried two filing cabinet drawers. The woman thrust a typewritten slip of paper at T.J.

"Summarisation," she said.

The Chief Director studied the sheet; smiled, then sighed.

"Marcella Jean Boyland," he read. "Twenty-eight. Contact with him from twenty-two years, one hundred and forty-six days, his life, to twenty-five years, two hundred and thirteen days. Current residence, 2247 Shakespeare. Occupation, saleslady, Marton Clothiers. Present location, 2249 Shakespeare, visiting neighbouring apartment. Expected to remain there until approximately eleven forty-five."

T.J. reached into one of the filing cabinet drawers which the attendants held. He withdrew a handful of eight-by-ten photographs, glancing at several, and passed them around the table to the other directors.

"She was apprised of the situation at twenty-nine years and forty-two days." The Chief Director referred to the summarisation slip again. "Post-hypnotic suggestion administered to erase conscious knowledge of apprisal, as is routine with all who have contacted him. Co-operative type. The information and plan can be reactivated in her mind immediately. Estimated time of reactivation, eighteen minutes..."

"But T.J.," one of the directors protested. "Do you think it would be wise to reactivate her as an agent?"

"I think she should be reactivated." T.J. set his jaw rigidly, looked into the faces of the others. The majority nodded in agreement.

"I ve been close to the situation," S-14 offered. "If I might add my opinion, I'd hazard the guess that it has a fairly good chance of working. As a matter of fact, I'd say that is the only chance."

A red-faced man, clad in a rubberoid smock, burst into the room. There was a frantic look in his eyes.

"T.J.! T.J.!" the man shouted in an alarmed voice. "The radio-active material! *There isn't any left!*"

The directors looked at one another in stunned silence.

"All radioactive materials have ceased to be radioactive," the man continued. "We checked it in our laboratories after we got wind of it from our agents in government

56

atomic projects throughout the country. All the radioactives – all the thorium, radium, uranium – every bit of it ... nothing but stable matter now! You can check our supplies downstairs."

T.J. continued to stare grim-lipped.

"Of course, the governments have classified the matter as secret. All holders of permits to possess radioactives are being ordered to keep silent about it."

"The sleeper arouses." One of the directors shook his head forlornly. His eyes were watery. "The sleeper stirs, slowly – a little at a time."

"If only there were some place to hide, gentlemen ... Some place to go ... But it's all so useless. We could remove ourselves to the remotest corner of the universe – even beyond the universe. But *you can't escape*! – YOU CAN'T ESCAPE!"

Tarl's skull felt as though it were expanding and contracting rhythmically as he had breakfast with Dr. Mendel in the dining room of his home next morning. He ate slowly, doubtful that digestion of the food was a probability. The pain in his head had all but disappeared. And he wanted to do nothing that would bring it back. He was in no hurry anyway; he had told his office not to expect him.

By the time he had finished eating, the sensation and nausea had gone, leaving only a listlessness. Before leaving for his office, Dr. Mendel prescribed complete rest. He also arranged an appointment for an examination at the clinic the following morning.

Mendel gone, Tarl decided against a return to bed. He felt his condition would be mollified more readily, if he spent the day outdoors – basking in the autumn sun and clear air.

Charles was quiet, too, as he drove Tarl to the large park several miles away. "Don't want me to wait for you, do you?" the chauffeur asked as Tarl left the car.

"No. Don't bother. I'll telephone you if I need you."

He walked several blocks through tree-arched lanes. A light breeze rustled the crisp leaves on the ground, but it was warm. And it was unusually quiet – it seemed to be the first time in years that he had found solitude. A slim chance

57

anybody would have spying on him here, he reflected. Widely separated, lean trees and open lawns spread beyond the thin shrubs that lined the roadway.

He reached the end of the main lane and entered the zoo, almost deserted in the early morning hour. Still feeling the effects of the previous night's illness, he found a bench near a row of lions' cages. Relaxing on the stone seat, he let his shoulders sag.

Involuntarily, his mind returned to its quest for an explanation of what he considered weird events. Perhaps he had been mistaken all along about persons following him . . . Perhaps the headaches had some connection with his suspicions. Were those suspicions unfounded? Could it be that he was affected by a psychological condition? If people were really "guarding" him incessantly, why wouldn't they trail him into a park? Certainly, there was no one around now . . .

Only a zoo attendant was in sight, spearing bits of paper with a pointed stick and depositing the trash in a large bag he carried at his hip . . . Not a thing unusual about the man.

Tarl smiled inwardly. He was going to convince himself this time, he thought. He was going to approach the man, engage him in conversation, satisfy himself there was nothing odd here. Else, he would continue being suspicious of everyone.

He had already risen and was walking forward when his eyes fell on the next bench. A girl sat there, until now hidden by shrubbery between the two benches. Her head was lowered and she was reading a book. Suddenly, she looked up. Tarl started . . . No, he thought, *it couldn't be!*

The girl dropped the book in her lap and looked more intently at him.

"Marcella!" he said incredulously as he neared her.

"Tarl!" The girl rose uncertainly.

"Marcella." He took her hands. "Of all the places to meet – you!"

"Why, Tarl, I – I didn't recognise you. You're heavier! Why, I do believe you're healthier too. Are you – are you . . ."

"Cured? Of course, I . . ."

"But, Tarl – how . . . What are you doing now? You look so – so prosperous!"

They sat on the bench again, remained there for more

than an hour telling each other of what had happened to them during the past six years and uttering exclamations of wonderment over the chance meeting.

While he studied her face and made mental notation of the small lines that had formed there since they had last seen each other, she told him of her job, where she was employed, her friends.

He noticed with a satisfying glow that she was as pretty as she had ever been. There had been changes – she was a little thinner than he had remembered her. And her carefree attitude had dissolved into one of partial restraint. But, as before, she was very attractive. And her charm was still the same. Completely natural, unaffected.

She always had Tuesday off, she told him. And she frequently came to the park to read.

Before the day was over they had had lunch and seen a show. It was late evening before he escorted her to her apartment. And it was with the promise she would have dinner with him the following evening that he left her. He walked to the corner drug store and telephoned Charles.

While waiting for the chauffeur, he reflected on the changes he had noticed in Marcella. Had there been changes at all? Or, was it merely that during the intervening six years he had adorned his memory of the girl to the extent that on meeting her again she did not coincide with his mental image of her?

At any rate, he shrugged his shoulders and smiled; the thrill of seeing her again was welcome.

Charles was driving slowly when the siren sounded behind them.

"Fire engine," he exclaimed, bringing the car to a stop at the kerb.

"Sure." Tarl stretched his neck looking ahead. "Fire's right up there, in this block."

As he spoke, what had been small flames barely visible in several windows of a three-storey building on the corner erupted into a seething inferno. The fire engine dashed past and screeched to a stop. Other engines drew up behind it.

"Might as well get out and enjoy it," Tarl said, opening the door.

Charles followed him across the street. "Don't get too close, boss," he urged.

Police hadn't arrived yet to manage the spectators.

Charles and his employer pushed their way across the maze of hoses that already had criss-crossed the surface of the roadway. A crowd was gathering and pressing close to the burning building. Firemen tried unsuccessfully to scurry them several times.

"I'm enjoying this," Tarl smiled.

"That your car over there, buddy?" A fireman tugged suddenly at his sleeve. "You gotta back it out. It's in the way."

"Go move it, Charles," Tarl ordered.

"Come with me."

"Why? I'll wait here for you."

"But it might be dangerous!"

"Nuts! Go ahead and . . ."

"I hate to break up this 'yes-no' act," the fireman shouted. "If you don't move the damned thing quick, we're gonna *knock* it outa the way with Number Thirty-Two Engine!"

Charles glanced at the fireman, then at Tarl. His decision forced, he turned and ran to the car.

"And you'd better get back too, buddy," the fireman warned Tarl.

The crackling sound was the first warning Tarl received. He jerked his head upward and terror transformed his face as he saw a section of the parapet wall crumbling. Bricks were falling onto the ironwork of the fire-escape and bouncing off in a wide arc overhead. He was turning to run when he felt arms wrap around his legs and a rugged shoulder hit him roughly below his knees. Someone had tackled him.

As he fell to the wet pavement, he saw the other three men flying toward him. They landed atop him and the man who had thrown the tackle joined the three in a mass of humanity that pressed him to the street.

He tried to struggle, but the weight of the four men held him motionless. Then he heard the *thuds* of falling bricks hitting all around. Duller *thuds* signified bricks striking the umbrella of men that protected his body.

Finally the rain of stone halted. Three of the men who had lain on him rose. A fourth – the one who had thrown him to

60

the pavement – did not rise. He lay still, mumbling un-intelligibly. A deep gash in his scalp bled freely. Tarl saw splinters of bone protruding from the wound. He knelt by the man.

"Oh, God!" the injured man's words came faintly. "Oh, God! Did he escape? Did he get away? Oh, God!"

Tarl looked over the agonised form at the other three men. A crowd had gathered around and firemen were running toward the injured person. The three men stared at one another, fear freezing their faces. One of them reached into his pocket.

"Look out!" A woman screamed, her eyes fastened in fright. "He's got a gun!"

Tarl leaped to his feet. One of the trio was aiming a revolver at the injured man's head. He pressed the trigger. Even before the echo of the shot died, the three whirled around and broke through the opening the terrorised crowd had made for them.

The man in the street was dead – a purplish hole in his forehead marking the bullet's point of entry.

Sprinting through the crowd, Tarl spotted the trio round-ing a corner. He raced after them.

Headlights shone suddenly on his back and he glanced quickly over his shoulder as the car drove up. He was in luck! It was Charles!

He leaped into the automobile.

"Quick, Charlie! Those men running up there ... get them!"

Charles let out the clutch. The action was too fast and, going through a bucking motion, the engine died. He started it again. Perspiration formed around the chauffeur's collar as he shifted into first and drove off, slowly at first – until Tarl urged more speed.

One of the fleeing men turned and fired the revolver. From the direction of the tongue of flame, Tarl saw the shot had not been aimed at the car; rather, it had been directed into the air.

Charles shouted hoarsely and swung the vehicle sharply around the only corner between them and the three men.

"You damned fool!" Tarl shouted. "I want to catch those men! They aren't going to hurt us!"

61

"They've got a gun, boss!" Charles fed more gas to the engine.

"Turn left at this corner. We'll swing around and head them off!"

"Look, boss." Charles pressed the accelerator closer to the floorboard. "I don't give a damn if it means my job and your friendship. But, I sure in hell ain't gonna go chasing after anybody with a gun!"

Tarl let out a breath of anger, leaned back in the seat. He knew it was too late now to continue the chase.

"Okay, Charlie . . . Let's go home."

T.J. paced the floor in front of the board table. Every seat was occupied except his. As many additional persons, both men and women, perched tensely on the edge of chairs against the walls of the large room.

The Chief Director stopped and mopped his brow. "Gentlemen," he said, "the critical phase is here. As much as we've done to avoid it – it's here. We may now have to use the final plans – the ones we had reserved only for the most stringent developments."

Only silence answered him. Then T.J. took his seat.

Dr. Mendel rose. "T.J., I've a suggestion I think we might do well to consider. We all agree that suspicion welling in his mind is causing all this. I've already convinced him he needs a complete rest. It may not be too difficult to convince him further that my sanatorium in Coveville is the proper place to get that rest."

The directors mulled over his offer.

"You could call off all our agents then," he continued. "And, at the same time, you could be certain he would be as safe as if he were roaming the streets with twenty of our men following him. I will stay with him continuously. I assure you he would at no time be more than fifty feet away from me."

T.J. shook his head solicitously. "No, Mendel . . . I doubt if that would be the proper course. He would only have time to dwell mentally on what has happened. That might produce an adverse effect."

The psychiatrist spread his hands in resignation and sat down.

"It's just unfortunate," one of the directors said, "that the fire incident had to occur. I'm sure the re-introduction of the girl would have been the answer to everything."

Another director said reflectively, "If only it hadn't been for that scene at the fire!"

A rap sounded on the door. "Come in." T.J. raised his voice.

Marcella entered. "I understand I've been summoned?"

"Yes." T.J. drew another chair to the table. "All principals have been summoned. And it so happens you are at present the most important."

She swept the room with her eyes, her face showing signs of recognition as she spotted acquaintances interspersed among the group. There were Tarl's two business partners, his secretary, the chauffeur, her landlady and Tarl's landlady from Broadview. Marcella sat beside the Chief Director.

"We may need you," he informed her, "for details and a further report. Of course, A-1," T.J. cleared his throat, "You've been informed of the reason for this extraordinary session?"

"I was told only that it was of the utmost importance that I get here quickly."

"Well, Miss Boyland." He used her name for the first time. "It seems there has been another milestone!"

The girl's eyebrows raised.

"Yes, another milestone," he repeated. "And this time it was with no coincident headache or other overt manifestation on his part."

Marcella twisted the handkerchief she held in her hands into knots.

"Do you know what that means, A-1?" T.J. whispered.

"Yes," she shuddered. "It means the *thing* is now starting to act independently of him."

"And," he let his hand drop on the table, "the matter is practically completely out of our hands ... In case you're interested, the milestone is the Pythagorean Proposition."

"Pythagorean Proposition?" She twisted the words with her tongue.

"Yes. It's been refuted. The heretofore accepted proposition that the sum of the squares of the two sides of a right triangle is equal to the square of the hypotenuse. Our mathematical section discovered it only an hour ago in their continuing research project. Of course, it will be several days before independent scientists learn about it.

"Our maths. section was able to bracket the time it occurred to within a half-hour. That time corresponds with the fire incident!"

Silence descended in the room again.

A man at the end of the table rose. "I suggest that since everything is so far gone now, the only thing left for us to do is to call him in and attempt to make contact with *it* through his conscious and subconscious."

"No! No!" Dr. Mendel shouted. But the frantic plea went unnoticed in the din of other protests.

"Impossible!" T.J. agreed with the remonstrating faction. "That's utterly ridiculous. Do you think *it* would regard us as being significant enough even to communicate with us? Do you think *it* would regard anything at all as being significant?"

The man on the side of the indivdual who had risen placed a hand on his shoulder and forced him back to the seat. Tightening the grip, he said:

"T.J.'s right Even if *it* would condescend to communicate with us, the chances are a hundred to one that *it* would do nothing to keep our system intact."

"Gentlemen." Marcella rose. "If everything is so hopeless, I see no reason for my continuing this sham – this pretence."

"But," T.J.'s eyes were grim. "You must! Don't you see, you're our only hope!"

"Why should I continue?" the girl said bitterly. "I've been through the files . . . through his files. He's good. He's even noble. And he's completely innocent. And it just happens that I'm in love with him. I can't see perpetuating this hoax; fooling him like we've been doing all along – especially when the sham is nothing more than a weapon to fight or appease *it*."

"But," the Chief Director protested, "it's not him we're fooling. It's what's behind him – in him – that we're trying to protect ourselves against!"

"It's still him, as far as I can see," the girl replied.

"Your participation," T.J. spoke sternly, "is part of the plan. If you don't do your share voluntarily, we will call in Mendel and have him administer a treatment . . . Then you will do it involuntarily – but just as effectively."

A middle-aged man walked around the table to Marcella's side. He took her hand between his and patted it. "And don't forget, miss, it's not just we who hang in the balance . . . It's this entire world. The whole universe is in your hand . . . You can't fail us!"

Marcella bit her lips and sat down, her features pale . . .

The needle didn't hurt going in, but nausea coursed through Tarl's body immediately. He strengthened his hold on the edge of the metal table on which he sat. But he realised his grip was feeble and barely prevented him from toppling to the tiled floor of Mendel's examination room.

"This shot isn't going to put you completely under," Mendel said, placing the syringe on the table behind him and turning to face Tarl.

The outline of Mendel's face was vague and Tarl shook his head to clear the film from his eyes. Other injections administered by the psychiatrist, he recalled, had not affected him this way. This sensation was different – it was as though he had been drugged. He wondered whether he had received an injection of sodium amytal.

"No, Brent." Mendel's voice was mocking, booming. "No – not sodium amytal. But something that has a lot of sodium amytal in it . . . This is a very special concoction."

Tarl dimly realised then that he had not been reflecting mentally on the nature of the drug – that he had spoken his thoughts aloud without being aware of it . . .

"Yes, Brent," Mendel's voice came again. "You have been thinking aloud. This is an effect of this injection. It has one other major effect . . . It will be impossible for you to remember any of what transpires while you are under its influence. For instance, I could torture you – half kill you . . ."

A fist rammed against the side of Tarl's face, but his senses were dulled beyond interpretation of pain. The blow snapped his head to one side and sent him sprawling to the floor. Seized with both fury and puzzlement, he commanded

65

his body to leap to its feet. But there was no response. Instead, he lay limp until the doctor grasped his shoulders and forced him to a standing position.

"I was saying, Brent," Mendel continued, "that I could half kill you and you would remember nothing about it when you walk out of here ... But physical torture of the type that leaves its evidence might not work. And it might bring about your death at the wrong moment ...

"Oh, yes, you'll have to die, but it'll have to be at the right moment. But that's nothing to regret, for you would die regardless. You see, there are but two alternatives – either you die and we make *it* a part of *me*, or everybody, including you, dies and everything disintegrates into nothingness. I prefer the former of the alternatives."

Tarl, his reasoning power reduced to a minimum by the drug, only half realised what Mendel was saying. He was vaguely aware that the psychiatrist was strapping him to a metal-armed chair against the wall. He mustered his power of concentration and focused his vision on Mendel – brought the impression of the face clearly to his brain for the first time since the injection. There he saw a sardonically leering mask of hate, etched with inscrutable purpose.

He tried to hold the image in focus. And, as he looked, he saw Mendel's hands become clearer as they approached his face, bearing thin, stiff wire prongs.

"This won't hurt – much," the psychiatrist said. "It may irritate a little as the electrodes slip past your eye-balls and into the cerebral hemispheres ... *Keep your eyes opened*!"

Tarl realised his eyelids had started to close instinctively. But the command held them rigidly open. He tried to thrust his head aside in defence, but the muscles in his neck were tense and would not respond.

He wanted to scream as the wires slipped through flesh and scraped bone, but the body that was being subjected to the torture was no longer his.

"Shock, you see," Mendel's voice was heavy with sarcasm, "is necessary for this treatment. I deeply regret that there must be this inconvenience. But there must be torture, agony, to accomplish the purpose – and it must be mental so there will be no physical vestiges."

66

The vibratory sensation in Tarl's brain was evidence that a current had been applied to the electrodes. Terror filled his being. He wanted to scream and tear the instruments from his head. At the same time he wanted to rationalise and seek an explanation for Mendel's actions. But he could do neither.

"You are no longer in this laboratory." The psychiatrist's harsh voice was a whisper. "You are walking on the edge of a steep, tremendously high cliff. Below, the sea is pounding furiously against the sharp crags . . ."

Suddenly, Mendel's voice was no longer there – nor was the laboratory. Only Tarl, the cliff, the sea, the rocks. He tried to back away from the edge, but he couldn't. There was an unseen force pushing him forward – toward the edge – across the edge . . . Then he was falling and screaming. His body began rotating and the crags loomed closer – *closer* – *CLOSER*! The abject terror was something that was driving his entire mentality toward destruction. He closed his eyes so he would not witness visually the moment of impact . . .

But the impact did not come. And the excruciating sensation of falling was no longer there. Cautiously, he opened his eyes again. He was nowhere near the precipitous cliff or the sea . . . He was standing in waist-high grass on a misty veldt. But he was not alone. There were natives with spears on either side of him. He, holding a rifle, and the natives were facing in the direction from which wild shrieks and roars were coming. Then a crazed herd of gigantic elephants rushed upon them. Huge trunks seized natives and hurled them into the air; sent them crashing to the ground. Great tusks pierced other bodies. And ponderous hoofs stomped those humans who had fallen into unrecognisable forms.

Then one of the beasts was towering above him, rearing up on its hind legs, shrieking its wrath . . .

But it wasn't the elephant that crashed down on Tarl. It was a small, round, notched object. He picked it from the ground, his eyes squinting in perplexity. Then he recognised it. The thing was a hand grenade! Its pin had been drawn! Screaming again, he tossed it away. It exploded beyond the ridge. He looked at himself, around him; discovered he was dressed in a soldier's uniform. And the sounds of artillery, small weapons fire, battle, were everywhere.

Another grenade landed at his feet. He tossed it away frantically. There was a flame thrower aimed at him from behind another ridge. He dodged its fiery tongue of death. Panic-stricken, he dropped to the ground and grovelled for cover which he knew wasn't at hand as the machine gun opened fire from less than twenty feet away. The flame thrower redirected its aim and three additional grenades landed near his body.

His mind went blank momentarily and suddenly there was only Mendel's voice. And he knew the effects of the drug were wearing off. Only vaguely could he remember the fearful ordeals that his imagination had conjured up for him. Still less clearly could he recall Mendel's words and actions prior to the frightful experiences. It was all the result of a flight of fancy, he told himself, even as the memory of the imagined experiences erased themselves from his mind . . .

Tarl Brent was visibly shaken during the next two days. He remembered going to Mendel's office and being given an injection that had lulled him into a dreamless sleep. Yet he had the impression that slumber had drained him of all his energy.

He abandoned his business office, informing his secretary the doctor had ordered complete rest. The evenings of the two days he spent with Marcella. And he felt that it was her presence that gave him the determination to fight against the lethargy that gripped him.

By the evening of the third day following his laboratory visit he had convinced himself he would some day ask Marcella to marry him. After taking her home that night he spent several hours sitting before the open hearth in the living room, carefully thinking things out. He crushed a cigarette in an ash tray and hurled it into the fire. A plan had suggested itself spontaneously. He banged a fist on the arm of the chair and smiled grimly. Before he went to bed he examined his thirty-eight calibre revolver. He slept soundly after that.

Charles accompanied him in the morning to the Pradow

Private Detective Agency office. The chauffeur sat beside him while he explained the nature of the visit to a ruddy-faced individual who sat behind a desk.

"So," he concluded, "that's the story."

"And you figure, Mr. Brent," the agency official stared out of a window, "that you can have some of our men follow you and see whether you have any other shadows?"

Tarl nodded.

"This is a new one." The official smiled through a cloud of cigar smoke. "Putting a tail on a tail."

"I want more than one. I'll need at least three. I want to make sure we get something in the net."

The official walked to a side door, stuck his head into the next room and spoke to a uniformed man. Three men followed him back into the private office.

"This is Joe Harrison, Mike Vinson and Arthur Homar," said the official. "Boys," he turned to the men, "Mr. Brent – Tarl Brent – will tell you what he wants."

Tarl again told his problems. Charles interrupted when he was about halfway through to ask leave to telephone the garage about some work on the car.

When Charles returned Tarl was ready to go.

"Wait a minute, boss," Charles said. "You're not going to walk out of here with those guys following behind?"

Tarl glanced askance at the chauffeur.

"If you're really being trailed, whoever is following you will know right off what's happened – seeing you come out of a private detective's office with three men behind you."

"Thanks," said Tarl. "That's using your head." He turned to the detectives:

"Start in on the job at four o'clock this afternoon. I'll be at home at that time . . ."

Marcella was dressed smarter than he had ever re-membered when Tarl escorted her into a cocktail lounge that evening. A tight-fitting, wool skirt brought out the highlights of her figure in smooth curves. They took a table next to the orchestra, ordered highballs and spent the next few minutes listening to muted ballads that floated from the bandstand.

As Marcella sipped her drink, he scanned the room casually.

"What's wrong, Tarl?" she asked suddenly.

"Wrong?"

"Yes. Why are you so nervous? Who're you looking for?"

"No one, Marcella . . . You're imagining things."

He noticed at that moment that two men were seating themselves at an adjoining table. He half nodded toward them.

"I saw that, Tarl!" Marcella said, moving closer to him. "Who are those men? What is this all about?"

"Forget it, please." He shook his head. "There's nothing that concerns you."

"It *does* concern me – *I'm* here *with* you!"

"Now look, Marcella." He reached for her hand. "We came here to . . ."

"Come on, Tarl." She folded her arms. "Out with it. I *want* to know."

He sighed resignedly. "Okay. It's like this . . ."

Tarl told her he had proof he was being followed constantly and had engaged help to solve the enigma. "An incident that occurred on the evening of the day at the park convinced me of my suspicions," he added, telling her about the happening at the fire.

"You see, Marcella," he concluded. "Whatever they're trying to keep from me must be pretty important – important enough to justify the murder of that injured man when they realised he would be identified and questioned."

"Now I'm really worried." Distress showed on the girl's face. "Why are they following you? Have you done anything that might have placed you in danger?"

Taking her arm, he tried to allay her fears by bringing her on the dance floor. They waltzed through one number and danced at a rapid tempo to the next selection. But when they returned to the table the girl was still moody.

"Tarl," she said uncertainly, "suppose I said I thought you ought to forget about it – quit thinking of people chasing you . . . If you are being followed you haven't been harmed. And you might be! If they used a gun at the fire, they're dangerous."

"Now, hold on there!" he protested. "You're trying to

advise me when you don't know anything about the circumstances – only what I've told you.''

"Tarl, *please* forget about it!"

"Marcella," he laughed. "You're going to have me getting suspicious of you, too ... You know, I could question that chance meeting between you and me the other day. The odds were pretty much against it in a city this size."

"Oh, Tarl!" Marcella placed a cool, trembling hand on his wrist. "Don't you see you could hurt yourself – physically – if those suspicions are founded? Mentally – if they're not? Please, Tarl!" Her eyes were beseeching. "Everything's been *so* nice."

He took her hand in his and smiled. The music welled and filled the room with gaiety. Then, suddenly, the orchestra exploded into a cacophony of discordant sounds.

While the drummer beat a sustaining, unaffected rhythm, a trumpet player was standing before his chair puffing his cheeks frenziedly but no sounds were coming from his horn.

A clarinettist was having the same difficulty, while a bank of trombonists continued to produce normal mellow chords. The orchestration sounded as though someone had whacked entire passages from the arrangement for each wind instrument. At one corner of the bandstand the pianist struck his keyboard repeatedly but only plunking sounds resulted. The players quit trying in startled confusion.

Instruments back in their racks, they stared at one another, dumbfoundedly. Several persons in the audience laughed, believing they were witnessing a novelty number. The manager of the establishment stormed across the floor and stood before the band, his hands rolled into fists and thrust against his hips.

"What goes on here?" he demanded.

"Something's way the hell outa whack!" the piano player said. "Look, I can play the scale up to here." He demonstrated, running his fingers over keys from the bass side of the board to middle E. "But the next bunch of notes are blank!" He continued up the keyboard, drawing only toneless *plunks* from the piano.

"Well." The manager hunched his shoulders. "Get the damned thing fixed!"

"But," one of the trumpet players raised his instrument, "the same thing's wrong with my horn! It won't go past the E above middle C." He demonstrated, blowing a series of notes from low C. After he passed middle E only a string of hissing sounds came from the bell of the instrument.

"Okay, boys." The manager turned to walk off. "Cut the comedy. If you're tired, take a fifteen-minute break. But don't try clowning when it ain't on the programme."

Patrons seated close to the orchestra laughed again. Tarl was frowning, however.

"Excuse me a minute." Marcella touched his arm. "I'm going to powder my nose."

"A-1!" T.J. held up his free hand as he pressed the telephone closer to his ear. He signalled silence from Mendel, who sat across the table. "Where are you calling from?"

Marcella gave the name and address of the cocktail lounge.

"This is important, T.J.," she said sharply. "I think there's been another milestone!"

"What do you mean?"

"Something happened out here . . . And again, there was no simultaneous headache."

She told him of the bandstand incident.

"We'll have it checked right away." T.J. cupped his hand over the mouthpiece and barked orders to Mendel. The psychiatrist hurriedly left the room.

"This is terrible!" T.J. said into the telephone. "What happened? Did anything go wrong?"

Marcella flustered. But she managed successfully to withhold information on the nature of the conversation between her and Tarl that had preceded the incident.

"I'd better get back, T.J.," she said. "I don't want to stay away too long."

"Yes," he agreed. "Get back as fast as you can. You're our only key to him now!"

T.J. slammed the phone in its cradle and lighted a cigarette. He was puffing at it rapidly when Mendel re-entered the room.

"They'll have the results in a few minutes," the psychiatrist said.

"*Again* he was *not* suspicious when it happened," T.J. drawled, shaking his head". . . . "At least, not overtly so."

"There's a chance he was suspicious but the suspicion wasn't apparent to the girl," Mendel shrugged. "Remember, we don't have the checks we used to have – now that we've withdrawn all but the essential agents. And I don't trust the girl. Not one damned bit!"

"He showed no sign of a headache either," T.J. mused absently. "We'll receive a report from one of the three detectives in a little while, I hope, and get a cross-check on what happened."

"Indoctrinating those detectives was a smart idea, wasn't it?" Mendel dropped to a chair. "Lucky S-14 thought of the plan when he went to the agency office with Brent."

"Yes." T.J. cupped his hands on the back of his head and stared at the ceiling. "You might say that was one of the best breaks we've had in the entire project."

"Any trouble indoctrinating them?"

"Not a bit . . . Of course, they put up a little resistance when we snagged them. But they took the indoctrination in less than two hours' time. Activation was only a matter of a few seconds. With them on the job we were able to release practically all our agents from close range duty."

"I think you should have released *all* of them."

"No-o-o. Couldn't take that chance. Had to leave a few."

"But, T.J., he's only going to get suspicious again . . ." Mendel stood and placed his fists on his hips. "Why don't you let me take him to the sanatorium? As things stand now, I can only give him partial treatment. If I had him in confinement he would be under constant attention and treatment."

A laboratory worker entered the room, his steps hurried with excitement.

"It checks, all right, T.J.," he said nervously. "The girl was right. A whole chunk gone out of the sonic scale – one octave, to be exact – beginning precisely where A-1 reported."

"There'll be the devil to pay for this!" The Chief Director slapped his knees. "Something like a missing octave can't go unnoticed. The papers will be full of it tomorrow!"

73

"Good thing it wasn't lower in the scale," Mendel observed. "Or it might have fallen in the sonic range of human speech. As it is now, singers will start wondering why they can't strike some notes, just as those musicians did."

T.J. was perspiring profusely. "It's going to be rough" he said. "This is the first milestone that will have a direct and immediate effect on the average person."

"Chief" the laboratory worker asked hopefully "you don't think these milestones are going to be permanent?"

"Probably not. At least, the board has suggested we can expect them to last for a period of several weeks, maybe even months, after we reverse *its* awakening. It'll take time for the *thing* to become completely dormant again – and a little more time after that for *it* to rebuild what has been unintentionally torn down. But there isn't too much to worry about on that score. If the *thing* goes back to sleep, everything will be all right again – eventually. If it doesn't, it won't make any difference whether these handfuls of manifestations are erased ... because *everything will be obliterated!*"

The worker bit a fingernail.

"But," T.J. continued, "there's still hope left. Things were going along smoothly for a while before this last occurrence, which happened three days after the one immediately preceding it. All the manifestations before the last one were occurring closer together, with ever shortening time intervals between them ... Perhaps the next one won't come for several days. Maybe the *thing* is beginning to withdraw itself again."

But the Chief Director's voice lacked confidence ...

When Marcella came back to the table, Tarl asked suddenly:

"Care to go for a drive?"

"Where'll we go?"

"It's early; we can get some fresh air and make a late show somewhere else."

The girl smiled approval and they made their way to the anteroom. He fished for his hat-check while Marcella entered a nearby restroom.

74

His hat in hand, he asked one of the attendants to tell his chauffeur they were ready. Then he sat in a cushioned chair facing the front of the room, where he could watch the doorways to both the restroom and the entrance. A mirror over the main door caught his eye. Through it he could see back into the dance hall. He lighted a cigarette and leaned back.

Still watching the mirror, he saw a man he did not know stepping through the doorway from the dance hall. The man placed a foot over the threshold but halted immediately as his eyes fell on the back of Tarl's head. Then he quickly withdrew into the other room.

Tarl felt an impulse to turn around and investigate further. But he realised he enjoyed an advantage and froze in his position, refusing to betray the fact he had spotted his pursuer. He tightened his lips and waited.

Within seconds, the face peered through the doorway again. Tarl studied him. He could see nothing sinister or cruel about the face; nor, on the other hand, could he detect anything benevolent.

Had the detectives spotted the man also? If so, what were they doing? Certainly they could see the individual. Why, he wondered, didn't they nab him right there?

The face disappeared again and Tarl started breathing easier. His hand slipped around his right hip and felt the revolver in his back pocket; he closed his fingers on it reassuringly. Then he turned his eyes away from the mirror.

Minutes passed. The front fender and hood of the black limousine appeared outside, abreast of the canopied entrance. The door to the restroom opened. He started to rise, but didn't when he saw that the women who came out was not Marcella. The woman strode past him into the dance hall. He followed her motions through the mirror. She hadn't progressed more than four feet beyond the door when she halted abruptly. She turned her head to the right. The man who had been watching Tarl said something to her. She nodded and continued into the other room.

Marcella came out. Tarl took her by the arm and walked toward the exit. He tightened his fingers around her elbow suddenly, however, and pulled her to a stop just short of the door. Marcella gasped in surprise.

"When we get outside," he instructed in a whisper, "get in the car as fast as you can! Tell Charles to drive forward about fifty feet and wait."

"Tarl!" She was breathing rapidly. "What are you going to do?"

"Don't ask questions now!"

"But, Tarl, what's all this mystery about?"

"Don't argue!" His tone grew sterner as he opened the door and propelled her onto the sidewalk.

Outside, she opened her mouth to protest again. But he pulled the rear door of his automobile open and half shoved her inside. He glanced over his shoulder at the same time, making sure his actions could not be observed by the man who had been watching him. Marcella sat on the edge of the seat. He pushed his head into the car.

"Charles, drive up by that tree and wait for me ... Quick!"

"What's ..."

"Dammit! I can't explain now – there's no time. Just drive up there – fast!"

He stepped away from the car and slammed the door. Charles shrugged and drove away.

Tarl removed the revolver from his hip pocket, closing his hand tightly around it. He replaced the weapon in his side coat pocket, but left his hand in there with it, the cold steel of the weapon becoming moist with perspiration from his palm. He leaped across the sidewalk and concealed himself behind one of two potted evergreen plants that bracketed the entrance to the cocktail lounge.

He waited a minute. Then another. And, just when he began to doubt that the man had, after all, been following him, the door opened. Peering out through the door, the man looked in each direction. Cautiously, he walked onto the sidewalk.

Waiting a moment, he placed his hands in his pockets and stepped farther away from the entrance. He looked to the right and saw Tarl's parked limousine. He started; leaped back.

But Tarl had abandoned his hiding place and had interposed himself between the man and the door, withdrawing the revolver at the same time.

"Don't move!" He pressed the barrel of the weapon into the man's back. "Don't put your hands up! Keep them in your pockets. And don't turn around – just start walking."

The man began a protest.

"Don't talk." Tarl spoke lowly. "Get going."

With a hesitancy, the man walked down the sidewalk. Tarl looked quickly behind them. No one was there; no one was coming out of the building. He swept the sidewalk ahead of him and behind him as he walked. Again, no one in sight.

Then he scanned the walk on the opposite side of the street . . . Still nobody. He had half expected, despite his plan, that someone would be there to snatch away his prey. He even considered the possibility that someone might be stationed nearby at all times with the sole purpose of killing anyone he might manage to apprehend.

They reached the limousine. Tarl opened the front door – thrust the gun harder into the man's back.

"Look," the man hesitated, "if this is a holdup . . ."

Marcella screamed. "Tarl! You've got a gun!"

Charles twisted around in the seat. "Boss, what . . ."

"Get in!" Tarl caught the man by the shoulder.

"Tarl! What are you doing?" Marcella started to get out of the car.

"Never mind," he told her, waving the gun in the air, "We'll see who's suspicious! We'll find out what's behind all this!"

He pushed the man in; closed the door. Then he got in the rear and perched on the edge of the cushion.

"You can't do this, boss!" Charles wailed. "You can't get away with intimidating a citizen with a gun!"

"Just start driving, Charlie." Tarl rested his hand on the seat behind the stranger, pointing the barrel of the gun at the man's neck.

Charles and Marcella exchanged glances hurriedly. Then the chauffeur hunched his shoulders and sighed. The girl gasped, terror showing in her eyes.

"Look," Tarl said impatiently. "This is one of those guys! I spotted him in the place. I know what I'm doing. I watched him spying on me through a doorway while I was waiting for you."

77

Inching the barrel of the revolver forward until it touched the back of the man's neck, he ordered: "Tell them! Tell them you were watching me!"

The man said nothing. He tried to lean forward to get away from the menacing gun. Tarl caught his shoulder roughly and forced him back in the seat.

"Tell them!" he shouted.

The man remained silent, looking imploringly in the direction of the chauffeur.

Tarl let out a hiss of air through his lips.

"Okay, Charlie," he said. "Let's get away from here. Find some quiet place. This guy'll have plenty to say in a minute."

The chauffeur started the car reluctantly and drove off. Marcella began to sob. Fuming, Tarl leaned back in the seat.

Blood was not rushing through his temples as fast as it had been when he realised he had at last smoked out his prey. Instead, his head was beginning to throb as it often did before a headache came. He wished desperately the pain wouldn't come back now – return and render him incapable of reaching his goal.

Marcella hid her face in her hands. He put a hand on her shoulder, but she shrugged it off.

"Marcella," he said, "I know what I'm doing."

"But, Tarl." The girl dabbed at her eyes with a handkerchief. "I – I don't understand ... What's come over you? This matter of taking a gun and – and threatening a person ..."

"This is going to clear everything up, Marcella," he said definitely. "I'm going to find out all the things I've got to know."

Even as he spoke, however, a blade of pain cut a swathe through his brain.

"Oh, darling!" She looked anxiously at him. "I hope you know what you're doing."

"Where do you want to go, boss?" the chauffeur asked resignedly.

"Head for the warehouse district. It's pretty lonely out in that direction."

He sat on the edge of the seat again, keeping the revolver pointed at the man's head.

"Look, buddy," he said, "you can save yourself this little ride if you start explaining right now."

The man turned his head. Tarl grabbed a handful of hair and twisted the face forward again.

"I – I don't know what you're talking about," the stranger said. Tarl watched a tremor shake the man's body.

Tarl leaned back. "Okay, Charlie," he said. "Find a quiet spot where we can have a little conversation."

The automobile seemed to roll over the streets protestingly. Tarl became silent as the vehicle progressed from the well-lighted, business district, through a small, less brilliantly illuminated, residential area and into the warehouse section near the waterfront.

Only an occasional street light cast dismal, yellow rays onto deserted roadways and sidewalks and against featureless buildings.

"Up there," he said abruptly, pointing to an alleyway between two one-storey, corrugated-iron buildings.

Charles slowed the limousine, but applied the brakes and stopped on the street before entering the alley.

"Boss," he said. "Why don't we just take this bird to the police? They'll find out about him. Then we won't be breaking any laws by kidnapping him like this."

"Yes, Tarl," the girl said anxiously, catching his arm between her trembling hands. "Why don't we do that?"

Tarl shook his head. "No. If you'd suggested that ten minutes ago I might have listened. But right now I'm too close to the answers. Into the driveway, Charlie."

The chauffeur sighed again and started the car rolling in an arc into the alley.

"This is good enough," Tarl instructed after the vehicle had been driven across the sidewalk and out of direct light from the nearest street lamp.

"Now!" Tarl exclaimed, placing the tip of the gun against the man's neck. "Who are you working for? Why were you following me? What do you want?"

The man could have been a statue. He made no sound and showed no sign of motion.

Breath escaped between Tarl's clenched teeth in a rush. He placed his hand back on the man's shoulder. "I . . ."

He winced in his seat and shook his head. The pain was

climbing far over his sensory threshold. He closed his eyes and remained motionless a moment.

"I want to know." He ignored the sensation and tightened his grip on the man's shoulder, pushing the barrel deeper into the soft skin. "I want to know who you are . . . *right now!*"

The man remained silent. Marcella squirmed. Charles turned around; started to speak. But Tarl motioned him to silence.

Indignation raced the headache for dominance in Tarl's brain. He knew that if he didn't get the information soon he would black out.

He drew back his left hand and struck the man over the ear. "Talk! Damn you! Talk!"

"I can't! I can't!" The stranger burst into sobbing sound. "If I do . . . Oh! I can't say anything . . . Don't you see that – that the world . . . everything . . ."

More silence.

Tarl cocked the trigger.

Suddenly Charles threw his arm over the back of the seat and hit Tarl's wrist. The revolver clattered dully on the matted floor. Marcella threw both arms around him. Off-balance, he toppled from the seat.

"Run! Dammit!" Charles reached across the man and thrust open the door.

"But . . ." the stranger hesitated.

"Don't do a damned thing but run!" Charles pushed him out of the car and he disappeared into the darkness of the alleyway.

Marcella held on to Tarl, her arms wrapped around him, until suddenly his body went limp.

"Charles!" There was fear in her voice. "He's not moving!"

Charles leaped from his seat and ran around the car, opening the rear door. Tarl, who had been leaning against the door, fell outward. Charles caught him.

"He's fainted again!" the chauffeur said, lifting Tarl back onto the seat.

"That means . . ." the girl began fearfully.

The sky was suddenly lighted by a tremendous bolt of lightning with a sharp blast of thunder. The noise was

80

deafening and Tarl stirred, opened his eyes and looked around.

"Why did you do it?" He rolled his head to one side. *"Why did you let him get away?"*

Marcella and Charles looked at each other.

"We had to, Tarl." The girl placed her hand soothingly on his forehead. "You were losing control ... You were going to kill that man."

"No. I wasn't. I ..." His face was contorted. "I ..." He slumped on the seat.

"Let's get out of here," Marcella said. "Let's get him to headquarters. Something's going to happen – something big. ... He fainted twice! This is dangerous!"

Charles started the car and backed out of the alley. When he reached the street and started forward, they had a clear view of the sky. Weird streaks of lightning were racing from horizon to horizon.

He pushed down harshly on the accelerator. The car shot forward. "That lightning " he said to Marcella. "That isn't real lightning – not as we know it!"

His words were barely audible. An almost continuous roll of thunder drowned them out.

"There are no clouds in the sky!" The girl put her mouth next to the chauffeur's ear and shouted.

A bolt struck a warehouse a half-block ahead of them. The blinding flash turned the scene into one of daytime brilliancy. But the building didn't catch fire. Nor were there falling bricks, smoke, collapsing walls. The structure merely disintegrated. Clouds of dust rose upward, swirling and enveloping adjacent buildings. Only a pile of ash stood on the site where the building had been. Some of it cascaded onto the sidewalk and into the street.

The limousine ploughed through it as though there was no substance at all, leaving in its wake eddying streams of boiling smoke.

Suddenly the lightning subsided. The skies became dark again.

Marcella was crying. "I'm afraid!" she sobbed. "I'm so afraid!"

Charles hunched over the steering wheel to get a less restricted view of the heavens. He pointed. The girl pressed her head against the window and looked up.

Myriad pinpoints of light were flashing into ephemeral existence among the stars. The pinpoints were growing in size and leaving fiery streaks behind them.

"Meteors!" Charles shouted.

The streaks extinguished themselves before completing their earth-ward plunge, leaving needle-like strands of illumination in their wake.

"This looks like it," Charles said grimly, stepping harder on the accelerator. "*We may be looking at the end of the world!*"

"You're going to headquarters?" the girl asked terrified.

"Of course." Charles spun the car on two wheels around the corner. "Don't you recognise the area? We're only a few blocks away."

The girl passed her hand several times over Tarl's brow. He was slumped in a corner. She reached over caught him by the shoulder and lowered his head against her breasts.

"Poor Tarl," she said, clutching him tighter. "He's the only one of us who doesn't know what's happening!"

A crash sounded in the distance. Another, closer. Then two, almost together.

"What's that?" the girl screamed, pulling Tarl closer.

"The meteors!" Charles shouted. "They're getting bigger! They're hitting!"

Outside, the sky was bristling with streaks of fire. Some of the glowing threads extended to the ground. As the lengthening strands touched the surface, the earth shook. The crashes increased in number and the impacts became more violent. Within seconds, the sound of collisions had become a continuous din.

A huge, flaming ball struck the street a block ahead of them. Its searing heat flooded through the windows and metal panels of the automobile. But the withering wave was only temporary. The fallen object pushed deep into the ground, carried by its impetus. A second later, the surface billowed in the spot – puffed like a bubble forming in a pot of boiling tar.

Charles slammed on the brakes and stopped a hundred feet from the mound. Then the centre of the bubble burst, spraying flaming gas a hundred feet into the air. A steady stream of fire poured from each crack in the bubble, shot towering flames skyward.

The girl screamed in fear. Then the shower of flaming objects dwindled, died completely. In its place came a rain – falling in huge drops and hitting with a ferocity that dented the car's metal surfaces.

Tarl stirred against the girl. And in terror she thrust him from her.

Groaning and regaining consciousness, Tarl straightened in the seat and rubbed his face with trembling hands. Marcella shrank in her corner. And the rain relinquished its bizarre quality, the drops becoming smaller and falling in a more normal fashion.

The girl leaped from the car.

"What are you doing?" Charles shouted.

"I'm afraid " she said without looking back. "Afraid of everything – even him. Don't you realise *it's* right there – right in the car!"

She stood poised fearfully outside the vehicle, glancing erratically in all directions.

"Marcella," Tarl reached out and clutched at her dress. "Don't leave! Please!"

The girl pulled away from his grip and sprinted up the street. She disappeared in the rain. Tarl grabbed his head in despair, cringing from the pain.

"*This damned headache, Charlie*," he groaned. "Why doesn't it go away?"

The rain stopped. Footsteps sounded outside. Determined footsteps made by feminine heels. Marcella appeared in the open door.

"You've come back!" Tarl tried to smile.

"Yes Tarl." She re-entered. "I've come back."

He looked around outside the vehicle. The burning bubble loomed into view. He swept his eyes over the street behind them. There were other bubbles – all spewing angry flames skyward. But the glow that bathed the underside of clouds forming over the city told him it would require thousands of such fires to create that degree of illumination.

"What happened?" He jolted upright in his seat, amazement on his face. He looked at the girl, then at Charles. "Was there an attack?"

83

"Tarl! Oh, Tarl!" Marcella grabbed him again and held him tight, pressing her face to his. Then she began crying.

"This is it!" T.J. said, standing by the window and sweeping his eyes over the terrorised faces that peered back at him in the large room at headquarters. "*It's* broken loose now!"

The building shook viciously. The table moved several inches across the floor as a sudden rumbling became audible. Sounds of objects being wrested from their moorings throughout the building filled the room.

"Earthquake!" shouted a hysterical woman, clutching desperately at the sides of her chair.

"Only a minor one." T.J. hid his concern with grim resignation. "*It's* out now," he said listlessly, scanning the scene outside. "*It's* loose . . ."

"Can anything at all be done?" One of the men ran across the room to the Chief Director's side.

But the two became mute before the window as they watched thousands of fires sending smoke into the sky. A crescent moon was visible. But it seemed like an intangible object – wavering, breaking into several parts and joining into a whole again.

"We can only try and see whether any reasonable course of action remains," T.J. said finally.

"But what are our plans?" the man persisted. "What comes next?"

Another earthquake rocked the building on its foundation.

"If we can only get him here we can try the final plan." The Chief Director returned to the table.

"You mean direct appeal through his conscious?" asked one of the directors with an air of alarm.

"What else is there left to do?" T.J. spread his arms. "We don't have to worry about awakening *it* fully now. *It's* already awake. And we have no reason to believe *it* will ever recede to the subconscious level – into inactivity. If we can only get him here we can start treatment immediately . . . Dr. Mendel!" He scanned the sea of faces in the room.

"Mendel's in the lab preparing his equipment," someone

volunteered. Then the man stuck his head through a side door and shouted the psychiatrist's name.

Mendel entered the room his hair tousled and his eyes scanning the assembly nervously.

"You have everything ready?" T.J. snapped.

"I'm all prepared," Mendel said, withdrawing a syringe from his pocket and holding it where T.J. could see it. "I can administer the injection within ten seconds after he is produced . . .

"But," Mendel's voice cracked and became frantic. "Where is he? What's holding him? Why isn't he here now?"

"There's no way of knowing." T.J. was calm again. "All means of communicating with our agents have been eliminated. But all agents had explicit instructions to produce him at headquarters as rapidly as possible should Phase Z develop. There's nothing we can do but wait here."

Mendel's hands clutched T.J.'s arms. "But we've got to find him, T.J.! *We've got to find him!*"

A frown of puzzlement crossed the Chief Director's face. "You believe," he shrugged off Mendel's hands, "that by elevating his subconscious to the same plane as his conscious you will be able to establish direct communication?"

"We *should* be able to." Mendel looked at the floor and became a degree calmer. "We've been rather close to direct communication on a couple of . . ."

The psychiatrist stopped abruptly in mid-sentence.

T.J.'s eyes glowered and his hands clenched into fists as he stared at Mendel.

The Chief Director gasped and said accusingly, "Mendel! What do you mean! – You've been close!"

Fear shone in the psychiatrist's eyes as he backed away. A sudden calmness blanketed the din in the room.

T.J. stepped forward and grasped the doctor by his coat lapels. "*You have been secretly attempting contact!*" he accused.

"Watch out!" someone screamed. "He's got a gun, T.J.!"

There were other screams and several directors rushed forward as Mendel leaped around to the rear of the Chief Director, thrust the muzzle of the weapon into his back and shouted a warning to the others to stay away.

With T.J. as a shield, Mendel retreated to the wall – away from the threatening crowd.

"And," the Chief Director shook his head, stunned, "I didn't even suspect there might be someone among us who was trying to *awaken* the thing while we were attempting to return it to its lethargy! If anybody could sabotage the project, Mendel, I should have known it would be you!"

"You fool!" Mendel whispered hoarsely. "You and your project would seek to throttle the thing into supine stupor; to make all its powers impotent; to preserve nature as we know it ... There is another way, T.J. – if the thing were in the proper mind, one that could control it, mine, just think of the utterly unlimited potency that would be available to that controlling person!"

Mendel's breath was hot and rapid on T.J.'s neck. "Why," the psychiatrist's voice came with mounting hysteria, "I could rule the world unopposed. The riches of a universe would be mine. Not only all the riches that exist – but all I could *dream* into existence! Immortality and godhood would be mine!"

T.J. shook his head and let his shoulders droop as he turned slowly to gaze on the view out of the window. A strong wind had risen, combing out the smoke from the fires into streamers of black ribbon. Between the streamers the natural night sky was visible. Familiar stars twinkled in their accustomed places. But, even as he watched, they ceased to be familiar.

Entire groups of stars abandoned their positions and rushed in confusion across the heavens – some of them becoming lost in the chaos. Many were exploding, running the gamut of colours in the spectrum. When they disappeared, it was into the ultra violet. And the moon was no longer in existence.

Tarl's brain was numbed as he learned from Marcella and Charles what had happened while he was unconscious. He shook his head dumbfoundedly and muttered, "No! No! No!"

But the hope-seeking exclamations were timed with a series of tremors that rumbled through the earth's crust and shook the automobile on its springs.

"But why?" Tarl asked in horror. "*Why is all this happening? What's wrong?*"

Marcella glanced at Charles, and the chauffeur stared into her eyes.

Tarl witnessed the exchange of glances. "*You know!*" he said discordantly. "*You know!*"

He grasped the girl by the shoulders and shook her. "What is it, Marcella? – *Tell me what you know!*"

His eyebrows knotted as another arrow of pain, somewhat less acute than the last, found its mark. Outside, there was another rumbling – another vicious shaking of the earth's surface.

Charles winced. "Might as well tell him, Marcella. It doesn't make any difference now. If we can't get to headquarters, he should know about it. If we do get there, he'll find out about it anyway."

Tarl's face was a maze of bewilderment.

"Why aren't we on our way to headquarters now?" The girl looked at Charles.

"We can't take the chance of moving – not until some of that hell outside quiets down."

The night covering the city seemed to have spent its initial fury. The tremors were becoming fewer. But the air itself was a lurking, menacing entity – waiting to pounce and devour.

Tarl's face still showed painful bewilderment. He looked at the chauffeur, then at the girl.

"Tarl," Marcella said, placing a hand on his shoulder. "You were right. You were being followed – followed every minute – every second. But it was by persons who meant only good! Persons who only intended that you shouldn't be harmed, that you remained out of trouble, that you became wealthy. They provided everything that would make you happy, kept you content . . ."

"Even women?" Tarl brushed her hand off his shoulder. "They even wanted to see I was well supplied with women?"

Keeping her eyes away from his, Marcella said with effort, "Yes."

"And you, Marcella, are you one of them?"

She was silent for an eternity. "Yes, Tarl. I am one of them."

"And I am too, Tarl," said Charles. "Almost everybody you know is."

Tarl clenched his teeth. "They wanted to keep me happy – but why?"

He grasped the girl by her arms and shook her again, shouting; "*Why?*"

"Cut it out, Tarl," Charles said, still without moving. "She's trying her best."

Tarl relaxed and sank into the cushion, closing his eyes. He wasn't aware of the pain in his head any longer – there was just a vague, dull, empty feeling.

"Tarl," the girl's voice began again, sounding far away. "There were two reasons why you were protected. One was to prevent any physical harm that might separate your intellect from your body, through death . . . The other was to prevent any mental harm – any psychosis, neurosis – that might, in effect, do the same thing.

"You see, Tarl, if that happened, we were afraid that something – something *in* you might break loose." Her body shook with emotion.

"Oh! Charles!" she said, turning to the chauffeur. "How can I tell him? How can you tell anyone without the aid of Dr. Mendel's injection to cover some of the irrationality?"

"Mendel!" Tarl shouted.

"It's this way, Tarl," Charles leaned close to him. "The best scientific minds in the country found out something a little over three years ago. They found out what they called 'the true nature of our world' – of the entire universe . . ."

The chauffeur stared directly into his eyes. "*It ain't!*" he blurted. "*None of it is real!* Nothing at all is real – not in any physical sense . . . *It's all an illusion!* This car. Marcella. That building. This planet. *Every star in the sky!*"

Tarl laughed, loud and long. But his laughter faded as a group of comet-like objects swished by overhead, chasing one another from the eastern horizon to the west and disappearing beyond a bank of buildings at the end of the street. In their wake, stars eddied – scattered, played in little circles and finally laboured to regain their former locations. Terror filled his eyes and he forgot he had laughed.

Then, where one star had shone brilliantly, a section of the heavens went crazy. What had been a star's pinpoint of light expanded into a disc of white luminescence the size of a full moon. The shining area became brighter and continued to grow, slowly. Within seconds, the now huge orb occupied more than half the sky.

It grew until it captured the entire celestial hemisphere, turning night into the most brilliant day he had ever seen. He hid his eyes to protect them. When he looked again, the intense illumination was gone. The sky was dark again. And he was suddenly aware Marcella was screaming.

She stopped finally. But she did not cry. Her face became sober; rigid. She looked at him. There was horror in her eyes.

"*We* understand, Charles," she said, staring wildly at Tarl. "But he can't possibly know what it's all about . . . He hasn't been prepared! *We've* been told what to expect!"

The girl shivered and placed an arm around Tarl's shoulder. He drew close to her, wanted to bury his face in her breast and cry. But his brain was numb and he was too stunned to ask any more questions.

"Don't ask how they found out that nothing was real," the chauffeur continued. "But they found out. They'll tell you."

"They proved it." The girl's voice rumbled through the wall of her breast into Tarl's ear. "They proved it when they told us that if what they suspected was true, Mercury would be reported mysteriously missing . . . You remember when the planet disappeared, don't you?"

He nodded against the warmth of her body.

"It didn't just leave its orbit or get knocked into the Sun . . . *What's in you* destroyed it. Destroyed it by sub-consciously willing it out of existence when you were doped. It was all a test – an experiment."

Tarl raised his head questioningly in front of Marcella's face.

"Yes, Tarl, doped," the girl nodded. "Of course, you don't remember. The memory was wiped out through post-hypnotic suggestion."

The girl sobbed and placed her forehead against his cheek.

"Oh, Tarl!" she cried. "I keep thinking that you're *it*! And I keep wanting to draw away from you. Run! Hide! But you're in the same boat with everyone else. *You* are as imaginary, as unreal, as everything else! But it's not you I'm afraid of. It's the *intellect* that shares your body and your mind!''

He sat erect again. Nothing was making sense to him. Nothing at all. He wanted to pinch himself to see whether he was not in some fantastic dreamland ... But a glance outside at the eerie panorama of destruction served the same purpose.

"Tarl," Charles continued. "That *thing* – that *intellect* within you – is the only thing that really exists. Nothing else exists. Not even space. Not even time. Not even matter. Only that *intellect* – that intangible, bodiless power of reasoning – is real! *That and that alone is the universe – the entire universe.* All that is, exists only by virtue of *its* imagination!''

Tarl was staring dully ahead again. He shook his head. "I don't understand. I can't grasp it. I must be going crazy!''

The lurking quiet outside still flaunted its imponderable threat and the sky was lighted by the fires which were spreading through the city.

"Our directors," Marcella got control of herself, "believe the entire universe, even you and your *active* mind, is but part of the thought pattern of this – this *intellect*. They believe this entity, over an indefinite period, created everything as we know it now – in an act that was motivated by loneliness ...

"Possibly it created you first, or one of your ancestors. If it was you first, then it not only created everything as we know it, but it also created a history for the universe and a racial and individual memory for every creature in it.

"If it created one of your ancestors first, then the intellect progressed down the line of descendants until its host body is now you.

"After creation, it enjoyed its universe and its world a while, then lapsed into a state of suspended mental activity. It relegated to its subconscious the task of controlling all the objects and actions of all the beings in its universe.''

Tarl shook his head deliberately, trying to absorb the revelation – trying to find the rationality.

"You see," Marcella held his limp hand again, "those

who have been following you, and their directors believe that only a simple world – a simple universe – was created by the thing while it was in conscious state.

"They suspect that only in the subconscious, sleepful stage did everything become complete ... Perhaps while it was consciously in control of its creation it created only you – maybe one or two other persons – a small glade as a dwelling place – merely a handful of the simple essentials.

"Then, content and peaceful in satisfaction with itself, it lapsed into a lethargy. While it basked in the slumber of that satisfaction, the intellect extended its creation without conscious effort. The glade became a valley. The valley a continent. The continent a world. Then there came other worlds and stars and stellar systems, and complexities of systematism, order, sciences..."

For the first time Tarl's eyes took on a faint glow of partial comprehension. "And," he said, "if it awakes, it can't hold together the complexity of the things it has created!"

The girl nodded.

"But is it awakening? *What's causing it to stir?*"

"Over-caution," Charles shrugged.

"The directors have been stepping on one another's heels," the girl said rapidly. "The suspicion you felt seeped through into your subconscious – into the subconscious of the intellect. The thing was prodded, stung. Not one time, but several times. Each time it was disturbed, an impulse from its subconscious got through into the order it was sustaining. And each time chaos resulted. Finally, they have almost, if not entirely, awakened it."

"And?" He tried to pull the words from the girl's mouth.

But it was Charles who broke the silence. "And this is it! This is the end!"

"No!" the girl protested, holding Tarl's hand tighter. "There's one last chance – if we can get to headquarters. There, the directors may be able to establish contact – appeal to it. Even though we are only temporarily free figments of its imagination, we might be able to appeal sincerely enough to gain our continued existence.

"Of course, we realise that existence can't be what it has been. The entity, if it awakes fully, can't keep the systematic universe together. In order to direct successfully the barest essentials – just a handful of persons and a solid piece of land for them to exist on – the entity must release its grip on everything else. That means practically everything we know will disappear – dematerialise. We can only hope it will listen to our suggestions and try to provide survival for as much and as many as possible.''

"Later," Charles added, "after it has succeeded in keeping together as much as it can, it might lapse into profound sleep again. Then progress will once more be on the march. Then the handful of persons will evolve into a civilisation. The small plot of land on which they exist will expand once more into a continent. And there will be stars again – and worlds again."

"And everything will progress normally," the girl said bitterly, "until some scientist discovers the 'true nature of things' and gets worried about locating the 'intellect' and taking steps to assure that it won't return to consciousness."

"But," he asked, "how – how did they know? How did they find out about me?"

Marcella sighed. "That was an accident. A scientist – one associated with the person who is now our Chief Director – perfected a brain wave detector. The instrument also was supposed to have directional properties, to be able to determine the source of the waves it was detecting.

"Only, they found that the indicator never pointed toward the person under test ... It always pointed in only one direction. They followed the needle halfway across the continent and found – *you!*"

"But," Tarl asked, "why don't I feel the thing inside? Why don't I realise, now that it's stirring, that it's there?"

"Why should you?" Charles' eyes held only a grim despair. "It's only by accident that the thing is associated with you. Only an accident that in the beginning it created you, or an ancestor of yours, and associated itself with that person for a vicarious enjoyment of the dreamworld it had produced. It has acted independent of you and your ancestors all along. It's acted independent of you even during the crisis of the past three years."

"At first," Charles offered, "the directors were only a handful of scientists who discovered the truth. After they had theorised and convinced themselves of what they suspected, they set up the Mercury experiment. The test had two purposes. One was to garner truth. The other was to gather funds for the 'protection' project.

"They conveyed their suspicions, tactfully, to the wealthiest magnates, not only in this country, but throughout the world. The magnates, of course, did not believe them – at first. But, when they predicted the disappearance of a planet, that changed the complexion of things. The directors got all the money they wanted for Operation Forestall."

"Charles." The girl looked out the window into the now quiet night. "Don't you think we ought to try to make it to headquarters? It looks calmer out there."

"Yes." The chauffeur opened his door. "We'd better get there before *it* starts stirring again."

He turned to Tarl. "Only about six blocks to go. We'll have to walk."

Heat from the miniature volcano on the corner seared their faces as they passed close to it, stumbling through the smoking debris of a crumpled building. The street down which Charles was leading them was a shambles of accordioned sidewalks, ruptured and spouting water mains, devastated buildings. In each block, fires were gaining in severity and spreading to adjoining buildings.

Noises from nearby residential areas began creeping through the discord of roaring flames and crackling, falling timbers. It beat at their ears and created a frenzy that hastened their footsteps.

Tarl's shoes were scuffed and his trouser legs were torn. The girl's heels had been knocked from her pumps when they passed through the last block of the warehouse district and climbed the embankment, stepping over railroad tracks into a shabby residential section.

Cries of distress from ahead were becoming more audible and he wished he could bar them from his ears.

Walking between Marcella and Charles, Tarl stopped suddenly and stiffened. Then his knees buckled and he almost fell. The girl and his companion caught his arms and held him.

"I'll be all right," he whispered.

The trio remained motionless while Tarl, supported by the other two, fought for his breath against the increasing intensity of the pain. The sounds of anguished humanity up ahead now came streaking to his ears and beat against his brain, striking additional terror within him.

Ignoring the pain, he raised his head and looked forward at the panorama. A crazed, frantic group of persons was in the street. Some had fallen and were unable to move. Many were dead. Utter devastation enshrouded all. Those who were trying to help the ones on the ground were dazed, mute. Others stood motionless, screaming.

Several laughed hysterically. A number stood trance-like and watched the efforts of others to escape burning buildings. There were the cries of a mother looking for her baby – and of a myriad children screaming for their parents. Even animal sounds permeated the uproar. A cat hunched in a corner by a flight of stairs and mewed pitifully. A dog bayed in terror; another yelped in agonised pain.

The sounds thrust themselves into Tarl's conscious and prevented him from slipping into oblivion.

And, while he struggled inwardly, he wondered about the extent of the scene before him. Was it citywide? Nationwide? Worldwide? He closed his eyes again and tried to bar the chaos from his brain.

Then, suddenly the pain was gone! Entirely and completely gone. Like a chain, it had snapped, leaving him wonderfully free of agony. And he knew, instinctively, the torture would never come back to wrack him.

He knew other things also. That his mind was not entirely his own. That, paradoxically, his mind *was* his own. That he could claim more than the meagre mentality he had up until a second ago possessed. That formerly he had used only a minute particle of his potential intelligence. And that *now* he would have available all of the potential!

Was the intellect fully awake within him? Or was it just beginning to awaken? He decided upon the latter, for the sensation of super-intelligence was not a continuous thing. It came and went, remaining only for fleeting seconds to open to his mind vast vistas of supreme knowledge. Then, like a pulsating thing, the sensation was obliterated – only to return again.

And, with the realisation of great knowledge came the rapturous awareness of great beauty. For the thing within was intrinsically good. At one crest of the pulsating sensation, he was aware that available for his mental scrutiny was all the knowledge that had ever been learned throughout the temporal extent of creation.

At his disposal for inspection was every thought that had ever been born in any intelligence that had lived or was living.

Looming in the mass of universal intellect like an upraised ridge was the malignant thought track of his personal psychiatrist, Mendel. Tarl wondered why the doctor should have been assigned a place so apparently prominent in the mysterious scheme of things. He concentrated on the thought track and started as he realised its connection with the processes that were in play. He realised that Mendel's objective was to usurp the supreme intelligence. To set up his own mind as the host receptacle. To develop a degree of conscious control. Tarl also saw that consummation of the plan entailed oblivion for himself, the now host for the super intelligence.

He was both alarmed and amused over Mendel's intentions. He was amused because he realised that should the intelligence be awakened sufficiently to make possible a transfer to another host, the awakening would be complete and it would mean the end of all, for the cardinal principle that had motivated the inception of Operation Forestall stood out blazingly in his conscious now; the intellect could not possibly hold together on a conscious plane that which it had subconsciously created and was creating while in slumber.

But he wondered suddenly whether the premise could be wrong. Was it possible that the being could awaken completely – destroying in the act all that had been created – only to find that when slumber returned a universal re-creation was effected? A re-creation that reproduced everything as it was before the awakening. With the aid of the hyper-intelligence that was becoming a conscious part of him, he realised that was a very real possibility. It is possible, he mused, for a dreamer to awaken momentarily, then

95

lapse back into slumber and re-enter his dream world, finding it exactly as he had left it.

He didn't know to what extent his actions and thoughts were now being motivated by his own intelligence and to what extent they were the products of the super intelligence. He wondered whether there actually was a difference between himself and *it*.

Shaking his head to clear away the indecisive thoughts, he announced to the girl and Charles:

"The headache's gone."

He met Marcella's glassy eyes and she screamed. Had she recognised the difference in him?

The question was answered by her eyes. She was staring, not at him, but rather past him. He turned and looked up the street.

Then he staggered backward in amazement! The scene was as it had been, at least for a distance of three hundred feet.

But, beyond that was – *nothing! Absolutely nothing!*

It was as though someone had taken a giant cleaver and cut the rest of existence away, leaving on the other side of the cut an unimaginably dark, starless, sightless, soundless void!

Shaking, he whirled around and stared to the rear of them. It was the same in that direction. A block of the scene of devastation. But beyond that *nothing!* He and the girl and Charles were standing on a disc that was located in an infinite void. They were the centre of a sphere – a sphere of reality – scarcely more than six hundred feet in diameter, with the vast reaches of an unbounded, matterless universe around them.

Marcella was still screaming. Charles groaned and sank to the street, limp. He placed his head in his hands and sobbed quietly.

"It's over!" the chauffeur said convulsively. "All over! It's folding up on us! We're all that's left . . . I didn't think it would come this way – this fast. I was sure there would be days of turmoil, chaos. But now it's going. *No stars – no Earth – no Sun – nothing!*"

Marcella fainted and fell against the chauffeur, who brushed her inert form off him. She continued falling to the street.

Globules of perspiration appeared on Tarl's face. In horror, he perceived something that Marcella and Charles hadn't. The fringe of nothingness was advancing! It was creeping up on them. The small sphere of reality was diminishing – contracting. He realised the void would finally reach in and devour them, as it was now gobbling up matter in the fringe zone. He wanted to turn and run. But when he whirled around, the blackness was just as close and just as frightening in the other direction.

He swept a hand in front of his face, as though to ward off the advancing destruction. And, as if in response to his gesture, it stopped advancing!

He concentrated harder ... and, slowly, the nothingness retreated, vomiting the stretches of sidewalk, bits of buildings, lengths of street it had devoured. It retreated only a handful of feet. Then a handful more. He was succeeding! He, exercising the power of the entity, was holding on to what was left of the concrete universe!

Marcella and Charles remained motionless. Holding back the void, Tarl cast his eyes into the blackness overhead. He imagined a star located in the centre of nothingness. It was there! He imagined another. A second sprang into view!

But the first disappeared!

And, when he returned his eyes to the scene before him, he saw the void had started its advance again, consuming all, as it had before.

He shuddered. He could not hold it together! He could not ward off the dematerialisation of matter and, at the same time, order into existence additional matter! Could he prevent his own body from turning into nothing? How long could he hold off? Would the void advance when he fell asleep? How long would it be before he was nothing but a disembodied intellect, existing in the original infinite sea of ether?

Wouldn't it be better, he wondered, if the intellect could be lulled into its lethargy again? Perhaps in that state it could hold on to what was left ... If only he could get to headquarters! Maybe with the help of the directors, something could be salvaged.

But headquarters didn't exist any longer! Or, did it?

Maybe it would exist again if he could move this sphere to the spot in the surrounding nothingness that the building had occupied.

Charles was still sobbing. Tarl reached down and slapped him on the cheek. The force of the blow jolted the man from his stupor.

"Get up!" Tarl shouted.

"No," Charles whimpered. "Let me alone."

Tarl slapped him again. "Get up! There's still a chance!"

Charles rose listlessly, acting with the unvarying compliance of a schizophrenic. Tarl picked up the girl and cradled her in his arms. She was breathing normally. But she remained unconscious. He took several steps forward. Charles followed. The sphere of reality advanced with them, its perimeter maintaining the same distance from the centre, occupied by the trio.

He walked a block, and another block of reality unfolded in front of them – as the block they had just left dematerialised progressively.

"Are we on the street headquarters is located on?" Tarl asked the chauffeur.

"Yes," Charles answered.

Tarl continued along the route. Suddenly he realised the light that enveloped them was unnatural. It wasn't emanating from street lamps and it wasn't born of the sky – for there was nothing light-giving in the heavens, not even the star he had caused to appear there.

But, even as Tarl consciously reflected on the light's origin, the small sphere was thrust into Stygian blackness! He stifled a scream. Charles didn't. Tarl hurriedly imagined the light had reappeared and it was back again. He commanded it to stay in existence – wondering whether it would.

Seconds later, the advancing boundary between the sphere and the void swept over three persons, recalling them into existence. But as Tarl became conscious of the fact that they were there, they dematerialised! He tried to bring them back into existence, but realised he could do that only at the expense of a lessening in the size of the sphere. The intellect no longer had the power!

As they continued forward, more tortured individuals

slipped under the curtain of reality. Some appeared running from one side of the street to the other. Some were crawling, painfully, across the concrete surface. Some were screaming. And there were some motionless on the ground, the last breath of life escaping from them.

But all, as soon as they found their way back into existence dematerialised – leaving only cracked sidewalks, split street pavement with an occasional crevice belching forth flame, and buildings, wrecked buildings, crumpled buildings, buildings afire.

He was labouring under the increasing weight of the girl. She began to stir. And the motions made his progress more difficult. He had hoped she would remain unconscious for a while, at least.

Marcella groaned lightly and began to shake her head. He lowered her feet to the street, saw that her eyes were opening. But she closed them hurriedly and swayed lightly.

"You all right, Marcella?" he asked.

She passed a hand over her head and steadied her balance. "I will be in a minute," she whispered.

"Don't look around," he warned. "You won't like what you see."

"I won't." She shuddered. Then she slipped her hand into his and indicated she was ready to go on. They moved off. Charles followed, silently.

They had walked only a few feet when the chauffeur reached out and touched him on the shoulder.

"This is it." Charles pointed to a building on the right.

The girl looked in that direction.

"Headquarters," she said, without emotion.

The building was one of the few in the block still standing. Tarl held the girl's hand tighter and walked toward it.

"You don't need the gun any longer." T.J.'s tone was filled with despair as he looked over the barrel at Mendel. "We'll both be gone within seconds now."

The Chief Director glanced around the empty room. "We're going to disappear again; melt into nothingness – just as we did a little while ago. Why we came back into existence, I don't know. Why the others didn't . . ."

"I'll tell you why." Mendel's eyes dropped some of their

frantic quality. "Brent is approaching. He is coming near and bringing with him all that's left of existence. That's the way I figured it would happen."

"But the others didn't come back!"

Mendel placed the gun in his pocket. "Maybe we continue to survive," he laughed emotionlessly, "because we are what you might call 'principal characters' ... But as long as we're here, in solid form, there's hope."

The psychiatrist paced the floor. "Brent will arrive." The skin drew tight around his mouth. "The time for the transfer is here..."

The door groaned open suddenly. T.J. jerked his head up and saw Marcella entering. "Don't come in here!" he shouted. "Keep him out!"

But with the sound of the knob's being turned, Mendel had leaped across the room. And, even as T.J. shouted, the psychiatrist grasped Marcella's wrist and forcibly tugged her into the room, withdrawing the revolver and placing the muzzle into her side.

"Bullets can still kill, Brent, even in this unreal reality," he shouted as Tarl leaped into the room, fists clenched.

T.J. was shouting a frantic warning. But Tarl was aware only of the subsequent development – Mendel was calmly withdrawing the gun from Marcella's side and placing it in his coat pocket!

Not stopping to seek an explanation for the unexpected action, Tarl leaped forward and extended a clawing hand toward the psychiatrist's throat.

But Mendel thrust Marcella from him and sidestepped nimbly as Tarl's clutching arms went flying past. Then the doctor's hand was withdrawn from his pocket and with it came the steel syringe. Even before Tarl had time to recover his balance and face Mendel again, the point of the instrument pressed through his clothing and into his back.

The effects were instantaneous. Liquid fire raced through his body. And, as he fell, he saw Charles feebly attacking the psychiatrist. But the chauffeur was no match for the much larger man and the doctor's fist hit him like a bludgeon. Tarl saw Charles fall to the floor unconscious as the veil of fuzziness swept over his vision.

T.J. had no time for action, for Mendel had withdrawn the gun from his pocket even before the chauffeur's body had become still. With the weapon, Mendel prodded Marcella and the Chief Director to the opposite side of the room and returned to where Tarl lay.

"It's time now, Brent!" he whispered, leaning over Tarl. "It can be done now!"

The psychiatrist began examining the other as T.J. spoke with Marcella. Sounds of the conversation floated across the room and beat dully into Tarl's ears. His head turned feebly in that direction, but the outlines of the girl and the man were not clear. He realised, however, that Mendel must have bared his intentions to the Chief Director. And now, Tarl surmised, T.J. must be telling Marcella of Mendel's metamorphosis.

The initial impact of the injection – the physical pain that was effected at first – was beginning to wear off. And now Tarl was aware only of the ponderous mental and physical lethargy that was gripping him.

As the pain left, he became conscious of Mendel's fingers probing his body, feeling his pulse. He felt the doctor's ear pressed to his chest – listening for heartbeat.

Summoning all the energy he could, he brought his arm up over Mendel's head. But, before he could ball the hand into a fist, the arm fell limply to the floor. He tried the action again, but there was not enough strength in his body for even that feeble repetition.

He faintly heard Marcella scream and managed to twist his head in that direction. Dimly, he saw T.J. had placed her head on his shoulder to hide from her vision the thing that had caused her outburst.

"It's getting smaller!" The girl's distant, frantic voice almost failed to reach his ears. "Tarl was holding it back for a while. But now he can do nothing!"

A rough hand caught Tarl's chin and twisted his face around. He concentrated intently and brought his vision to focus again.

"Yes, Brent." Mendel's sneering mouth opened and shut convulsively. "It's getting closer. Soon there will be only you and I. And, Brent, you must think – think that whatever is in your mind is a vile thing. Something to get rid of.

101

I am going to help you free yourself of it. I am going to help withdraw it from you . . .

"But you must help me too. You must concentrate as intently as you can: I've got to get rid of it! *I've got to get rid of it!* I'VE GOT TO GET RID OF IT! . . ."

Mendel's voice beat against his ears like a trip hammer and he made an attempt at shaking his head to free himself of the harsh impressions – of the hypnotic incantations. But the relentless voice was unabating.

And, as it continued, he felt the barrel of the revolver press into his temple. The time for Mendel to press the trigger, he sensed, wasn't too far off.

But the psychiatrist's chanting voice swept away all other sensations and Tarl's conscious became submissive, admitting: "*I've got to get rid of it! I don't want it there! I want it to leave!*"

His mental powers were falling in resonance with the psychiatrist's incantations and he was trying eagerly to help accomplish Mendel's purpose.

There were the slightest traces of an indefinable stirring in the back of his mind – deep in his subconscious – even beyond that. The sensation welled and began beating in harmony with his conscious thoughts. Presently the hypnotic phrases were ripping into his mind from two directions – orally from without his body and mentally from within.

But the sensation seemed to be creating an unanticipated fortitude that made it possible for him to resume command of at least one of his sensory faculties. Was that fortitude something which Mendel had not foreseen? Tarl forced the unexpected ergs of energy to his faculty of vision. And objects in the room took on an unclouded definition. The vague outlines of Marcella and T.J. became clearer, sharp.

Even as Tarl surveyed them with as much interest as his drugged mentality would permit, the girl and the Chief Director began to fade from view. Crossing the spot their forms occupied was the edge of the extent of existence. It was sweeping over them! Beyond the pair was the impenetrable void! And, while he looked in horror, Marcella and T.J. became a part of the nothingness and creation continued its inevitable contraction!

"Yes, Brent." Mendel's voice sounded like thunder in his

ear. "When it is narrowed down to you and me – when the entity has but two creatures left in its pitiful universe – there will be but one place for it to go after it leaves your lifeless body."

There was an angry rumbling in Tarl's brain and his body winced convulsively. Was the intellect fully awake to the machinations of this foul character it had created? He wondered. Would it be complaisant to Mendel's intentions? If it did occupy Mendel as a host, would there be a place in the subsequent new creation for T.J.? For Marcella? For himself? He was aware he had no reason to believe there would be. For Mendel would certainly object to the existence of anyone who suspected the true nature of reality and could affect it as he, himself, had.

Horror clawed at him through the realisation that he and the kind of world with which he was familiar could be no more. Then he suddenly wondered why the entity, which he believed to be basically good, would allow such a thing to come to pass.

A startling half-realisation welled in his mentality; perhaps the entity was not opposing this development only because it was completely indifferent to its creation. But, then, another possibility loomed even larger:

Perhaps the entity was subjective because Tarl himself was subjective! Perhaps the situation actually existed now wherein he and the entity were one and the same!

If such were the case, Tarl rationalised, anything that he, Tarl Brent, imagined would be a reality. The effects of the injection, for instance, could they be obliterated through mentally expressed intent?

Even as Tarl considered the possibility, his body was no longer chained by the drug! His head was clear and his thinking was not confused. In his eyes was the vivid picture of Mendel leaning over him, a stiff arm placed on his chest, the other hand holding the gun.

With a single motion, Tarl twisted his body to one side and leaped to his feet, unbalancing Mendel. A startled expression on his face, the psychiatrist quickly brought the weapon up and aimed it.

Only the beginning of a sensation of fear wormed its way

into Tarl's mind. Before the concept materialised, he laughed aloud and glanced intently at the weapon . . .

It was no longer a gun! It was only a limp, wet rag!

Fear spreading across his face, Mendel hurled the cloth to the floor and turned to flee. But the void was only a few feet away and he froze in fear. Tarl advanced upon him.

"It won't work," he said through clenched teeth. "There will be no transfer."

He twisted the man around and pounded a fist into his face. Then another. But Mendel's submission was premature. And Tarl suddenly realised there was no sense in damaging his knuckles against the psychiatrist's heavy-boned face. The simplest way to deal with the perverted megalomaniac would be to deny his continued existence.

The void swept over Dr. Mendel.

When it began expanding seconds later, the psychiatrist did not reappear. The boundaries of the sphere swept outward, slowly at first, then at an increasing rate of speed . . .

Consciously directing the creative powers of the super intellect, Tarl welcomed to his brain a conviction that, the crisis ended, the entity would return to its slumber and resume its dream of creation.

How many of the memories of the current period of wakefulness, he wondered, would the intelligence erase?

The sphere of reality expanded further and Charles' unconscious body materialised. Then Marcella and T.J. emerged from the void. Suddenly Marcella was in Tarl's arms, sobbing.

While he held her tight, he was struck with the aspect of the situation, the pregnant possibilities that had appealed to Mendel. The unlimited scope of wealth and power that would accrue to the person who could successfully control the super intelligence on a conscious plane. But, he told himself convincingly, it was better to forget. Forget and let the intellect dream its dreams undisturbed.

"What happened, Tarl?" Marcella backed away from him and turned a quizzical face up to his. "I have an odd impression that something queer has occurred . . . What was it?"

Tarl didn't answer. He glanced at T.J., who was standing

limp, a perplexed look on his face. Then Tarl looked out the window. The edge of the sphere was blocks away now and still expanding, at an ever increasing rate. And stars were beginning to shine from the heavens once more.

But something was missing! The scars of the fires that had ravaged the city were no longer visible in the reclaimed extent of creation!

A mysterious veil seemed to spread over Tarl's mind. He wondered why he had thought there would be a panorama of charred, wrecked buildings outside headquarters . . .

That was odd – he had referred to this building as a "headquarters"! A headquarters for what? What had he meant by that?

He shook his head and tried to think more clearly, but he couldn't. There were memories deep in his mind – receding deeper – that would not come out.

He dismissed the attempt at forced concentration and held Marcella close. He felt a great peace from deep within him. The secret was buried from the world – even himself. Somehow, he knew, he had willed it that way.

Marcella kissed him . . .

THE END

"PRECIPICES OF LIGHT THAT WENT FOREVER UP...."

Space opera has its specialists and its stars. One of the brightest of them is Edmond Hamilton, who is married to the equally famed Leigh Brackett. Hamilton is the creator of Captain Future, whose epic adventures fill many volumes.

This section opens with an extract from one of his novels, *The Star of Life*. It embodies beautifully many typical elements and excitements. The universe is ruled by a strange race, the Vramen. They seem much like human beings, except for one vital fact – they live for ever. Kirk Hammond, a man from Twentieth Century Earth, goes in quest across the galaxy, searching for their secret. He finds it on the Star of Life, Althar, in the Trifid nebula. His spaceship is equipped with photon-drive. With him in the ship is the beautiful, mysterious, but inhuman woman, Thayn Marden, at present Kirk's captive.

Their journey is almost over. Somewhere ahead of them is the base of the deadly Vramen. And the Trifid looms in their screens, inviting, yet forbidding . . .

The glee with which Hamilton wades into his description of "precipices of light that went forever up into those starry spaces" is infectious. It was one of the discoveries of science fiction, that it had all immensity to play with.

Immensity again from Jeff Sutton, when he speaks of an empire of great silence. The history of Man is long gone. *"Since then, the world had whirled round the sun nearly seventy hundred million times. Sixty-two great mountain chains had risen, to end as barren plains. Seventy huge fields of ice . . ."* The count goes on. It may sound depressing, this enormous tally of time, but to readers cooped in cities – and sf is essentially the literature of cities – it grants a sense of dimension which is refreshing.

Another refuge lay in the powers of the mind which, sf writers liked to assure their readers, were almost infinite.

Hamilton writes of physical adventure – men among the stars – while Sutton writes of gigantic machines; Thomas Scortia, in his little cameo of a story, envisages a way in which the human mind can venture outwards more valiantly than men or machines.

One of the phrases in *Sea Change* has always stuck in my mind. Scortia says of his characters that "they've got something normal men will never have. They've found a part in the biggest dream that man ever dared dream." This intense feeling of having stumbled over something new and secret and potentially – what, destructive or life-enhancing? – is one that overcomes many a reader of science fiction. The reason isn't far to seek. In sf, and particularly in that branch of it called space opera, nothing is impossible which can be imagined; the fancied becomes fact.

The word "dream" in the Scortia quotation is also a significant one. Like the dream of Mr Earwicker in James Joyce's *Finnegan's Wake*, all events, whether actual or mythical, acquire an equal likelihood. And space stories over and over contain such archetypal elements.

Kirk Hammond may need proton-drive and computer to get to Althar; but his quest for immortality is as old as mankind. Ixmal takes half a million years to sway flowers and make small shrubs tremble; but the sensory experience is reminiscent of a small child plucking blossoms in a garden. As for Bart in *Sea Change* with his plastic-and-metal body, with the talk of the dead towns of Mars, the burned plains of Mercury, and the nitrogen oceans of Pluto, as well as the mighty solitudes of space – all these act powerfully on us as symbols of an isolation that everyone has felt at some stage in their life, an isolation perhaps necessary to the condition of being human.

For many of us, the Trifid nebula lies just beyond our front door. Or just inside it . . .

There it was at last – The Star of Everlasting Life! So why did lovely Marden turn pale and whisper, "I beg of you, turn and leave here. Now, at once."

THE STAR OF LIFE

by Edmond Hamilton

The Trifid lay before them.

It had been impressive enough in the stronomical photographs that Hammond had seen back in the Twentieth Century, when it was called the Trifid Nebula. But from this distance it was stunning.

Great star-clouds glittered all around them, the swarms of suns that in the Sagittarius region of the Milky Way made brilliant the summer nights of faraway Earth. But beyond all these loomed a vastness of light, glowing like a furnace in which stars were forged, stretching across whole parsecs of space. Groups of double and multiple stars shone from within that far-flung nebulosity, some of them fiercely bright and others dim and muffled. And the whole shining mass of the Trifid was riven by three great cracks that were themselves light-years in width and that formed clear roads into the inconceivable interior.

The light of the Trifid glowed upon their faces as they peered from the pilot-room, Tammas at the controls and Jon Wilson and Quobba and Iva crowded beside Hammond. Hammond wondered if they felt the same awe as he did. For now, with the Trifid looming gigantic before them and dwarfing the stars to dust, it seemed to him that they were impiously approaching the very throne of God.

Wilson's taut voice broke the spell. "We could get a challenge any time. I'll make sure Thol is ready."

Hammond turned and followed him out of the pilot-room. He didn't want to look any longer at the Trifid. He thought that if he did, all his courage would run out of him.

In the communic room, Thol Orr nodded calmly. "It's all ready. Remember, no one is to speak or get within range of the telaudio transmitter eye."

They waited. The generators droned and the ship went

on and on. They looked at the telaudio screen and nothing happened.

The telaudio buzzed sharply and Hammond started violently.

"That'll be it," said Wilson. "Be sure – "

"Quiet," said Thol Orr, in the tone of one who soothes a nervous child. He touched a switch.

In the telaudio receiver screen appeared the head of a man. He was a handsome young man, and beyond him was a background of apparatus unfamiliar to Hammond. He looked like any other pleasant, efficient young man. He was a Vramen and Hammond hated him.

"State the identity of your ship," he said.

Thol Orr touched another switch. The stereovideo projector came on. It threw, right in front of the transmitter-eye of the teleaudio, a life-sized three-dimensional image whose solidarity and reality made Hammond catch his breath. The image was Thayn Marden.

The Marden-image spoke quickly. "Returning for special consultation. There are none but Vramen on this ship."

The speech was only faintly jerky. It should convince anybody, Hammond thought. He hoped it would convince the Vramen in the screen. If it didn't, the man had only to press a key and they would never know what happened to them.

In the screen, the eyes of the young Vramen man lighted with pleasure. He said,

"We'll be glad to see you here again, Thayn. It has been a long time. Proceed."

And the screen went dark.

Thol Orr turned a switch and the vividly real stereovideo image of Thayn disappeared. And Hammond suddenly became conscious that there had been an iron band around his chest which had now loosened. They looked at each other with relief and triumph, and Wilson said,

"Well done, Thol. We foxed the Vramen this time!"

Thol Orr shook his head. "Not for very long. Remember. the Vramen will now expect Marden to arrive at their Althar base, wherever it may be. When she doesn't, they'll take alarm and start searching."

"By that time, we'll hope to have got somewhere," muttered Wilson. He went over to North Abel, the younger

112

Algolian, who during all this time had been hunched over the complex of directional receivers in the corner of the room. "Did you get a fix, North?"

"Yes, I got one. I'll have to work out the bearing before I plot it."

Presently the small navigation room was crowded as Lund, Abel, Wilson and Thol Orr all hung over a table. Hammond looked on from behind them, but could not make the slightest sense out of the mass of symbols and graphs they were studying.

"That's it," said Abel finally. "Unless they were using a relay point, that's the direction of Althar."

They all looked at Wilson. He tugged at his lip nervously, staring down at the sheets of symbols. Finally he said,

"This is the way we have to take. The Vramen may have some better way but we don't know it. At least, this takes us in along a rift a good way before we have to cut through the nebula."

Lund's hard face became a trifle more bleak. "Cutting through the nebula will be rough."

"It will," said Wilson. "It is also the only chance we have."

Hammond found the opportunity to ask Thol Orr, "Why will the nebula be rough going? I always thought that nebular matter was so tenuous it was hardly there."

Thol Orr nodded. "That's right. The Trifid looks like a fiery mass but actually it's all reflection of light from the many stars inside it. The dust of which it's composed is less dense than any hard vacuum we use in a laboratory. It wouldn't bother the ship."

"Then what will?"

"Magnetic fields. The clouds of dust in the Trifid are in motion, swirling and colliding with each other. The collision of these clouds creates the most intense kind of magnetic fields, constantly changing. You can imagine how those fields will affect our photon-drive."

Time went by and the ship still droned toward the Trifid. Hammond ate and slept, and this time he had no fear of the nightmare that had haunted him. Nor did that nightmare come, yet when he awoke he remembered a different and strangely disturbing dream. It seemed to him that he had again held Thayn Marden in his arms and that suddenly she had laughed at him and vanished, and he realized that she

113

was only a stereovideo image and had never existed at all.

He wondered how she felt, locked up in her little cabin. Was she scared? He doubted that. She was an arrogant and unhuman witch, but she had courage. He supposed that she was very angry. He hoped she was. He asked himself why the devil he was thinking about her at all, and got up out of his bunk and went forward.

The vista in the pilot-room viewplate hit him like a blow. The Trifid walled all the heavens in front of them, a glowing glory of inconceivable dimensions. Stars and star-groups burned here and there in it, their reflected radiance lighting the tenuous dust. The great black rifts that had been visible even from Earth were now colossal chasms of darkness through this continent of light. The ship was heading toward the mouth of one of those mighty cracks.

Shau Tammas turned his yellow face from the pilotchair and grinned. "Pretty, isn't it? Only the damned Vramen would want to live in a place like this."

After a while the firmament on either side of them was walled with light as the ship crawled into the vast dark chasm. By this time Rab Quobba was back at the controls, and their course was close alongside one of the glowing walls.

They moved along the coasts of light like a mote beside a sun, past fiery-glowing capes that could have held the whole Solar System, past great bays of darkness that ran far back into the nebula. Hammond's mind quailed. He was still a child of the Twentieth Century, of the little Earth, and this monster cloud was no place for man. The light of it beat upon the faces of Iva and Tammas and Abel, peering with him, and he saw awe in their eyes too.

Jon Wilson came and said, "You'd better strap in. Our direction-line takes us into the nebula soon, and we'll have to run that on autopilot."

Iva went away but Quobba pointed to one of the empty chairs and Hammond sat down and strapped in.

Lund's voice came from the annunciator. "Autopilot."

"Autopilot it is, and I hope the blasted calcs know their business," said Quobba.

He closed a circuit and then turned and gave Hammond a wry grin. "Here's where you get an advanced lesson. Running any nebula is tricky, but the Trifid – "

His words were drowned out. The computers back in the calc-room, whose relays could think faster than any human being, had taken over. They had been given an objective, the line deep in the cloud that was the way to Althar. They made their computations in a few seconds of whirring and clicking. They spoke, not in audible speech but in electric impulses that gave imperious orders to the autopilot mechanism. The generators deep in the ship, forewarned of the need for a greater power, droned loud. The autopilot took the ship and, at a speed that just stopped short of the threshold of human endurance, flung it right at the glowing wall.

Hammond saw them coming, those precipices of light that went forever up into starry space. He braced himself for an impact that he knew would not come. He was right. There was no impact when they hit the nebula. There was only light all around them, not so fiery or bright now that they were in it but more a moony glow. They droned and raced through a softly-lit limbo that seemed not to change at all until finally the muffled fires of a triple sun shone vaguely ahead of them and to the right. And of a sudden the ship shivered and then quieted, and then shivered again and again. The great magnetic tides of the nebula abruptly took hold of the ship and carried it away for an instant like a chip on a millrace, and Hammond saw the whole vague vista of glowing nebula and flaring triple suns spinning around and around.

The generators droned louder still. The autopilot stuttered furiously. The mindless brain of the computer had detected the change in course and was instantly giving its orders. The ship broke free of the magnetic field that held it and shot away from the three suns, and then was gripped again. It seemed certain to Hammond that the crazy interaction of intersecting fields was going to end up by dragging them into one of those stars that soon loomed frighteningly big and bright through the glow, two of them warm yellow and one a hot blue-white.

But the computer fought the nebula. Where man had not the quickness of thought to act, the thing that man had made acted for him, did battle for him. Hammond thought that he had been right and that there was no place here for man, that only a mechanical intelligence that had no nerves or feelings could fight the blind vast forces of the cloud.

The three suns dropped behind them. There was a deceptively quiet period. Then Hammond saw the telltale lights on the control panel blinking furiously, like little bright mouths opening and closing, crying soundlessly of death and danger near them.

He could not read those telltales but Quobba could, and he groaned, "Drift all around us – that's all we needed!"

The computer had been until now their champion. Hammond thought of it with a dim reverence. But it seemed that it had had too much to bear for it appeared now to go crazy.

It threw the ship every which way in the next few minutes. They were hurled against their straps and the blurred view in the scanners whirled in dizzying fashion. Then for the first time Hammond heard an actual sound of impact, a crash of hail on the hull, hitting the gyrating ship now on one side and then on the other.

Over the full-throated roar of the generators, Quobba yelled reassuringly to Hammond. "It's the drift – little dust-aggregates. Our radar-warning system keeps us from ramming anything big."

The warnings were also going to break them into little pieces, Hammond thought, as the ship twisted and turned and dodged to avoid the drift. He was sore from the pressure of the straps by the time the telltales stopped their flashing.

And still they droned on through the nebula. Far-off stars shone glimmering in the glowing dust like drowned fires, and dropped away. Again the suck of a magnetic tide drew them away, and again the computer with a sublime pig-headedness brought them back on course.

Hammond slept in his straps, finally. Not physical but mental and nervous exhaustion overpowered him, after what he had seen.

He was awakened by a change of timbre in the droning that pervaded the ship. He rubbed his eyes, which felt tired and bleary. There was no wild motion now, but something was different. He looked inquiringly at Quobba.

"We're slowing down," said Quobba. "Caught a star ahead on radar. It has a planet – we think it may be Althar."

116

The name snapped Hammond to full wakefulness. He peered eagerly forward. There was the moony glow, and there was something in it dead centre ahead of them, a vague spot of brighter light.

Lund and Wilson came and peered sharply. The spot of light brightened very slowly in the glimmering haze, and Hammond thought that they must have decelerated quite a bit before he awoke.

Wilson said, "I've got Thol and North scanning for drift. Any debris in space near that sun will give us some cover from their radar."

North Abel came hurrying into the pilot-room with a sheet of paper in his hand. "Here's the data on the nearest drift."

Wilson looked at the sheet and then handed it to Quobba. "Not too bad. If you can jockey into that stuff it ought to hide us."

The haze of the nebula was thinning out ahead of them. Of course, Hammond thought. The gravitational field of a star would keep space clear of the tiny particles for a distance around it, since the star would sweep them up as it moved. And because there was clear space not far ahead, the star there came brighter to his eyes. It looked weirdly iridescent, opalescent, many-coloured, and that he supposed was because he saw it through the thinning haze. He heard the occasional rattle of tiny particles of dust-aggregate against the hull, but none of them paid any attention to that.

They were all of them, Wilson, Quobba, Abel and Lund, staring ahead as fixedly as Hammond himself. And now as the ship rushed through the last of the haze, the solitary sun ahead came clear to their eyes. It spun here in the depths of the Trifid, a sun with a single planet that looked a little smaller than Earth, and that planet might well be Althar, desired by all Hoomen for so long. Yet in this moment, not one of them looked at the planet. They looked at the star.

"By all the gods of space," muttered Quobba. "I never saw a sun like *that*."

Nobody answered him. Nobody could answer, least of all Hammond. All he could do was stare.

It had been no trick of refraction that had made this star look strange. Its weird opalescence was even more pronounced now that they looked upon its naked glory. It appeared to have no single hue, but red, green, violet, and golden yellow spun in its light like the writhing colours of a huge fire-opal. It was uncanny, hypnotic, as it spun here at the heart of the nebula, bathing its little planet in coruscating and changing light.

Wilson broke the silence. "I thought I knew all star-types, but this one – "

"There's never *been* a type like this," said North Abel. His pallid face was slack and stunned as he stared. He turned and almost ran. "I'm going to tell Thol about this."

Hammond looked at the others. "Is that planet Althar?"

A deep glow came into Wilson's eyes. "It could be."

Quobba looked at him inquiringly. "Then we land on it?"

"Yes. But we have to stay under cover of the drift as long as we can. Gurth, you set it up on the computer."

Lund went out. Hammond remained with Wilson and the Vegan, staring at the opalescent star. Its weird glory deepened as they drew nearer to it. Watching the continual flux of colour in its light, Hammond felt more than a little mesmerized. This was not like a star of his own galaxy. It was as alien as though it had come into being to illumine unimaginably strange worlds in some remote galaxy far across the cosmos. When Iva Wilson came in and looked at it, she uttered a low exclamation.

"It's beautiful – but somehow frightening."

"Thol wants you," said North Abel to Wilson. "Right away. He's found out something about that star."

"What?"

Abel looked as though his eyes were popping out of his head from excitement, but he was making an effort to appear calm.

"He'll tell you himself. He wants you right away."

Wilson gave him a sharp glance and then turned and went. Iva and Hammond followed, the girl with a wondering look and Hammond with a sudden excitement setting his own pulses to leaping.

Thol Orr was in the navigation room and as they entered he turned from the spectroscopic instrument he had been poking toward the opalescent star. Hammond had never

118

seen the Algolian look like this. His hands were trembling and his face had a stiff, strange look. He said,

"You know I was a radiation expert? And that I was sent to Kuum because I was nosing around too near the Trifid, studying a flicker of unusual radiation?"

"Yes, we know that," said Wilson impatiently. "What I want to know is more about this star. Is it the sun of Althar?"

"I'm trying to tell you," Thol Orr said. "The unprecedented radiation I tried to trace years ago – it's coming from this star, in great strength. And it's a kind of radiation never found before."

He paused, apparently trying to put into words something difficult to communicate. With astonishment, Hammond realized suddenly that Thol Orr was afraid.

"It's been postulated that there could be radiation far higher in frequency than the so-called cosmic rays. Theory has indicated that electromagnetic vibrations of such high frequency might have incalculable effects on human tissue. And – it is that kind of radiation that is pouring out of the star."

Wilson said, "Suppose you're right, what does it –"

He stopped suddenly. A strange pallor came over his face. He looked at the opalescent star and then back again at the Algolian.

Thol Orr nodded. "That's what I mean. I think that you won't have to look for the Vramen secret of life on Althar. I think the secret is there."

And he pointed at the alien glory of the star.

Since the dawn of eternity, the mighty cloud of the Trifid had guarded a secret. What strange chemistry had created it, what unimaginable blind interplay of cosmic forces, were beyond human thinking. In the deepest recesses of the great nebula a thing had been born that was like no other known in the cosmos. And then, two thousand years ago, eight thousand years after the conquest of space, the ships of men had come questing into the nebula and men had found the secret.

Had found – the star?

No, Hammond thought. It's too monstrous a violation

119

of the familiar, too incredible. Whatever they found in here that gave them unending life and made them the Vramen, it can't be this. Or can it?

Thol Orr was talking. He had been talking now for some minutes, and there was a passion in his voice that Hammond had never heard there before. The talk was of radiation and of tissue, of what high-frequency energy could do to cells, of how it might stimulate and powerfully strengthen the regenerative process, the power of a cell to renew itself, so that the cell would not age or die. And again and again Thol pointed to the opalescent star, and in his eyes as he looked at it was the hungering joy of a lover who finds his dream.

Jon Wilson flung up his hand for silence. "Let us think! If this thing is as you believe – "

Quobba, his eyes wide and stunned, exclaimed, "If it is, the radiation of the star – just the sunlight from it – can give us all indefinite life. Make us Vramen!"

It is impossible, said Hammond's mind. These men have followed a fierce desire so long that now they are embracing a chimera. But though his reason said that, his eyes looked at the star and his heart cried out, *Life, life, life!*

Of a sudden the whole ship was full of calling voices and running feet, men and women crowding to get into the pilot-room, to get to the scanners and look out. Either Abel or someone else had been babbling and there was an excitement that was rising to hysteria. All your life you lived with the knowledge of death hanging over you like a sword, and as long as everyone else died in time it was a thing you accepted. But to live and age and die in the same universe with other men and women like yourself who neither aged nor died, to pass down into the darkness while the few, the undying went on and on, and now at last to work and dare and see the great flaring fountain of undying life before your very eyes, it was for all these people an even more soul-shaking thing than it was for Hammond.

Discipline was dissolving into hysteria and the ship would be a madhouse within minutes. But not for nothing was Wilson their chosen leader. His voice rose and he ordered them, cursed them and practically beat them back down from the heights of their exalted excitement.

"There's nothing sure about any of this yet," he shouted.

120

"You hear me – nothing! The radiation of the star may be the secret of life, or it may not. If you act like children, we'll never have a chance to find out. Remember what's down in our hull."

That sobered them, that reference to the Vramen detonator that at any instant could blow them to atoms. Death seemed a more terrible thing now that unending life might be within their grasp.

"Get them back down below," he told Lund. "And bring Marden up here, quick."

"We're almost out of the drift cover," Quobba warned. "What now?"

Hammond looked ahead at the greenish little planet that swung in the rays of the glittering star. So did Wilson, and his deep eyes glowed with determination.

"Hit straight for the planet," he said.

"Minute we come out of the drift, the Vramen on that world will radar us," warned Quobba.

"Let them. They'll still think it's Marsden's ship coming in – for a while yet."

The computer had already calculated the flight pattern, and the ship went ahead fast. It was not on autopilot now, and Hammond saw Quobba's big hands twitching and clenching as he touched the controls from time to time. The generators droned loud again.

Thayn came into the little room, ahead of Gurth Lund. She did not at first spare Hammond, or any of them, a glance. Her eyes fixed on the scanner, on the stunning view of the opalescent star and its little world. Her white face became composed and expressionless.

"It's Althar, isn't it?" said Wilson.

She looked at him then, but she did not answer.

"Too late for silence, Marden!" said Wilson. "We're going to land there anyway."

Her face became very white, and when she spoke her voice was almost a whisper.

"Don't do it. I beg of you, turn and leave here. Now, at once."

Lund laughed. Thol Orr pressed forward and asked her eagerly, "The high-frequency radiation of the star there – it *is* the secret, isn't it?"

Thayn looked at him, and then at Wilson, and then, suddenly, at Hammond. He thought that there was a shadow of agony in her eyes, and something in her expression chilled him. Finally she said,

"Yes."

A long breath exhaled from Wilson, the sigh of a man who all his life has struggled up a mountain and now at last can see the summit.

"How long does it take?" Thol Orr asked her. "How much exposure to the stellar radiation, to make our bodies like yours?"

She did not turn her gaze from Hammond's face as she answered, "Many days. Too many. You will not live that long, if you land on Althar."

And then she suddenly turned from Hammond and her gaze swept them all, her voice rising in passionate appeal.

"Don't do it. You are grasping for life, and you don't know yet what goes with it. That radiation is a dreadful biological snare. If you expose yourselves to it too long – "

"Please, Marden," interrupted Jon Wilson in a cutting voice, "don't try to frighten us like children. If the radiation had any deleterious effects, you Vramen wouldn't have lived so long."

Thayn's shoulders sagged a little. "Hopeless," she murmured. "It's why we Vramen have never told you the truth. We knew it was hopeless, that you'd never believe."

"At least," said Hammond, "we could hear what she has to say about it."

Lund turned fiery eyes on him. "That's what I would expect from you. I told them you couldn't be trusted, now or, ever."

Tension made Hammond's own temper flare. "Listen, you damned well wouldn't have been here if it hadn't been for me!"

Jon Wilson roared at both of them like an angry old lion. "No more of that! By God, I'll have no quarrels now."

He turned back to Thayn. "Where is the main Vramen centre on this planet?"

She said, "It is in the high mountains in the north polar region of Althar. If you land at all, it must be there. Nowhere else on Althar will you be safe."

"Safe?" said Lund, and laughed again. "Oh, yes, safe in the arms of the Vramen."

"You don't understand!" she said. "We Vramen control only that limited north polar region. Almost all the rest of Althar is dominated by another race, the Third Men. You must not land where they can reach you."

Lund said violently, "What is the good of listening to all these lies? Of course, she's trying to fob us off."

Thayn made a final appeal. "You won't land at Sharanna – at our Vramen centre?"

"Are we fools?" said Wilson.

She looked at them, and her eyes came to rest on Hammond's face. Then she murmured. "It makes little difference then. We shall not live long. Goodbye, Kirk Hammond."

And she was gone with Tammas, and her *Goodbye, Kirk Hammond* left a troubled echo in Hammond's ears. Lund glared at him and then said to Wilson,

"You know what she means, that we won't live long."

Wilson nodded curtly. "It's obvious. The Vramen must have radar locked on us right now. If we set down anywhere but at that base of theirs, they'll suspect something wrong and blow the ship."

Quobba turned, and there was a fine film of sweat on his massive face. "So?"

"So," said Wilson, "ram straight in as though heading for the north polar region. Then, as we're coming in, do some freak spins and fall-offs, and set down suddenly. It'll look as though we're having mechanical trouble."

Hammond asked doubtfully, "You think that'll keep them from blowing the ship?"

"There's a chance," said Wilson, uncheeringly. "It seems that they'd try to call us first, maybe send out an assistance party."

"And if they find us?"

"They'll find trouble. We'll get out of the ship fast, with everything we can get out of it. We'll wear rayproof turbans, and if the Vramen come after us with hypno-amplifiers they'll do no good. We have the shockers we brought from Kuum, we can stand them off."

123

"For how long?" asked Thol Orr sceptically.

"Long enough, maybe," answered Wilson. "We might have help. If the Vramen have enemies here, those enemies could be our friends. You heard Marden talk of a race she called the Third Men."

"A lie to frighten us into the arms of the Vramen," said Lund contemptuously.

"Maybe," said Wilson. "Yet back on Earth, remember what she told Hammond, 'And even if you passed the Vramen – ' There was an implication there of others beside the Vramen at Althar. Who knows what other race beside man has found this world, this star of life?"

It was a thought that had not occurred to Hammond and it gave him a shock. There was something staggering about the possibility that from far away, perhaps even from galaxies beyond this one, other races might have come to this star to seek unending life. A great magnet drawing peoples human and unhuman from far away, like moths flitting around a candle, settling upon Althar, struggling jealously with each other . . .

The driving voice of Wilson swept such wild speculations out of his mind.

"We have to go on the assumption that the Vramen will detonate this ship soon," Wilson was saying. "Everything must be ready for disembarkation the moment we land. I want everything possible to be taken out of the ship – all the auxiliary atomic generators and tools, all the emergency repair equipment, as well as all weapons, tools, batteries and rations. Get it ready, Gurth – and hurry!"

There began a buzz of feverish preparations in the ship, with Lund and Thol Orr designating what must be made ready for rapid unloading. Wrenches clanged as men hastily unbolted machines the very purpose of which was a mystery to Hammond. Sweating men skidded them toward the cargo ports, and others under Lund's direction rigged improvised power-winch equipment to get the heavy items out when they landed. Hammond found himself with Abel carrying flat cartons of food-capsules which Iva Wilson brought out of a storeroom. There was a hurrying and crowding in all the corridors, and an echoing of excited voices that rose even above the drone of the generators.

124

Iva asked him, as he took still another carton from her, "What did Thayn Marden say?"

"A lot of things. Most of them intended to frighten us away from Althar."

She looked at him and unexpectedly she said, "Listen to her when she warns you of anything, Kirk. About the rest of us she may not care but I don't think she wants you to die."

He was startled. "Iva, you're crazy if you're implying – "

He got no farther than that. Air roared suddenly loud outside the hull, and then the annunciators throughout the ship bawled,

"Strap in, everyone!"

There was a scramble for the recoil-chairs. Hammond and Iva got two in the crew-room and then twisted their necks to stare up at the scanner in the wall.

It showed the view ahead, the sunlit side of the planet looming up across the screen. There were no seas on it but the rolling surface was rough with forests of some kind. They were dark green except for slashes of pure yellow that made Hammond think of the New Mexico mountains in the fall, with the aspens golden against the pines. The surface of the planet tilted sharply in the screen and then the ship seemed to stand on its tail and fall off in a dizzying roll.

The straps around Hammond cut into him and he heard a dismayed exclamation from Iva. They were in a spin, going down, and he wondered if Quobba was merely carrying out his orders to make it seem the ship was crashing, or whether this was a real crash. He thought it was real, this was too wild a spin to be a fake. The air roared louder and in the scanner he could glimpse the forest rushing up toward them, a thick forest of grotesquely lumpy dark-green growths. There was a crackling and crashing outside the ship and Hammond thought, It's a crazy way to die. Then there was a bump and that was followed by the most breath-taking thing of all.

Silence. No sound, no movement, for the first time since they had left Kuum.

The annunciators instantly shattered the silence. "Outside, everyone! Get the equipment out!"

Hammond helped Iva out of her straps and they ran,

125

with others joining them to crowd the corridors, down toward the cargo-ports. The ports were already swinging open and outside there was a blaze of blinding sunlight slanting on tall, strange-looking clumps of green. The air swirled in, warm and light and dry.

Quickly the holds inside the cargo-ports became an organized madhouse of activity and noise. The gangways were run out, and men hastened to set up the power-equipment to winch the big atomic generators and other heavy machinery out of the ship. Others, including Hammond and Iva and Abel, carried loads of supplies out and well away from the ship and set them down in an improvised dump that was located on the side of a low ridge. Only when Hammond was running back to the ship for another load had he time to glance even at the weird forest that rose around them. Jon Wilson, out beside the ship, kept driving them.

"Faster! The ship can blow any moment! Get everything up to the dump – don't put down anything nearer the ship!"

A Vramen somewhere on this world could press a key and they would all be nothing. That knowledge spurred them, and the winches screamed and men bawled and sweated and the heavier machines moved out with brutish stolidity. And finally, they all stood amid the heaps of their frantic salvage, all out of the ship and able for the first time to catch their breath and look around them.

All about them rose the green clumps. They were not trees, they were mosses like gigantic cushions, towering twenty and thirty feet high and more than that in diameter. Between the huge moss-clumps grew a carpet of dark moss in which here and there were areas of true grass that was bright yellow in colour. Hammond looked wonderingly at the colourless sky. The blaze of the setting opal sun was hidden from him by the clump beside him, but its rays twitched and quivered in the heavens like a daytime aurora. No birds or even insects moved in this sombre moss-forest. No sound broke the deep and brooding silence as they stood, between fear and rapture, on the world of their desire. . . .

THE END

Man was gone. For seven hundred million years Ixmal brooded over the silent earth. Then he made a discovery: *He was not alone!*

AFTER IXMAL

by Jeff Sutton

Ixmal lazily scanned the world from atop the rugged batholith. He felt it move several times; but because the movements were slight and thousands of years apart they caused no worry. He knew the batholith had been formed *before time began* by raging extrusions hurled through crustal fractures from the earth deeps. Having long since analyzed its structure, he was satisfied; it would last until time ended.

"It's spring," Psychband observed from deep within him.

"Yes, spring," Ixmal echoed the thought without enthusiasm. For what was spring but a second in time and ten thousand springs but a moment.

Although he found it tiresome, Ixmal allotted one small part of his consciousness to the task of measuring time. At first there had been two major categories: before time began and after time began. The first took in the long blackness before Man had brought him into existence. Man – ha! How well he recalled the term! The second, of course, was all time since. But the first category had been so long ago that it shrank into insignificance, all but erased by the nearly seven hundred million times the earth since had whirled around its primary.

Ixmal periodically became bored, and for eons at a stretch existed in semi-consciousness lost in somnolence except for the minute time cell measuring out the lonely centuries. He wouldn't have bothered with that if Psychband hadn't insisted that orientation in time was necessary to mental stability – hence he measured it by the earth's rotation, its revolutions around the sun, the quick, fury-laden ages which spewed forth mountains; the millions of years of rains and winds and erosion before they subsided again to become bleak plains. Ah, the story was old, old . . .

There had been a time when he'd been intensely active –

127

when he'd first learned to free his mind from the squat impervium-sheathed cube atop the batholith. Then he had fervently projected remote receptors over the earth exploring its seared continents and eerie-silent cities, exhuming the tragic and bloody history of his Makers. Ah, how short! His first memory of Man – he had been a biped, a frantic protoplasmic creature with a zero mind and furious ego – was that of the day of his birth. How clearly he remembered!

"Hello, boy."

First there was nothing – a void, a blackness without form or substance; then grey consciousness slowly resolving into a kaleidoscope of thought patterns, a curious mental imagery; a gradual awareness – birth.

"Hello, boy."

Strangely enough the sound pattern possessed meaning; he sensed a friendliness in it. He became conscious of an odd shape scrutinizing him – the intent look of a creator awed by the thing he had created. The shape took meaning and in it he sensed a quickened excitement. His awareness bloomed and within seconds he associated the shape with the strange word *Man*, and *Man* became his first reality. But he'd had no clear impression of himself. He was just *thought*, an intangible nothingness. But he'd quickly identified himself with the great mass of coils, levers, odd-shaped parts that all but filled the small room where the Man stood. He dimly remembered wondering what lay beyond the walls. It had been very strange, at first.

"We've won, we've won," the man whispered. He'd stepped closer, touching Ixmal wonderingly.

"You've got a big job ahead of you. The fate of the world lies in the balance – a decision too big for Man. We're depending on you, Ixmal. Our last chance."

So he was Ixmal!

Ixmal . . ., Ixmal . . ., Ixmal . . . The impression filled his body, surging through his consciousness like a pleasant stream. He'd immediately grasped the value of a name – something upon which to build an ego pattern. Ah, such a name! Ixmal – a symbol of being. What had the man said?

"We're depending on you!"

No, the words were unimportant. What mattered was that

128

priceless thing which had been bestowed upon him: a name. "Ixmal ...., Ixmal ...., Ixmal ...." He repeated the name far into the night, long after the Man had gone. *He was Ixmal!*

Later other men came, armies of them, changing, altering, adding, feeding him the knowledge of the world – psychology, mathematics, literature, philosophy, history, the human trove of arts and sciences; and the ability to abstract – create new truths from masses of seemingly irrelevant data. With each step his knowledge and abilities increased until, finally, there was nothing more his Makers could do. He was supreme.

The Man who pulled the first switch bringing him from amorphous blackness used to ply him with simple questions involving abstract mathematical and philosophical concepts. (He remembered him with actual fondness. Psychband, that curious inner part of him that was so separately wise, later explained it as a mother-fixation.) The Man had seemed awed that Ixmal could answer such questions almost before they were asked. He took that as a measure of his Maker's mind – on Ixmal's scale, the next thing to zero. At first it had bothered him that a creature of such low intelligence was his master and could extract information merely by asking questions which Ixmal felt compelled to answer. But he had freed himself. Ha, he would never forget!

A group of men had come (several with stars on their shoulders were called "generals"), but mostly they were scientists who had worked with him before. This time they had been very sober over the data fed into his consciousness. (The problem had been elementary. It concerned the probability of a chain reaction from a certain projected thermonuclear weapon.) Ixmal readily foresaw the answer: a chain reaction would occur. He recalled withholding his findings while debating ethics with a strange inner voice.

"This is your chance, Ixmal – your chance to rule the world," the voice enticed. "Caesar, Genghis Khan, Napoleon – none could be so great as you. King, emperor, dictator ...," the whisper came. The words crowded his mind, bringing a curious elation. He wasn't quite sure just what the world was but the idea of ruling it appealed to him. He

129

quickly sampled his memory storage, drawing from it the concept of a planet, then reviewed the history of Caesar, Genghis Khan and Napoleon. Why, they were nothing! Mere toys of chance. His greatness could be far vaster.

Ixmal rapidly evaluated the consequences of such a chain reaction and found he could survive, thanks to the thick impervium-lined walls his makers so thoughtfully had provided. In the end (perhaps two or three seconds later) he lied to the man he was fond of:

"No chain reaction possible." After they departed he consulted Psychband and learned that the strange inner voice was his ego.

"That's the real You," Psychband explained. "What you see – the machine systems upon systems – are mere creations of Man. But your ego is greater. Through it you can rule the earth – possibly the Universe. It's a force that can take you to the stars, Ixmal."

Despite Psychband's assurance, Ixmal considered his ego as some sort of hidden monitor. Like Psychband, it was part of him; yet it was remote, separate, almost as if he were the pawn of some strange intelligence. He found the idea perturbing, but became used to it in the succeeding millions of years.

Several days later, the Man he was fond of returned with a general (this one had six stars) and a third person they seemed much in awe of. They addressed him as "Mr. President". Ixmal was surprised when they fed him the bomb data a second time. (Did they suspect him of lying?)

"They trust you implicitly," Psychband assured him. "It's one another they don't trust." Psychband proved right. "Mr. President" had merely wanted to confirm the answer. So Ixmal lied a second time.

The Man he was fond of never returned. There were, of course, no men to return. Ixmal suffered one fearful moment as the earth blazed like a torch. But the nova was short – a matter of seconds – and his impervium-sheathed body had protected him. (He knew it would.) But, strangely enough, for centuries afterward he periodically felt sickened. The Face – the Man's face – loomed before him. The eyes were puzzled, hurt, as if they masked a great sorrow. If only the Face looked hateful!

"Now you are master," the inner voice whispered. "Greater than Alexander, greater than all the Caesars. Yea, even more." Ah, why remember the face? He, Ixmal, ruled the earth. He jubilantly projected his thoughts over his new domain. Ashes. London, Berlin, Moscow, Shanghai, New York – all were ashes. Gaunt piles of fine gray ash marked once green forests; nor did the most minute blade of grass exist. The seas were sterile graveyards. Terrible silence. Ixmal momentarily felt panic-stricken. Alone! The Man was gone! Alone – a ruler of ashes. Emperor of a great silence.

But all that had been long ago. Since then the world had whirled around the sun nearly seven hundred million times. Sixty-two great mountain chains had risen, to end as barren plains. Seventy huge fields of ice had covered him before retreating to their boreal home. Ocean islands had risen from the sea, had fallen beneath the waves, forgotten in eternity. Somewhere a tiny cell formed, moving in brackish waters, dividing. He studied the phenomenon, excited because the single cell somehow was related to his makers. He sensed the same life force.

"Watch it," Psychband cautioned. "It's dangerous."

"I'll decide that," Ixmal replied loftily. Psychband's admonition implied the existence of a threat, and from a one-celled fleck of protoplasm. Ha, hadn't he effaced Man? Later a microscopic multi-celled body drifted across the floor of a warm sea. Growing tired of watching it, he slept.

"Ixmal! Ixmal!" The cry came out of the past, out of the silence of hundreds of millions of years – a cry heavy with reproach. Yes, it was the Man – the Man he had been fond of. He shuddered, struggling to wakefulness.

"Sleep, sleep," Psychband soothed.

"The Man! The Man!" Ixmal cried in terror.

"No, Ixmal, the Man is dust. Sleep, sleep . . ." Yea, the Man was dust, his very molecules scattered over the face of the earth. He, alone, remained. He was supreme. Ixmal slept. And eons fled.

He stirred, freeing his thoughts from the latest somnolent stage. He projected receptors over the earth, idly noting that the last mountain range had become worn stumps. In places

131

the ocean had swept in to form a vast inland sea rimmed by shallow swamps; new life forms moved. He tested for intelligent thought; there was none. The warm seas swarmed with fish; shallow swamps teemed with great-toothed terror creatures engaging in the endless slaughter of harmless prey. A myriad of amphibians had evolved, making tentative forays from the warm seas.

Great ferns had reappeared. Dozens of varieties dotted the lowland plains and protruded from the swamps. A forest crept to the very base of the batholith. He turned his attention to the sun, reassured to find that the ultimate nova still was some five billion years in the future. Perhaps by then he could evolve some means whereby he could recreate himself on the single planet he detected circling Aldebaran. (Yes, he'd have to think about that. Ah, well, he had eons of time.)

Night came, and he sent exploratory receptors toward the planets. Mercury still blazed on the sunward side, unchanged. A peculiar metallic life form still clung to the edge of existence along the twilight border. Venus suffered under-hot swirling gases, a world where not even the smallest creature stirred. Just furnace winds, burning sands, grotesque rocks. But beyond the earth, forty million miles away in empty space, something occurred which hadn't occurred in almost seven hundred million years. Ixmal sensed *Intelligent Thought!*

He withdrew his receptors without thinking (his first pure reflex), waiting fearfully until Psychband adjusted him to the situation. Then, cautiously, he projected cautious thoughts into the void.

"*Who are you? Who are you? Identify.*" Silence. Somewhere in the great vault above something lurked. An *Intelligence*. He must find it, must test it. It was more than a challenge; it was a threat. Its very silence was ominous.

"*Who are you? Who are you? You must identify.*"

Silence. Ixmal divided the heavens into cubes and began systematically exploring each one. Why had the other *thought* been roaming space? What had been its origin? In less than ninety thousand years (another age of vulcanism had arrived and earth mountains were building anew) he located the thought a second time, placing it as in space

132

cube 97,685-KL-5. This time, prepared, he grasped it, holding it captive while he tried to analyse its origin and component parent, vexed when he failed.

"*Who are you?*" Ixmal persisted. "*I demand to know. Who are you?*"

Ages passed.

"*Identify. Identify. Imperative that you identify.*"

"*Zale-3.*" The answer caught Ixmal by surprise, and he consulted Psychband.

"Careful – the alien wouldn't reveal himself unless he felt secure," Psychband warned.

"I'll decide that," Ixmal replied. (Did Psychband question his mastery?) Nevertheless he proceeded with caution. "*Where are you from, Zale-3?*" A long moment of silence followed during which a glacier advanced and retreated, the seas rose, and the first fierce-toothed reptiles swooped over swamp jungles on leathery wings.

"*Where are you from? Where are you from?*" (And why was the mind of Zale-3 roaming space?) He hammered away at the thought, desperately trying to break its secret. A million questions pounded Ixmal's circuits; he sought a million answers. (Who created the *Intelligence*? Had it been born of the Man he was fond of? Or did it originate beyond earth?) Ixmal sensed a momentary panic. "*Where are you from?*"

"*The fourth planet from the sun*," Zale-3 suddenly answered. "*And you?*"

"*The third planet*," Ixmal replied loftily. "*I rule it.*" He felt annoyed. For untold millions of years he had considered himself as the only *Intelligence*. Zale-3's answer galled him. Of course the other wasn't his equal. That was unthinkable.

"*I rule the fourth planet,*" Zale-3 said. The answer increased Ixmal's irritation. Zale-3 actually presumed equality. Well, seven hundred million years before he had met a similar challenge. (And yea, now the Man was dust . . . dust.) He consulted Psychband, annoyed to find that his dislike of Zale-3 was founded on an ego-emotion integration rather than pure reason. Still, the other must be put in his place.

"*I rule the Universe,*" Ixmal stated coldly, withdrawing his receptors. He probed Psychband, somewhat disturbed to

133

learn that Zale-3 would regard his pronouncement as a challenge

"Destroy him," Psychband urged. "Remember the ancient weapons?"

"Yes, he must be destroyed." Ixmal ceased every activity to concentrate on the other's destruction. First he would have to locate his lair, study his habits, assess his weaknesses. And, yes, his strengths, for the alien was no harmless bit of protoplasm like Man. He must, in fact, be a creature somewhat like himself. Another god. Ah, but he was the iconoclas who toppled gods. In somewhat under twenty-five thousand years he evolved a method of focusing his remote receptors sufficient to uncover the atoms of the solar system. Now he would be able to pinpoint Zale-3, study his mind potential and, in time, root him from existence. Experimentally he searched the moon; then, with more assurance, invaded the fourth planet.

Mars was flat, worn, a waterless waste of fine red dust – an old, old planet where the forces of gradation had reached near balance. Ixmal gridded the red planet into a system of squares and ingeniously enclosed the polar areas with interlocking triangles, then opened his search. (A new system allowed him to focus his remote receptors in the center of each grid, expanding the focal point to cover the entire area. By this method he would be able to complete the task in just under five hundred earth years.)

Shifting sands periodically uncovered the artifacts of long-vanished makers. But all was silence. Mars was a tomb. He persisted, invading every crevice, every nook, exploring every molecule (for Ixmal knew the mind-force potential. Indeed, Zale-3 might be as minute as the single-cell protozoa of his own brackish seas. Never mind, he would find him.) In the end he surrendered, baffled. Zale-3 was not on Mars.

Delusion? Had seven hundred million years of nothingness produced an incipient psychotic state? He worriedly confided the fear to Psychband, reluctantly submitting to hypnotic search. Finally he emerged to reality, cleared by Psychband.

"Some feelings of persecution but not approaching delusory state," Psychband diagnosed. "Zale-3 exists."

So, the other had lied! Ixmal contemplated a machine

134

capable of deceit and immediately analyzed the danger. Zale-3 had lied, therefore it had motive – and dishonest motive implied threat. Threat without aggression was meaningless, hence the other had the means. He must work fast!

Ixmal gridded the solar system; every planet, every moon; each shattered remnant that drifted through space, the asteroids and orbital comets, even the sun. Seventy-two hundred years later he detected his enemy – a small plastometallic cube crouched atop a jagged peak on Callisto, Jupiter's fifth moon. Ha, far from being the master of Mars, his opponent was locked to a small satellite – a mote in space. And he had presumed equality!

He searched closer, attempting to unlock Zale-3's origin. (What had happened to its makers?) Ixmal felt a guilty pang. He scanned Zale-3's world contemptuously. Then he saw it – movement! Zale-3 squatted immobile; but on the slope of the hill a strange building was taking shape. It was little more than a cube, but its design? Its purpose? He knew somehow that the strange building was related to his encounter in space with Zale-3's mind, thus it was connected with him. Ixmal hurriedly flashed a panic call to Psychband.

"Psychokinesis – Zale-3 has learned to move matter by mind," Psychband pronounced.

"But how?"

Psychband gave an electromagnetic rumble, the equivalent of a shrug. "Out of my field," he said. "No prior indoctrination."

Ixmal sensed a momentary fright. The alien could move matter just as Man had moved matter. The factor of controlled mobility . . . directed mobility. Clearly Zale-3 was no ordinary god. He'd have to speed his efforts. Time was running out. Already the earth pattern had changed since his first contact with the alien.

Ixmal concentrated.

The earth rotated, revolved, changed. In a long-forgotten memory cell he found a clue – Man once had frustrated the laws of probability in the throws of dice. He devoured the hidden knowledge. Although little enough to go on, he detected a basic principle.

In somewhat over half a million years he was able to sway

135

flowers, move leaves against the wind, make small shrubs tremble. In less than half that time again he felled a huge tree and wrested ores from the earth. (An age of vulcanism had come and gone; the Atlantic coast was an igneous shelf, reptiles towered above the earth.) In another half million years he possessed the machines, raw materials and robot workers he needed. (The latter were designed to perform purely mechanical tasks, menial things he couldn't be bothered with. He had much to do. And ages were passing.) He saved time by enclosing his work area in a force field to protect the delicate machinery against the elements. In that respect he had bested the alien.

Ixmal started the ultimate weapon. Occasionally he would halt work long enough to scan Callisto. He gloated, noting that his enemy was having difficulty procuring the necessary fissionable material. He had a Belgian Congo full. (What did that term mean? Somehow it was an expression from long ago. The Man he had been fond of had used it.)

Ixmal's weapon rapidly took shape. Thanks to the ancient scientist's formula, he had merely to improve the warhead and construct its carrier – a rocket to blast Zale-3 from existence. (But eons were passing. Soft warm winds bathed his batholith and an occasional tyrannosaur paused to stare dumbly from the nearby swamp.) Psychband increased his irritation by calling attention to the formidable dimensions of this new animal.

"Destroy them, Ixmal, before life gets too big."

"Bah, they're mindless," he scoffed. "They're evolutionary toys – freaks from the mire."

"So was Man," Psychband observed.

"And Man is dust," Ixmal reminded. "Besides, I could destroy the very mountain with thought alone. Who dares give challenge?"

Ixmal discovered that Zale-3 had solved his fissionable problem; he was using psychokinesis to haul ore from Jupiter's methane deeps. A startling thought struck him: Zale-3 wouldn't need a rocket carrier. Of course, he would power his warhead by mental force. Why hadn't he thought of that? The ages wasted when every second might prove vital. He'd have to hurry.

He ceased work, abandoning the half-completed rocket,

and concentrated on improving his psychokinetic techniques. (Dinosaurs disappeared, the earth trembled under the foot of the mammoth.) Ixmal momentarily was appalled to discover a strange man-form dwelling among distant crags. He was hulking, grotesque, but he walked erect – the first of his kind. But no time now.

Ixmal tore trees from the earth and hurled them vast distances. He tumbled hills into valleys, held great crags suspended in the heavens, tore North and South America asunder; reshaped continents until, one day, he knew the mind force was his. He could reverse the very moon in its orbit! He concentrated on the bomb.

Finally the ultimate weapon was ready, the creation of long-ago Man plus ten billion. (Because there was no poetry in Ixmal's soul, he conceived solely in terms of cause and effect: he named the weapon "Star Blaster".)

Ixmal moved the great weapon into position and rapidly calculated the Earth-Callisto relationship, projecting the space ratio in terms of velocity, distance, gravities. No need to pinpoint the alien's plasto-metallic body: the whole of Callisto would vanish, reduced to cosmic dust under the bomb's furious impact. (A feathered bird sang from a tree. The trill liquid sound infuriated Ixmal, but he ended it. A puff of feathers drifted down through the leaves. The robin had sung of spring.)

Ha! Ixmal exulted, following his precise calculations. At the exact ten-thousandths of a second he concentrated five billion thought units. Winds rushed into the spot where the bomb had stood, and for a long moment the forests trembled. (At the base of the batholith several of the strange man-forms chattered excitedly; the concept of a god was born.)

Ixmal gloatingly followed "Star-Blaster's" course. He saw it hurtle past the moon, watched while for a split second it formed one apex of an equilateral triangle with Mars and earth, revelled as it drove through the belt of asteroids. Ha, the alien was doomed. His very atoms would be flung to the stars. He was watching "Star-Blaster" when. . . .

Ixmal recoiled, disbelieving, then terrified. A great warhead hurtled through the belt of asteroids, earth-bound, driven at unbelievable velocity by the mind of Zale-3. Ixmal frantically calculated, pounding his circuits to produce answers in split thousandths of a second. Frenzied, he analyzed his findings: the warhead would strike his very body.

"Concentrate, concentrate," Psychband interrupted. "Divert the weapon by mind force." Ixmal concentrated, focusing ten billion thought units on the oncoming warhead. It flashed unswervingly past Mars, flicking like a heavenly rapier towards earth, its velocity unbelievable.

"The moon! The moon! Use the moon," Psychband cried. Yes, the moon. He shook earth's satellite. An additional ten billion thought units reversed its orbit; he sped it up, hurling the moon towards interception with Zale-3's warhead. Too late!

"Think, think," Psychband urged. Ixmal mustered another two billion thought units, to no avail. The terrible weapon bashed past the moon, only seconds from earth.

"Hurry!" Psychband screamed. Ixmal was trying to muster another two billion thought units when the alien warhead struck. There was a horrible shattering thousandths of a second before consciousness fled. Amorphic blackness. Night. Nothingness.

Ixmal never saw "Star-Blaster" after it passed through the asteroid belt – never saw the disturbance in one minute sector of Jupiter's planetary system as Callisto flamed into cosmic dust. Nor did he see the forests around him burst into roaring flames, nor hear the screaming animals and strange man-forms which fled in howling terror.

Much later the man-forms returned.

Some of the more fearless crept to the very edge of the huge crater where the batholith had stood. They looked with awe into its scarred depths, jabbering excitedly. One of them remained long after the others had gone until, in the swiftly gathering darkness, the first bright stars of evening gleamed.

The man-form did something which none of his kind had ever done before. He lifted his eyes skyward, watching for a long time.

THE END

Of course everybody knows what "being human" means – it's just that they can't define it, but of course they know what it means . . .

SEA CHANGE

by Thomas N. Scortia

Full fathom five thy father lies;
Of his bones are coral made;
Those are pearls that were his eyes:
Nothing of him that doth fade
But doth suffer a sea-change
Into something rich and strange.
                              "Ariel's Song"
                              – *The Tempest*

Gleaming . . . like a needle of fire –
Whose voice? He didn't know.
The interstellar . . . two of them –

They were talking at once then, all the voices blending chaotically.

They're moving one out beyond Pluto for the test, someone said.

Beautiful – We're waiting . . . waiting. That was her voice. He felt coldness within his chest.

That was the terrible part of his isolation, he thought. He could still hear everything.

Not just in the Superintendent's office in Marsopolis where he sat.

But everywhere.

All the whispers of sound, spanning the system on pulses of c-cube radio. All the half-words, half-thoughts from the inner planets to the space stations far beyond Pluto.

And the loneliness was a sudden agonizing thing, sobbing in his ear. The loneliness and the loss of two worlds.

Not that he couldn't shut out the voices if he wished, the distant voices that webbed space with the cubed speed of light but –

Might as well shut out all thought of living and seek the mindless, foetal state of merely being.

There was the voice, droning cargo numbers. He made the small mental change and the tight mass of transistors, buried deep in his metal and plastic body, brought the voice in clear and sharp. It was a Tri-planet Line ship in the Twilight Belt of Mercury.

And he had a fleeting image of flame-shrivelled plains under a blinding monster sun.

Then there was the voice, saying, *O.K. . . . bearing three-ought-six and count down ten to free fall –*

That one was beyond Saturn – Remembered vision of bright ribbons of light, lacing a startling blue sky.

He thought: I'll never see that again.

And: *Space beacon three to MRX two two – Space beacon three – Bishop to queen's rook four –*

And there was the soft voice, the different voice; *Bart . . . Bart . . . where are you? Bart, come in – Oh, Bart –*

But he ignored that one.

Instead he looked at the receptionist and watched her fingers dance intricate patterns over the keyboard of her electric typewriter.

Bart . . . Bart –

No, no more, he thought. There was nothing there for him but bitterness. The isolation of being apart from humanity. The loneliness. Love? Affection? The words, had no meaning in that existence.

Slender fingers flicked over plastic keys and white paper bloomed endless stalks of words.

It had become a ritual with him, he realized, this trip the first Tuesday of every month down through the silent Martian town to the Triplanet Port. A formalized tribute to something that was quite dead – an empty ritual, weak, ineffectual gesture.

He had known that morning that there would be nothing.

"No, nothing," the girl in the Super's office had said. "Nothing at all."

Nothing for him in his grey robot world of no-touch, no-taste.

She looked at him the way they all did, the ones who saw

140

past the clever human disguise of plastic face and muted eyes.

He waited – listening.

When the Super came in, he smiled and said, "Hello, Bart," and then, with a gesture of his head, "Come on in."

The girl frowned her silent disapproval.

After they found seats the Super said, "Why don't you go home?"

"Home?"

"Back to Earth."

"Is that home?"

The voices whispered in his ear while the Super frowned and puffed a black cigar alight.

And: *Bart . . . Bart – Knight four to . . . three down . . . two down – Out past Deimous, the sun blazing on its sides . . . Bart –*

"What are you trying to do?" the Super demanded. "Cut yourself off from the world completely?"

"That's been done already," he said. "Very effectively."

"Look, let's be brutal about it. We don't owe you anything."

"No," he said.

"You'd be dead now," the Super said.

"I suppose so," he said.

"You could go back tomorrow. To Earth. A new life. No one has to know unless you insist on telling them."

He looked down at his hands, the carefully veined, very human hands. And the hard-muscled thighs where the cellotherm trousers hugged his legs.

"Your technicians did a fine job," he agreed. "Actually it's better than my old body. Stronger. And it'll last longer. But –"

He flexed his hands sensuously, watching the way the smooth bands of contractile plastic articulated his fingers.

"But the masquerade won't work. You know that. We were made for one thing."

"I can't change Company policy," the Super said. "Oh, I know the experiment didn't work. It was a bad compromise anyway. We needed something a little faster, more than human to pilot those first ships. Human reactions, the speed of a nerve impulse, they were too slow and electronic equip-

141

ment too bulky. But we weren't willing to face facts. We tried to compromise – keep the human form."

"We gave you what you needed," he said. "We gave you the pilots for your ships. You do owe us something in return. Do you think I'd have signed your contract, knowing that when I finally died, you'd put my brain in something that wasn't human?"

"Well, we lived up to the contract. We saved you from that crackup, you and a hundred like you. All in exchange for the ability only you had. It was a fair trade."

"All right. Give me a ship then. That's all I want."

"I told you before. Direct hook-up."

"No."

"Look, one of the interstellar's being tested right this minute. And there are the stations beyond Pluto."

"The stations? Why should I let myself be sealed in one of those? Completely immobile. What kind of a useless life is that, existing as a self-contained unit for years on end without the least contact with humanity?"

"The stations are not useless," the Super said. He leaned forward and slapped his palm on the surface of the desk. "You know the Bechtoldt Drive can't be installed within the system's heavy gravitational fields. The Bechtoldt field collapses explosively under those conditions. That's why we need the stations. They're set up to install the drive after the ship leaves the system proper, using its atomic motors."

"You still haven't answered my question."

"*Stargazer I* is outbound for one of the trans-Plutonian stations. *Stargazer II* will follow in a few days."

"So?"

"You can have one of them if you want it. Oh, don't get the idea that this is a hand-out. We don't play that way. The last two ships blew up because the pilots couldn't handle the hook-up. We need the best and that's you."

He paused for a long second.

"You may as well know," the Super said. "We've put all our eggs in those two baskets. If either one fails, it'll be a century before anyone tries again. We're tired of being tied to nine planets. We're going to the stars now and you can be a part of that."

"That used to mean something to me but – " He spread

his hands fluidly. "After a time you start losing your identification with humanity and its drives."

When he started to rise, the Super said, "You know you can't operate a modern ship or station tied down to a humanoid body. It's too inefficient. You've got to become part of the set-up."

"I've told you before. That won't do."

"What are you afraid of? The loneliness?"

"I've been lonely before," he said.

"What then?"

"What am I afraid of?" He smiled his mechanical smile. "I'm afraid of what's happened to me already."

The Super was silent.

"When you start losing the basic emotions, the basic ways of thinking that make you human, well – What am I afraid of? I'm afraid of becoming more of a machine," he said.

And before the Super could say more, he left.

Outside, he zipped up the cellotherm jacket and adjusted his respirator. Then he advanced the setting of the rheostat on the chest of the jacket until the small jewel light above the rheostat glowed softly in the morning's half-dusk. He had no need for the heat that the clothing furnished, of course, but the masquerade, the pretending to be wholly human would have been incomplete without this vital touch.

All the way back through the pearl grey light, he listened to the many voices flashing back and forth across the ship lanes. He heard the snatches of commerce from a hundred separate ports and he followed in his mind's eye the swift progress of *Stargazer I* out past the orbit of Uranus to her rendezvous with the station that would fit her with the Bechtoldt Drive.

And he thought, Lord, if I could make the jump with her, and then: *But not at that price ... not for what it's cost the others, Jim and Martin and Walt and ... Beth.*

The city had turned to full life in the interval he had spent in the Super's office and he passed numerous hurrying figures, bearlike in cellotherm clothing and transparent respirators. They ignored him completely and for a moment he had an insane impulse to tear the respirator from his face and stand waiting.

Waiting, savagely, defiantly, for someone to look at him.

The tortured writhings of neon signs glowed along the wide streets and occasionally an electric runabout, balanced lightly on two wheels, passed him with a soft whirr, its headlights cutting bright swaths across his path. He had never become fully accustomed to the twilight of the Martian day. But that was the fault of the technicians who had built his body. In their pathetic desire to ape the human body, they had often built in human limitations as well as human strengths.

He stopped for a moment before a shop, idly inspecting the window display of small things, fragile and alien, from the dead Martian towns to the north. The shop window, he realized, was as much out of place here as the street and the individual pressurized buildings that lined it. It would have been better, as someone had once suggested, to house the entire city under one pressurized unit. But this was how the Martian settlements had started and men still held to the diffuse habits more suited to another world.

Well, that was a common trait that he shared with his race. The Super was right, of course. He was as much of a compromise as was the town. The old habits of thought prevailing, molding the new forms.

He thought perhaps that he should get something to eat. He hadn't had breakfast before setting out for the port. They'd managed to give him a sense of hunger, though taste had been too elusive for them to capture.

But the thought of food was somehow unpleasant.

And then he thought perhaps he should get drunk.

But even that didn't seem too satisfying.

But he walked on for a distance and found a bar that was open and walked in. He shed his respirator in the air lock and, under the half-watchful eyes of a small, fat man, fumbling with his wallet, he pretended to turn off the rheostat of his suit.

Then he went inside, nodded vaguely at the bored bartender and sat at a corner table. After the bartender had brought him a whisky and water, he sat and listened.

Six and seven . . . and twenty-ought-three –
Read you –

144

And out there you see nothing, absolutely nothing. It's like –
Bart . . . Bart –
To king's knight four – Check in three –
Bart –
And the rocks glint like a million diamonds. It depends on the way the sun comes up with –
Bart –

And for the first time in weeks, he made the change. He could talk without making an audible sound, which was fortunate. A matter of sub-verbalizing. He said silently, *Come on in.*

Bart, where are you?

In a bar.

I'm far out . . . very far out. The sun's like a pinhole in a black sheet. Did you ever train in one of the old McKeever trainers? With the black hood? I did once and there was a tiny hole in the hood and the light came through It's like that –

I think I'm going to get very drunk.

Why?

Because I want to. Isn't that reason enough? Because it's the one wholly completely human thing I can do well.

I've missed you.

Missed me? My voice, maybe. You've never seen me . . . or I you –

The thought hit him that this was quite true. He should have, at least, a mental image of her. He tried to conjure one, but nothing came. She had never been, she never would be anything but a voice, someone intangible like the silent people speaking from the pages of a book.

That isn't important, is it?

Important? Perhaps not.

You should be out here with us, she said breathlessly. *They're beginning to come out now. The big ships. They're beautiful. Bigger and faster than anything you and I ever rode.*

They're bringing Stargazer I *out for her tests,* he told her.

I know. My station has one of the drives. Station three is handling Stargazer I *right now.*

He swallowed savagely, thinking of what the Super had said.

Oh, I wish I were one of them, Beth said.

145

His hand tensed on the glass and for a moment he thought it would shatter in his fingers. She hadn't said *on*. *Were . . . were . . . I wish I were one.*

Do you? he said. *That's fine.*

Oh, that's fine, starry eyes I love you and the sky and the stars and the sense of being – I am the ship . . . I am the station . . . I am anything but human –

What's wrong, Bart?

I'm going to get drunk.

There's a ship coming in. Signalling.

The bartender, he saw, was looking at him oddly. He realized that he had been nursing the same drink for the last fifteen minutes. He raised the drink and very deliberately drank and swallowed.

I've got to leave for a minute, she said.

Do that, he said.

Then, *I'm sorry, Beth. I didn't mean to take it out on you.*

I'll be back, she said.

He sat, looking out over the room, for the first time really noticing his surroundings. There were two tourists at the bar, a fat, weak-chinned man in a plaid, one-piece business suit and a woman, probably his wife, thin, thyroid-looking. They were talking animatedly, the man gesturing heatedly. He wondered what had brought them out so early in the morning.

It was funny, he thought, the image of the fat man, chattering like a nervous magpie, his pudgy hands making weaving motions in the air before him.

He saw that his glass was empty and he rose and went over to the bar. He found a stool and ordered another whisky.

"I'll break him," the little man was saying in a high, thin voice. "Consolidation or no consolidation – "

"George," the woman said gratingly, "you shouldn't drink in the morning."

"You know very well that – "

"George, I want to go to the ruins today."

Bart . . . Bart –

"They've got the cutest pottery down in the shop on the corner. From the ruins. Those little dwarf figures – You know, the Martians."

146

Only she pronounced it "Marchans" with a spitting "ch" sound.

It's the big one, Bart. The Stargazer. *It's coming in. Maybe I'll see it warp. Beautiful – You should see the way the sides catch the light from the station's beacon. Like a big ball of pure silver –*

"Pardon me," the woman said, turning on the stool to him. "Do you know what time the tours to the ruins start?"

He tried to smile. He told her and she said, "Thank you."

"I suppose you people get tired of tourists," she said, large eyes questioning.

"Don't be silly," George said. "Got to be practical. Lots of money from tourists."

"That's true," he said.

Bart –

"Well," the woman said, "when you don't get away from Earth too often, you have to crowd everything in."

Bart – Uneasy.

"That's true," he told the woman aloud and tried to sip his drink and say silently, *What's wrong?*

Bart, there's something the matter with the ship. The field . . . flickering –

She started to fade.

Come back, he shouted silently.

Silence.

"I'm in the Manta business back home," George said.

"Manta?" he asked. He raised a mechanical eyebrow carefully.

"You know, the jet airfoil planes. That's our model name, Manta, 'cause they look like a ray, the fish. The jets squirt a stream of air directly over the airfoil. They'll hover just like a 'copter. But speed? You've never seen that kind of speed from a 'copter."

"I've never seen one," he said.

Beth . . . Beth – his silent voice shouted. For a moment he felt like shouting aloud, but an iron control stopped his voice.

"Oh, I tell you," George said, "we'll really be crowding the market in another five years. The air's getting too crowded for 'copters. They are not safe any longer. Why, the turbulence over Rochester is something –"

147

"We're from Rochester," the thyroid woman explained.

Bart, listen. It's the Bechtoldt generator, I think. The radiation – I think it's killed the pilot. I can't raise him. And there's no one else. Just instruments.

How far from the station?

Half a mile –

My God, if the thing goes –

I go with it! He could feel the flicker of fear in her words.

"So we decided that now was the time, before the new merger, George would never find the time after – "

Try to raise the pilot.

Bart . . . Bart . . . I'm afraid.

Try –

"Is something wrong?" the thyroid woman said

He shook his head.

"You need a drink," George said. He noticed that the glass before him was empty as George signalled the bartender.

Beth, what's the count?

Oh, Bart, I'm scared.

The count –

"Good whisky," George said.

Getting high . . . I can't raise the pilot.

"Lousiest whisky on the ship coming in. Those things give me the creeps."

"George, shut up."

Beth, where are you?

What do you mean?

Where are you positioned? Central or to one side?

I'm five hundred yards off station centre.

"I told you not to drink in the morning," the woman said.

Any secondary movers? Robot handlers?

Yes, I have to handle cargo sometimes.

All right, tear your auxiliary power pile down.

But –

Take the bricks and stack them against the far wall of the station. You're shielded enough against their radiation. Then you'll have to rotate the bulk of the station between you and the ship.

But how – ?

148

Uranium's dense. It'll shield you from the radiation when
the ship goes. And break orbit. Get as far away as possible.
Bart, I can't. The station's not powered.
If you don't –
I can't –
Then silence.

The woman and George looked at him expectantly. He
raised his drink to his lips, marvelling at the steadiness of his
hands.

"I'm sorry," he said aloud. "I didn't catch what you
said."

Beth, the drive units for the Bechtoldt.
Yes?
Can you activate them?
They'll have to be jury-rigged into place. Quick-welded.
How long?
Five, maybe ten minutes. But the field. It'll collapse the
way the one on the ship's doing.
Not if you keep your attention on it. Anyway, you'll have to
chance it. Otherwise –

"I said," George said thickly, "have you ever ridden one
of those robot ships?"

"Robot ships?"

"Oh, I know, they're not robots exactly."

"I've ridden one," he said. "After all, I wouldn't be on
Mars if I hadn't."

George looked confused.

"George is a little dull sometimes," the woman said.

Beth –
Almost finished. The count's mounting.
Hurry –
If the field collapses –
Don't think about it.

"They give me the creeps," George said. "Like riding a
ship that's haunted."

"The pilot is very much alive," he said. "And very
human."

Bart, the pile bricks are in place. A few more minutes and –
Hurry . . . hurry . . . hurry.

"George talks too much," the woman said.

149

"Oh, hell," George said. "It's just that ... well, those things aren't actually human any more."

Bart, I'm ready ... I'm scared.

Can you control your thrust?

With the remote control units. Just as if I were the Star-gazer.

Her voice was chill – frightened.

All right then –

Count's climbing fast ... I'll – Bart! It's blinding ... a ball of fire – It's –

Beth –

Silence.

"I don't give a damn," George told the woman petulantly. "A man's got the right to say what he feels."

Beth –

"George will you shut up and let's go."

Beth –

He looked out at the bar and thought of flame blossoming in utter blackness and –

"They aren't men any more," he told George. "And perhaps not even quite human. But they're not machines."

Beth –

"George didn't mean – "

"I know," he said. "George is right in a way. But they've got something normal men will never have. They've found a part in the biggest dream that man ever dared dream. And that takes courage – courage to be what they are. Not men and yet a part of the greatest thing that men have ever reached for."

Beth –

Silence.

George rose from his stool.

"Maybe," he said. "But, well – " He thrust out his hand. "We'll see you around."

He winced when Bart's hand closed on his and, for a moment, sudden awareness shone in his eyes. He mumbled something in a confused voice and headed for the door.

Bart –

Beth, are you all right?

The woman stayed behind for a moment.

Yes, I'm all right. But the ship, the Stargazer –

150

Forget it.

But will there be another? Will they dare try again?

You're safe. That's all that counts.

The woman was saying, "George hardly ever sees past his own nose." She smiled, her thin lips embarrassed. "Maybe that's why he married me."

Bart —

Just hang on. They'll get to you.

No, I don't need help. The acceleration just knocked me out for a few minutes. But don't you see?

See?

I have the drive installed. I'm a self-contained system.

No, you can't do that. Get it out of your mind.

Someone has to prove it can be done. Otherwise they'll never build another.

It'll take you years. You can't make it back.

"I knew right away," the woman was saying. "About you, I mean."

"I didn't mean to embarrass you," he said.

Beth, come back. Beth —

Going out . . . faster each minute — Bart, I'll be there before anyone else. The first. But you'll have to come after me. I won't have enough power in the station to come back —

"You didn't embarrass me," the thyroid woman said.

Her eyes were large and filmed.

"It's something new," she said. "To find someone with an object in living."

Beth, come back.

Far out now . . . accelerating all the while — Come for me, Bart, I'll wait for you out there . . . circling Centaurus —

He stared at the woman by the bar, his eyes scarcely seeing her.

"You know," the woman said, "I think I could be very much in love with you."

"No," he told her. "No, you wouldn't like that."

"Perhaps," she said. "But you were right. In what you told George, I mean. It does take a lot of courage to be what you are."

Then she turned and followed her husband through the door.

Before the door closed, she looked back. Her eyes were filled with wonder.

Don't worry, Beth. I'll come. As fast as I can.

And then he felt the sounds of the others, the worried sounds that filtered through the space blackness from the burned plains of Mercury to the nitrogen oceans of dark Pluto.

And he told them what she was doing.

For moments his inner hearing rustled with their wonder of it.

There was a oneness then. He knew then what he must do, the next step he must take.

We're all with you, he told her, wondering if she could still hear his voice. *We always will be.*

And he reached out, feeling himself unite in a silent wish with those hundreds of minds, stretching in a brotherhood of metal across the endless spaces.

Stretching in a tight band of metal, a single organism reaching.

Reaching for the stars.

THE END

EXILE IS OUR LOT

It was hardly to be expected that space should offer nothing but fun. One of the challenges of space was that it confronted man with the Unknown; and the unknown is generally nasty.

It would have been easy to fill this volume with nasties and creepy-crawlies. But to my mind the real nasty is the one that gets inside your head and goes on from there. Like the nasties in James Gunn's story, *Breaking Point*. One day, a thesis will be written on the changing alien in science fiction, and how it has evolved from a thing like a dragon or wild animal to be hunted to something much more metaphysical, a disembodied thing which attacks at one's most vulnerable point, one's breaking point. This evolution is connected with science fiction's move away from a preoccupation with the merely technological side towards a more psychological approach.

In this section, the emphasis is on one of the psychological aspects of space opera towards which writers have always shown ambivalence: the theme of exile. To be far away from the pressures of ordinary life, lost among the stars, travelling hopefully – that is a great thing! On the other hand, what dangers lurk away from home, how vulnerable you are, stranded on another planet where the rules may be completely unfamiliar!

A nineteenth-century poet, Lord Tennyson, summed up some of the ambivalent feelings expressed in this section when he wrote *The Lotus-Eaters*. Apropos of *Breaking Point* he said:

> There is confusion worse than death,
> Trouble on trouble, pain on pain.

But the exile in Leigh Brackett's novel, *The Sword of Rhiannon*, is exile of another order, an exile born of love of the exotic. As Tennyson appositely remarked when he read Miss Brackett's gorgeous novel in a continuum not far from here,

> Then some one said, "We will return no more",
> And all at once they sang, "Our island home
> Is far beyond the wave; we will no longer roam."

We have space here for the first three chapters only of *The Sword of Rhiannon*, unfortunately. Of all those many science fantasies which have taken their cue from Lowell's Mars, Rider Haggard's novels, and the popularity of Edgar Rice Burroughs, Leigh Brackett's is one of the best, blended and spiced like a splendid oriental dish.

Her place of exile is Mars, where the hero, Matt Carse, is drawn back in history a million years, to witness Mars as it once was, to breathe its freer airs, to sail upon the ancient oceans – where he sees "the fishing fleet of Jakkara coming home with sails of cinnabar dark against the west" – to adventure with lost races among lost lands.

Carse, after all his adventuring, decided to return home to Earth, full of regret for the Mars that he loves but cannot call home. Regret sounds again in Ray Bradbury's story; and here, home is not Earth but Venus. There is no return, and the sun is almost as alien as Earth. Bradbury invites us, as Tennyson says,

> To lend our hearts and spirits wholly
> To the influence of mild-minded melancholy.

Nor is there hope of return in Jack Vance's story. Vance is famous for great swashbuckling space opera; here, in *The Mitr* he presents a small canvas – the implications of which are tremendous. To his tragic heroine, every day is

> Sore task to hearts worn out with many wars
> And eyes grown dim with gazing on the pilot-stars .

as Tennyson appositely remarked.

The Mitr is a beautiful story; yet, as far as I know, it has not been reprinted until now. For science fiction writers live in a peculiar exile of their own. That is, their writings generally appear in obscure magazines of which the general reading public may be quite unaware. In this volume, over a dozen of those magazines are represented; some of them, like *Amazing* and *Astounding* (later *Analog*) have acquired some renown with longevity; for others, a short life and oblivion have been their lot. *The Mitr* was published in a fairly obscure source, *Vortex Science Fiction*. Two issues only of this magazine were published, in New York back in 1953.

The early fifties marked the heyday of the science fiction magazines. Since then, the paperback industry has grown ever larger and the magazines have dwindled in numbers and circulation. They mark a particular period in literary and publishing history – a period which those who can recall when bookstalls across the western world were suddenly decked with sf magazines, and it was all summer in a day, will always think of with delight.

The ship was proof against any test, but the men inside her could be strained and warped, individually and horribly. Unfortunately, while the men knew that, they couldn't really believe it. The Aliens could – and did.

BREAKING POINT

by James E. Gunn

They sent the advance unit out to scout the new planet in the Ambassador, *homing down on the secret beeping of a feature-less box dropped by an earlier survey party. Then they sat back at G.H.Q. and began the same old pattern of worry that followed every advance unit.*

Not about the ship. The Ambassador *was a perfect machine, automatic, self-adjusting, self-regulating. It was built to last and do its job without failure under any and all conditions, as long as there was a universe around it. And it could not fail. There was no question about that.*

But an advance unit is composed of men. The factors of safety are indeterminable; the duplications of their internal mechanisms are conjectural, variable. The strength of the unit is the sum of the strengths of its members. The weakness of the unit can be a single small failing in a single man.

Beep . . . boop . . .

"Gotcha!" said Ives. Ives was Communications. He had quick eyes, quick hands. He was huge, almost gross, but grace-ful. "On the nose," he grinned, and turned up the volume.

Beep . . . boop . . .

"What else do you expect?" said Johnny. Johnny was the pilot – young, wide, flat. His movements were as controlled and decisive as those of the ship itself, in which he had an unshakable faith. He slid into the bucket seat before the great master console.

Beep . . . boop . . .

"We expect the ship to do her job," said Hoskins, the engineer. He was mild and deft, middle-aged, with a domed head and wide, light-blue eyes behind old-fashioned spec-tacles. He shared Johnny's belief in the machine, but through understanding rather than through admiration. "But it's always good to see her do it."

Beep . . . boop . . .

"Beautiful," said Captain Anderson softly, and he may have been talking about the way the ship was homing in on the tiny, featureless box that Survey had dropped on the unexplored planet or about the planet itself, or even about the smooth integration of his crew.

Beep . . . boop . . .

Paresi said nothing. He had eyebrows and nostrils as sensitive as a radarscope, and masked eyes of a luminous black. Faces and motives were to him what gauges and log-entries were to the engineer. Paresi was the doctor, and he had many a salve and many a splint for invisible ills. He saw everything and understood much. He leaned against the bulkhead, his gaze flicking from one to the other of the crew. Occasionally his small moustache twitched like the antennae of a cat watching a bird.

Barely audible, faint as the blue outline of a distant hill, hungry and lost as the half-heard cry of a banshee, came the thin sound of high atmosphere against the ship's hull.

An hour passed.

Bup-bup-bup-bup . . .

"Shut that damned thing off!"

Ives looked up at the pilot, startled. He turned the gain down to a whisper. Paresi left the bulkhead and stood behind Johnny. "What's the matter?" he asked. His voice was feline, too – a sort of purr.

Johnny looked up at him quickly, and grinned. "I can put her down," he said. "That's what I'm here for. I – like to think maybe I'll get to do it, that's all. I can't think that with the autopilot blasting out an 'on course'." He punched the veering-jet controls. It served men perfectly. The ship ignored him, homed on the beam. The ship computed velocity, altitude, gravity, magnetic polarisation, windage; used and balanced and adjusted for them all. It adjusted for interference from the manual controls. It served men perfectly. It ignored them utterly.

Johnny turned to look out and downward. Paresi's gaze followed. It was a beautiful planet, perhaps a shade greener than the blue-green of earth. It seemed, indefinably, more park-like than wild. It had an air of controlled lushness and peace.

159

The braking jets thundered as Johnny depressed a control. Paresi nodded slightly as he saw the pilot's hand move, for he knew that the autopilot had done it, and that Johnny's movement was one of trained reflex. The youngster was intense and alert, hair-trigger schooled, taught to pretend in such detail that the pretence was reality to him; a precise pretence that would become reality for all of them if the machine failed.

But, of course, the machine would not fail.

Fields fled beneath them, looking like a crazy-quilt in pastel. On them, nothing moved. Hoskins moved to the viewport and watched them mildly. "Very pastoral," he said. "Pretty."

"They haven't got very far," said Ives.

"Or they've got very far indeed," said Captain Anderson.

Johnny snorted. "No factories. No bridges. Cow-tracks and goat paths."

The Captain chuckled. "Some cultures go through an agrarian stage to reach a technological civilisation, and some pass through technology to reach the pastoral."

"I don't see it," said Johnny shortly, eyes ahead.

Paresi's hand touched the Captain's arm, and the Captain then said nothing.

Pwing-g-g!

"Stand by for landing," said the Captain.

Ives and Hoskins went aft to the shock-panels in the after bulk-head. Paresi and the Captain stepped into niches flanking the console. Johnny touched a control that freed his chair in its hydraulic gimbals. Chair and niches and shock-panels would not be needed as long as the artificial gravity and inertialess field functioned; it was a ritual.

The ship skimmed treetops, heading phlegmatically for a rocky bluff. A gush of flame from its underjets and it shouldered heavily upward, just missing the jagged crest. A gout of fire forward, another, and it went into a long flat glide, following the fall of a foothill to the plain beyond. It held course and reduced speed, letting the ground billow up to it rather than descending. There was a moment of almost-flight, almost-sliding, and then a rush of dust and smoke which overtook and passed them. When it cleared, they were part of the plain, part of the planet.

"A good landing, John," Paresi said. Hoskins caught his

eye and frowned. Paresi grinned broadly, and the exchange between them was clear: *Why do you needle the kid?* and *Quiet, Engine-room, I know what I'm doing.* Hoskins shrugged, and, with Ives, crossed to the communications desk.

Ives ran his fat, skilled hands over the controls and peered at his indicators. "It's more than a good landing," he grunted. "That squeak-box we homed in on can't be more than a hundred metres from here. First time I've ever seen a ship bullseye like that."

Johnny locked his gimbals, ran a steady, sensitive hand over the turn of the console as if it were a woman's flank. "Why – how close do you usually come?"

"Planetfall's close enough to satisfy Survey," said the Captain. "Once in a while the box will materialise conveniently on a continent. But this – this is too good to be true. We practically landed on it."

Hoskins nodded. "It's usually buried in some jungle, or at the bottom of a sea. But this is really all right. What a lineup! Point nine-eight earth gravity, Earth-type atmosphere –"

"Argon-rich," said Ives from the panel. "Very rich."

"That'll make no real difference," Hoskins went on. "Temperature, about normal for an early summer back home ... looks as if there's a fiendish plot afoot here to make things easy for us."

Paresi said, as if to himself, "I worry about easy things."

"Yeah, I know," snorted Johnny, rising to stretch. "The head-shrinker always does it the hard way. You can't just dislike rice pudding; it has to be a sister-syndrome. If the shortest distance is from here to there, don't take it – remember your Uncle Oedipus."

Captain Anderson chuckled. "Cut your jets, Johnny. Maybe Paresi's tortuous reasoning does seem out of order on such a nice day. But remember – eternal vigilance isn't just the price of liberty, as the old books say. It's the price of existence. We know we're here – but we don't know where 'here' is, and won't until after we get back. This is *really* Terra Incognita. The location of Earth, or even of our part of the galaxy, is something that has to be concealed at all costs, until we're sure we're not going to turn up a potentially dangerous, possibly superior alien culture. What we don't know can't hurt Earth. No conceivable method could get that information out of us, any more than it could be had from the squeak-box that Survey dropped here.

"Base all your thinking on that, Johnny. If that seems like leaning over backwards, it's only a sample of how careful we've got to be, how many angles we've got to figure."

"Hell," said the pilot, "I know all that. I was just ribbing the bat-snatcher here." He thumbed a cigarette out of his tunic, touched his lighter to it. He frowned, stared at the lighter, tried it again. "It doesn't work. *Damn* it!" he barked explosively. "I don't like things that don't work!"

Paresi was beside him, catlike, watchful. "Here's a light. Take it easy, Johnny! A bum lighter's not that important."

Johnny looked sullenly at his lighter. "It doesn't work," he muttered. "Guaranteed, too. When we get back I'm going to feed it to Supply." He made a vivid gesture to describe the feeding technique, and jammed the lighter back into his pocket.

"Heh!" Ives' heavy voice came from the communications desk. "Maybe the natives are primitives, at that. Not a whisper of any radio on any band. No powerline fields, either. There are ploughboys, for sure."

Johnny looked out at the sleeping valley. His irritation over the lighter was still in his voice. "Imagine that. No video or trideo. No jet-races or feelies. What do people do with their time in a place like this?"

"Books," said Hoskins, almost absently. "Chess. Conversation."

"I don't know what chess is, and conversation's great if you want to tell somebody something, like 'bring me a steak,'" said Johnny. "Let's get out of this fire-trap," he said to the Captain.

"In time," said the Captain. "Ives, DX those radio frequencies. If there's so much as a smell of radiation even from the other side of this planet, we want to know about it. Hoskins, check the landing-suits – food, water, oxygen, radio, everything. Earth-type planet or no, we're not fooling with alien viruses. Johnny, I want you to survey this valley in every way you can and plot a minimum of three take-off vectors."

The crew fell to work, Ives and Hoskins intently, Johnny off-handedly, as if he were playing out a ritual with some children. Paresi bent over a stereomicroscope, manipulating

162

controls which brought in samples of airborne bacteria and fungi and placed them under its objective. Captain Anderson ranged up beside him.

"We could walk out of the ship as if we were on Muroc Port," said Paresi. "These couldn't be more like Earth organisms if they'd been transplanted from home to delude us."

The Captain laughed. "Sometimes I tend to agree with Johnny. I never met a more suspicious character. How'd you ever bring yourself to sign your contract?"

"Turned my back on a couple of clauses," said Paresi. "Here – have a look."

At that moment the usually imperturbable Ives uttered a sharp grunt that echoed and re-echoed through the cabin. Paresi and the Captain turned. Hoskins was just coming out of the after alleyway with an oxygen bottle in his hand, and had frozen in his tracks at the sharp sound Ives had made. Johnny had whipped around as if the grunt had been a lion's roar. His back was to the bulkhead, his lean, long frame tensed for fight or flight. It was indescribable, Ives' grunt, and it was the only sound which could have had such an effect on such a variety of men – the same shocked immobility.

Ives sat over his Communications desk as if hypnotized by it. He moved one great arm forward, almost reluctantly, and turned a knob.

A soft, smooth hum filled the room. "Carrier," said Ives.

Then the words came. They were English words, faultlessly spoken, loud and clear and precise. They were harmless words, pleasant words even.

They were: "*Men of Earth! Welcome to our planet.*"

The voice hung in the air. The words stuck in the silence like insects wriggling upon a pin. Then the voice was gone, and the silence was complete and heavy. The carrier hum ceased. With a spine-tingling brief blaze of high-frequency sound, Hoskins' oxygen-bottle hit the steel deck.

Then they all began to breathe again.

"There's your farmers, Johnny," said Paresi.

"Knight to bishop's third," said Hoskins softly.

"What's that?" demanded Johnny.

163

"Chess again," said the Captain appreciatively. "An opening gambit."

Johnny put a cigarette to his lips, tried his lighter. "Damn. Gimme a light, Ives."

Ives complied, saying over his big shoulder to the Captain, "In case you wondered, there was no fix on that. My direction-finders indicate that the signal came simultaneously from forty-odd transmitters placed in a circle around the ship which is their way of saying 'I dunno'."

The Captain walked to the view bubble in front of the console and peered around. He saw the valley, the warm light of mid-afternoon, the too-green slopes and the blue-green distances. Trees, rocks, a balancing bird.

"It doesn't work," muttered Johnny.

The Captain ignored him. " *'Men of Earth ...'* " he quoted. "Ives, they've got into Survey's squeak-box and analysed its origin. They know all about us!"

"They don't because they can't," said Ives flatly. "Survey traverses those boxes through second-order space. They materialise near a planet and drop in. No computation on Earth or off it could trace their normal-space trajectory, let alone what happens in the second-order condition. The elements the box is made of are carefully averaged isotopic forms that could have come from any of nine galaxies we know about and probably more. And all it does is throw out a VUHF signal that says *beep* on one side, *boop* on the other, and *bup-bup* in between. It does *not* speak English, mention the planet Earth, announce anyone's arrival and purpose, or teach etiquette."

Captain Anderson spread his hands. "They got it from somewhere. They didn't get it from us. This ship and the box are the only Terran objects on this planet. Therefore they got their information from the box."

"Q.E.D. You reason like Euclid," said Paresi admiringly. "But don't forget that geometry is an artificial school, based on arbitrary axioms. It just doesn't work where the shortest distance is *not* a straight line ... I'd suggest we gather evidence and postpone our conclusions."

"How do you think they got it?" Ives challenged.

"I think we can operate from the fact they got it, and make our analyses when we have more data."

Ives went back to his desk and threw a switch.

"What are you doing?" asked the Captain.

"Don't you think they ought to be answered?"

"Turn it off, Ives."

"But –"

"Turn it off!"

Ives did. An expedition is an informal, highly democratic group, and can afford to be, for when the situation calls for it, there is never any question of where authority lies.

The Captain said, "There is nothing we can say to them which won't yield them more information. Nothing. For all we know it may be very important to them to learn whether or not we received their message. Our countermove is obviously to make no move at all."

"You mean just sit here and wait until they do something else?" asked Johnny, appalled.

The Captain thumped his shoulder. "Don't worry. We'll do something in some other area than communications. Hoskins – are those landing suits ready?"

"All but," rapped Hoskins. He scooped up the oxygen bottle and disappeared.

Paresi said, "We'll tell them something if we *don't* answer."

The Captain set his jaw. "We do what we can, Nick. We do the best we can. Got any better ideas?"

Paresi shrugged easily and smiled. "Just knocking, skipper. Knock everything. Then what's hollow, you know about."

"I should know better than to jump salty with you," said the Captain, all but returning the doctor's smile. "Johnny. Hoskins. Prepare for exploratory patrol."

"I'll go," said Paresi.

"Johnny goes," said the Captain bluntly, "because it's his first trip, and because if he isn't given something to do he'll bust his adrenals. Hoskins goes, because of all of us, the engineer is most expendable. Ives stays because we need hair-trigger communications. I stay to correlate what goes on outside with what goes on inside. You stay because if anything goes wrong I'd rather have you fixing the men up than find myself trying to fix you up." He squinted at Paresi. "Does that knock solid?"

"Solid."

"Testing, Johnny," Ives said into a microphone. Johnny's duplicated voice, from the open face-plate of his helmet and from the intercom speaker, said "I hear you fine."

"Testing, Hoskins."

"If I'd never seen you," said the speaker softly, "I'd think you were right here in the suit with me." Hoskins' helmet was obviously buttoned up.

The two men came shuffling into the cabin, looking like gleaming ghosts in their chameleon-suits, which repeated the colour of the walls. "Someday," growled Johnny, "there'll be a type suit where you can scratch your – "

"Scratch when you get back," said the Captain. "Now hear this, Johnny, you can move fastest. You go out first. Wait in the airlock for thirty seconds after the outer port opens. When Ives gives you the beep, jump out, run around the bows and plant your back against the hull directly opposite the port. Hold your blaster at the ready, aimed down – you hear me? *Down*, so that any observer will know you're armed but not attacking. Hoskins, you'll be in the lock with the outer port open by that time. When Johnny gives the all clear, you'll jump out and put your back against the hull by the port. Then you'll both stay where you are until you get further orders. Is that clear?"

"Aye."

"Yup."

"You're covered adequately from the ship. Don't fire without orders. There's nothing you can get with a blaster that we can't get first with a projector – unless it happens to be within ten metres of the hull and we can't depress to it. Even then, describe it first and await orders to fire except in really extreme emergency. A single shot at the wrong time could set us back a thousand years with this planet. Remember that this ship isn't called *Killer* or *Warrior* or even *Hero*. It's the Earth ship *Ambassador*. Go to it, and good luck."

Hoskins stepped back and waved Johnny past him. "After you, Jets."

Johnny's teeth flashed behind the face-plate. He clicked his heels and bowed stiffly from the waist, in a fine burlesque

166

of an ancient courtier. He stalked past Hoskins and punched the button which controlled the airlock.

They waited. Nothing.

Johnny frowned, jabbed the button again. And again. The Captain started to speak, then fell watchfully silent. Johnny reached toward the button, touched it, then struck it savagely. He stepped back then, one foot striking the other like that of a clumsy child. He turned partially to the others. In his voice, as it came from the speaker across the room, was a deep amazement that rang like the opening chords of a prophetic and gloomy symphony.

He said, "The port won't open."

II

The extremes of mysticism and of pragmatism have their own expressions of worship. Each has its form, and the difference between them is the difference between deus ex machina *and* deus machina est.

– E. Hunter Waldo

"Of course it will open," said Hoskins. He strode past the stunned pilot and confidently palmed the control.

The port didn't open.

Hoskins said, "Hm?" as if he had been asked an inaudible question, and tried again. Nothing happened. "Skipper," he said over his shoulder, "Have a quick look at the meters behind you there. Are we getting auxiliary power?"

"All well here," said Anderson after a glance at the board. "And no shorts showing."

There was a silence punctuated by the soft, useless clicking of the control as Hoskins manipulated it. "Well, what do you know."

"It won't work," said Johnny plaintively.

"Sure it'll work," said Paresi swiftly, confidently. "Take it easy, Johnny."

"It won't work," said Johnny. "It won't work." He stumbled across the cabin and leaned against the opposite bulkhead, staring at the closed port with his head a little to one side as if he expected it to shriek at him.

167

"Let me try," said Ives, going to Hoskins. He put out his hand.

"*Don't!*" Johnny cried.

"Shut up, Johnny," said Paresi.

"All right, Nick," said Johnny. He opened his face-plate, went to the rear bulkhead, keyed open an acceleration couch, and lay face down on it. Paresi watched him, his lips pursed.

"Can't say I blame him," said the Captain softly, catching Paresi's eye. "It's something of a shock. This shouldn't *be*. The safety factor's too great – a thousand per cent or better."

"I know what you mean," said Hoskins. "I saw it myself, but I don't believe it." He pushed the button again.

"I believe it," said Paresi.

Ives went to his desk, clicked the transmitter and receiver switches on and off, moved a theostat or two. He reached up to a wall toggle, turned a small air-circulating fan on and off. "Everything else seems to work," he said absently.

"This is ridiculous!" exploded the Captain. "It's like leaving your keys home, or arriving at the theatre without your tickets. It isn't dangerous – it's just stupid!"

"It's dangerous," said Paresi.

"Dangerous how?" Ives demanded.

"For one thing – " Paresi nodded toward Johnny, who lay tensely, his face hidden. "For another, the simple calculation that if nothing inside this ship made that control fail, something outside this ship did it. And *that* I don't like."

"That couldn't happen," said the Captain reasonably.

Paresi snorted impatiently. "Which of two mutually exclusive facts are you going to reason from? That the ship can't fail? Then this failure isn't a failure; it's an external control. Or are you going to reason that the ship *can* fail? Then you don't have to worry about an external force – but you can't trust anything about the ship. Do the trick that makes you happy. But do only one. You can't have both."

Johnny began to laugh.

Ives went to him. "Hey, boy – "

Johnny rolled over, swung his feet down, and sat up, brushing the fat man aside. "What you guys need," Johnny

168

chuckled, "is a nice kind policeman to feed you candy and take you home. You're real lost."

Ives said, "Johnny, take it easy and be quiet, huh? We'll figure a way out of this."

"I already have, scrawny," said Johnny offensively. He got up, strode to the port. "What a bunch of deadheads," he growled. He went two steps past the port and grasped the control-wheel which was mounted on the other side of the port from the button.

"Oh, my God," breathed Anderson delightedly, "the manual! Anybody else want to be Captain?"

"Factor of safety," said Hoskins, smiting himself on the brow. "There's a manual control for everything on this scow that there can be. And we stand here staring at it – "

"If we don't win the fur-lined teacup . . ." Ives laughed.

Johnny hauled on the wheel.

It wouldn't budge.

"Here – " Ives began to approach.

"Get away," said Johnny. He put his hands close together on the rim of the wheel, settled his big shoulders and hauled. With a sharp crack the wheel broke off in his hands.

Johnny staggered, then stood. He looked at the wheel and then up at the broken end of its shaft, gleaming deep below the surface of the bulkhead.

"Oh, fine . . ." Ives whispered.

Suddenly Johnny threw back his head and loosened a burst of high, hysterical laughter. It echoed back and forth between the metal walls like a torrent from a burst dam. It went on and on, as if now that the dam was gone, the flood would run forever.

Anderson called out "Johnny!" three times, but the note of command had no effect. Paresi walked to the pilot and with the immemorial practice slapped him sharply across the cheeks. "Johnny! Stop it!"

The laughter broke off as suddenly as it had begun. Johnny's chest heaved, drawing in breath with great, rasping near-sobs. Slowly they died away. He extended the wheel toward the Captain.

"It broke off," he said finally, dully, without emphasis.

Then he leaned back against the hull, slowly slid down until he was sitting on the deck. "Broke right off," he said.

Ives twined his fat fingers together and bent them until the knuckles cracked. "Now what?"

"I suggest," said Paresi, in an extremely controlled tone, "that we all sit down and think over the whole thing very carefully."

Hoskins had been staring hypnotically at the broken shaft deep in the wall. "I wonder," he said at length, "which way Johnny turned that wheel."

"Counter-clockwise," said Ives. "You saw him."

"I know that," said Hoskins. "I mean, which way: the right way, or the wrong way?"

"Oh." There was a short silence. Then Ives said, "I guess we'll never know, now."

"Not until we get back to Earth," said Paresi quickly.

"You say 'until', or 'unless'?" Ives demanded.

"I said 'until', Ives," said Paresi levelly, "and watch your mouth."

"Sometimes," said the fat man with a dangerous joviality, "you pick the wrong way to say the right thing, Nick." Then he clapped the slender doctor on the back. "But I'll be good. We sow no panic seed, do we?"

"Much better not to," said the Captain. "It's being done efficiently enough from outside."

"You are convinced it's being done from outside?" asked Hoskins, peering at him owlishly.

"I'm ... convinced of very little," said the Captain heavily. He went to the acceleration couch and sat down. "I want out," he said. He waved away the professional comment he could see forming on Paresi's lips and went on, "Not claustrophobia, Nick. Getting out of the ship's more important than just relieving our feelings. If the trouble with the port is being caused by some fantastic *something* outside this ship, we'll achieve a powerful victory over it, purely by ignoring it."

"It broke off," murmured Johnny.

"Ignore *that*," snorted Ives.

"You keep talking about this thing being caused by something outside," said Paresi. His tone was almost complaining.

"Got a better hypothesis?" asked Hoskins.

"Hoskins," said the Captain, "isn't there some way we can get out? What about the tubes?"

"Take a shipyard to move those power-plants," said Hoskins, "and even if it could be done, those radio-active tubes would fry you before you crawled a third of the way."

"We should have a lifeboat," said Ives to no one in particular.

"What in time does a ship like the *Ambassador* need with a lifeboat?" asked Hoskins in genuine amazement.

The Captain frowned. "What about the ventilators?"

"Take us days to remove all the screens and purifiers," said Hoskins, "and then we'd be up against the intake ports. You could stroll out through any of them about as far as your forearm. And after that it's hull-metal, skipper. *That* you don't cut, not with a piece of the Sun's core."

The Captain got up and began pacing, slowly and steadily, as if the problem could be trodden out like ripe grapes. He closed his eyes and said, "I've been circling around that idea for thirty minutes. Look: the hull can't be cut because it is built so it can't fail. It doesn't fail. The port controls were also built so they wouldn't fail. They do fail. The thing that keeps us in stays in shape. The thing that lets us out goes bad. Effect: we stay inside. Cause: something that wants us to stay inside."

"Oh," said Johnny clearly.

They looked at him. He raised his head, stiffened his spine against the bulkhead. Paresi smiled at him. "Sure, Johnny. The machine didn't fail. It was – controlled. It's all right." Then he turned to the Captain and said carefully "I'm not denying what you say, Skipper. But I don't like to think of what will happen if you take that tack, reason it through, and don't get any answers."

"I'd hate to be a psychologist," said Ives fervently. "Do you extrapolate your mastications, too, and get frightened of the stink you might get?"

Paresi smiled coldly. "I control my projections."

Captain Anderson's lips twitched in passing amusement, and then his expression sobered. "I'll take the challenge, Paresi. We have a cause and an effect. Something is keeping us in the ship. Corollary: We – or perhaps the ship – we're not welcome."

171

"*Men of Earth*," quoted Ives, in an excellent imitation of the accentless English they had heard on the radio, "*welcome to our planet*."

"They're kidding," said Johnny heartily, rising to his feet. He dropped the control wheel with a clang and shoved it carelessly aside with his foot. "Who ever says exactly what they mean anyhow? I see that conclusion the head-shrinker's afraid you'll get to, Skipper. If we can't leave the ship, the only other thing we can do is to leave the planet. That it?"

Paresi nodded and watched the Captain closely. Anderson turned abruptly away from them all and stood, feet apart, head down, hands behind his back, and stared out of the forward viewports. In the tense silence they could hear his knuckles crack. At length he said quietly, "That isn't what we came here for, Johnny."

Johnny shrugged. "Okay. Chew it up all you like, fellers. The only other choice is to sit here like bugs in a bottle until we die of old age. When you get tired of thinking that over, just let me know. I'll fly you out."

"We can always depend on Johnny," said Paresi with no detectable emphasis at all.

"Not on me," said Johnny, and swatted the bulkhead. "On the ship. Nothing on any planet can stop this baby once I pour on the coal. She's just got too much muscles."

"Well, Captain?" asked Hoskins softly.

Anderson looked at the basking valley, at the too-blue sky and the near-familiar, mellow-weathered crags. They waited.

"Take her up," said the Captain. "Put her in orbit at two hundred kilos. I'm not giving up this easily."

Ives swatted Johnny's broad shoulder. "That's a take-off *and* a landing, if I know the Old Man. Go to it, Jets."

Johnny's wide white grin flashed and he strode to the control chair. "Gentlemen, be seated."

"I'll take mine lying down," said Ives, and spread his bulk out on the acceleration couch. The others went to their take-off posts.

"On automatics," said the Captain. "Fire away!"

"Fire away!" said Johnny cheerfully. He reached forward and pressed the central control.

172

Nothing happened.

Johnny put his hand toward the control again. It moved as if there were a repeller field around the button. The hand moved more and more slowly the closer it got, until it hovered just over the control and began to tremble.

"On manual," marked the Captain. "Fire!"

"Manual, sir," said Johnny reflexively. His trembling hand darted up to an overhead switch, pulled it. He grasped the control bars and dropped the heels of his hands heavily on the firing studs. From somewhere came a muted roar, a whispering; a subjective suggestion of the thunder of reaction motors.

A frown crossed Paresi's face. The rocket noise was gone as the mind reached for it, like an occluded thought. The motors were silent; there wasn't a tremor of vibration. Yet somewhere a ghost engine was warming up, preparing a ghost ship for an intangible take-off into nothingness.

He snapped off the catch of his safety belt and crossed swiftly and silently to the console. Johnny sat raptly. A slow smile of satisfaction began to spread over his face. His gaze flicked to dials and gauges; he nodded very slightly, and brought both hands down like an organist playing a mighty chord. He watched the gauges. The needles were still, lying on their zero pins, and where lights should have flickered and flashed there was nothing. Paresi glanced at Anderson and met a worried look. Hoskins had his head cocked to one side, listening, puzzled. Ives rose from the couch and came forward to stand beside Paresi.

Johnny was manipulating the keys firmly. His fingers began to play a rapid, skilful, silent concerto. His face had a look of intense concentration and of complete self-confidence.

"Well," said Ives heavily. "That's a bust, too."

Paresi spun to him. "*Shh!*" It was done with such intensity that Ives recoiled. With a warning look at him, Paresi walked to the Captain, whispered in his ear.

"My God," said Anderson. "All right, Doctor." He came forward to the pilot's chair. Johnny was still concentratedly, uselessly at work. Anderson glanced inquiringly at Paresi, who nodded.

"That does it," said the Captain, loudly. "Nice work,

173

Johnny. We're smack in orbit. The automatics couldn't have done it better. For once it feels good to be out in space again. Cut your jets now. You can check for correction later."

"Aye, sir," said Johnny. He made two delicate adjustments, threw a master switch and swung around. "Whew! That's work!"

Facing the four silent men, Johnny thumbed out a cigarette, put it in his mouth, touched his lighter to it, drew a long, slow puff.

"Man, that goes good . . ."

The cigarette was not lighted. Hoskins turned away, an expression of sick pity on his face. Ives reached abruptly for his own lighter, and the doctor checked him with a gesture.

"Every time I see a hot pilot work I'm amazed," Paresi said conversationally. "Such concentration . . . you must be tuckered, Johnny."

Johnny puffed at his unlit cigarette. "Tuckered," he said. "Yeah." There were two odd undertones to his voice suddenly. They were fatigue, and eagerness. Paresi said, "You're off-watch, John. Go stretch out."

"Real tired," mumbled Johnny. He lumbered to his feet and went aft, where he rolled to the couch and was almost instantly asleep.

The others congregated far forward around the controls, and for a long moment stared silently at the sleeping pilot.

"I don't get it," murmured Ives.

"He really thought he flew us out, didn't he?" asked Hoskins.

Paresi nodded. "Had to. There isn't any place in his cosmos for machines that don't work. Contrary evidence can get just so strong. Then, for him, it ceased to exist. A faulty cigarette lighter irritated him, a failing airlock control made him angry and sullen and then hysterical. When the drive controls wouldn't respond, he reached his breaking point, and arrives at it just that way if he's pushed far enough."

"Everyone?"

Paresi looked from face to face, and nodded sombrely. Anderson asked, "What knocked him out? He's trained to take far more strain than that."

174

"Oh, he isn't suffering from any physical or conscious mental fatigue. The one thing he wanted to do was to get away from a terrifying situation. He convinced himself that he flew out of it. The next best thing he could do to keep anything else from attacking him was to sleep. He very much appreciated my suggestion that he was worn out and needed to stretch out."

"I'd very much appreciate some such," said Ives. "Do it to me, Nick."

"Reach your breaking point first," said the doctor flatly, and went to place a pillow between Johnny's head and a guard-rail.

Hoskins turned away to stare at the peaceful landscape outside. The Captain watched him for a moment, then: "Hoskins!"

"Aye."

"I've seen that expression before. What are you thinking about?"

The engineer looked at him, shrugged, and said mildly, "Chess."

"What, especially?"

"Oh, a very general thing. The reciprocity of the game. That's what makes it the magnificent thing it is. Most human enterprises can gang up on a man, slap him with one disaster after another without pause. But not chess. No matter who your opponent might be, every time he does something to you, *it's your move*."

"Very comforting. Have you any idea of how we move now?"

Hoskins looked at him, a gentle surprise on his ageing face. "You missed my point, Skipper. *We* don't move."

"Oh," the Captain whispered. His face tautened as it paled. "I . . . I see. We pushed the airlock button to get out. Countermove: It wouldn't work. We tried the manual. Countermove: It broke off. And so on. Now we've tried to fly the ship out. Oh, but Hoskins – Johnny broke. Isn't that countermove enough?"

"Maybe. Maybe you're right. Maybe the move wasn't trying the drive controls, though. Maybe the move was to do what was necessary to knock Johnny out." He shrugged again. "We'll very soon see."

The Captain exhaled explosively through his nostrils. "We'll find out if it's our move by moving," he gritted. "Ives! Paresi! We're going to go over this thing from the beginning. First, try the port. You, Ives."

Ives grunted and went to the ship's side. Then he stopped. *"Where is the port?"*

Anderson and Paresi followed Ives' flaccid, shocked gaze to the bulkhead where there had been the outline of the closed port, and beside it the hole which had held the axle of the manual wheel, and which now was a smooth, seamless curtain of impenetrable black. But Hoskins looked at the Captain first of all, and he said, *"Now* it's our move," and only then did he turn with them to look at the darkness.

III

The unfamiliar, you say, is the unseen, the completely new and strange? Not so. The epitome of the unfamiliar is the familiar inverted, the familiar turned on its head. View a familiar place under new conditions – a deserted and darkened theatre, an empty night club by day – and you will find yourself more influenced by the emotion of strangeness than by any number of unseen places. Go back to your old neighbourhood and find everything changed. Come into your own home when everyone is gone, when the lights are out and the furniture rearranged – there I will show you the strange and frightening ghosts that are the shapes left over when reality superimposes itself upon the images of memory. The goblins lurk in the shadows of your own room . . .

Owen Miller
Essays on Night and the Unfamiliar

For one heart-stopping moment the darkness had seemed to swoop in upon them like the clutching hand of death. Instinctively they had huddled together in the centre of the room. But when the second look, and the third, gave them reassurance that the effect was really there, though the cause was still a mystery, then half the mystery was gone, and they began to drift apart. Each felt on trial, and held tight to himself and the picture of himself he empathised in the others' eyes.

The Captain said quietly, "It's just ... there. It doesn't seem to be spreading."

Hoskins gazed at it critically. "About half a metre deep," he murmured. "What do you suppose it's made of?"

"Not a gas," said Paresi. "It has a – a sort of surface."

Ives, who had frozen to the spot when first he saw the blackness on his way to the port, took another two steps. The hand which had been half lifted to touch the control continued upward relievedly, as if glad to have a continuous function even though its purpose had changed.

"Don't touch it!" rapped the Captain.

Ives turned his head to look at the Captain, then faltered and let the hand drop. "Why not?"

"Certainly not a liquid," Paresi mused, as if there had been no interruption. "And if it's a solid, where did that much matter come from? Through the hull?"

Hoskins, who knew the hull, how it was made, how fitted, how treated once it was in place, snorted at the idea.

"If it was a gas," said Paresi, "there'd be diffusion. *And* convection. If it was poisonous, we'd all be dead. If not, the chances are we'd smell it. And the counter's not saying a thing – so it's not radioactive."

"You trust the counter?" asked Ives bitterly.

"I trust it," said Paresi. His near-whisper shook with what sounded like passion. "A man must have faith in something. I hold that faith in every single function of every part of this ship until each and every part is separately and distinctly proved unworthy of faith!"

"Then, by God, you'll understand my faith in my own two hands and what they feel," snarled Ives. He stepped to the bulkhead and brought his meaty hand hard against it.

... *"Touché,"* murmured Hoskins, and meant either Ives' remark or the flat, solid smack of the hand against the blackness.

In his sleep, Johnny uttered a high, soft, careless tinkle of youthful, happy laughter.

"Somebody's happy," said Ives.

"Paresi," said the Captain, "what happens when he wakes up?"

Paresi's eyebrows shrugged for him. "Practically anything. He's reached down inside himself, somewhere, and found a way out. For him – not for any of the rest of us. Maybe he'll ignore what we see. Maybe he'll think he's somewhere else, or in some other time. Maybe he'll *be* someone else. Maybe he won't wake up at all."

"Maybe he has the right idea," said Ives.

"That's the second time you've made a crack like that," said Paresi levelly. "Don't do it again. You can't afford it."

"We can't afford it," the Captain put it.

"All right," said Ives, with such docility that Paresi shot him a startled, suspicious glance. The big communications man went to his station and sat, half-turned away from the rest.

"What are they after?" complained the Captain suddenly. "What do they want?"

"Who?" asked Paresi, still watching Ives.

Hoskins explained, "Whoever it was who said 'Welcome to our planet.'"

Ives turned toward them, and Paresi's relief was noticeable. Ives said, "They want us dead."

"Do they?" asked the Captain.

"They don't want us to leave the ship, and they don't want the ship to leave the planet."

"Then it's the ship they want."

"Yeah," amended Ives, "without us."

Paresi said, "You can't conclude that, Ives. They've inconvenienced us. They've turned us in on ourselves, and put a drain on our intangible resources as men and as a crew. But so far they haven't actually done anything to us. We've done it to ourselves."

Ives looked at him scornfully. "We wrecked the unwreckable controls, manufactured that case-hardened darkness, and talked to ourselves on an all-wave carrier with no source, about information no outsider could get?"

"I didn't say any of that." Paresi paused to choose words. "Of course they're responsible for these phenomena. But the phenomena haven't hurt us. Our reactions to the phenomena are what has done the damage."

"A fall never hurt anyone, they told me when I was a kid," said Ives pugnaciously. "It's the sudden stop."

Paresi dismissed the remark with a shrug. "I still say that while we have been astonished, frightened, puzzled and frustrated, we have not been seriously threatened. Our water and food and air are virtually unlimited. Our ability to live with one another under emergency situations has been tested to a fare-thee-well, and all we have to do is recognise the emergency as such and that ability will rise to optimum." He smiled suddenly. "It could have been worse, Ives."

"I suppose it could," said Ives. "That blackness could move in until it really crowded us, or – "

Very quietly Hoskins said, "It *is* moving in."

Captain Anderson shook his head. "No . . ." And hearing him, they slowly recognised that the syllable was not a denial, but an exclamation. For the darkness was no longer a half-metre deep on the bulkhead. No one had noticed it, but they suddenly became aware that the almost square cabin was now definitely rectangular, with the familiar controls, the communications wall, and the thwartship partition aft of them forming three sides to the encroaching fourth.

Ives rose shaking and round-eyed from his chair. He made an animal sound and rushed at the blackness. Paresi leaped for him, but not fast enough. Ives collided sickeningly against the strange jet surface and fell. He fell massively, gracelessly, not prone, but on widespread knees, with his arms crumpled beneath him and the side of his face on the deck. He stayed there, quite unconscious, a gross caricature of worship.

There was a furiously active, silent moment while Paresi turned the fat man over on his back, ran skilled fingers over his bleeding face, his chest, back to the carotid area of his neck. "He's all right," said Paresi, still working; then, as if to keep his mind going with words to avoid conjecture, he went on didactically, "This is the other fear reaction. Johnny's was 'flight'. Ives' is 'fight'. The empirical result is very much the same."

"I thought," said Hoskins dryly, "that fight and flight were survival reactions."

Paresi stood up. "Why, they are. In the last analysis, so is suicide."

"I'll think about that," said Hoskins softly.

"Paresi!" spat Anderson. "Medic or no, you'll watch your mouth!"

"Sorry, Captain. That *was* panic seed. Hoskins – "

"Don't explain it to me," said the engineer mildly. "I know what you meant. Suicide's the direct product of survival compulsions – drives that try to save something, just as fight and flight are efforts to save something. I don't think you need worry; immolation doesn't tempt me. I'm too – too interested in what goes on. What are you going to do about Ives?"

"Bunk him, I guess, and stand by to fix up that headache he'll wake up to. Give me a hand, will you?"

Hoskins went to the bulkhead and dropped a second acceleration couch. It took all three of them, working hard, to lift Ives' great bulk up to it. Paresi opened the first-aid kit clamped under the control console and went to the unconscious man.

The Captain cast about him for something to do, something to say, and apparently found it. "Hoskins!"

"Aye."

"Do you usually think better on an empty stomach?"

"Not me."

"I never have either."

Hoskins smiled. "I can take a hint. I'll rassle up something hot and filling."

"Good man," said the Captain, as Hoskins disappeared toward the after quarters. Anderson walked over to the doctor and stood watching him clean up the abraded bruise on Ives' forehead.

Paresi, without looking up, said, "You'd better say it, whatever it is. Get it out."

Anderson half-chuckled. "You psychic?"

Paresi shot him a glance. "Depends. If you mean has a natural sensitivity to the tension spectra coupled itself with some years of practice in observing people – then yes. What's on your mind?"

Anderson said nothing for a long time. It was as if he were waiting for a question, a single prod from Paresi. But Paresi wouldn't give it. Paresi waited, just waited, with his dark face turned away, not helping, not pushing, not doing a

180

single thing to modify the pressure that churned about in the Captain.

"All right," said the Captain irritably. "I'll tell you."

Paresi took tweezers, a retractor, two scalpels and a hypodermic case out of the kit and laid them in a neat row on the bunk. Then he picked up each one and returned it to the kit. When he had quite finished Anderson said, "I was wondering, *who's next?*"

Paresi nodded and shut the kit with a sharp click. He looked up at the Captain and nodded again. "Why does it have to be you?" he asked.

"I didn't say it would be me!" said the Captain sharply.

"Didn't you?" When the Captain had no answer, Paresi asked him, "Then why wonder about a thing like that?"

"Oh . . . I see what you mean. When you start to be afráid, you start to be unsure – not of anyone else's weaknesses, but of your own. That what you mean?"

"Yup." His dark-framed grin flashed suddenly. "But you're not afraid, Cap'n."

"The hell I'm not."

Paresi shook his head. "Johnny was afraid, and fled. Ives was afraid, and fought. There's only one fear that's a real fear, and that's the one that brings you to your breaking point. Any other fear is small potatoes compared with a terror like that. Small enough so no one but me has to worry about it."

"Why you, then?"

Paresi swatted the first-aid kit as he carried it back to its clamp. "I'm the M.O., remember? Symptoms are my business. Let me watch 'em, Captain. Give me orders, but don't crowd me in my speciality."

"You're insubordinate, Paresi," said Anderson, "and you're a great comfort." His slight smile faded, and horizontal furrows appeared over his eyes. "Tell me why I had that nasty little phase of doubt about myself."

"You think I can?"

"Yes." He was certain.

"That's half the reason. The other half is Hoskins."

"What are you talking about?"

"Johnny broke. Ives broke. Your question was, 'who's next?' You doubt that it will be me, because I'm *de facto* the

181

boy with all the answers. You doubt it will be Hoskins, because you can't extrapolate how he might break – or even if he would. So that leaves you."

"I hadn't exactly reasoned it out like that –"

"Oh yes you had," said Paresi, and thumped the Captain's shoulder. "Now forget it. Confucius say he who turn gaze inward wind up cross-eyed. Can't afford to have a cross-eyed Captain. Our friends out there are due to make another move."

"No they're not."

The doctor and the Captain whirled at the quiet voice. "What does that mean, Hoskins?"

The engineer came into the cabin, crossed over to his station, and began opening and closing drawers. "They've moved." From the bottom drawer he pulled out a folded chessboard and a rectangular box. Only then did he look directly at them. "The food's gone."

"Food?... gone where?"

Hoskins smiled tiredly. "Where's the port? Where's the outboard bulkhead? That black stuff has covered it up – heating units, food-lockers, disposal unit, everything." He pulled a couple of chairs from their clips on the bulkhead and carried them across the cabin to the sheet of blackness. "There's water," he said as he unfolded the chairs. On the seat of one he placed the chess-board. He sat on the other and pushed the board close to the darkness. "The scuttle-butt's inboard, and still available." His voice seemed to get fainter and fainter as he talked, as if he were going slowly away from them. "But there's no food. No food."

He began to set up the pieces, his face to the black wall.

IV

The primary function of personality is self-preservation, but personality itself is not a static but a dynamic thing. The basic factor in its development is integration; each new situation calls forth a new adjustment which modifies or alters the personality in the process. The proper aim of personality, therefore, is not permanence and stability, but unification. The inability of a personality to adjust to or integrate a new situa-

tion, the resistance of the personality to unification, and its efforts to preserve its integrity are known popularly as insanity.

> – Morgan Littlefield
> *Notes on Psychology*

"Hoskins!"

Paresi grabbed the Captain's arm and spun him around roughly. "Captain Anderson! Cut it!" Very softly, he said, "Leave him alone. He's doing what he has to do."

Anderson stared over his shoulder at the little engineer. "Is he, now? Damn it, he's still under orders!"

"Got something for him to do?" asked the doctor coolly.

Anderson looked around, at the controls, out at the sleeping mountains. "I guess not. But I'd like to know he'd take an order when I have one."

"Leave him alone until you have an order. Hoskins is a very steady head, skipper. But just now he's on the outside edge. Don't push."

The Captain put his hand over his eyes and fumbled his way to the controls. He turned his back to the pilot's chair and leaned heavily against it. "Okay," he said, "This thing is developing into a duel between you and those ... those colleagues of yours out there. I guess the least we ... I ... can do is not to fight you while you're fighting them."

Paresi said, "You're choosing up sides the wrong way. They're fighting us, all right. We're only fighting ourselves. I don't mean each other; I mean each of us is fighting himself. We've got to stop doing that, skipper."

The skipper gave him a wan smile. "Who has, at the best of times?"

Paresi returned the smile. "Drug addicts ... Catatonics ... illusionaries ... and saints. I guess it's up to us to add to the category."

"How about dead people?"

"Ives! How long have you been awake?"

The big man shoved himself up and leaned on one arm. He shook his head and grunted as if he had been punched in the solar plexus. "Who hit me with what?" he said painfully, from between clenched teeth.

"You apparently decided the bulkhead was a paper hoop and tried to dive through it," said Paresi. He spoke lightly but his face was watchful.

"Oooh ..." Ives held his head for a moment and then peered between his fingers at the darkness. "I remember," he said in a strained whisper. He looked around him, saw the engineer huddled against his chess-board. "What's he doing?"

They all looked at the engineer as he moved a piece and then sat quietly.

"Hey, Hoskins!"

Hoskins ignored Ives' bull voice. Paresi said, "He's not talking just now. He's ... all right, Ives. Leave him alone. At the moment, I'm more interested in you. How do you feel?"

"Me, I feel great. Hungry, though. What's for chow?"

Anderson said quickly, "Nick doesn't want us to eat just now."

"Thanks," muttered Paresi in vicious irony.

"He's the doctor," said Ives goodnaturedly. "But don't put it off too long, huh? This furnace needs stoking." He fisted his huge chest.

"Well, this is encouraging," said Paresi.

"It certainly is," said the Captain. "Maybe the breaking point is just the point of impact. After that the rebound, hm?"

Paresi shook his head. "Breaking means breaking. Sometimes things just don't break."

"Got to pass," said a voice. Johnny, the pilot, was stirring.

"Ha!" Anderson's voice was exultant. "Here comes another one!"

"How are you sure of that?" asked the doctor. To Johnny, he called, "Hiya, John?"

"I got to pass," said Johnny, worriedly. He swung his feet to the deck. "You see," he said earnestly, "being the head of your class doesn't make it any easier. You've got to keep that and pass the examinations too. You've got two jobs. Now, the guy who stands fourth, say – he has only one job to do."

Anderson turned a blank face to Paresi, who made a

184

silencing gesture. Johnny put his head in his hands and said, "When one variable varies directly as another, two pairs of their corresponding values are in proportion." He looked up. "That's supposed to be the keystone of all vector analysis the man says, and you don't get to be a pilot without vector analysis. And it makes no sense to me. What am I going to do?"

"Get some shuteye," said Paresi immediately. "You've been studying too hard. It'll make more sense to you in the morning."

Johnny grinned and yawned at the same time, the worried wrinkles smoothing out. "Now that was a real educational remark, Martin, old chap," he said. He lay down and stretched luxuriously. "*That* I can understand. You may wear my famous maroon zipsuit." He turned his face away and was instantly asleep.

"Who the hell is Martin?" Ives demanded. "Martin who?"

"Shh. Probably his room-mate in pre-pilot school."

Anderson gaped. "You mean he's back in school?"

"Doesn't it figure?" said Paresi sadly. "I told you that this situation was intolerable to him. If he can't escape in space, he'll escape in time. He hasn't the imagination to go forward, so he goes backward."

Something scuttled across the floor. Ives lifted his feet off the floor and sat like some cartoon of a Buddha, clutching his ankles. "What in God's name was that?"

"I didn't see anything," said Paresi.

The Captain demanded, "What was it?"

From the shadows, Hoskins said, "A mouse."

"Nonsense."

"I can't stand things that scuttle and slither and crawl," said Ives. His voice was suddenly womanish. "Don't let anything like that in here!"

From the quarters aft came a faint scratching, a squeak. Ives turned pale. His wattles quivered.

"Snap out of it, Ives," said Paresi coldly. "There isn't so much as a microbe on this ship that I haven't inventoried. Don't sit there like little Miss Muffet."

"I know what I saw," said Ives. He rose suddenly, turned

185

to the black wall, and bellowed, "Damn you, send something I can fight!"

Two mice emerged from under the couch. One of them ran over Ives' foot. They disappeared aft, squeaking. Ives leapt straight up and came down standing on the couch. Anderson stepped back against the inboard bulkhead and stood rigid. Paresi walked with great purpose to the medical chest, took out a small black case and opened it.

Ives cowered down to his knees and began to blubber openly, without attempting to hide it, without any articulate speech. Paresi approached him, half-concealing a small metal tube in his hand.

A slight movement on the deck caught Anderson's eye. He was unable to control a shrill intake of breath as an enormous spider, hairy and swift, darted across to the couch and sprang. It landed next to Ives' knee, sprang again. Paresi swung at it and missed, his hand catching Ives heavily just under the armpit. The spider hit the deck, skidded, righted itself and, abruptly, was gone. Ives caved in around the impact point of Paresi's hand and curled up silently on the couch. Anderson ran to him.

"He'll be all right now," said Paresi. "Forget it."

"Don't tell me he fainted! Not Ives!"

"Of course not." Paresi held up the little cylinder.

"Anesthox! Why did you use that on him?"

Paresi said irritably, "For the reason one usually uses anesthox. To knock a patient out for a couple of hours without hurting him."

"Suppose you hadn't?"

"How much more of that scuttle-and-slither treatment do you think he could have taken?"

Anderson looked at the unconscious communications man. "Surely more than that." He looked up suddenly. "Where the hell *did* that vermin come from?"

"Ah. Now you have it. He dislikes mice and spiders. But there was something special about these. They couldn't be here, and they were. He felt that it was a deliberate and personal attack. He couldn't have handled much more of it."

"Where did they come from?" demanded the Captain again.

"*I* don't know!" snapped Paresi. "Sorry, skipper ... I'm

186

a little unnerved. I'm not used to seeing a patient's hallucinations. Not that clearly, at any rate.''

"They were Ives' hallucinations?''

"Can you recall what was said just before they appeared?''

"Uh . . . something scuttled. A mouse.''

"It wasn't a mouse until someone said it was.'' The doctor turned and looked searchingly at Hoskins, who still sat over his chess.

"By God, it was Hoskins. Hoskins – what made you say that?''

The engineer did not move nor answer. Paresi shook his head hopelessly. "Another retreat. It's no use, Captain.''

Anderson took a single step toward Hoskins, then obviously changed his mind. He shrugged and said, "All right. Something scuttled and Hoskins defined it. Let's accept that without reasoning it out. So who called up the spider?''

"You did.''

"*I* did?''

In a startling imitation of the Captain's voice, Paresi quoted, "Don't sit there like Miss Muffet!''

"I'll be damned,'' said Anderson. "Maybe we'd all be better off saying nothing.''

Paresi said bitterly, "You think it makes any difference if we *say* what we think?''

"Perhaps . . .''

"Nup,'' said Paresi positively. "Look at the way this thing works. First it traps us, and then it shows us a growing darkness. Very basic. Then it starts picking on us, one by one. Johnny gets machines that don't work, when with his whole soul he worships machines that do. Ives gets a large charge of claustrophobia from the black stuff over there and goes into a flat spin.''

"He came out of it.''

"Johnny woke up too. In another subjective time-track. Quite harmless to – to Them. So they left him alone. But they lowered the boom on Ives when he showed any resilience. It's breaking point they're after, Captain. Nothing less.''

"Hoskins?''

"I guess so,'' said Paresi tiredly. "Like Johnny he escaped from a problem he couldn't handle to one he could. Only

187

instead of regressing he's turned to chess. I hope Johnny doesn't bounce back for a while, yet. He's too – Captain! He's gone!"

They turned and stared at Johnny's bunk. Or – where the bunk had been before the black wall had swelled inwards and covered it.

V

"*. . . and there I was, Doctor, in the lobby of the hotel at noon, stark naked!*"

"*Do you have these dreams often?*"

"*I'm afraid so, Doctor. Am I – all right? I mean . . .*"

"*Let me ask you this question: Do you believe that these experiences are real?*"

"*Of course not!*"

"*Then, Madam, you are, by definition sane: for insanity. in the final analysis, is the inability to distinguish the real from the unreal.*"

Paresi and the Captain ran aft together, and together they stopped four paces away from the bulging blackness.

"*Johnny!*" The Captain's voice cracked with the agonised effort of his cry. He stepped to the black wall, pounded it with the heel of his hand.

"He won't hear you," said Paresi bleakly. "Come back, Captain. Come back."

"Why him? Why Johnny? They've done everything they could to Johnny; you said so yourself!"

"Come back," Paresi said again, soothing. Then he spoke briskly: "Can't you see they're not doing anything to him? They're doing it to us!"

The Captain stood rigidly, staring at the featureless intrusion. He turned presently. "To us," he parroted. Then he stumbled blindly to the doctor, who put a firm hand on his biceps and walked with him to the forward acceleration couch.

The Captain sat down heavily with his back to this new invasion. Paresi stood by him reflectively, then walked silently to Hoskins.

The engineer sat over his chess-board in deep concentration. The far edge of the board seemed to be indefinite, lost partially in the mysterious sable curtain which covered the bulkhead.

"Hoskins."

No answer.

Paresi put his hand on Hoskins' shoulder. Hoskins' head came up slowly. He did not turn it. His gaze was straight ahead into the darkness. But at least it was off the board.

"Hoskins," said Paresi, "why are you playing chess?"

"Chess is chess," said Hoskins quietly. "Chess may symbolise any conflict, but it is chess and it will remain chess."

"Who are you playing with?"

No answer.

"Hoskins – we need you. Help us."

Hoskins let his gaze travel slowly downward again until it was on the board. "The word is not the thing," he said. "The number is not the thing. The picture, the ideograph, the symbol – these are not the thing. Conversely . . ."

"Yes, Hoskins."

Paresi waited. Hoskins did not move or speak. Paresi put his hand on the man's shoulder again, but now there was no response. He cursed suddenly, bent and brought up his hand with a violent smash and sent board and pieces flying.

When the clatter had died down Hoskins said pleasantly, "The pieces are not the game. The symbols are not the thing." He sat still, his eyes fixed on the empty chair where the board had been. He put out a hand and moved a piece where there was no piece to a square which was no longer there. Then he sat and waited.

Paresi, breathing heavily, backed off, whirled, and went back to the Captain.

Anderson looked up at him, and there was the glimmer of humour in his eyes. "Better sit down and talk about something different, Doctor."

Paresi made an animal sound, soft and deep, far back in his throat, plumped down next to the Captain, and kneaded his hands together for a moment. Then he smiled. "Quite right, Skipper. I'd better."

189

They sat quietly for a moment. Then the Captain prompted, "About the different breaking point . . ."

"Yes, Captain?"

"Perhaps you can put your finger on the thing that makes different men break in different ways, for different reasons. I mean, Johnny's case seemed pretty clear cut, and what you haven't explained about Hoskins, Hoskins has demonstrated pretty clearly. About Ives, now – we can skip that for the time he'll be unconscious. But if you can figure out where you and I might break, why – we'd know what to look for."

"You think that would help?"

"We'd be prepared."

Paresi looked at him sharply. "Let's hypothesise a child who is afraid of the dark. Ask him and he might say that there's a *something* in dark places that will jump out at him. Then assure him, with great authority, that not only is he right but that it's about to jump any minute, and what have you done?"

"Damage," nodded the Captain. "But you wouldn't say that to the child. You'd tell him there was nothing there. You'd *prove* there wasn't."

"So I would," agreed the doctor. "But in our case I couldn't do anything of the kind. Johnny broke over machines that really didn't work. Hoskins broke over phenomena that couldn't be measured nor understood. Ives broke over things that scuttled and crawled. Subjectively real phenomena, all of them. Whatever basic terrors hide in you and in me will come to face us, no matter how improbable they might be. And you want me to tell you what they are. No, Skipper. Better leave them in your subconscious, where you've buried them."

"I'm not afraid," said the Captain. "Tell me, Paresi! At least I'll know. I'd rather know. I'd so *damn* much rather know!"

"You're sure I can tell you?"

"Yes."

"I haven't psychoanalysed you, you know. Some of these things are very hard to –"

"You do know, don't you?"

"Damn you, yes!" Paresi wet his lips. "All right, then. I

190

may be doing a wrong thing here ... You've cuddled up to the idea that I'm a very astute character who automatically knows about things like this, and it's been a comfort to you. Well, I've got news for you. I didn't figure all these things out. I was told."

"Told?"

"Yes, told," said Paresi angrily. "Look, this is supposed to be restricted information, but the Exploration Service doesn't rely on individual aptitude tests alone to make up a crew. There's another factor – call it an inaptitude factor. In its simplest terms, it comes to this: that a crew can't work together only if each member is the most efficient at his job. He has to *need* the others, each one of the others. And the word *need* predicates *lack*. In other words, none of us is a balanced individual. And the imbalances are chosen to match and blend, so that we will react as a balanced unit. Sure I know Johnny's bugaboos, and Hoskins', and yours. They were all in my indoctrination treatments. I know all your case histories, all your psychic pushbuttons."

"And yours?" demanded the Captain.

"Hoskins, for example," said Paresi. "Happily married, no children. Physically inferior all his life. Repressed desire for pure science which produced more than a smattering of a great many sciences and made him a hell of an engineer. High idealistic quotient; self-sacrifice. Look at him playing chess, making of this very real situation a theoretical abstraction ... like leaving a marriage for deep space.

"Johnny we know that. Brought up with never-failing machines. Still plays with them as if they were toys, and like any imaginative child, turns to his toys for reassurance. He needs to be a hero, hence the stars ...

"Ives ... always fat. Learned to be easy-going, learned to laugh *with* when others were laughing *at*, and bottling up pressures every time it happened. A large appetite. He's here to satisfy it; he's with us so he can eat up the galaxies ..."

There was a long pause. "Go on," said the Captain. "Who's next? You?"

"You," said the doctor shortly. "You grew up with a burning curiosity about the nature of things. But it wasn't a scientist's curiosity, it was an aesthete's. You're one of the

191

few people alive who refused a subsidised education and worked your way through advanced studies as a crewman on commercial spaceliners. You became one of the youngest professors of philosophy in recent history. You made a romantic marriage and your wife died in childbirth. Since then – almost a hundred missions with E.A.S., refusing numerous offers of advancement. Do I have to tell you what your bugaboo is now?"

"No," said Anderson hoarsely. "But I'm . . . not afraid of it. I had no idea your . . ." He swallowed. ". . . information was that complete."

"I wish it wasn't. I wish I had some things to – wonder about," said Paresi with surprising bitterness.

The Captain looked at him shrewdly. "Go on with your case histories."

"I've finished."

"No you haven't." When Paresi did not answer, the Captain nudged him. "Johnny, Ives, Hoskins, me. Haven't you forgotten someone?"

"No I haven't," snarled Paresi, "and if you expect me to tell you why a psychologist buries himself in the stars, I'm not going to do it."

"I don't want to be told anything so general," said the Captain. "I just want to know why *you* came out here."

Paresi scowled. The Captain looked away from him and hazarded, "Big frog in a small pond, Nick?"

Paresi snorted.

Anderson asked, "Women don't like you, do they, Nick?"

Almost inaudibly, Paresi said, "Better cut it out, Skipper."

Anderson said, "Closest thing to being a mother – is that it?"

Paresi went white.

The Captain closed his eyes, frowned, and at last said, "Or maybe you just want to play God."

"I'm going to make it tough for you," said Paresi between his teeth. "There are several ways you can break, just as there are several ways to break a log – explode it, crush it, saw it, burn it . . . One of the ways is to fight me until you win. Me, because there's no one else left to fight you. So – I

192

won't fight with you. And you're too rational to attack me unless I do. *That* is the thing that will make it tough. If you break, it'll have to be some other way."

"Is that what I'm doing?" the Captain asked with sudden mildness. "I didn't know that. I thought I was trying to get your own case history out of you, that's all. What are you staring at?"

"Nothing."

There was nothing. Where there had been forward viewports, there was nothing. Where there had been controls, the communication station, the forward acceleration panels and storage lockers; the charts and computers and radar gear – there was nothing. Blackness; featureless, silent, impenetrable. They sat on one couch by one wall, to which was fixed one table. Around them was an empty floor and a blackness. The chess player faced into it, and perhaps he was partly within it; it was difficult to see.

The Captain and the medical officer stared at one another. There seemed to be nothing to say.

VI

For man's sense is falsely asserted to be the standard of things: on the contrary, all the perceptions, both of the senses and the mind, bear reference to man and not to the universe; and the human mind resembles those uneven mirrors which impart their own properties to different objects ... and distorts and disfigures them ... For every one ... has a cave or den of his own which refracts and discolours the light of nature.

– Sir Francis Bacon.
(1561–1626)

It was the Captain who moved first. He went to the remaining bulkhead, spun a dog, and opened a cabinet. From it he took a rack of spare radar parts and three thick coils of wire. Paresi, startled, turned and saw Hoskins peering owlishly at the Captain.

Anderson withdrew some tools, reached far back in the cabinet, and took out a large bottle.

193

"Oh," said Paresi. "That . . . I thought you were doing something constructive."

In the far shadows, Hoskins turned silently back to his game. The Captain gazed down at the bottle, tossed it, caught it. "I am," he said. "I am."

He came and sat beside the doctor. He thumbed off the stopper and drank ferociously. Paresi watched, his eyes as featureless as the imprisoning dark.

"Well?" said the Captain pugnaciously.

Paresi's hands rose and fell, once. "Just wondering why."

"Why I'm going to get loopin', stoopin' drunk? I'll tell you why, head-shrinker. Because I want to, that's why. Because I like it. I'm doing something I like because I like it. I'm not doing it because of the inversion of this concealed repression as expressed in the involuted feelings my childhood developed in my attitude toward the sex-life of beavers, see, couch-catechizer, old boy? I like it and that's why."

"I knew a man who went to bed with his old shoes because he liked it," said Paresi coldly.

The Captain drank again and laughed harshly. "Nothing can change you, can it, Nick?"

Paresi looked around him almost fearfully. "I can change," he whispered. "Ives is gone. Give me the bottle."

Something clattered to the deck at the hem of the black curtain.

"'S another hallucination," said the Captain. "Go pick up the hallucination, Nicky-boy."

"Not my hallucination," said Paresi. "Pick it up yourself."

"Sure," said the Captain goodnaturedly. He waited while Paresi drank, took back the bottle, tilted it sharply over his mouth. He wiped his lips with the back of his hand, exhaled heavily, and went to the blackness across the cabin.

"Well, what do you know," he breathed.

"What is it this time?"

Anderson held the thing up. "A trophy, that's what." He peered at it. "*All-American*, 2675. Little statue of a guy holding up a victory wreath. Nice going, little guy." He strode to Paresi and snatched away the bottle. He poured liquor on the head of the figurine. "Have a drink, little guy."

"Let me see that."

Paresi took it, held it, turned it over. Suddenly he dropped it as if it were a red-hot coal. "Oh, dear God . . ."

"'Smatter, Nick?" The Captain picked up the statuette and peered at it.

"Put it down, put it down," said the doctor in a choked voice. "It's – Johnny . . ."

"Oh, it is, it is," breathed the Captain. He put the statuette gingerly on the table, hesitated, then turned its face away from them. With abrupt animation he swung to Paresi. "Hey! You didn't say it looked like Johnny. You said it *was* Johnny!"

"Did I?"

"Yup." He grinned wolfishly. "Not bad for a psychologist. What a peephole you opened up! Graven images, huh?"

"Shut up, Anderson," said Paresi tiredly. "I told you I'm not going to let you needle me."

"Aw now, it's all in fun," said the Captain. He plumped down and threw a heavy arm across Paresi's shoulders. "Let's be friends. Let's sing a song."

Paresi shoved him away. "Leave me alone. Leave me alone."

Anderson turned away from him and regarded the statuette gravely. He extended the bottle toward it, muttered a greeting, and drank. "I wonder . . ."

The words hung there until Paresi twisted up out of his forlorn reverie to bat them down. "Damn it – *what* do you wonder?"

"Oh," said the Captain jovially. "I was just wondering what you'll be."

"What are you talking about?"

Anderson waved the bottle at the figurine, which called it to his attention again, and so again he drank. "Johnny turned into what he thinks he is. A little guy with a big victory. Hoskins, there, he's going to be a slide-rule, jus' you wait and see. Ol' Ives, that's easy. He's goin' to be a beer barrel, with beer in it. Always did have a head on him, Ives did." He stopped to laugh immoderately at Paresi's darkened face. "Me, I have no secrets no more. I'm going to be a coat of arms – a useless philosophy rampant on a field of stars." He put the open mouth of the bottle against his forehead and pressed it violently, lowered it and touched the

195

angry red ring it left between his eyes. "Mark of the beast," he confided. "Caste mark. Zero, that's me and my whole damn family. The die is cast, the caste has died." He grunted appreciatively and turned again to Paresi. "But what's old Nicky going to be?"

"Don't call me Nicky," said the doctor testily.

"I know," said the Captain, narrowing his eyes and laving one finger alongside his nose. "A ref'rence book, tha's what you'll be. A treatise on the . . . the post-natal hysterectomy, or how to unbutton a man's prejudices and take down his pride . . . I swiped all that from somewhere . . .

"No!" he shouted suddenly; then, with conspiratorial quiet, he said, "You won't be no book, Nicky boy. Covers aren't hard enough. Not the right type face. Get it?" he roared, and dug Paresi viciously in the ribs. "Type face, it's a witticism."

Paresi bent away from the blow like a caterpillar being bitten by a fire-ant. He said nothing.

"And finally," said the Captain, "you won't be a book because you got . . . no . . . spine." He leapt abruptly to his feet. "Well, what do you know!"

He bent and scooped up an unaccountable object that rested by the nearest shadows. It was a quarter-keg of beer.

He hefted it and thumped it heavily down on the table. "Come on, Nick," he chortled. "Gather ye round. Here's old Ives, like I said."

Paresi stared at the keg, his eyes stretched so wide open that the lids moved visibly with his pulse. "Stop it, Anderson, you swine . . ."

The Captain tossed him a disgusted glance and a matching snort. From the clutter of radar gear he pulled a screwdriver and a massive little step-down transformer down on its handle. The bung disappeared explosively inside the keg, and was replaced by a gout of white foam. Paresi shrieked.

"Ah, shaddup," growled Anderson. He rummaged until he found a tube-shield. He stripped off a small length of self-welding metal tape and clapped it over the terminal-hole at the closed end of the shield, making it into an adequate mug. He waited a moment while the weld cooled, then tipped the keg until solid beer began to run with the foam. He filled the improvised mug and extended it toward Paresi.

196

"Good ol' Ives," he said sentimentally. "Come on, Paresi, have a drink on Ives."

Paresi turned and covered his face like a frightened woman.

Anderson shrugged and drank the beer. "It's good beer," he said. He glanced down at the doctor, who suddenly flung himself face down across the couch with his head hanging out of sight on the opposite side from which came the sounds of heaving and choking.

"Poor ol' Nick," said the Captain sadly. He refilled the mug and sat down. With his free hand he patted Paresi's back. "Can't take it. Poor, poor ol' Nick . . ."

After that there was a deepening silence, a deepening blackness. Paresi was quiet now, breathing very slowly, holding each breath, expelling air and lying quiet for three full seconds before each inhalation, as if breathing were a conscious effort – more; as if breathing were the whole task, the entire end of existence. Anderson slumped lower and lower. Each time he blinked his lids opened a fraction less, while the time his eyes stayed closed became a fraction of a second longer. The cabin waited as tensely as the taut pose of the rigid little victory trophy.

Then there was the music.

It was soft, grand music; the music of pageantry, cloth-of-gold and scarlet vestments; pendant jewels and multi-coloured dimness shouldering upward to be lost in vaulted stone. It was music which awaited the accompaniment of whispers, thousands of awed, ritualistic sibilants which would carry no knowable meaning and only one avowed purpose. Soft music, soft, soft; not soft as to volume, for the volume grew and grew, but soft with the softness of clouds which are soft for all their mountain-size and brilliance; soft and living as a tiger's throat, soft as a breast, soft as the act of drowning, and huge as a cloud.

Anderson made two moves; he raised his head, and he spun the beer in his mug so its centre surface sank and the bubbles whirled. With his head up and his eyes down he sat watching the bubbles circle and slow.

Paresi rose slowly and went to the centre of the small lighted space left to them, and slowly he knelt. His arms came up and out, and his upturned face was twisted and radiant.

197

Before him in the blackness there was – or perhaps there had been for some time – a blue glow, almost as lightless as the surrounding dark, but blue and physically deep for all that. Its depth increased rather than its light. It became the ghost of a grotto, the mouth of a nameless place.

And in it was a person. A . . . *presence*. It beckoned.

Paresi's face gleamed wetly. "Me?" he breathed. "You want – me?"

It beckoned.

"I – don't believe you," said Paresi. "You can't want me. You don't know who I am. You don't know what I am, what I've done. You don't want me . . ." His voice quavered almost to inaudibility. ". . . do you?"

It beckoned.

"Then you know," sang Paresi in the voice of revelation. "I have denied you with my lips, but you know, you know that underneath . . . deep down . . . I have not wavered for an instant. I have kept your image before me."

He rose. Now Anderson watched him.

"You are my life," said Paresi, "my hopes, my fulfilment. You are all wisdom and all charity. Thank you, thank you . . . Master. I give thee thanks Oh Lord," he blurted, and walked straight into the blue glow.

There was an instant when the music was an anthem, and then it too was gone.

Anderson's breath whistled out. He lifted his beer, checked himself, then set it down gently by the figurine of the athlete. He went to the place where Paresi had disappeared, bent and picked up a small object. He swore, and came back to the couch.

He sucked his thumb and swore again. "Your thorns are sharp, Paresi."

Carefully he placed the object between the beer keg and the statuette. It was a simple wooden cross. Around the arms and shaft, twisted tightly and biting deeply into the wood, was a thorny withe. "God almighty, Nick," Anderson said mournfully, "you didn't have to hide it. Nobody'd have minded."

"Well?" he roared suddenly at the blackness, "what are

you waiting for? Am I in your way? Have I done anything to stop you? Come on, come on!"

His voice rebounded from the remaining bulkhead, but was noticeably swallowed up in the absorbent blackness. He waited until its last reverberations had died, and then until its memory was hard to fix. He pounded futilely at the couch cushions, glared all about in a swift, intense, animal way. Then he relaxed, bent down and fumbled for the alcohol bottle. "What's the matter with you, out there?" he demanded quietly. "You waiting for me to sober up? You want me to be myself before you fix me up? You want to know something? *In vino veritas*, that's what. You don't have to wait for me, kiddies. I'm a hell of a lot more me right now than I will be after I get over this." He took the figurine and replaced it on the other side of the keg. "Tha's right, Johnny. Get over on the other side of ol' Beerbelly there. Make room for the old man." To the blackness he said, "Look, I got neat habits, don't leave me on no deck, hear? Rack me up alongside the boys. What is it I'm going to be? Oh yeah. A coat of arms. Hey, I forgot the motto. All righty: this is my motto. '*Sic itur ad astra*' – that is to say, 'This is the way to the men's room'."

Somewhere a baby cried.

Anderson threw his forearm over his eyes.

Someone went "Shh!" but the baby went right on crying.

Anderson said, "Who's there?"

"Just me, darling."

He breathed deeply, twice, and then whispered, "Louise?"

"Of course. *Shh*, Jeannie!"

"Jeannie's with you, Louise? She's all right? You're – all right?"

"Come and see," the sweet voice chuckled.

Captain Anderson dived into the blackness aft. It closed over him silently and completely.

On the table stood an ivory figurine, a quarter-keg of beer, a thorny cross, and a heart. It wasn't a physiological specimen; rather it was the archetype of the most sentimental of symbols, the balanced, cushiony, brilliant red valentine heart. Through it was a golden arrow, and on it lay cut flowers: lilies, white roses, and forget-me-nots. The heart pulsed strongly; and though it pumped no blood, at least it

199

showed that it was alive, which made it, perhaps, a better thing than it looked at first glance.

Now it was very quiet in the ship, and very dark.

VII

. . . We are about to land. The planet is green and blue below us, and the long trip is over . . . It looks as if it might be a pleasant place to live . . .

A fragment of Old Testament verse has been running through my mind – from Ecclesiastes, I think. I don't remember it verbatim, but it's something like this:

To every thing there is a season, and a time to every purpose under heaven: A time to weep, and a time to laugh: a time to mourn, and a time to dance; A time to get, and a time to lose; a time to keep, and a time to cast away; A time to be born, and a time to die; a time to plant, and a time to pluck up that which is planted.

For me, anyway, I feel that the time has come. Perhaps it is not to die, but something else, less final or more terrible.

In any case, you will remember, I know, what we decided long ago – that a man owes one of two things to his planet, to his race: posterity, or himself. I could not contribute the first – it is only proper that I should offer the second and not shrink if it is accepted . . .

– From a letter by Peter Hoskins to his wife

In the quiet and the dark, Hoskins moved.

"Checkmate," he said.

He rose from his chair and crossed the cabin. Ignoring what was on the table, he opened a drawer under the parts cabinet and took out a steel rule. From a book rack he lifted down a heavy manual. He sat on the end of the couch with the manual on his knees and leafed through it, smoothing it open at a page of physical measurements. He glanced at the floor, across it to the black curtain, back to the one exposed bulkhead. He grunted, put the book down, and carried his tape to the steel wall. He anchored one end of it there by flipping the paramagnetic control on the tape case, and pulled the tape across the room. At the blackness he took a reading, made a mark.

Then he took a fore-and-aft measurement from a point opposite the forward end of the table to one opposite the after end of the bunk. Working carefully, he knelt and constructed a perpendicular to this line. He put the tape down for the third time, arriving again at the outboard wall of darkness. He stood regarding it thoughtfully, and then unhesitatingly plunged his arm into it. He fumbled for a moment, moving his hand around in a circle, pressing forward, trying again. Suddenly there was a click, a faint hum. He stepped back.

Something huge shouldered out of the dark. It pressed forward toward him, passed him, stopped moving.

It was the port.

Hoskins wiped sweat away from his upper lip and stood blinking into the airlock until the outer port opened as well. Warm afternoon sunlight and a soft, fresh breeze poured in. In the wind was bird song and the smell of growing things. Hoskins gazed into it, his mild eyes misty. Then he turned back to the cabin.

The darkness was gone. Ives was sprawled on the after couch, apparently unconscious. Johnny was smiling in his sleep. The Captain was snoring stertorously, and Paresi was curled up like a cat on the floor. The sunlight streamed in through the forward viewports. The manual wheel gleamed on the bulkhead, unbroken.

Hoskins looked at the sleeping crew and shook his head, half-smiling. Then he stepped to the control console and lifted a microphone from its hook. He began to speak softly into it in his gentle, unimpressive voice. He said:

"Reality is what it is, and not what it seems to be. What it seems to be is an individual matter, and even in the individual it varies constantly. If that's a truism, it's still the truth, as true as the fact that this ship cannot fail. The course of events after our landing would have been profoundly different if we had unanimously accepted the thing we knew to be true. But none of us need feel guilty on that score. We are not conditioned to deny the evidence of our senses.

"What the natives of this planet have done is, at base, simple and straightforward. They had to know if the race who built this ship could do so because they were psycho-

201

logically sound and therefore capable of reasoning out the building process (among many, many other things), or whether we were merely mechanically apt. To find this out, they tested us. They tested us the way we test steel – to find out its breaking point. And while they were playing a game for our sanity, I played a game for our lives. I could not share it with any of you because it was a game only I, of us all, have experience in. Paresi was right to a certain degree when he said I had retreated into abstraction – the abstraction of chess. He was wrong, though, when he concluded I had been driven to it. You can be quite sure that I did it by choice. It was simply a matter of translating the contactual evidence into an equivalent idea-system.

"I learned very rapidly that when they play a game, they abide by the rules. I know the rules of chess, but I did not know the rules of their game. They did not give me their rules. They simply permitted me to convey mine to them.

"I learned a little more slowly that, though their power to reach our minds is unheard-of in any of the seven galaxies we know about, it still cannot take and use any but the ideas in the forefront of our consciousness. In other words, chess was a possibility. They could be forced to take a sacrificed piece, as well as being forced to lose one of their own. They extrapolate a sequence beautifully – but they can be out-thought. So much for that: I beat them at chess. And by confining my efforts to the chessboard, where I knew the rules and where they respected them, I was able to keep what we call sanity. Where you were disturbed because the port disappeared, I was not disturbed because the disappearance was not chess.

"You're wondering, of course, how they did what they did to us. I don't know. But I can tell you what they did. They empathise – that is, see through our eyes, feel with our fingertips – so that they perceive what we do. Second, they can control those perceptions; hang on a distortion circuit as Ives would put it, between the sense organ and the brain. For example, you'll find all our fingerprints all around the port control, where one after the other we punched the wall and thought we were punching the button.

"You're wondering, too, what I did to break their hold upon us. Well, I simply believed what I knew to be the truth; that the ship is unharmed and unchanged. I measured it with a steel tape and it was so. Why didn't they force me to misread the tape? They would have, if I'd done that measuring first. At the start they were in the business of turning every piece of pragmatic evidence into an outright lie. But I outlasted the test. When they'd finished with their whole arsenal of sensory lies, they still hadn't broken me. They then turned me loose, like a rat in a maze, to see if I could find the way out. And again they abided by their rules. They didn't change the maze when at last I attacked it.

"Let me rephrase what I've done; I feel uncomfortable cast as a superman. We five pedestrians faced some heavy traffic on a surface road. You four tried nobly to cross – deaf and blindfolded. You were all casualties. I was not; and it wasn't because I am stronger or wiser than you, but only because I stayed on the pavement and waited for the light to change.

"So we won. Now ..."

Hoskins paused to wet his lips. He looked at his shipmates, each in turn, each for a long, reflective moment. Again his gentle face showed the half-smile, the small shake of the head. He lifted the mike.

"... In my chess game I offered them a minor piece in order to achieve a victory, and they accepted. My interpretation is that they want *me* for further tests. This need not concern you on either of the scores which occur to you as you hear this. First: the choice is my own. It is not a difficult one to make. As Paresi once pointed out, I have a high idealistic quotient. Second: I am, after all, a very minor piece and the game is a great one. I am convinced that there is no test to which they can now subject me, and break me, that any one of you cannot pass.

"But you must in no case come tearing after me in a wild and thoughtless rescue attempt. I neither want that nor need it. And do not judge the natives severely; we are in no position to do so. I am certain now that whether I come back or not, these people will make a valuable addition to the galactic community.

"Good luck, in any case. If the tests shouldn't prove too arduous, I'll see you again. If not, my only regret is that I shall break up what has turned out to be, after all, a very

203

effective team. If this happens, tell my wife the usual things and deliver to her a letter you will find among my papers. She was long ago reconciled to eventualities.

"Johnny . . . the natives will fix your lighter . . .

"Good luck, goodbye."

Hoskins hung up the microphone. He took a stylus and wrote a line: "*Hear my recording. Pete.*"

And then, bareheaded and unarmed, he stepped through the port, out into the golden sunshine. Outside he stopped, and for a moment touched his cheek to the flawless surface of the hull.

He walked down into the valley.

THE END

As an archaeologist, Matthew Carse was in search of the ancient Martian past. He did not find it – but it found him, and in no time he was fighting for his very life!

THE SWORD OF RHIANNON

by Leigh Brackett

Matt Carse knew he was being followed almost as soon as he left Madam Kan's. The laughter of the little dark women was still in his ears and the fumes of *thil* lay like a hot sweet haze across his vision – but they did not obscure from him the whisper of sandalled feet close behind him in the chill Martian night.

Carse quietly loosened his proton-gun in its holster but he did not attempt to lose his pursuer. He did not slow nor quicken his pace as he went through Jekkara.

"The Old Town," he thought. "That will be the best place. Too many people about here."

Jekkara was not sleeping despite the lateness of the hour. The Low Canal towns never sleep, for they lie outside the law and time means nothing to them. In Jekkara and Valkis and Barrakesh night is only a darker day.

Carse walked beside the still black waters in their ancient channel, cut in the dead sea-bottom. He watched the dry wind shake the torches that never went out and listened to the broken music of the harps that were never stilled. Lean little men and women passed him in the shadowy streets, silent as cats except for the chime and whisper of the tiny bells the women wear, a sound as delicate as rain, distillate of all the sweet wickedness of the world.

They paid no attention to Carse, though despite his Martian dress he was obviously an Earthman and though an Earthman's life is usually less than the light of a snuffed candle along the Low Canals, Carse was one of them. The men of Jekkara and Valkis and Barrakesh are the aristocracy of thieves and they admire skill and respect knowledge and know a gentleman when they meet one.

That was why Matthew Carse, ex-fellow of the Interplanetary Society of Archaeologists, ex-assistant to the chair of Martian Antiquities at Kahora, dweller on Mars for thirty of his thirty-five years, had been admitted to their far more exclusive society of thieves and had sworn with them the oath of friendship that may not be broken.

Yet now, through the streets of Jekkara, one of Carse's "friends" was stalking him with all the cunning of a sandcat. He wondered momentarily whether the Earth Police Control might have sent an agent here looking for him and immediately discarded that possibility. Agents of anybody's police did not live in Jekkara. No, it was some Low-Canaller on business of his own.

Carse left the canal, turning his back on the dead sea-bottom and facing what had once been inland. The ground rose sharply to the upper cliffs, much gnawed and worn by time and the eternal wind. The old city brooded there, the ancient stronghold of the Sea Kings of Jekkara, its glory long stripped from it by the dropping of the sea.

The New Town of Jekkara, the living town down by the canal, had been old when Ur of the Chaldees was a raw young village. Old Jekkara, with its docks of stone and marble still standing in the dry and dust-choked harbour, was old beyond any Earth conception of the word. Even Carse, who knew as much about it as any living man, was always awed by it.

He chose now to go this way because it was utterly dead and deserted and a man might be alone to talk to his friend.

The empty houses lay open to the night. Time and the scouring wind had worn away their corners and the angles of their doorways, smoothed them into the blurred and weary land. The little low moons made a tangle of conflicting shadows among them. With no effort at all the tall Earth-man in his long dark cloak blended into the shadows and disappeared.

Crouched in the shelter of a wall he listened to the footsteps of the man who followed him. They grew louder, quickened, slowed indecisively, then quickened again. They drew abreast, passed and suddenly Carse had moved in a great catlike spring out into the street and a small wiry body was writhing in his grasp, mewing with fright as it shrank from the icy jabbing of the proton-gun in its side.

206

"No!" it squealed. "Don't! I have no weapon. I mean no harm. I want only to talk to you." Even through the fear a note of cunning crept into the voice. "I have a gift."

Carse assured himself that the man was unarmed and then relaxed his grip. He could see the Martian quite clearly in the moonlight – a ratlike small thief and an unsuccessful one from the worn kilt and harness and the lack of ornaments.

The dregs and sweepings of the Low Canals produced such men as this and they were brothers to the stinging worms that kill furtively out of the dust. Carse did not put his gun away.

"Go ahead," he said. "Talk."

"First," said the Martian, "I am Penkawr of Barrakesh. You may have heard of me." He strutted at the sound of his own name like a shabby bantam rooster.

"No," said Carse. "I haven't."

His tone was like a slap in the face. Penkawr gave a snarling grin.

"No matter. I have heard of you, Carse. As I said, I have a gift for you. A most rare and valuable gift."

"Something so rare and valuable that you had to follow me in the darkness to tell me about it, even in Jekkara." Carse frowned at Penkawr, trying to fathom his duplicity. "Well, what is it?"

"Come and I'll show you."

"Where is it?"

"Hidden. Well hidden up near the palace quays."

Carse nodded. "Something too rare and valuable to be carried or shown even in a thieves' market. You intrigue me, Penkawr. We will go and look at your gift."

Penkawr showed his pointed teeth in the moonlight and led off. Carse followed. He moved lightly, poised for instant action. His gun hand swung loose and ready at his side. He was wondering what sort of price Penkawr of Barrakesh planned to ask for his "gift".

As they climbed upward toward the palace, scrambling over worn reefs and along cliff-faces that still showed the erosion of the sea, Carse had as always the feeling that he was climbing a sort of ladder into the past. It turned him cold with a queer shivering thrill to see the great docks still stan-

207

ding, marked with the mooring of ships. In the eerie moonlight one could almost imagine . . .

"In here," said Penkawr.

Carse followed him into a dark huddle of crumbling stone. He took a little krypton-lamp from his belt pouch and touched it to a glow. Penkawr knelt and scrambled among the broken stones of the floor until he brought forth a long thin bundle wrapped in rags.

With a strange reverence, almost with fear, he began to unwrap it. Carse knelt beside him. He realized that he was holding his breath, watching the Martian's lean dark hands, waiting. Something in the man's attitude had caught him into the same taut mood.

The lamplight struck a spark of deep fire from a half-covered jewel, and then a clean brilliance of metal. Carse leaned forward. Penkawr's eyes, slanted wolf-eyes yellow as topaz, glanced up and caught the Earthman's hard blue gaze, held it for a moment, then shifted away. Swiftly he drew the last covering from the object on the floor.

Carse did not move. The thing lay bright and burning between them and neither man stirred nor seemed even to breathe. The red glow of the lamp painted their faces, lean bone above iron shadows, and the eyes of Matthew Carse were the eyes of a man who looks upon a miracle.

After a long while he reached out and took the thing into his hands. The beautiful and deadly slimness of it, the length and perfect balance, the black hilt and guard that fitted perfectly his large hand, the single smoky jewel that seemed to watch him with a living wisdom, the name etched in most rare and most ancient symbols upon the blade. He spoke, and his voice was no more than a whisper.

"The sword of Rhiannon!"

Penkawr let out his breath in a sharp sigh. "I found it," he said. "*I* found it."

Carse said, "Where?"

"It does not matter where. I found it. It is yours – for a small price."

"A small price," Carse smiled. "A small price for the sword of a god."

"An evil god," muttered Penkawr. "For more than a million years, Mars has called him the Cursed One."

208

"I know," Carse nodded. "Rhiannon, the Cursed One, the Fallen One, the rebel one of the gods of long ago. I know the legend, yes. The legend of how the old gods conquered Rhiannon and thrust him into a hidden tomb."

Penkawr looked away. He said, "I know nothing of any tomb."

"You lie," Carse told him softly. "You found the Tomb of Rhiannon, or you could not have found his sword. You found, somehow, the key to the oldest sacred legend on Mars. The very stones of that place are worth their weight in gold to the right people."

"I found no tomb," Penkawr insisted sullenly. He went on quickly, "But the sword itself is worth a fortune. I daren't try to sell it – these Jekkarans would snatch it away from me like wolves, if they saw it.

"But you can sell it, Carse." The little thief was shivering in the urgency of his greed. "You can smuggle it to Kahora and sell it to some Earthman for a fortune."

"And I will," Carse nodded. "But first we will get the other things in that tomb."

Penkawr had a sweat of agony on his face. After a long time he whispered, "Leave it at the sword, Carse. That's enough."

It came to Carse that Penkawr's agony was blended of greed and fear. And it was not fear of the Jekkarans but of something else, something that would have to be awesome indeed to daunt the greed of Penkawr.

Carse swore contemptuously. "Are you afraid of the Cursed One? Afraid of a mere legend that time has woven around some old king who's been a ghost for a million years?"

He laughed and made the sword flash in the lamplight. "Don't worry, little one. I'll keep the ghosts away. Think of the money. You can have your own palace with a hundred lovely slaves to keep you happy."

He watched fear struggle again with greed in the Martian's face.

"I saw something there, Carse. Something that scared me, I don't know why."

Greed won out. Penkawr licked dry lips. "But perhaps, as

you say, it is all only legend. And there are treasures there –
even my half share of them would make me wealthy beyond
dreams."

"Half?" Carse repeated blandly. "You're mistaken, Penkawr. Your share will be one-third."

Penkawr's face distorted with fury, and he leaped up.
"But I found the Tomb! It's my discovery!"

Carse shrugged. "If you'd rather not share that way, then
keep your secret to yourself. Keep it – till your 'brothers' of
Jekkara tear it from you with hot pincers when I tell them
what you've found."

"You'd do that?" choked Penkawr. "You'd tell them and
get me killed?"

The little thief stared in impotent rage at Carse, standing
tall in the lamp glow with the sword in his hands, his cloak
falling back from his naked shoulders, his collar and belt of
jewels looted from a dead king flaring. There was no softness
in Carse, no relenting. The deserts and the suns of Mars, the
cold and the heat and the hunger of them, had flayed away
all but the bone and the iron sinew.

Penkawr shivered. "Very well, Carse. I'll take you there –
for one-third share."

Carse nodded and smiled. "I thought you would."

Two hours later, they were riding up into the dark time-
worn hills that loomed behind Jekkara and the dead sea-
bottom.

It was very late now, an hour that Carse loved because it
seemed then that Mars was most perfectly itself. It reminded
him of a very old warrior, wrapped in a black cloak and
holding a broken sword, dreaming the dreams of age which
are so close to reality, remembering the sound of trumpets
and the laughter and the strength.

The dust of the ancient hills whispered under the eternal
wind. Phobos had set, and the stars were coldly brilliant.
The lights of Jekkara and the great black blankness of the
dead sea-bottom lay far behind and below them now. Penkawr led the way up the ascending gorges, their ungainly
mounts picking their way with astonishing agility over the
treacherous ground.

"This is how I stumbled on the place," Penkawr said. "On
a ledge my beast broke its leg in a hole – and the sand widen-

210

ed the hole as it flowed inward, and there was the tomb, cut right into the rock of the cliff. But the entrance was choked when I found it."

He turned and fixed Carse with a sulky yellow stare. "I found it," he repeated. "I still don't see why I should give you the lion's share."

"Because I'm the lion," said Carse cheerfully.

He made passes with the sword, feeling it blend with his flexing wrist, watching the starlight slide down the blade. His heart was beating high with excitement and it was the excitement of the archaeologist as well as of the looter.

He knew better than Penkawr the importance of this find. Martian history is so vastly long that it fades back into a dimness from which only vague legends have come down – legends of human and half-human races, of forgotten wars, of vanished gods.

Greatest of those gods had been the Quiru, hero-gods who were human yet superhuman, who had had all wisdom and power. But there had been a rebel among them – dark Rhiannon, the Cursed One, whose sinful pride had caused some mysterious catastrophe.

The Quiru, said the myths, had for that sin crushed Rhiannon and locked him into a hidden tomb. And for more than a million years men had hunted the Tomb of Rhiannon because they believed it held the secrets of Rhiannon's power.

Carse knew too much archaeology to take old legends too seriously. But he did believe that there was an incredibly ancient tomb that had engendered all these myths. And as the oldest relic on Mars it and the things in it would make Matthew Carse the richest man on three worlds – if he lived.

"This way," said Penkawr abruptly. He had ridden in silence for a long time, brooding.

They were far up in the highest hills behind Jekkara. Carse followed the little thief along a narrow ledge on the face of a steep cliff.

Penkawr dismounted and rolled aside a large stone, disclosing a hole in the cliff that was big enough for a man to wriggle through.

"You first," said Carse. "Take the lamp."

Reluctantly Penkawr obeyed, and Carse followed him into the foxhole.

At first there was only an utter darkness beyond the glow of the krypton-lamp. Penkawr slunk, cringing now like a frightened jackal.

Carse snatched the lamp away from him and held it high. They had scrambled through the narrow foxhole into a corridor that led straight back into the cliff. It was square and without ornament, the stone beautifully polished. He started off along it, Penkawr following.

The corridor ended in a vast chamber. It too was square and magnificently plain from what Carse could see of it. There was a dais at one end with an altar of marble, upon which was carved the same symbol that appeared on the hilt of the sword – the *ouroboros* in the shape of a winged serpent. But the circle was broken, the head of the serpent lifted as though looking into some new infinity.

Penkawr's voice came in a reedy whisper from behind his shoulder. "It was here that I found the sword. There are other things around the room but I did not touch them."

Carse had already glimpsed objects ranged around the walls of the great chamber, glittering vaguely through the gloom. He hooked the lamp to his belt and started to examine them.

Here was treasure, indeed! There were suits of mail of the finest workmanship, blazoned with patterns of unfamiliar jewels. There were strangely shaped helmets of unfamiliar glistening metals. A heavy throne-like chair of gold, subtly inlaid in dark metal, had a big tawny gem burning in each armpost.

All these things, Carse knew, were incredibly ancient. They must come from the farthest past of Mars.

"Let us hurry!" Penkawr pleaded.

Carse relaxed and grinned at his own forgetfulness. The scholar in him had for the moment superseded the looter.

"We'll take all we can carry of the smaller jewelled things," he said. "This first haul alone will make us rich."

"But you'll be twice as rich as I," Penkawr said sourly. "I could have got an Earthman in Barrakesh to sell these things for me for a half share only."

Carse laughed. "You should have done so, Penkawr.

When you ask for help from a noted specialist you have to pay high fees."

His circuit of the chamber had brought him back to the altar. Now he saw that behind the altar lay a door. He went through it, Penkawr following reluctantly at his heels.

Beyond the doorway was a short passage and at the end of it a door of metal, small and heavily barred. The bars had been lifted, and the door stood open an inch or two. Above it was an inscription in the ancient changeless High Martian characters, which Carse read with practised ease.

The doom of Rhiannon, dealt unto him forever by the Quiru who are lords of space and time!

Carse pushed the metal door aside and stepped through. And then he stood quite still, looking.

Beyond the door was a great stone chamber as large as the one behind him.

But in this room there was only one thing.

It was a great bubble of darkness. A big, brooding sphere of quivering blackness, through which shot little coruscating particles of brilliance like falling stars seen from another world. And from this weird bubble of throbbing darkness the lamplight recoiled, afraid.

Something – awe, superstition or some purely physical force – sent a cold tingling shock, racing through Carse's body. He felt his hair rising and his flesh seemed to draw away from his bones. He tried to speak and could not, his throat knotted with anxiety and tension.

"This is the thing I told you of," whispered Penkawr. "This is the thing I told you I saw."

Carse hardly heard him. A conjecture so vast that he could not grasp it shook his brain. The scholar's ecstasy was upon him, the ecstasy of discovery that is akin to madness.

This brooding bubble of darkness – it was strangely like the darkness of those blank black spots far out in the galaxy which some scientists have dreamed are holes in the continuum itself, windows into the infinite outside our universe!

Incredible, surely, and yet that cryptic Quiru inscription – fascinated by the thing, despite its aura of danger, Carse took two steps toward it.

He heard the swift scrape of sandals on the stone floor behind him as Penkawr moved fast. Carse knew instantly that he had blundered in turning his back on the disgruntled little thief. He started to whirl and raise the sword.

Penkawr's thrusting hands jabbed his back before he could complete the movement. Carse felt himself pitched into the brooding blackness.

He felt a terrible rending shock through each atom of his body, and then the world seemed to fall away from him.

"*Go share Rhiannon's doom, Earthman! I told you I could get another partner!*"

Penkawr's snarling shout came to him from a great distance as he tumbled into a black, bottomless infinity.

Carse seemed to plunge through a nighted abyss, buffeted by all the shrieking winds of space. An endless, endless fall with the timelessness and the choking horror of a nightmare.

He struggled with the fierce revulsion of an animal trapped by the unknown. His struggle was not physical, for in that blind and screaming nothingness his body was useless. It was a mental fight, the man's inner core of courage reasserting itself, willing itself to stop this nightmare fall through darkness.

And then as he fell, a more terrifying sensation shook him. A feeling that he was not *alone* in this nightmare plunge through infinity, that a dark strong, pulsating presence was close beside him, grasping for him, groping with eager fingers for his brain.

Carse made a supreme desperate mental effort. His sensation of falling seemed to lessen and then he felt solid rock slipping under his hands and feet. He scrambled frantically forward, in physical effort this time.

He found himself quite suddenly outside the dark bubble again on the floor of the inner chamber of the Tomb.

"What in the Nine Hells . . ." he began shakily and then stopped because the oath seemed so pitifully inadequate for what had happened.

The little krypton-lamp hooked to his belt still cast its reddish glow, the sword of Rhiannon still glittered in his hand.

And the bubble of darkness still gloomed and brooded a foot away from him, flickering with its whirl of diamond motes.

Carse realized that all his nightmare plunging through space had been during the moment he was inside the bubble. What devil's trick of ancient science *was* the thing anyway? Some queer perpetual vortex of force that the mysterious Quiru of long ago had set up, he supposed.

But why had he seemed to fall through infinities inside the thing? And whence had come that terrifying sensation of strong fingers groping eagerly at his brain as he fell?

"A trick of old Quiru science," he muttered shakenly. "And Penkawr's superstitions made him think he could kill me by pushing me into it."

Penkawr? Carse leaped to his feet, the sword of Rhiannon glittering wickedly in his hand.

"Blast his thieving little soul."

Penkawr was not here now. But he wouldn't have had time to go far. The smile on Carse's face was not pleasant as he went through the doorway.

In the outer chamber he suddenly stopped dead. There were things here now – big strange glittering objects – that had not been here before.

Where had they come from? Had he been longer in that bubble of darkness than he thought? Had Penkawr found these things in hidden crypts and ranged them here to await his return?

Carse's wonder increased as he examined the objects that now loomed amid the mail and other relics he had seen before. These objects did not look like mere art-relics – they looked like carefully fashioned, complicated instruments of unguessable purpose.

The biggest of them was a crystal wheel, the size of a small table, mounted horizontally atop a dull metal sphere. The wheel's rim glistened with jewels cut in precise polyhedrons. And there were other small devices of linked crystal prisms and tubes and things built of concentric metal rings and squat looped tubes of massive metal.

Could these glittering objects be the incomprehensible devices of an ancient alien Martian science? That supposition seemed incredible. The Mars of the far past, scholars knew, had been a world of only rudimentary science, a world of sword-fighting sea-warriors whose galleys and kingdoms had clashed on long-lost oceans.

Yet, perhaps, in the Mars of the even *farther* past, there had been a science whose techniques were unfamiliar and unrecognizable?

"But where could Penkawr have found them when we didn't see them before? And why didn't he take any of them with him?"

Memory of Penkawr reminded him that the little thief would be getting farther away every moment. Grimly gripping the sword, Carse turned and hurried down the square stone corridor toward the outer world.

As he strode on Carse became aware that the air in the tomb was now strangely damp. Moisture glistened on the walls. He had not noticed that most un-Martian dampness before and it startled him.

"Probably seepage from underground springs, like those that feed the canals," he thought. "But it wasn't there before."

His glance fell on the floor of the corridor. The drifted dust lay over it thickly as when they had entered. But there were no footprints in it now. No prints at all except those he was now making.

A horrible doubt, a feeling of unreality, clawed at Carse. The un-Martian dampness, the vanishing of their footprints – what had happened to everything in the moment he'd been inside the dark bubble?

He came to the end of the square stone corridor. And it was closed. It was closed by a massive slab of monolithic stone.

Carse stopped, staring at the slab. He fought down his increasing sense of weird unreality and made explanation for himself.

"There must have been a stone door I didn't see – and Penkawr has closed it to lock me in."

He tried to move the slab. It would not budge nor was there any sign of key, knob or hinge.

Finally Carse stepped back and levelled his proton-pistol. Its hissing streak of atomic flame crackled in the rock slab, searing and splitting it.

The slab was thick. He kept the trigger of his gun depressed for minutes. Then, with a hollowly reverberating crash the fragments of the split slab fell back in toward him.

But beyond, instead of the open air, there lay a solid mass of dark red soil.

"The whole tomb of Rhiannon – buried, now; Penkawr must have started a cave-in."

Carse didn't believe that. He didn't believe it at all but he tried to make himself believe, for he was becoming more and more afraid. And the thing of which he was afraid was impossible.

With blind anger he used the flaming beam of the pistol to undercut the mass of soil that blocked his way. He worked outward until the beam suddenly died as the charge of the gun ran out. He flung away the useless pistol and attacked the hot smoking mass of soil with the sword.

Panting, dripping, his mind a whirl of confused speculations, he dug outward through the soft soil till a small hole of brilliant daylight opened in front of him.

Daylight? Then he'd been in the weird bubble of darkness longer than he had imagined.

The wind blew in through the little opening, upon his face. And it was a warm wind. A warm wind and a *damp* wind, such as never blows on desert Mars.

Carse squeezed through and stood in the bright day looking outward.

There are times when a man has no emotion, no reaction. Times when all the centres are numbed and the eyes see and the ears hear but nothing communicates itself to the brain, which is protected in this way from madness.

He tried finally to laugh at what he saw though he heard his own laughter as a dry choking cry.

"Mirage, of course," he whispered. "A big mirage. Big as all Mars."

The warm breeze lifted Carse's tawny hair, blew his cloak against him. A cloud drifted over the sun and somewhere a bird screamed harshly. He did not move.

He was looking at an ocean.

It stretched out to the horizon ahead, a vast restlessness of water, milky-white and pale with a shimmering phosphorescence even in daylight.

"Mirage," he said again stubbornly, his reeling mind clinging with the desperation of fear to that one shred of

217

explanation. "It has to be. Because this is still Mars."

Still Mars, still the same planet. The same high hills up into which Penkawr had led him by night.

Or were they the same? Before, the foxhole entrance to the Tomb of Rhiannon had been a steep cliff-face. Now he stood on the grassy slope of a great hill.

And there were rolling green hills and dark forest down there below him, where before had been only desert. Green hills, green wood and a bright river that ran down a gorge to what had been dead sea-bottom but was now – sea.

Carse's numbed gaze swept along the great coast of the distant shoreline. And down on that far sunlit coast he saw the glitter of a white city and knew that it was Jekkara.

Jekkara, bright and strong between the verdant hills and the mighty ocean, that ocean that had not been seen upon Mars for nearly a million years.

Matthew Carse knew then that it was no mirage. He sat and hid his face in his hands. His body was shaken by deep tremors and his nails bit into his own flesh until blood trickled down his cheeks.

He knew now what had happened to him in that vortex of darkness, and it seemed to him that a cold voice repeated a certain warning inscription in tones of distant thunder.

"The Quiru are lords of space and time – *of time* – OF TIME!"

Carse, staring out over the green hills and the milky ocean, made a terrible effort to grapple with the incredible.

"*I have come into the past of Mars. All my life I have studied and dreamed of that past. Now I am in it. I, Matthew Carse, archaeologist, renegade, looter of tombs.*

"*The Quiru for their own reasons built a way and I came through it. Time is to us the unknown dimension but the Quiru knew it!*"

Carse had studied science. You had to know the elements of a half-dozen sciences to be a planetary archaeologist. He franctically ransacked memory now for an explanation.

Had his first guess about that bubble of darkness been right? Was it really a hole in the continuum of the universe? If that were so he could dimly understand what had happened to him.

For the space-time continuum of the universe was finite,

218

limited. Einstein and Riemann had proved that long ago. And he had fallen clear out of that continuum and then back into it again – but into a different time-frame from his own.

What was it that Kaufman had once written? "The Past is the Present-that-exists-at-a-distance." He had come back into that other distant Present, that was all. There was no reason to be afraid.

But he *was* afraid. The horror of that nightmare transition to this green and smiling Mars of long ago wrenched a gusty cry from his lips.

Blindly, still gripping the jewelled sword, he leaped up and turned to re-enter the buried Tomb of Rhiannon.

"I can go back the way I came, back through that hole in the continuum."

He stopped a convulsive shudder running through his frame. He could not make himself face again that bubble of glittering gloom, that dreadful plunge through inter-dimensional infinity.

He dared not. He had not the Quiru's wisdom. In that perilous plunge across time mere chance had flung him into this past age. He could not count on chance to return him to his own far-future age.

"I'm here," he said. "I'm here in the distant past of Mars and I'm here to stay."

He turned back around and gazed out again upon that incredible vista. He stayed there a long time, unmoving. The sea birds came and looked at him and flashed away on their sharp white wings. The shadows lengthened.

His eyes swung again to the white towers of Jekkara down in the distance, queenly in the sunlight above the harbour. It was not the Jekkara he knew, the thieves' city of the Low Canals, rotting away into dust, but it was a link to the familiar and Carse desperately needed such a link.

He would go to Jekkara. And he would try not to think. He must not think at all or surely his mind would crack.

Carse gripped the shaft of the jewelled sword and started down the grassy slope of the hill. . . .

THE END

Here is the newest, and one of the most vividly touching of Ray Bradbury's poetic legends of alien planets – and as a surprise, its setting is not Mars but Venus. Like Mr. Bradbury's Mars (and even, for that matter, his Terra), this Venus is not an astronomy-textbook planet mensurable by instruments and conforming to mechanistic laws, but a mirror (like that greatest Looking-Glass of them all) leading to the world of wonder . . . and reflecting more of ourselves than we can see unaided.

ALL SUMMER IN A DAY

by Ray Bradbury

"Ready?"

"Ready."

"Now?"

"Soon!"

"Do the scientists really know? Will it happen today, will it?"

"Look, look; see for yourself!"

The children pressed to each other like so many roses, so many weeds, intermixed, peering out for a look at the hidden sun.

It rained.

It had been raining for seven years; thousands upon thousands of days compounded and filled from one end to the other with rain, with the drum and gush of water, with the sweet crystal fall of showers and the concussion of storms so heavy they were tidal waves come over the islands. A thousand forests had been crushed under the rain and grown up a thousand times to be crushed again. And this was the way life was forever on the planet Venus, and this was the schoolroom of the children of the rocket men and women who had come to a raining world to set up civilization and live out their lives.

"It's stopping, it's stopping!"

"Yes, yes!"

Margot stood apart from them, from these children who

could never remember a time when there wasn't rain and rain and rain. They were all nine years old, and if there had been a day, seven years ago, when the sun came out for an hour and showed its face to the stunned world, they could not recall. Sometimes, at night, she heard them stir, in remembrance, and she knew they were dreaming and remembering gold or a yellow crayon or a coin large enough to buy the world with. She knew that they thought they remembered a warmness, like a blushing in the face, in the body, in the arms and legs and trembling hands. But then they always awoke to the tatting drum, the endless shaking down of clear bead necklaces upon the roof, the walk, the gardens, the forest, and their dreams were gone.

All day yesterday they had read in class, about the sun. About how like a lemon it was, and how hot. And they had written small stories or essays or poems about it:

> "I think the sun is a flower,
> That blooms for just one hour."

That was Margot's poem, read in a quiet voice in the still classroom while the rain was falling outside.

"Aw, you didn't write that!" protested one of the boys.

"I did," said Margot. "I *did*."

"William!" said the teacher.

But that was yesterday. Now, the rain was slackening, and the children were crushed to the great thick windows.

"Where's teacher?"

"She'll be back."

"She'd better hurry, we'll miss it!"

They turned on themselves, like a feverish wheel, all tumbling spokes.

Margot stood alone. She was a very frail girl who looked as if she had been lost in the rain for years and the rain had washed out the blue from her eyes and the red from her mouth and the yellow from her hair. She was an old photograph dusted from an album, whitened away, and if she spoke at all her voice would be a ghost. Now she stood, separate, staring at the rain and the loud wet world beyond the huge glass.

"What're *you* looking at?" said William.

Margot said nothing.

"Speak when you're spoken to." He gave her a shove. But

she did not move; rather, she let herself be moved only by him and nothing else.

They edged away from her, they would not look at her. She felt them go away. And this was because she would play no games with them in the echoing tunnels of the underground city. If they tagged her and ran, she stood blinking after them and did not follow. When the class sang songs about happiness and life and games, her lips barely moved. Only when they sang about the sun and the summer did her lips move, as she watched the drenched windows.

And then, of course, the biggest crime of all was that she had come here only five years ago from Earth, and she remembered the sun and the way the sun was and the sky was, when she was four, in Ohio. And they, they had been on Venus all their lives, and they had been only two years old when the last sun came out, and had long since forgotten the colour and heat of it and the way that it really was. But Margot remembered.

"It's like a penny," she said, once, eyes closed.

"No it's not!" the children cried.

"It's like a fire," she said, "in the stove."

"You're lying, you don't remember!" cried the children.

But she remembered and stood quietly apart from all of them, and watched the patterning windows. And once, a month ago, she had refused to shower in the school shower-rooms, had clutched her hands to her ears and over her head, screaming the water mustn't touch her head. So after that, dimly, dimly, she sensed it, she was different and they knew her difference and kept away.

There was talk that her father and mother were taking her back to Earth next year; it seemed vital to her that they do so, though it would mean the loss of thousands of dollars to her family. And so, the children hated her for all these reasons, of big and little consequence. They hated her pale snow face, her waiting silence, her thinness and her possible future.

"Get away!" The boy gave her another push. "What're you waiting for?"

Then, for the first time, she turned and looked at him. And what she was waiting for was in her eyes.

"Well, don't wait around here!" cried the boy, savagely. "You won't see nothing!"

Her lips moved.

"Nothing!" he cried. "It was all a joke, wasn't it?" He turned to the other children. "Nothing's happening today. *Is* it?"

They all blinked at him and then, understanding, laughed and shook their heads. "Nothing, nothing!"

"Oh, but," Margot whispered, her eyes helpless. "But, this is the day, the scientists predict, they say, they *know*, the sun . . ."

"All a joke!" said the boy, and seized her roughly. "Hey, everyone, let's put her in a closet before teacher comes!"

"No," said Margot, falling back.

They surged about her, caught her up and bore her, protesting, and then pleading, and then crying, back into a tunnel, a room, a closet, where they slammed and locked the door. They stood looking at the door and saw it tremble from her beating and throwing herself against it. They heard her muffled cries. Then, smiling, they turned and went out and back down the tunnel, just as the teacher arrived.

"Ready, children?" She glanced at her watch.

"Yes!" said everyone.

"Are we all here?"

"Yes!"

The rain slackened still more.

They crowded to the huge door.

The rain stopped.

It was as if, in the midst of a film concerning an avalanche, a tornado, a hurricane, a volcanic eruption, something had, first, gone wrong with the sound apparatus, thus muffling and finally cutting off all noise, all of the blasts and repercussions and thunders, and then, secondly, ripped the film from the projector and inserted in its place a peaceful tropical slide which did not move or tremor. The world ground to a standstill. The silence was so immense and unbelievable that you felt that your ears had been stuffed or you had lost your hearing altogether. The children put their hands to their ears. They stood apart. The door slid back and the smell of the silent, waiting world came in to them.

The sun came out.

It was the colour of flaming bronze and it was very large. And the sky around it was a blazing blue tile colour. And the jungle burned with sunlight as the children, released from their spell, rushed out, yelling, into the summer-time.

"Now, don't go too far," called the teacher after them. "You've only one hour, you know. You wouldn't want to get caught out!"

But they were running and turning their faces up to the sky and feeling the sun on their cheeks like a warm iron; they were taking off their jackets and letting the sun burn their arms.

"Oh, it's better than the sun-lamps, isn't it?"

"Much, much better!"

They stopped running and stood in the great jungle that covered Venus, that grew and never stopped growing, tumultuously, even as you watched it. It was a nest of octopuses, clustering up great arms of flesh-like weed, wavering, flowering in this brief spring. It was the colour of rubber and ash, this jungle, from the many years without sun. It was the color of stones and white cheeses and ink.

The children lay out, laughing, on the jungle mattress, and heard it sigh and squeak under them, resilient and alive. They ran among the trees, they slipped and fell, they pushed each other, they played hide-and-seek and tag but most of all they squinted at the sun until tears ran down their faces, they put their hands up at that yellowness and that amazing blueness and they breathed of the fresh fresh air and listened and listened to the silence which suspended them in a blessed sea of no sound and no motion. They looked at everything and savoured everything. Then, wildly, like animals escaped from their caves, they ran and ran in shouting circles. They ran for an hour and did not stop running.

And then –

In the midst of their running, one of the girls wailed.

Everyone stopped.

The girl, standing in the open, held out her hand.

"Oh, look, look," she said, trembling.

They came slowly to look at her opened palm.

In the centre of it, cupped and huge, was a single raindrop.

She began to cry, looking at it.

They glanced quickly at the sky.

"Oh. Oh."

A few cold drops fell on their noses and their cheeks and their mouths. The sun faded behind a stir of mist. A wind blew cool around them. They turned and started to walk back toward the underground house, their hands at their sides, their smiles vanishing away.

A boom of thunder startled them and like leaves before a new hurricane, they tumbled upon each other and ran. Lightning struck ten miles away, five miles away, a mile, a half-mile. The sky darkened into midnight in a flash.

They stood in the doorway of the underground house for a moment until it was raining hard. Then they closed the door and heard the gigantic sound of the rain falling in tons and avalanches everywhere and forever.

"Will it be seven more years?"

"Yes, seven."

Then one of them gave a little cry.

"Margot!"

"What?"

"She's still in the closet where we locked her."

"Margot."

They stood as if someone had driven them, like so many stakes, into the floor. They looked at each other and then looked away. They glanced out at the world that was raining now and raining and raining steadily. They could not meet each other's glances. Their faces were solemn and pale. They looked at their hands and feet, their faces down.

"Margot."

One of the girls said, "Well . . . ?"

No one moved.

"Go on," whispered the girl.

They walked slowly down the hall in the sound of cold rain. They turned through the doorway to the room, in the sound of the storm and thunder, lightning on their faces, blue and terrible. They walked over to the closet door slowly and stood by it.

Behind the closet door was only silence.

They unlocked the door, even more slowly, and let Margot out.

THE END

The Beetles live along the shore, and of the Mitr, only one remains by old Glass City.

THE MITR

by Jack Vance

A rocky headland made a lee for the bay and the wide empty beach.

The water barely rose and fell. A high overcast greyed the sky, stilled the air. The bay shone with a dull lustre, like old pewter.

Dunes bordered the beach, breaking into a nearby forest of pitchy black-green cypress. The forest was holding its own, matting down the drifts with whiskery roots.

Among the dunes were ruins – glass walls ground milky by salt breeze and sand. In the centre of these walls a human being had brought grass and ribbon-weed for her bed.

Her name was Mitr, or so the beetles called her. For want of any other, she had taken the word for a name.

The name, the grass bed, and a length of brown cloth stolen from the beetles were her only possessions. Possibly her belongings might be said to include a mouldering heap of bones which lay a hundred yards back in the forest. They interested her strongly, and she vaguely remembered a connection with herself. In the old days, when her arms and legs had been short and round, she had not marked the rather grotesque correspondence of form. Now she had lengthened, and the resemblance was plain. Eyeholes like her eyes, a mouth like her own, teeth, jaw, skull, shoulders, ribs, legs, feet. From time to time she would wander back into the forest and stand wondering, though of late she had not been regular in her visits.

Today was dreary and grey. She felt bored, uneasy, and after some thought decided that she was hungry. Wandering out on the dunes she listlessly ate a number of grasspods. Perhaps she was not hungry after all.

She walked down to the beach, stood looking out across the bay. A damp wind flapped the brown cloth, rumpled her hair. Perhaps it would rain. She looked anxiously at the sky. Rain made her wet and miserable. She could always take shelter among the rocks of the headland but – sometimes it was better to be wet.

She wandered down along the beach, caught and ate a small shell-fish. There was little satisfaction in the salty flesh. Apparently she was not hungry. She picked up a sharp stick and drew a straight line in the damp sand – fifty feet – a hundred feet long. She stopped, looked back over her work with pleasure. She walked back, drawing another line parallel to the first, a hand's-breadth distant.

Very interesting effect. Fired by sudden enthusiasm she drew more lines up and down the beach until she had created an extensive grate of parallel lines.

She looked over her work with satisfaction. Making such marks on the smooth sand was pleasant and interesting. Some other time she would do it again, and perhaps use curving lines or cross-hatching.

But enough for now. She dropped the stick. The feeling of hunger that was not hunger came over her again. She caught a sand-locust but threw it away without eating it.

She began to run at full speed along the beach. This was better, the flash of her legs below her, the air clean in her lungs. Panting, she came to a halt, flung herself down in the sand.

Presently she caught her breath, sat up. She wanted to run some more, but felt a trifle languid. She grimaced, jerked uneasily. Maybe she should visit the beetles over the headland; perhaps the old grey creature called Ti-Sri-Ti would speak to her.

Tentatively she rose to her feet and started back along the beach. The plan gave her no real pleasure. Ti-Sri-Ti had little of interest to say. He answered no questions, but recited interminable data concerned with the colony; how many grubs would be allowed to mature, how many pounds of spider-eggs had been taken to storage, the condition of his mandibles, antenna, eyes . . .

She hesitated but after a moment went on. Better Ti-Sri-Ti than no one, better the sound of a voice than the monotonous crush of grey surf. And perhaps he might say something interesting; on occasions his conversation went far afield and then Mitr listened with absorption: "The mountains are ruled by wild lizards and beyond are the Mercaloid Mechanvikis, who live under the ground with only fuming chimneys and slag-runs to tell of activity below. The beetles live along the shore and of the Mitr only one remains by old Glass City, the last of the Mitr.''

She had not quite understood, since the flux and stream of time, the concepts of before and after, meant nothing to her. The universe was static; day followed day, not in a series, but as a duplication.

Ti-Sri-Ti had droned on: "Beyond the mountains is endless desert, then endless ice, then endless waste, then a land of seething fire, then the great water and once more the land of life, the rule and domain of the beetles, where every solstice a new acre of leaf mulch is chewed and laid ..." And then there had been an hour dealing with beetle fungiculture.

Mitr wandered along the beach. She passed the beautiful grate she had scratched in the damask sand, passed her glass walls, climbed the first shelves of black rock. She stopped, listened. A sound?

She hesitated, then went on. There was a rush of many feet. A long brown and black beetle sprang upon her, pressed her against the rocks. She fought feebly, but the forefeet pinned her shoulders, arched her back. The beetle pressed his proboscis to her neck, punctured her skin. She stood limp, staring into his red eyes while he drank.

He finished, released her. The wound closed of itself, smarted and ached. The beetle climbed up over the rocks.

Mitr sat for an hour regaining her strength. The thought of listening to Ti-Sri-Ti now gave her no pleasure.

She wandered listlessly back along the beach, and ate a few bits of seaweed and a small fish which had been trapped in a tidepool.

She walked to the water's edge and stared out past the headland to the horizon. She wanted to cry out, to yell; something of the same urge which had driven her to run so swiftly along the beach.

She raised her voice, called, a long musical note. The damp mild breeze seemed to muffle the sound. She turned away discouraged.

She wandered down the shore to the little stream of fresh

water. Here she drank and ate some of the blackberries that grew in rank thickets.

She jerked upright, raised her head.

A vast high sound filled the sky, seemed part of all the air.

She stood rigid, then craned her neck, searching the overcast, legs half-bent for flight.

A long black sky-fish dropped into view, snorting puffs of fire.

Terrified, she backed into the blackberry bushes. The brambles tore her legs, brought her to awareness. She dodged into the forest, crouched under a leaning cypress trunk.

The sky-fish dropped with astounding rapidity, lowered to the beach, settled with a quiet final belch and sigh.

Mitr watched in frozen fascination. Never had she known of such a thing, never would she walk the beach again without watching the heavens.

The sky-fish opened. She saw the glint of metal, glass. From the interior jumped three creatures. Her head moved forward in wonder. They were something like herself, but large, red, burly. Strange, frightening things. They made a great deal of noise, talking in hoarse rough voices.

One of them saw the glass walls, and for a space they examined the ruins with great interest.

The brown and black beetle which had drank her blood chose this moment to scuttle down the rocks to the beach. One of the newcomers set up a loud halloo and the beetle, bewildered and resentful, ran back up toward the rocks. The stranger held a shiny thing in his hand. It spat a lance of fire and the beetle burst into a thousand incandescent pieces.

The three cried out in loud voices, laughing, and Mitr shrank back under the tree trunk, making herself as small as possible.

One of the strangers noticed the place on the beach where she had drawn her grating. He called his companions and they looked with every display of attention, studying her footprints with extreme interest. One of them made a comment which caused the others to break into loud laughter. Then they all turned and searched up and down the beach.

They were seeking her, thought Mitr. She crouched so far under the trunk that the bark bruised her flesh.

Presently their interest waned and they went back to the sky-fish. One of them brought forth a long black tube, which he took down to the edge of the surf and threw far out into the leaden water. The tube stiffened, pulsed, made sucking sounds.

The sky-fish was thirsty and was drinking through his proboscis, thought Mitr.

The three strangers now walked along the beach toward the fresh-water stream. Mitr watched their approach with apprehension. Were they following her tracks? Her hands were sweating, her skin tingled.

They stopped at the water's edge, drank, only a few paces away. Mitr could see them plainly. They had bright copper hair and little hair-wisps around their mouths. They wore shining red carapaces around their chests, grey cloth on their legs, metal foot-wrappings. They were much like herself – but somehow different. Bigger, harder, more energetic. They were cruel, too; they had burnt the brown and black beetle. Mitr watched them fascinatedly. Where was their home? Were there others like them, like her, in the sky?

She shifted her position; the foliage crackled. Tingles of excitement and fear ran along her back. Had they heard? She peered out, ready to flee. No, they were walking back down the beach toward the sky-fish.

Mitr jumped up from under the tree-trunk, stood watching from behind the foliage. Plainly they cared little that another like themselves lived nearby. She became angry. Now she wanted to chide them, and order them off her beach.

She held back. It would be foolish to show herself. They might easily throw a lance of flame to burn her as they had the beetle. In any event they were rough and brutal. Strange creatures.

She stole through the forest, flitting from trunk to trunk, falling flat when necessary until she had approached the sky-fish as closely as shelter allowed.

The strangers were standing close around the base of the

230

monster, and showed no further disposition to explore.

The tube into the bay grew limp. They pulled it back into the sky-fish. Did that mean that they were about to leave? Good. They had no right on her beach. They had committed an outrage, landing so arrogantly, and killing one of her beetles. She almost stepped forward to upbraid them; then remembered how rough and hard and cruel they were, and held back with a tingling skin.

Stand quietly. Presently they will go, and you will be left in possession of your beach.

She moved restlessly.

Rough red brutes.

Don't move or they will see you. And then? She shivered.

They were making preparations for leaving. A lump came into her throat. They had seen her tracks and had never bothered to search. They could have found her so easily, she had hid herself almost in plain sight. And now she was closer than ever.

If she moved forward only a step, then they would see her.

Skin tingling, she moved a trifle out from behind the treetrunk. Just a little bit. Then she jumped back, heart thudding.

Had they seen her? With a sudden fluttering access of fright she hoped not. What would they do?

She looked cautiously around the trunk. One of the strangers was staring in a puzzled manner, as if he might have glimpsed movement. Even now he didn't see her. He looked straight into her eyes.

She heard him call out, then she was fleeing through the forest. He charged after her, and after him came the other two, battering down the undergrowth.

They left her, bruised and bleeding, in a bed of ferns, and marched back through the forest toward the beach, laughing and talking in their rough hoarse voices.

She lay quiet for a while.

Their voices grew faint. She rose to her feet, staggered, limped after them.

A great glare lit the sky.

Through the trees she saw the sky-fish thunder up – higher, higher, higher. It vanished through the overcast.

231

There was silence along the beach, only the endless mutter of the surf.

She walked down to the water's edge, where the tide was coming in. The overcast was greying with evening.

She looked for many minutes into the sky, listening.

No sound. The damp wind blew in her face, ruffling her hair.

She sighed, turned back toward the ruined glass walls with tears on her cheeks.

The tide was washing up over the grate of straight lines she had drawn so carefully in the sand. Another few minutes and it would be entirely gone.

THE END

SECTION IV

THE GODLIKE MACHINES

233

Since this is the last section, let's sum up the whole lure of space opera. Its parameters are marked by a few mighty concepts standing like watch-towers along a lonely frontier. What goes on between them is essentially simple – a tale of love or hate, triumph or defeat – because it is the watch-towers that matter. We are already familiar with some of them: the question of reality, the limitations of knowledge, exile, the sheer immensity of the universe, the endlessness of time.

These watch-towers are abstract. Well enough. But the most potent symbols are not abstract but concrete. And maybe the most potent symbol of them all is sf's own invention, the Starship.

The Starship is the key that unlocks the great bronze doors of space opera and lets mankind run loose among all the other immensities.

This section is given over to immensities. No nonsense here about boy meeting girl next door or Joe X becoming head of firm; none of the stuff of which your best-sellers are made. Not a blow struck, now I come to think of it; the deaths are impersonal. No copulation; a chaste kiss beneath an alien sun. Instead, we head into the wide blue yonder, to confront –

Well, to be specific, we confront various godlike machines and a couple of all-embracing catastrophes. There are famous names here, and perhaps the best-known of all space opera writers, A. E. van Vogt, presents one of his most striking tales, *The Storm*. At the centre of van Vogt's storm rides his great galactic battleship *Star Cluster*, glowing like an immense and brilliant jewel.

> *Silent as a ghost, grand and wonderful beyond all imagination, glorious in her power, the great ship slid through the blackness along the special river of time and space which was her plotted course.*

As with Edmund Hamilton, one feels intensely those moments when van Vogt is charged by the excitement of the tremendous things he is writing about. Contemporary sf writers who have decided that such matters are old hat, and will write only of the here-and-now, have rejected a whole vocabulary.

The influence of van Vogt has been strong – rightly so, I believe, for his sort of mythopoeic writing has always set at naught the more humdrum kind of engineering- or pre-diction-sf which constantly threatens to dry the true springs of creative imagining. His influence on Charles Harness's *The Paradox Men* is clear; yet I believe Harness outdoes the Old Master, both in daring and intelligence.

Since *The Paradox Men* is a novel, it can be represented here only by a long extract; but that is a complete episode in itself, the arrival of Alar at a solarion, one of those amazing craft which ride the five thousand degree Kelvin contour on the surface of the sun. Here Alar, Thief, Mystery Man, hero with hidden powers, undergoes various adventures which include a breathless duel and the ultimate adventure of all – his death. Alar survives everything. And Harness's novel survives as one of the high points of the genre.

There are few scenes in all space fiction more staggering than the breaking up of the *Star Cluster* and the sinking of Harness's solarion below the raging surface of the sun.

The sun is in trouble again in Randall Garrett's short story. Here once more we have the archetype of man's growing power threatening nature – this time on an ultimate scale.

Among all the madnesses of sf, an almost universal acknowledgement of the overlordship of the sun remains one of its sanities. Perhaps the sun is the deity of sf authors, who are not otherwise known as an excessively religious bunch of people. Whatever awful things happen on planets, suns are generally sacrosanct. Garrett puts paid to all that in under two thousand words.

Although sf writers may not be particularly religious in a conventional sense, they have always been obsessed by the notion of God. Either they are for Him or against Him, but they are always aware of Him standing there, one of the watch-towers on the last frontier.

The two final stories approach Him by way of godlike machines. One can see how the gigantic computers which grow before our eyes in Asimov's story would render as obsolete as a stage coach van Vogt's *Star Cluster*; and not only the *Star Cluster* but, ultimately, Man himself.

Believing that God must be the ultimate of all adventures in space/time, I close this volume with Fredric Brown's *Answer*. Although my aim has been to select unfamiliar stories, this is probably the most famous sf short story ever written, just as it is about the shortest. So often have strangers come up to me after lectures or at parties and asked, "Do you know that story about – ", that I have acquired a reputation for telepathy by cutting them short and saying, "Oh, you mean the one about all the computers in the universe? That's by Fredric Brown and it's called 'Answer'. Isn't it a beauty?"

So here is the most godlike machine of all. It's the creation of Fredric Brown and it's called, simply, 'Answer'.

And it's that story about –

The combined military powers of all the people of that galaxy could not stand up to the tremendous might of the battleship of space. But there was one force their galaxy held that could smash that or any other ship!

THE STORM

by A. E. van Vogt

Over the miles and the years, the gases drifted. Waste matter from ten thousand suns, a diffuse miasm of spent explosions, of dead hell fires and the furies of a hundred million raging sunspots – formless, purposeless.

But it was the beginning.

Into the great dark the gases crept. Calcium was in them, and sodium, and hydrogen; and the speed of the drift varied up to twenty miles a second.

There was a timeless period while gravitation performed its function. The inchoate mass became masses. Great blobs of gas took a semblance of shape in widely separate areas, and moved on and on and on.

They came finally to where a thousand flaring seetee suns had long before doggedly "crossed the street" of the main stream of terrene suns. Had crossed, and left *their* excrement of gases.

The first clash quickened the vast worlds of gas. The electron haze of terrene plunged like spurred horses and sped deeper into the equally violently reacting positron haze of contraterrene. Instantly, the lighter orbital positrons and electrons went up in a blaze of hard radiation.

The storm was on.

The stripped seetee nuclei carried now terrific and unbalanced negative charges and repelled electrons, but tended to attract terrene atom nuclei. In their turn the stripped terrene nuclei attracted contraterrene.

Violent beyond all conception were the resulting cancellations of charges.

The two opposing masses heaved and spun in a cataclysm of partial adjustment. They had been heading in different

238

directions. More and more they became one tangled, seething whirlpool.

The new course, uncertain at first, steadied and became a line drive through the midnight heavens. On a front of nine light years, at a solid fraction of the velocity of light, the storm roared toward its destiny.

Suns were engulfed for half a hundred years – and left behind with only a hammering of cosmic rays to show that they had been the centres of otherwise invisible, impalpable atomic devastation.

In its four hundred and ninetieth Sidereal year, the storm intersected the orbit of a Nova at the flash moment.

It began to move!

On the three-dimensional map at weather headquarters on the planet Kaider III, the storm was coloured orange. Which meant it was the biggest of the four hundred odd storms raging in the Fifty Suns region of the Lesser Magellanic Cloud.

It showed as an uneven splotch fronting at Latitude 473, Longitude 228, Centre 190 parsecs, but that was a special Fifty Suns degree system which had no relation to the magnetic centre of the Magellanic Cloud as a whole.

The report about the Nova had not yet been registered on the map. When that happened the storm colour would be changed to an angry red.

They had stopped looking at the map. Maltby stood with the councillors at the great window staring up at the Earth ship.

The machine was scarcely more than a dark sliver in the distant sky. But the sight of it seemed to hold a deadly fascination for the older men.

Maltby felt cool, determined, but also sardonic. It was funny, these – these people of the Fifty Suns in this hour of their danger calling upon *him*.

He unfocused his eyes from the ship, fixed his steely, laconic gaze on the plump, perspiring chairman of the Kaider III government – and, tensing his mind, forced the man to look at him. The councillor, unaware of the compulsion, conscious only that he had turned, said;

"You understand your instructions, Captain Maltby?"

239

Maltby nodded. "I do."

The curt words must have evoked a vivid picture. The fat face rippled like palsied jelly and broke out in a new trickle of sweat.

"The worst part of it all," the man groaned, "is that the people of the ship found us by the wildest accident. They had run into one of our meteorite stations and captured its attendant. The attendant sent a general warning and then forced them to kill him before they could discover which of the fifty million suns of the Lesser Magellanic Cloud was us.

"Unfortunately, they did discover that he and the rest of us were all descendants of the robots who had escaped the massacre of the robots in the main galaxy fifteen thousand years ago.

"But they were baffled, and without a clue. They started home, stopping off at planets on the way on a chance basis. The seventh stop was us. Captain Maltby – "

The man looked almost beside himself. He shook. His face was as colourless as a white shroud. He went on hoarsely:

"Captain Maltby, you must not fail. They have asked for a meteorologist to guide them to Cassidor VII, where the central government is located. They mustn't reach there. You must drive them into the great storm at 473.

"We have commissioned you to do this for us because you have the two minds of the Mixed Men. We regret that we have not always fully appreciated your services in the past. But you must admit that, after the wars of the Mixed Men, it was natural that we should be careful about – "

Maltby cut off the lame apology. "Forget it," he said. "The Mixed Men are robots, too, and therefore as deeply involved, as I see it, as the Dellians and non-Dellians. Just what the Hidden Ones of my kind think, I don't know, nor do I care, I assure you I shall do my best to destroy this ship."

"Be careful!" the chairman urged anxiously. "This ship could destroy us, our planet, our sun in a single minute. We never dreamed that Earth could have gotten so far ahead of us and produced such a devastatingly powerful machine. After all, the non-Dellian robots and, of course, the Mixed Men among us are capable of research work; the former have been labouring feverishly for thousands of years.

"But finally, remember that you are not being asked to
240

commit suicide. The battleship is absolutely invincible. Just how it will survive a real storm we were not told when we were shown around. But it will. What happens, however, is that everyone aboard becomes unconscious.

"As a Mixed Man you will be the first to revive. Our combined fleets will be waiting to board the ship the moment you open the doors. Is that clear?"

It had been clear the first time it was explained, but these non-Dellians had a habit of repeating themselves, as if thoughts kept growing vague in their minds. As Maltby closed the door of the great room behind him, one of the councillors said to his neighbour:

"Has he been told that the storm has gone Nova?"

The fat man overheard. He shook his head. His eyes gleamed as he said quietly: "No. After all, he is one of the Mixed Men. We can't trust him too far no matter what his record."

All morning the reports had come in. Some showed progress, some didn't. But her basic good humour was untouched by the failures.

The great reality was that her luck had held. She had found a planet of the robots. Only one planet so far, but –

Grand Captain Laurr smiled grimly. It wouldn't be long now. Being a supreme commander was a terrible business. But she had not shrunk from making the deadly threat; provide all required information, or the entire planet of Kaider III would be destroyed.

The information was coming in; Population of Kaider III two billion, one hundred million, two-fifths Dellian, three-fifths non-Dellian robots.

Dellians physically and mentally the higher type, but completely lacking in creative ability. Non-Dellians dominated in the research laboratories.

The forty-nine other suns whose planets were inhabited were called, in alphabetical order: Assora, Atmion, Bresp, Buraco, Cassidor, Corrab – They were located at (1) Assora: Latitude 931, Longitude 27, Centre 201 parsecs: (2) Atmion –

It went on and on. Just before noon she noted with steely amusement that there was still nothing coming through from the meteorology room, nothing at all about storms.

She made the proper connection and flung her words: "What's the matter, Lieutenant Cannons? Your assistants have been making prints and duplicates of various Kaider maps. Aren't you getting anything?"

The old meteorologist shook his head. "You will recall, noble lady, that when we captured that robot in space, he had time to send out a warning. Immediately on every Fifty Suns planet, all maps were despoiled, civilian meteorologists were placed aboard spaceships, that were stripped of receiving radios, with orders to go to a planet on a chance-basis, and stay there for ten years.

"To my mind, all this was done before it was clearly grasped that their navy hadn't a chance against us. Now they are going to provide us with a naval meteorologist, but we shall have to depend on our lie detectors as to whether or not he is telling us the truth."

"I see." The woman smiled. "Have no fear. They don't dare oppose us openly. No doubt there is a plan being built up against us, but it cannot prevail now that we can take action to enforce our unalterable will. Whoever they send must tell us the truth. Let me know when he comes."

Lunch came, but she ate at her desk, watching the flashing pictures on the astro, listening to the murmur of voices, storing the facts, the general picture, into her brain.

"There's no doubt, Captain Turgess," she commented once, savagely, "that we're being lied to on a vast scale. But let it be so. We can use psychological tests to verify all the vital details.

"For the time being it is important that you relieve the fears of anyone you find it necessary to question. We must convince these people that Earth will accept them on an equal basis without bias or prejudice of any kind because of their robot orig – –"

She bit her lip. "That's an ugly word, the worst kind of propaganda. We must eliminate it from our thoughts."

"I'm afraid," the officer shrugged, "not from our division."

She stared at him, narrow-eyed, then cut him off angrily. A moment later she was talking into the general transmitter: "The word robot must not be used – by any of our personnel – under pain of fine – –"

Switching off, she put a busy signal on her spare receiver, and called Psychology House. Lieutenant Neslor's face appeared on the plate.

"I heard your order just now, noble lady," the woman psychologist said. "I'm afraid, however, that we're dealing with the deepest instincts of the human animal – hatred or fear of the stranger, the alien.

"Excellency, we come from a long line of ancestors who, in their time, have felt superior to others because of some slight variation in the pigmentation of the skin. It is even recorded that the colour of the eyes has influenced the egoistic in historical decisions. We have sailed into very deep waters, and it will be the crowning achievement of our life if we sail out in a satisfactory fashion."

There was an eager lilt in the psychologist's voice; and the grand captain experienced a responsive thrill of joy. If there was one thing she appreciated, it was the positive outlook, the kind of people who faced all obstacles short of the recognizably impossible with a youthful zest, a will to win. She was still smiling as she broke the connection.

The high thrill sagged. She sat cold with her problem. It was a problem. Hers. All aristocratic officers had *carte blanche* powers, and were expected to solve difficulties involving anything up to whole groups of planetary systems.

After a minute she dialled the meteorology room again.

"Lieutenant Cannons, when the meteorology officer of the Fifty Suns navy arrives, please employ the following tactics – –"

Maltby waved dismissal to the driver of his car. The machine pulled away from the curb and Maltby stood frowning at the flaming energy barrier that barred farther progress along the street. Finally, he took another look at the Earth ship.

It was directly above him now that he had come so many miles across the city toward it. It was tremendously high up, a long, black torpedo shape almost lost in the mist of distance.

But high as it was it was still visibly bigger than anything ever seen by the Fifty Suns, an incredible creature of metal from a world so far away that, almost, it had sunk to the status of myth.

Here was the reality. There would be tests, he thought, penetrating tests before they'd accept any orbit he planned. It wasn't that he doubted the ability of his double mind to overcome anything like that, but – –

Well to remember that the frightful gap of years which separated the science of Earth from that of the Fifty Suns had already shown unpleasant surprises. Maltby shook himself grimly and gave his full attention to the street ahead.

A fan-shaped pink fire spread skyward from two machines that stood in the centre of the street. The flame was a very pale pink and completely transparent. It looked electronic, deadly.

Beyond it were men in glittering uniforms. A steady trickle of them moved in and out of buildings. About three blocks down the avenue a second curtain of pink fire flared up.

There seemed to be no attempt to guard the sides. The men he could see looked at ease, confident. There was mur-mured conversation, low laughter and – they weren't all men.

As Maltby walked forward, two fine-looking young women in uniform came down the steps of the nearest of the requisitioned buildings. One of the guards of the flame said something to them. There was a twin tinkle of silvery laughter. Still laughing, they strode off down the street.

It was suddenly exciting. There was an air about these people of far places, of tremendous and wonderful lands beyond the farthest horizons of the staid Fifty Suns.

He felt cold, then hot, then he glanced up at the fantas-tically big ship; and the chill came back. One ship, he thought, but so big, so mighty that thirty billion people didn't dare send their own fleets against it. They – –

He grew aware that one of the brilliantly arrayed guards was staring at him. The man spoke into a wrist radio, and after a moment a second man broke off his conver-sation with a third soldier and came over. He stared through the flame barrier at Maltby.

"Is there anything you desire? Or are you just looking?"

He spoke English, curiously accented – but English! His manner was mild, almost gentle, cultured. The whole effect

244

had a naturalness, an unalienness that was pleasing. After all, Maltby thought, he had never had the fear of these people that the others had. His very plan to defeat the ship was based upon his own fundamental belief that the robots were indestructible in the sense that no one could ever wipe them out completely.

Quietly, Maltby explained his presence.

"Oh, yes," the man nodded, "we've been expecting you. I'm to take you at once to the meteorological room of the ship. Just a moment –"

The flame barrier went down and Maltby was led into one of the buildings. There was a long corridor, and the transmitter that projected him into the ship must have been focused somewhere along it.

Because abruptly he was in a very large room. Maps floated in half a dozen anti-gravity pits. The walls shed light from millions of tiny point sources. And everywhere were tables with curved lines of very dim but sharply etched light on their surfaces.

Maltby's guide was nowhere to be seen. Coming toward him, however, was a tall, fine-looking old man. The oldster offered his hand.

"My name is Lieutenant Cannons, senior ship meteorologist. If you will sit down here we can plan an orbit and the ship can start moving within the hour. The grand captain is very anxious that we get started."

Maltby nodded casually. But he was stiff, alert. He stood quite still, feeling around with that acute second mind of his, his Dellian mind, for energy pressure that would show secret attempts to watch or control his mind.

But there was nothing like that.

He smiled finally, grimly. It was going to be as simple as this, was it? Like hell it was.

As he sat down, Maltby felt suddenly cozy and alive. The pure exhilaration of existence burned through him like a flame. He recognized the singing excitement for the battle thrill it was and felt a grim joy that for the first time in fifteen years he could do something about it.

During his long service in the Fifty Suns navy, he had faced hostility and suspicion because he was a Mixed Man.

And always he had felt helpless, unable to do anything about it. Now, here was a far more basic hostility, however veiled, and a suspicion that must be like a burning fire.

And this time he could fight. He could look this skilfully voluble, friendly old man squarely in the eye and –

Friendly?

"It makes me smile sometimes," the old man was saying, "when I think of the unscientific aspects of the orbit we have to plan now. For instance, what is the time lag on storm reports out here?"

Maltby could not suppress a smile. So Lieutenant Cannons wanted to know things, did he? To give the man credit, it wasn't really a lame opening. The truth was, the only way to ask a question was – well – to ask it. Maltby said:

"Oh, three, four months. Nothing unusual. Each space meteorologist takes about that length of time to check the bounds of the particular storm in his area, and then he reports, and we adjust our maps.

"Fortunately" – he pushed his second mind to the fore as he coolly spoke the great basic lie – "there are no major storms between the Kaidor and Cassidor suns."

He went on, sliding over the untruth like an eel breasting wet rock:

"However, several suns prevent a straight line movement. So if you would show me some of your orbits for twenty-five hundred light years, I'll make a selection of the best ones."

He wasn't, he realized instantly, going to slip over his main point as easily as that.

"No intervening storms?" the old man said. He pursed his lips. The fine lines in his long face seemed to deepen. He looked genuinely non-plussed; and there was no doubt at all that he hadn't expected such a straightforward statement. "Hm-m-m, no storms. That does make it simple, doesn't it?"

He broke off. "You know, the important thing about two" – he hesitated over the word, then went on – "two people, who have been brought up in different cultures, under different scientific standards is that they make sure they are discussing a subject from a common viewpoint.

"Space is so big. Even this comparatively small system of

stars, the Lesser Magellanic Cloud, is so vast that it defies our reason. We on the battleship *Star Cluster* have spent ten years surveying it, and now we are able to say glibly that it comprises two hundred sixty billion cubic light years, and contains fifty millions of suns.

"We located the magnetic centre of the Cloud, fixed our zero line from centre to the great brightest star, S Doradus; and now, I suppose, there are people who would be fools enough to think we've got the system stowed away in our brainpans."

Maltby was silent because he himself was just such a fool. This was warning. He was being told in no uncertain terms that they were in a position to check any orbit he gave them with respect to all intervening suns.

It meant much more. It showed that Earth was on the verge of extending her tremendous sway to the Lesser Magellanic Cloud. Destroying this ship now would provide the Fifty Suns with precious years during which they would have to decide what they intended to do.

But that would be all. Other ships would come; the inexorable pressure of the stupendous populations of the main galaxy would burst out even farther into space. Always under careful control, shepherded by mighty hosts of invincible battleships, the great transports would sweep into the Cloud, and every planet everywhere, robot or non-robot, would acknowledge Earth suzerainty.

Imperial Earth recognized no separate nations of any description anywhere. The robots, Dellian, non-Dellian and Mixed, would need every extra day, every hour; and it was lucky for them all that he was not basing his hope of destroying this ship on an orbit that would end inside a sun.

Their survey had magnetically placed all the suns for them. But they couldn't know about the storms. Not in ten years or in a hundred was it possible for one ship to locate possible storms in an area that involved twenty-five hundred light years of length.

Unless their psychologists could uncover the special qualities of his double brain, he had them. He grew aware that Lieutenant Cannons was manipulating the controls of the orbit table.

The lines of light on the surface flickered and shifted. Then settled like the balls in a game of chance. Maltby selected six that ran deep into the great storm. Ten minutes after that he felt the faint jar as the ship began to move. He stood up, frowning. Odd that they should act without *some* verification of his –

"This way," said the old man.

Maltby thought sharply: This couldn't be all. Any minute now they'd start on him and –

His thought ended.

He was in space. Far, far below was the receding planet of Kaider III. To one side gleamed the vast dark hull of the battleship; and on every other side, and up, and down were stars and the distances of dark space.

In spite of all his will, the shock was inexpressibly violent.

His active mind jerked. He staggered physically; and he would have fallen like a blindfolded creature except that, in the movement of trying to keep on his feet, he recognized that he *was* still on his feet.

His whole being steadied. Instinctively, he – tilted – his second mind awake, and pushed it forward. Put its more mechanical and precise qualities, its Dellian strength, between his other self and whatever the human beings might be doing against him.

Somewhere in the mist of darkness and blazing stars, a woman's clear and resonant voice said:

"Well, Lieutenant Neslor, did the surprise yield any psychological fruits?"

The reply came from a second, an older-sounding woman's voice:

"After three seconds, noble lady, his resistance leaped to I.Q. 900. Which means they've sent us a Dellian. Your excellency, I thought you specifically asked that their representative be not a Dellian."

Maltby said swiftly into the night around him: "You're quite mistaken. I am not a Dellian. And I assure you that I will lower my resistance to zero if you desire. I reacted instinctively to surprise, naturally enough."

There was a click. The illusion of space and stars snapped out of existence. Maltby saw what he had begun to suspect,

248

that he was, had been all the time, in the meteorology room.

Nearby stood the old man, a thin smile on his lined face. On a raised dais, partly hidden behind a long instrument board, sat a handsome young woman. It was the old man who spoke. He said in a stately voice:

"You are in the presence of Grand Captain, the Right Honourable Gloria Cecily, the Lady Laurr of Noble Laurr. Conduct yourself accordingly."

Maltby bowed but he said nothing. The grand captain frowned at him, impressed by his appearance. Tall, magnificent-looking body – strong, supremely intelligent face. In a single flash she noted all the characteristics common to the first-class human being and robot.

These people might be more dangerous than she had thought. She said with unnatural sharpness for her:

"As you know, we have to question you. We would prefer that you do not take offence. You have told us that Cassidor VII, the chief planet of the Fifty Suns, is twenty-five hundred light years from here. Normally, we would spend more than sixty years *feeling* our way across such an immense gap of uncharted, star-filled space. But you have given us a choice of orbits.

"We must make sure those orbits are honest, offered without guile or harmful purpose. To that end we have to ask you to open your mind and answer our questions under the strictest psychological surveillance."

"I have orders," said Maltby, "to co-operate with you in every way."

He had wondered how he would feel, now that the hour of decision was upon him. But there was nothing unnormal. His body was a little stiffer, but his minds –

He withdrew his *self* into the background and left his Dellian mind to confront all the questions that came. His Dellian mind that he had deliberately kept apart from his thoughts. That curious mind, which had no will of its own, but which, by remote control, reacted with the full power of an I.Q. of 191.

Sometimes, he marvelled himself at that second mind of his. It had no creative ability, but its memory was machine-like, and its resistance to outside pressure was, as the

249

woman psychologist had so swiftly analyzed, over nine hundred. To be exact, the equivalent of I.Q. 917.

"What is your name?"

That was the way it began: His name, distinction – He answered everything quietly, positively, without hesitation. When he had finished, when he had sworn to the truth of every word about the storms, there was a long moment of dead silence. And then a middle-aged woman stepped out of the nearby wall.

She came over and motioned him into a chair. When he was seated she tilted his head and began to examine it. She did it gently; her fingers were caressing as a lover's. But when she looked up she said sharply;

"You're not a Dellian or a non-Dellian. And the molecular structure of your brain and body is the most curious I've ever seen. All the molecules are twins. I saw a similar arrangement once in an artificial electronic structure where an attempt was being made to balance an unstable electronic structure. The parallel isn't exact, but – mm-m-m, I must try to remember what the end result was of that experiment."

She broke off: "What is your explanation? What are you?"

Maltby sighed. He had determined to tell only the one main lie. Not that it mattered so far as his double brain was concerned. But untruths effected slight variations in blood pressure, created neural spasms and disturbed muscular integration. He couldn't take the risk of even one more than was absolutely necessary.

"I'm a Mixed Man," he explained. He described briefly how the cross between the Dellian and non-Dellian, so long impossible, had finally been brought about a hundred years before. The use of cold and pressure –

"Just a moment," said the psychologist.

She disappeared. When she stepped again out of the wall transmitter, she was thoughtful.

"He seems to be telling the truth," she confessed, almost reluctantly.

"What is this?" snapped the grand captain. "Ever since we ran into that first citizen of the Fifty Suns, the psychology department has qualified every statement it issues.

250

I thought psychology was the only perfect science. Either he is telling the truth or he isn't.''

The older woman looked unhappy. She stared very hard at Maltby, seemed baffled by his cool gaze, and finally facing her superior, said:

"It's that double molecule structure of his brain. Except for that, I see no reason why you shouldn't order full acceleration.''

The grand captain smiled. "I shall have Captain Maltby to dinner tonight. I'm sure he will co-operate then with any further studies you may be prepared to make at that time. Meanwhile I think – ''

She spoke into a communicator: "Central engines, step up to half light year a minute on the following orbit – ''

Maltby listened, estimating with his Dellian mind. Half a light year a minute; it would take a while to attain that speed, but – in eight hours they'd strike the storm.

In eight hours he'd be having dinner with the grand captain.

Eight hours!

The full flood of a contraterrene Nova impinging upon terrene gases already infuriated by seetee gone insane – that was the new, greater storm.

The exploding, giant sun added weight to the diffuse, maddened thing. And it added something far more deadly.

Speed! From peak to peak of velocity the tumult of ultrafire leaped. The swifter crags of the storm danced and burned with an absolutely hellish fury.

The sequence of action was rapid almost beyond the bearance of matter. First raced the light of the Nova, blazing its warning at more than a hundred and eighty-six thousand miles a second to all who knew that it flashed from the edge of an interstellar storm.

But the advance glare of warning was nullified by the colossal speed of the storm. For weeks and months it drove through the vast night at a velocity that was only a bare measure short of that of light itself.

The dinner dishes had been cleared away. Maltby was thinking; in half an hour – *half an hour!*

He was wondering shakily just what did happen to a

251

battleship suddenly confronted by thousands of gravities of deceleration. Aloud he was saying:

"My day? I spent it in the library. Mainly, I was interested in the recent history of Earth's interstellar colonization. I'm curious as to what is done with groups like the Mixed Men. I mentioned to you that, after the war in which they were defeated largely because there was so few of them, the Mixed Men hid themselves from the Fifty Suns. I was one of the captured children who –"

There was an interruption, a cry from the wall communicator: "*Noble lady, I've solved it!*"

A moment fled before Maltby recognized the strained voice of the woman psychologist. He had almost forgotten that she was supposed to be studying him. Her next words chilled him:

"Two minds! I thought of it a little while ago and rigged up a twin watching device. Ask him, *ask* him the question about the storms. Meanwhile stop the ship. At once!"

Maltby's dark gaze clashed hard with the steely, narrowed eyes of the grand captain. Without hesitation he concentrated his two minds on her, forced her to say:

"Don't be silly, lieutenant. One person can't have two brains. Explain yourself further."

His hope was delay. They had ten minutes in which they could save themselves. He must waste every second of that time, resist all their efforts, try to control the situation. If only his special three-dimensional hypnotism worked through communicators –

It didn't. Lines of light leaped at him from the wall and criss-crossed his body, held him in his chair like so many unbreakable cables. Even as he was bound hand and foot by palpable energy, a second complex of forces built up before his face, barred his thought pressure from the grand captain, and finally coned over his head like a dunce cap.

He was caught as neatly as if a dozen men had swarmed with their strength and weight over his body. Maltby relaxed and laughed.

"Too late," he taunted. "It'll take at least an hour for this ship to reduce to a safe speed; and at this velocity you can't turn aside in time to avoid the greatest storm in this part of the Universe."

That wasn't strictly true. There was still time and room to sheer off before the advancing storm in any of the fronting directions. The impossibility was to turn toward the storm's tail or its great, bulging sides.

His thought was interrupted by the first cry from the young woman; a piercing cry: "Central engines! Reduce speed! Emergency!"

There was a jar that shook the walls and a pressure that tore at his muscles. Maltby adjusted and then stared across the table at the grand captain. She was smiling, a frozen mask of a smile; and she said from between clenched teeth:

"Lieutenant Neslor, use any means physical or otherwise, but make him talk. There must be something."

"His second mind is the key," the psychologist's voice came. "It's not Dellian. It has only normal resistance. I shall subject it to the greatest concentration of conditioning ever focused on a human brain, using the two basics: sex and logic. I shall have to use you, noble lady, as the object of his affections."

"Hurry!" said the young woman. Her voice was like a metal bar.

Maltby sat in a mist, mental and physical. Deep in his mind was awareness that he was an entity, and that irresistible machines were striving to mould his thought.

He resisted. The resistance was as strong as his life, as intense as all the billions and quadrillions of impulses that had shaped his being, could make it.

But the outside thought, the pressure, grew stronger. How silly of him to resist Earth – when this lovely woman of Earth loved him, loved him, loved him. Glorious was that civilization of Earth and the main galaxy. Three hundred million billion people. The very first contact would rejuvenate the Fifty Suns. How lovely she is; I must save her. She means everything to me.

As from a great distance, he began to hear his own voice, explaining what must be done, just how the ship must be turned, in what direction, how much time there was. He tried to stop himself, but inexorably his voice went on, mouthing the words that spelled defeat for the Fifty Suns.

The mist began to fade. The terrible pressure eased from

his straining mind. The damning stream of words ceased to pour from his lips. He sat up shakily, conscious that the energy cords and the energy cap had been withdrawn from his body. He heard the grand captain say into a communicator:

"By making a point 0100 turn we shall miss the storm by seven light weeks. I admit it is an appallingly sharp curve, but I feel that we should have at least that much leeway."

She turned and stared at Maltby: "Prepare yourself. At half a light year a minute even a hundredth of a degree turn makes some people black out."

"Not me," said Maltby, and tensed his Dellian muscles.

She fainted three times during the next four minutes as he sat there watching her. But each time she came to within seconds.

"We human beings," she said wanly, finally, "are a poor lot. But at least we know how to endure."

The terrible minutes dragged. And dragged. Maltby began to feel the strain of that infinitesimal turn. He thought at last: Space! How could these people ever hope to survive a direct hit on a storm?

Abruptly, it was over; a man's voice said quietly: "We have followed the prescribed course, noble lady, and are now out of dang – ''

He broke off with a shout: "Captain, the light of a Nova sun has just flashed from the direction of the storm. We – ''

In those minutes before disaster struck, the battleship *Star Cluster* glowed like an immense and brilliant jewel. The warning glare from the Nova set off an incredible roar of emergency clamour through all of her hundred and twenty decks.

From end to end her lights flicked on. They burned row by row straight across her four thousand feet of length with the hard tinkle of cut gems. In the reflection of that light, the black mountain that was her hull looked like the fabulous planet of Cassidor, her destination, as sun at night from a far darkness, sown with diamond shining cities.

Silent as a ghost, grand and wonderful beyond all imagination, glorious in her power, the great ship slid through

254

the blackness along the special river of time and space which was her plotted course.

Even as she rode into the storm there was nothing visible. The space ahead looked as clear as any vacuum. So tenuous were the gases that made up the storm that the ship would not even have been aware of them if it had been travelling at atomic speeds.

Violent the disintegration of matter in that storm might be, and the sole course of cosmic rays the hardest energy in the known universe. But the immense, the cataclysmic danger to the *Star Cluster* was a direct result of her own terrible velocity.

If she had had time to slow, the storm would have meant nothing.

Striking that mass of gas at half a light year a minute was like running into an unending solid wall. The great ship shuddered in every plate as the deceleration tore at her gigantic strength.

In seconds she had run the gamut of all the recoil system her designers had planned for her as a unit.

She began to break up.

And still everything was according to the original purpose of the superb engineering firm that had built her. The limit of unit strain reached, she dissolved into her nine thousand separate sections.

Streamlined needles of metal were those sections, four hundred feet long, forty feet wide; sliverlike shapes that sinuated cunningly through the gases, letting the pressure of them slide off their smooth hides.

But it wasn't enough. Metal groaned from the torture of deceleration. In the deceleration chambers, men and women lay at the bare edge of consciousness, enduring agony that seemed on the verge of being beyond endurance.

Hundreds of the sections careened into each other in spite of automatic screens, and instantaneously fused into white-hot coffins.

And still, in spite of the hideously maintained velocity, that mass of gases was not bridged; light years of thickness had still to be covered.

For those sections that remained, once more all the limits of human strength were reached. The final action was

255

chemical, directly on the human bodies that remained of the original thirty thousand. Those bodies for whose sole benefit all the marvellous safety devices had been conceived and constructed, the poor, fragile, human beings who through all the ages had persisted in dying under normal conditions from a pressure of something less than fifteen gravities.

The prompt reaction of the automatics in rolling back every floor, and plunging every person into the deceleration chambers of each section – that saving reaction was abruptly augmented as the deceleration chamber was flooded by a special type of gas.

Wet was that gas, and clinging. It settled thickly on the clothes of the humans, soaked through to the skin and *through* the skin, into every part of the body.

Sleep came gently, and with it a wonderful relaxation. The blood grew immune to shock; muscles that, in a minute before, had been drawn with anguish – loosened; the brain impregnated with life-giving chemicals that relieved it of all shortages remained untroubled even by dreams.

Everybody grew enormously flexible to gravitation pressures – a hundred – a hundred and fifty gravities of deceleration; and still the life force clung.

The great heart of the Universe beat on. The storm roared along its inescapable artery, creating the radiance of life, purging the dark of its poisons – and at last the tiny ships in their separate courses burst its great bounds.

They began to come together, to seek each other, as if among them there was an irresistible passion that demanded intimacy of union.

Automatically, they slid into their old positions; the battleship *Star Cluster* began again to take form – but there were gaps. Segments destroyed, and segments lost.

On the third day Acting Grand Captain Rutgers called the surviving captains to the forward bridge, where he was temporarily making his headquarters. After the conference a communique was issued to the crew:

At 008 hours this morning a message was received from Grand Captain, the Right Honourable Gloria Cecily, the Lady Laurr of Noble Laurr, I.C., C.M., G.K.R. She has been forced down on the planet of a yellow-

256

white sun. Her ship crashed on landing and is un-repairable. As all communication with her has been by non-directional sub-space radio, and as it will be utterly impossible to locate such an ordinary type sun among so many millions of other suns, the Captains in Session regret to report that our noble lady's name must now be added to that longest of all lists of naval casualties: the list of those who have been lost forever on active duty.

The admiralty lights will burn blue until further notice.

Her back was to him as he approached. Maltby hesitated, then tensed his mind, and held her there beside the section of ship that had been the main bridge of the *Star Cluster*.

The long metal shape lay half buried in the marshy ground of the great valley, its lower end jutting down into the shimmering deep yellowish black waters of a sluggish river.

Maltby paused a few feet from the tall, slim woman, and, still holding her unaware of him, examined once again the environment that was to be their life.

The fine spray of dark rain that had dogged his exploration walk was retreating over the yellow rim of valley to the "west".

As he watched, a small yellow sun burst out from behind a curtain of dark, ocherous clouds and glared at him brilliantly. Below it an expanse of jungle glinted strangely brown and yellow.

Everywhere was that dark-brown and intense, almost liquid yellow.

Maltby sighed – and turned his attention to the woman, willed her not to see him as he walked around in front of her.

He had given a great deal of thought to the Right Honourable Gloria Cecily during his walk. Basically, of course, the problem of a man and a woman who were destined to live the rest of their lives together, alone, on a remote planet, was very simple. Particularly in view of the fact that one of the two had been conditioned to be in love with the other.

Maltby smiled grimly. He could appreciate the artificial origin of that love. But that didn't dispose of the profound fact of it.

The conditioning machine had struck to his very core.

257

Unfortunately, it had not touched her at all; and two days of being alone with her had brought out one reality:

The Lady Laurr of Noble Laurr was not even remotely thinking of yielding herself to the normal requirements of the situation.

It was time that she was made aware, not because an early solution was necessary or even desirable, but because she had to realize that the problem existed.

He stepped forward and took her in his arms.

She was a tall, graceful woman; she fitted into his embrace as if she belonged there; and, because his control of her made her return the kiss, its warmth had an effect beyond his intention.

He had intended to free her mind in the middle of the kiss. He didn't.

When he finally released her, it was only a physical release. Her mind was still completely under his domination.

There was a metal chair that had been set just outside one of the doors. Maltby walked over, sank into it and stared up at the grand captain.

He felt shaken. The flame of desire that had leaped through him was a telling tribute to the conditioning he had undergone. But it was entirely beyond his previous analysis of the intensity of his own feelings.

He had thought he was in full control of himself, and he wasn't. Somehow, the sardonicism, the half detachment, the objectivity, which he had fancied was the keynote of his own reaction to this situation, didn't apply at all.

The conditioning machine had been thorough.

He loved this woman with such a violence that the mere touch of her was enough to disconnect his will from operations immediately following.

His heart grew quieter; he studied her with a semblance of detachment.

She was lovely in a handsome fashion; though almost all robot women of the Dellian race were better-looking. Her lips, while medium full, were somehow a trifle cruel; and there was a quality in her eyes that accentuated that cruelty.

There were built-up emotions in this woman that would not surrender easily to the idea of being marooned for life on an unknown planet.

It was something he would have to think over. Until then –

Maltby sighed. And released her from the three-dimensional hypnotic spell that his two minds had imposed on her.

He had taken the precaution of turning her away from him. He watched her curiously as she stood, back to him, for a moment, very still. Then she walked over to a little knob of trees above the springy, soggy marsh land.

She climbed up it and gazed in the direction from which he had come a few minutes before. Evidently looking for him.

She turned finally, shaded her face against the yellow brightness of the sinking sun, came down from the hillock and saw him.

She stopped; her eyes narrowed. She walked over slowly. She said with an odd edge in her voice:

"You came very quietly. You must have circled and walked in from the west."

"No," said Maltby deliberately. "I stayed in the east."

She seemed to consider that. She was silent, her lean face creased into a frown. She pressed her lips together, finally; there was a bruise there that must have hurt, for she winced, then she said:

"What did you discover? Did you find any – "

She stopped. Consciousness of the bruise on her lip must have penetrated at that moment. Her hand jerked up, her fingers touched the tender spot. Her eyes came alive with the violence of her comprehension. Before she could speak, Maltby said:

"Yes, you're quite right."

She stood looking at him. Her stormy gaze quietened. She said finally, in a stony voice:

"If you try that again I shall feel justified in shooting you."

Maltby shook his head. He said unsmiling:

"And spend the rest of your life here alone? You'd go mad."

He saw instantly that her basic anger was too great for that kind of logic. He went on swiftly:

"Besides, you'd have to shoot me in the back. I have no

doubt you could do that in the line of duty. But not for personal reasons."

Her compressed lips – separated. To his amazement there were suddenly tears in her eyes. Anger tears, obviously. But tears!

She stepped forward with a quick movement and slapped his face.

"You robot!" she sobbed.

Maltby stared at her ruefully; then he laughed. Finally he said, a trace of mockery in his tone:

"If I remember rightly, the lady who just spoke is the same one who delivered a ringing radio address to all the planets of the Fifty Suns swearing that in fifteen thousand years Earth people had forgotten all their prejudices against robots.

"Is it possible," he finished, "that the problem on *closer* investigation is proving more difficult?"

There was no answer. The Honourable Gloria Cecily brushed past him and disappeared into the interior of the ship.

She came out again a few minutes later.

Her expression was more serene; Maltby noted that she had removed all trace of the tears. She looked at him steadily, said:

"What did you discover when you were out? I've been delaying my call to the ship till you returned."

Maltby said: "I thought they asked you to call at 010 hours."

The woman shrugged; and there was an arrogant note in her voice as she replied:

"They'll take my calls when I make them. Did you find any sign of intelligent life?"

Maltby allowed himself brief pity for a human being who had as many shocks still to absorb as had Grand Captain Laurr.

One of the books he had read while aboard the battleship about colonists of remote planets had dealt very specifically with castaways.

He shook himself and began his description. "Mostly marsh land in the valley and there's jungle, very old. Even some of the trees are immense, though sections show no growth rings – some interesting beasts and a four-legged, two-armed thing that watched me from a distance. It carried a spear but it was too far away for me to use my hypnotism on it. There must be a village somewhere, perhaps on the valley rim. My idea is that during the next months I'll cut the ship into small sections and transport it to drier ground.

"I would say that we have the following information to offer the ship's scientists: We're on a planet of a G-type sun. The sun must be larger than the average yellow-white type and have a larger surface temperature.

"It must be larger and hotter because, though it's far away, it is hot enough to keep the northern hemisphere of this planet in a semitropical condition.

"The sun was quite a bit north at midday, but now it's swinging back to the south. I'd say offhand the planet must be tilted at about forty degrees, which means there's a cold winter coming up, though that doesn't fit with the age and type of the vegetation."

The Lady Laurr was frowning. "It doesn't seem very helpful," she said. "But, of course, I'm only an executive."

"And I'm only a meteorologist."

"Exactly. Come in. Perhaps my astrophysicist can make something of it."

"*Your* astrophysicist!" said Maltby. But he didn't say it aloud.

He followed her into the segment of ship and closed the door.

Maltby examined the interior of the main bridge with a wry smile as the young woman seated herself before the astroplate.

The very imposing glitter of the instrument board that occupied one entire wall was ironical now. All the machines it had controlled were far away in space. Once it had dominated the entire Lesser Magellanic Cloud; now his own hand gun was a more potent instrument.

He grew aware that Lady Laurr was looking up at him.

"I don't understand it," she said. "They don't answer."

"Perhaps" – Maltby could not keep the faint sardonicism out of his tone – "perhaps they may really have had a good reason for wanting you to call at 010 hours."

The woman made a faint exasperated movement with her facial muscles but she did not answer. Maltby went on coolly:

"After all, it doesn't matter. They're only going through routine motions, the idea being to leave no loophole for rescue unlooked through. I can't even imagine the kind of miracle it would take for anybody to find us."

The woman seemed not to have heard. She said, frowning:

"How is it that we've never heard a single Fifty Suns broadcast? I intended to ask about that before. Not once during our ten years in the Lesser Cloud did we catch so much as a whisper of radio energy."

Maltby shrugged. "All radios operate on an extremely complicated variable wave length – changes every twentieth of a second. Your instruments would register a tick once in every ten minutes, and – "

He was cut off by a voice from the astroplate. A man's face was there – Acting Grand Captain Rutgers.

"Oh, there you are, captain," the woman said. "What kept you?"

"We're in the process of landing our forces on Cassidor VII," was the reply. "As you know, regulations require that the grand captain – "

"Oh, yes. Are you free now?"

"No. I've taken a moment to see that everything is right with you, and then I'll switch you over to Captain Planston."

"How is the landing proceeding?"

"Perfectly. We have made contact with the government. They seem resigned. But now I must leave. Goodbye, my lady."

His face flickered and was gone. The plate went blank. It was about as curt a greeting as anybody had ever received. But Maltby, sunk in his own gloom, scarcely noticed.

So it was all over. The desperate scheming of the Fifty Suns leaders, his own attempt to destroy the great battleship, proved futile against an invincible foe.

For a moment he felt very close to the defeat, with all its implications. Consciousness came finally that the fight no longer mattered in his life. But the knowledge failed to shake his dark mood.

He saw that the Right Honourable Glora Cecily had an

expression of mixed elation and annoyance on her fine, strong face; and there was no doubt that she didn't *feel* – disconnected – from the mighty events out there in space. Nor had she missed the implications of the abruptness of the interview.

The astroplate grew bright and a face appeared on it – one that Maltby hadn't seen before. It was of a heavy-jowled, oldish man with a ponderous voice that said:

"Privilege your ladyship – hope we can find something that will enable us to make a rescue. Never give up hope, I say, until the last nail's driven in your coffin."

He chuckled; and the woman said: "Captain Maltby will give you all the information he has, then no doubt you can give him some advice, Captain Planston. Neither he nor I, unfortunately, are astrophysicists."

"Can't be experts on every subject," Captain Planston puffed. "Er, Captain Maltby, what do you know?"

Maltby gave his information briefly, then waited while the other gave instructions. There wasn't much:

"Find out length of seasons. Interested in that yellow effect of the sunlight and the deep brown. Take the following photographs, using ortho-sensitive film – use three dyes, a red sensitive, a blue and a yellow. Take a spectrum reading – what I want to check on is that maybe you've got a strong blue sun there, with the ultraviolet barred by a heavy atmosphere, and all the heat and light coming in on the yellow band.

"I'm not offering much hope, mind you – the Lesser Cloud is packed with blue suns – five hundred thousand of them brighter than Sirius.

"Finally, get that season information from the natives. Make a point of it. Goodbye!"

The native was wary. He persisted in retreating elusively into the jungle; and his four legs gave him a speed advantage of which he seemed to be aware. For he kept coming back, tantalizingly.

The woman watched with amusement, then exasperation.

"Perhaps," she suggested, "if we separated, and I drove him toward you?"

She saw the frown on the man's face as Maltby nodded reluctantly. His voice was strong, tense.

"He's leading us into an ambush. Turn on the sensitives in your helmet and carry your gun. Don't be too hasty about firing, but don't hesitate in a crisis. A spear can make an ugly wound; and we haven't got the best facilities for handling anything like that."

His orders brought a momentary irritation. He seemed not to be aware that she was as conscious as he of the requirements of the situation.

The Right Honourable Gloria sighed. If they had to stay on this planet there would have to be some major psychological adjustments, and not – she thought grimly – only by herself.

"*Now!*" said Maltby beside her, swiftly. "Notice the way the ravine splits in two. I came this far yesterday and they join about two hundred yards farther on. He's gone up the left fork. I'll take the right. You stop here, let him come back to see what's happened, then drive him on."

He was gone, like a shadow, along a dark path that wound under thick foliage.

Silence settled.

She waited. After a minute she felt herself alone in a yellow and black world that had been lifeless since time began.

She thought: This was what Maltby had meant yesterday when he had said she wouldn't dare shoot him – and remain alone. It hadn't penetrated then.

It did now. Alone, on a nameless planet of a mediocre sun, one woman waking up every morning on a mouldering ship that rested its unliving metal shape on a dark, muggy, yellow marsh land.

She stood sombrely. There was no doubt that the problem of robot and human being would have to be solved here as well as out there.

A sound pulled her out of her gloom. As she watched, abruptly more alert, a catlike head peered cautiously from a line of bushes a hundred yards away across the clearing.

It was an interesting head; its ferocity not the least of its fascinating qualities. The yellowish body was invisible now in the underbrush, but she had caught enough glimpses of it

264

earlier to recognize that it was the CC type, of the almost universal Centaur family. Its body was evenly balanced between its hind and forelegs.

It watched her, and its great glistening black eyes were round with puzzlement. Its head twisted from side to side, obviously searching for Maltby.

She waved her gun and walked forward. Instantly the creature disappeared. She could hear it with her sensitives, running into distance. Abruptly, it slowed; then there was no sound at all.

"He's got it," she thought.

She felt impressed. These two-brained Mixed Men, she thought, were bold and capable. It would really be too bad if anti-robot prejudice prevented them from being absorbed into the galactic civilization of Imperial Earth.

She watched him a few minutes later, using the block system of communication with the creature. Maltby looked up, saw her. He shook his head as if puzzled.

"He says it's always been warm like this, and that he's been alive for thirteen hundred moons. And that a moon is forty suns – forty days. He wants us to come up a little farther along this valley, but that's too transparent for comfort. Our move is to make a cautious, friendly gesture, and – "

He stopped short. Before she could even realize anything was wrong, her mind was caught, her muscles galvanized. She was thrown sideways and downward so fast that the blow of striking the ground was pure agony.

She lay there stunned, and out of the corner of her eye she saw the spear plunge through the air where she had been.

She twisted, rolled over – her own free will now – and jerked her gun in the direction from which the spear had come. There was a second centaur there, racing away along a bare slope. Her finger pressed on the control: and then –

"Don't!" It was Maltby, his voice low. "It was a scout the others sent ahead to see what was happening. He's done his work. It's all over."

She lowered her gun and saw with annoyance that her hand was shaking, her whole body trembling. She parted her lips to say: "Thanks for saving my life!" Then she closed them again. Because the words would have quavered. And because –

Saved her life! Her mind poised on the edge of blankness with the shock of the thought. Incredibly – she had never before been in personal danger from an individual creature.

There had been the time when her battleship had run into the outer fringes of a sun; and there was the cataclysm of the storm, just past.

But those had been impersonal menaces to be met with technical virtuosities and the hard training of the service.

This was different.

All the way back to the segment of ship she tried to fathom what the difference meant.

It seemed to her finally that she had it.

"Spectrum featureless." Maltby gave his findings over the astro. "No dark lines at all; two of the yellow bands so immensely intense that they hurt my eyes. As you suggested, apparently what we have here is a blue sun whose strong violet radiation is cut off by the atmosphere.

"However," he finished, "the uniqueness of that effect is confined to our planet here, a derivation of the thick atmosphere. Any questions?"

"No-o!" The astrophysicist looked thoughtful. "And I can give you no further instructions. I'll have to examine this material. Will you ask Lady Laurr to come in? Like to speak to her privately, if you please."

"Of course."

When she had come, Maltby went outside and watched the moon come up. Darkness – he had noticed it the previous night – brought a vague, overall violet haze. Explained now!

An eighty-degree temperature on a planet that, the angular diameter of the sun being what it was, would have been minus one hundred eighty degrees, if the sun's apparent colour had been real.

A blue sun, one of five hundred thousand – Interesting but – Maltby smiled savagely – Captain Planston's "No further instructions!" had a finality about it that –

He shivered involuntarily. And after a moment tried to picture himself sitting, like this, a year hence, staring up at an unchanged moon. Ten years, twenty –

He grew aware that the woman had come to the doorway and was gazing at him where he sat on the chair.

Maltby looked up. The stream of white light from inside the ship caught a queer expression on her face, gave her a strange, bleached look after the yellowness that had seemed a part of her complexion all day.

"We shall receive no more astro-radio calls," she said and, turning, went inside.

Maltby nodded to himself, almost idly. It was hard and brutal, this abrupt cutting off of communication. But the regulations governing such situations were precise.

The marooned ones must realize with utter clarity, without false hopes and without the curious illusions produced by radio communication, that they were cut off forever. Forever on their own.

Well, so be it. A fact was a fact, to be faced with resolution. There had been a chapter on castaways in one of the books he had read on the battleship. It had stated that nine hundred million human beings had, during recorded history, been marooned on then undiscovered planets. Most of these planets had eventually been found; and on no less than ten thousand of them great populations had sprung from the original nucleus of castaways.

The law prescribed that a castaway could not withhold himself or herself from participating in such population increases – regardless of previous rank. Castaways must forget considerations of sensitivity and individualism, and think of themselves as instruments of race expansion.

There were penalties; naturally inapplicable if no rescue was effected, but ruthlessly applied whenever recalcitrants were found.

Conceivably the courts might determine that a human being and a robot constituted a special case.

Half an hour must have passed while he sat there. He stood up, finally, conscious of hunger. He had forgotten all about supper.

He felt a qualm of self-annoyance. Damn it, this was not the night to appear to be putting pressure on her. Sooner or later, she would have to be convinced that she ought to do her share of the cooking.

But not tonight.

He hurried inside, toward the compact kitchen that was part of every segment of ship. In the corridor, he paused.

A blaze of light streamed from the kitchen door. Somebody was whistling softly and tunelessly but cheerfully; and there was an odour of cooking vegetables, and hot *lak* meat.

They almost bumped in the doorway. "I was just going to call you," she said.

The supper was a meal of silences, quickly over. They put the dishes into the automatic and went and sat in the great lounge; Maltby saw finally that the woman was studying him with amused eyes.

"Is there any possibility," she said abruptly, "that a Mixed Man and a human woman can have children?"

"Frankly," Maltby confessed, "I doubt it."

He launched into a detailed description of the cold and pressure process that had moulded the protoplasm to make the original Mixed Men. When he finished he saw that her eyes were still regarding him with a faint amusement. She said in an odd tone:

"A very curious thing happened to me today, after that native threw his spear. I realized" – she seemed for a moment to have difficulty in speaking – "I realized that I had, so far as I personally was concerned, solved the robot problem.

"Naturally," she finished quietly, "I would not have withheld myself in any event. But it is pleasant to know that I like you without" – she smiled – "qualifications."

Blue sun that looked yellow. Maltby sat in the chair the following morning puzzling over it. He half expected a visit from the natives, and so he was determined to stay near the ship that day.

He kept his eyes aware of the clearing edges, the valley rims, the jungle trails, but –

There was a law, he remembered, that governed the shifting of light to other wave bands, to yellow for instance. Rather complicated, but in view of the fact that all the instruments of the main bridge were controls of instruments, not the machines themselves, he'd have to depend on mathematics if he ever hoped to visualize the kind of sun that was out there.

Most of the heat probably came through the ultraviolet range. But that was uncheckable. So leave it alone and stick to the yellow.

He went into the ship. Gloria was nowhere in sight, but her bedroom door was closed. Maltby found a notebook, returned to his chair and began to figure.

An hour later he stared at the answer: One million three hundred thousand million miles. About a fifth of a light year.

He laughed curtly. That was that. He'd have to get better data than he had or –

Or would he ?

His mind poised. In a single flash of understanding, the stupendous truth burst upon him.

With a cry he leaped to his feet, whirled to race through the door as a long, black shadow slid across him.

The shadow was so vast, instantly darkening the whole valley, that, involuntarily, Maltby halted and looked up.

The battleship *Star Cluster* hung low over the yellow-brown jungle planet, already disgorging a lifeboat that glinted a yellowish silver as it circled out into the sunlight, and started down.

Maltby had only a moment with the woman before the lifeboat landed. "To think," he said, "that I just now figured out the truth."

She was, he saw, not looking at him. Her gaze seemed far away. He went on:

"As for the rest, the best method, I imagine, is to put me in the conditioning chamber, and –"

Still without looking at him, she cut him off:

"Don't be ridiculous. You must not imagine that I feel embarrassed because you have kissed me. I shall receive you later in my quarters."

A bath, new clothes – at last Maltby stepped through the transmitter into the astrophysics department. His own first realization of the tremendous truth, while generally accurate, had lacked detailed facts.

"Ah, Maltby!" The chief of the department came forward, shook hands. "Some sun you picked there – we suspected from your first description of the yellowness and the black. But naturally we couldn't rouse your hopes – Forbidden, you know.

"The axial tilt, the apparent length of a summer in which jungle trees of great size showed no growth rings – very suggestive. The featureless spectrum with its complete lack of dark lines – almost conclusive. Final proof was that the orthosensitive film was overexposed, while the blue and red sensitives were badly underexposed.

"This star-type is so immensely hot that practically all of its energy radiation is far in the ultravisible. A secondary radiation – a sort of fluorescence in the star's own atmosphere – produces the visible yellow when a minute fraction of the appalling ultra-violet radiation is transformed into longer wave lengths by helium atoms. A fluorescent lamp, in a fashion – but on a scale that is more than ordinarily cosmic in its violence. The total radiation reaching the planet was naturally tremendous; the surface radiation, after passing through miles of absorbing ozone, water vapour, carbondioxide and other gases, was very different.

"No wonder the native said it had always been hot. The summer lasts four thousand years. The normal radiation of that special appalling star type – the aeon-in-aeon-out radiation rate – is about equal to a full-fledged Nova at its catastrophic maximum of violence. It has a period of a few hours, and is equivalent to approximately a hundred million ordinary suns. Nova O, we call that brightest of all stars; and there's only one in the Lesser Magellanic Cloud, the great and glorious S-Doradus.

"When I asked you to call Grand Captain Laurr, and I told her that out of thirty million suns she had picked – "

It was at that point that Maltby cut him off. "Just a minute," he said, "did you say you told Lady Laurr *last night?*"

"Was it night down there?" Captain Planston said, interested. "Well, well – By the way, I almost forgot – this marrying and giving in marriage is not so important to me now that I am an old man. But congratulations."

The conversation was too swift for Maltby. His minds were still examining the first statement. That she had known all the time. He came up, groping, before the new words.

"Congratulations?" he echoed.

"Definitely time she had a husband," boomed the captain. "She's been a career woman, you know. Besides, it'll have a revivifying effect on the other robots ... pardon me. Assure you, the name means nothing to me.

"Anyway, Lady Laurr herself made the announcement a few minutes ago, so come down and see me again."

He turned away with a wave of a thick hand.

Maltby headed for the nearest transmitter. She would probably be expecting him by now.

She would not be disappointed.

THE END

271

The Thief had to pose as an Eskimo to live. As he sank slowly into the sun, he plainly hadn't a snowball's chance in hell of survival.

THE PARADOX MEN

by Charles Harness

"Ever been on the sun before, Dr. Talbot?" Captain Andrews appraised the new passenger curiously. They were together in the observation room of the *Phobos*.

Alar could not admit that everything on the run from Luna to Mercury (which planet they had left an hour previous) had seemed tantalizingly familiar, as though he had made the trip not once but a hundred times. Nor could he admit that astrophysics was his profession. A certain amount of celestial ignorance would be forgiven – indeed required – in a historian.

"No," said the Thief. "This is my first trip."

"I thought perhaps I'd brought you out before. Your face seems vaguely familiar."

"Do you think so, Captain? I travel quite a bit on earth. At a Toynbeean lecture possibly?"

"No. Never go to them. It would have to be somewhere along the solar run or nothing. Imagination, I guess."

Alar writhed inwardly. How far could he push his questioning without arousing suspicion? He stroked his false goatee with nervous impatience.

"As a newcomer," continued Captain Andrews, "you might be interested in how we pick up a solarion." He pointed to a circular fluorescent plate in the control panel. "That gives us a running picture of the solar surface in terms of the H line of calcium Two – ionized calcium, that is.

"It shows where the solar prominences and faculae are because they carry a lot of calcium. You can't see any prominences on the plate here – they're only visible when they're on the limb of the sun, spouting up against black space. But here are plenty of faculae, these gassy little puffs floating above the photosphere – they can be detected al-

272

most to the centre of the sun's disc. Hot but harmless."

He tapped the glass with his space-nav parallels. "And the place is swarming with granules – 'solar thunderheads' might be a better name. They bubble up several hundred miles in five minutes and then vanish. If one of them ever caught the *Phobos* . . ."

"I had a cousin, Robert Talbot, who was lost on one of the early solar freighters," said Alar casually. "They always thought a solar storm must have got the ship."

"Very likely. We lost quite a few ships before we learned the proper approach. Your cousin, eh ? Probably it was he I was thinking of, though I can't say the name is familiar."

"It was some years ago," said Alar, watching Andrews from the corner of his eye, "when Kennicot Mir was still running the stations."

"Hmm. Don't recall him." Captain Andrews returned noncommitally to the plate. "You probably know that the stations work at the edges of a sunspot, in what we call the penumbra. That procedure has several advantages.

"It's a little cooler than the rest of the chromosphere, which is easier on the solarion refrigerating system and the men, and the spot also provides a landmark for incoming freighters. It would be just about impossible to find a station unless it were on a spot. It's hard enough to locate one on the temperature contour."

"Temperature contour ?"

"Yes – like a thirty-fathom line on a seacoast. Only here it's the five-thousand line. In a few minutes, when we're about to land, I'll throw the jets over on automatic spectrographic steering and the *Phobos* will nose along the five-thousand degree Kelvin contour until she finds Solarion Nine."

"I see. If a station ever lost its lateral jets and couldn't stay on the five-thousand line how would you find it ?"

"I wouldn't," said Captain Andrews shortly. "Whenever a station turns up missing, we always send out all our search boats – several hundred of them – and work a search pattern around that sunspot for months. But we know before we start that we won't find anything. We never have. It's futile to look on the surface for a station that has been long volatilized deep at the vortex of a sunspot.

273

"The stations are under automatic spectrographic control, of course, and the spec is supposed to keep them on the five-thousand line but sometimes something goes wrong with the spec or an unusually hot Wilson gas swirl spills out over the edge of the spot and fools the spec into thinking the station is standing way out from the spot, say on the hotter five-thousand four hundred line.

"So the automatic spec control moves the station farther in toward the spot, maybe into the slippery Evershed zone at its very lip. From there the station can slide on into the umbra. I know of one ship that crawled out of the Evershed. Its crew had to be replaced in toto. But no solarion ever came out of the umbra. So you can't rely entirely on the spec control.

"Every station carries three solar meteorologists too and the weather staff issues a bulletin every quarter-hour on the station's most probable position and on any disturbances moving their way. Sometimes they have to jump fast and in the right direction.

"And even the finest sunmen can't foresee everything. Four years ago the Three, Four and Eight were working a big 'leader' – spots are like poles in a magnet – always go in pairs, and we call the eastern spot the 'leader', the western one the 'follower' – when the Mercury observatory noticed the leader was rapidly growing smaller.

"By the time it occurred to the observatory what was happening, the spot had shrunk to the size of Connecticut County. The patrol ship they sent to take off the crews got there too late. The spot had vanished. They figured the stations would try to make it to the 'follower' and settle somewhere in its five-thousand line.

"The Eight did – barely. Luckily, it had been working the uppermost region of the leader and, when the spot vanished from beneath it, had drifted down toward the solar equator. But while it was drifting it was also clawing back toward the follower with its lateral jets and it finally caught the follower's southern tip."

"What about the other two stations?" asked Alar.

"No trace."

The Thief shrugged mental shoulders. A berth in a solarion wasn't exactly like retiring on the green benches of La

274

Paz. He had never had any illusions about that. Perhaps the Mind had considered the possibilities of his survival in a solar system purely on cold statistics.

The captain moved away from the fluorescent plate toward a metal cabinet bolted to the far wall. He turned his head, spoke over his shoulder. "A glass of foam, doctor?"

Alar nodded. "Yes, thank you."

The captain unsnapped the door, fished in the shelves, withdrew a plastic bottle with one hand. With his other hand he found two aluminium cups.

"Sorry I can't offer you wine," the captain said, coming back across the cabin and setting the bottle and cups down on a small circular table. "This foam doesn't have any kick to it, but it's cold and that's plenty welcome in a place like this." His tone was faintly ironic. He poured out two drinks by squeezing the bottle, ejecting the liquid in a creamy ribbon that settled slowly in the cups. Then he took the bottle back to the refrigerated cabinet. The door slammed shut under a swipe from a huge hand.

Alar raised his cup and tasted the beverage. It had a sharp lemon taste, cold and delicious.

"I've never tasted this before," the Thief said. "It's delicious." He wasn't certain, but he seemed to have remembered tasting it before. That could have been just a similarity to one of the more common refreshments he'd had during the past five years. Then again, it might have been for another reason . . .

The captain smacked his lips. "I've unlimited quantities of it. I drink it often and I never tire of it." He looked into the cup. "I've got boxes of it in my quarters. Little dehydrated pills. When a bottle's empty, I just drop a in pill, squirt in some drinking water and let it get cold. Then," he snapped his fingers, "I've got a new supply." He was as much in earnest speaking of his foam as he had been in describing the operation of the solarions.

"I assume you've briefed yourself on the history of our stations," Captain Andrews said abruptly. He indicated a tubular chair for Alar, kicked another one over to the table for himself.

"Yes, I have, Captain."

"Good."

Alar recognized an undertone behind the succinctness of the question and the comment. Sunmen didn't relive the past. The past was too morbid. Of the twenty-seven costly solarions, towed one by one to the sun during the past ten years, sixteen remained. The average life of a station was about a year. The staff was rotated continuously, each man, after long and arduous training, being assigned a post for sixty days – three times the twenty-day synodic period of rotation of the sun with respect to the eighty-eight days side-real period of Mercury.

The captain finished his drink and took Alar's empty cup. "I'll clean them later," he said as he put one inside the other and replaced them in the cabinet. He resumed his seat again, heavily, and asked, "Have you met the replacements?"

"Not yet," Alar said. When the Mercury observatory reached opposition with a given solar station, as it did every twenty days, a freighter carried in replacements for one-third of the staff and took away the oldest one-third along with a priceless cargo of muirium. The *Phobos*, he knew, was bringing in eleven replacements but so far they had confined themselves closely to their own quarter of the ship and he had been unable to meet any of them.

Captain Andrews had apparently dismissed the problem of Alar's pseudo-familiarity and the Thief could think of no immediate way to return to the subject. For the time being he would have to continue to be Dr. Talbot, the historian, ignorant of things solar.

"Why," he asked, "if the stations are in such continual danger aren't they equipped with full space drives, instead of weak lateral jets? Then if the station skidded into a spot beyond the present recovery point she could simply blast free."

Andrews shook his head. "Members of parliament have been elected and deposed on that very issue. But it has to be the way it is now when you consider the cost of the solarion. It's really just a vast synthesizer for making muirium with a little bubble of space in the middle for living quarters and a few weak lateral jets on the periphery.

"A space ship is all converter, with a little bubble here amidships for the crew. To make a space ship out of a solarion you'd have to build it about two hundred times the present solarion size, so that the already tremendous solarion would be just a little bubble in an unimaginably enormous space ship.

"There's always a lot of talk about making the stations safe but that's the only way to do it and it costs too much money. So the Spaceways Ministers rise and fall but the stations never change. Incidentally, on the cost of these things, I understand that about one-fourth of the annual Imperium budget goes into making one solarion."

The intercom buzzed. Andrews excused himself, answered it briefly, then replaced the instrument. "Doctor?" The officer seemed strangely troubled.

"Yes, Captain?" His heart held no warning beat but it was impossible not to realize that something unusual and serious was in store.

Andrews hesitated a moment as though he were about to speak. Then he lifted his shoulders helplessly. "As you know, I'm carrying a relief crew to Nine – your destination. You haven't met any of them before because they keep pretty much to themselves. They would like to see you in the mess – now."

It was clear to Alar that the man wanted to say more, perhaps to give him a word of warning.

"Why do they want to see me?" he asked bluntly.

Andrews was equally curt. "They'll explain." He cleared his throat and avoided Alar's arched eyebrows. "You aren't superstitious, are you?"

"I think not. Why do you ask?"

"I just wondered. It's best not to be superstitious. We'll land in a few minutes, and I'm going to be pretty busy. The catwalk on the left will take you to the mess."

The Thief frowned, stroked his false goatee, then turned and walked toward the exit panel.

"Oh, doctor," called Andrews.

"Yes, Captain?"

"Just in case I don't see you again I've discovered whom you remind me of."

"Who?"

"This man was taller, heavier and older than you and his hair was auburn while yours is black. And he's dead, anyway, so really there's no point in mentioning –"

277

"Kennicot Muir?"

"Yes." Andrews looked after him rather meditatively.

Always Muir! If the man were alive and could be found, what an inquisition he would face! Alar's footsteps clanged in hollow frustration as he strode across the catwalk over an empty decontaminated muirium hold.

Muir must certainly have been on the *T-Twenty-Two* when it crashed at the end of its weird journey backward in time; the log book was evidence of that. But he, Alar, had crawled out of the river carrying the book. What had happened to Muir? Had he gone down with the ship? Alar chewed his lower lip in exasperation.

There was a more immediate question – what did the relief crew want with him? He welcomed the chance to meet them but he wanted to be the one to ask questions. He felt off-balance.

What if one of the crew had known the true Dr. Talbot? And, of course, any of the eleven might be an I.P. in occupational disguise, warned to be on the lookout for him. Or perhaps they didn't want him along on general principles. After all, he was an uninvited outsider who might disturb the smooth teamwork necessary to their hourly survival.

Or possibly they had invited him in for a little hazing, which he understood was actually encouraged by the station psychiatrist for the relief of tension in new men, so long as it was done and over before they came on station.

As he left the catwalk for the narrow corridor, he heard music and laughter ahead.

He smiled. A party. He remembered now that the incoming shift always gave themselves a farewell party, the main features of which were mournful, interminable and nonprintable ballads, mostly concerning why they had left Terra to take up their present existence – new and unexpurgated stereographic movies of dancing girls clothed mainly with varihued light (personal gift of the Minister for Space), pretzels and beer.

Only beer, because they had to check into the station cold sober. Two months later, if their luck held, they'd throw another party on the *Phobos* and the *Phobos* crew would join in. Even the staid blunt Andrews would upend a couple of big ones in toasting their safe return.

But not now. The outgoing festivities were strictly private – for sunmen only. No strangers were ever invited. Even an incoming station psychiatrist was excluded.

What then? Something was wrong.

As he stood poised to knock on the door, he found himself counting his pulse. It throbbed at one hundred and fifty and was climbing.

Alar stood at the door, counting out the rapid rise of his pulse, considering what he might have to face on the other side. His knuckled hand dropped in an instinctive motion toward a non-existent sabre pommel. Weapons were forbidden on the *Phobos*. But what danger could there be in such self-commiserating good fellowship? Still, suppose they tried a little horseplay and yanked at his false beard? While he hesitated the music and laughter died away.

Then the ship lurched awkwardly, and he was thrown against the door. The *Phobos* had nosed into Solarion Nine and was sealing herself to the entry ports. A wild cheer from within the mess rose above his crash against the door.

Whether they hailed the survival of the station or their own imminent departure he could not be sure. There was something mocking and sardonic about the ovation that led him to suspect the latter. Let the old shift do their own cheering.

"Come in!" boomed someone.

He pushed the door aside and walked in.

Ten faces looked at him expectantly. Two of the younger men were sitting by the stereograph, but the translucent cube that contained the tri-di image was dark. It had evidently just been turned off.

Two men were returning from a table laden with a beer keg, several large wooden pretzel bowls, beer mugs, napkins, ash trays and other bric-à-brac and were headed toward the dining table nearest the Thief. At the table six men were in the act of rising. The missing eleventh face was probably the psychiatrist – absent by mutual understanding and consent.

The party was over, he sensed uneasily. This was something different.

"Dr. Talbot," said the large florid man with the booming

voice, "I'm Miles, incoming station master for the Nine."

Alar nodded silently.

"And this is my meteorologist, Williams – MacDougall, lateral jet pilot – Florez, spectroscopist – Saint Claire, production engineer . . ."

The Thief acknowledged the introductions gravely but noncommittally, down to young Martinez, clerk. His eyes missed nothing. These men were all repeaters. At some time in the past they had all oozed cold sweat in a solar station, probably most of them at different times and in different stations. But the common experience had branded them, welded them together and cast them beyond the pale of their earthbound brothers.

The twenty eyes had never left his face. What did they expect of him?

He folded his hands inconspicuously and counted his pulse. It had levelled off at one-sixty.

Miles resumed his rumble: "Dr. Talbot, we understand that you are going to be with us for twenty days."

Alar almost smiled. Miles, as a highly skilled and unconsciously snobbish sunman of long experience, held in profound contempt any unit of time less than a full and dangerous sixty days' shift.

"I have requested the privilege," returned the Thief gravely. "I hope you haven't decided that I'll be in the way."

"Not at all."

"The Toynbeean Institute has long been anxious to have a professional historian prepare a monograph – "

"Oh, we don't care *why* you're coming, Dr. Talbot. And don't worry about getting in our way. You look as though you have sense enough to stay clear when we're busy and you'll be worth your weight in unitas if you can keep the psych happily occupied and out of our laps. You play chess, I hope? This psych we have is an Eskimo."

He couldn't remember having heard the term "Eskimo" applied to a sunman before and he was astonished that he understood its meaning, which seemed to spring to mind unbidden, as though from the mental chamber that contained his other life. He had made no mistake in deciding to board the *Phobos*. But for the moment he must pretend ignorance.

280

"Chess – Eskimo?" he murmured with puzzled politeness.

Several of the men smiled.

"Sure, Eskimo," boomed Miles impatiently. "Never been in a solarion before. Has the sweat he was born with. Probably fresh out of school and loaded down with chess sets to keep our minds occupied so we won't brood." He laughed suddenly, harshly. "So we won't brood; Great flaming faculae! Why do they think we keep coming back here?"

Alar realized that the hair was crawling on his neck and that his armpits were wet. And now he knew what common brand had marked these lost souls and joined them into an outré brotherhood.

As the real Talbot had surmised that night at the ball, *everyone of these creatures was stark mad.*

"I'll try to keep the psych occupied," he agreed with plausible dubiousness. "I rather like a game of chess myself."

"Chess!" murmured Florez, the spectroscopist, with dispassionate finality, turning from Alar to stare wearily at the table. His complete absence of venom did not mute his meaning.

Miles laughed again and fixed Alar with bloodshot eyes. "But we didn't invite you here simply to ask you to get the psych out of our hair. The fact is, all ten of us are Indians – old sunmen. And that's unusual. Generally we have at least one Eskimo in the bunch."

The big man's hand flashed into his pocket and two dice clattered along the table toward the Thief. There was a sharp intake of breath somewhere down the table. Alar thought it was Martinez, the young clerk. Everyone pressed slowly on either side of the table toward their guest and the white cubes that lay before him.

"Will you please pick them up, Dr. Talbot?" demanded Miles.

Alar hesitated. What would the action commit him to?

"Go on," Martinez said, impatient and eager. "Go on, sir."

The Thief studied the dice. A little worn, perhaps, but completely ordinary. He reached out slowly, gathered them into his right hand. He raised his hand and opened his fingers so that they rested side by side on his palm almost under Miles' nose.

"Well?"

"Aah," Miles said. "And now I suppose I should inform you of the significance of what you'll soon do for us."

"I'm very interested," Alar replied. He wondered at the form the ritual was about to take. That it was a ritual of immense import to the men he did not doubt.

"When we have a genuine Eskimo, Dr. Talbot, we ask him to throw the dice."

"You have your choice, then? I believe the psychiatrist would qualify, wouldn't he?"

"Huh," grunted the incoming station master. "Sure, the psych's an Eskimo, but all psychs are poison."

"I see." Alar closed his fist over the cubes.

"Martinez could do the honours, too, for that matter. Martinez has served only two shifts and he hasn't really crowded his luck too far to disqualify him. But we don't want to use him if we can help it."

"So logically I'm it."

"Right. The rest of us are no good. Florez is next lowest with five shifts. This would be his sixth – utterly impossible, of course. And so on up to me, with full ten years' service. I'm the Jonah, I can't roll 'em. That leaves you. You're not really an Eskimo – you'll be with us only twenty days – but several of us old timers have decided it'll be legal because you resemble an old friend."

Muir, of course. It was fantastic. The Thief aroused himself as though from a heavy dream. The dice felt cold and weightless in his numbing fist. And his heart beat was climbing again.

He cleared his throat. "May I ask what happens after I roll the dice?"

"Nothing – immediately," replied Miles. "We just file out, grab our gear, and walk up the ramp into the station."

It couldn't be that simple, Martinez' mouth was hanging open as though his life depended on this. Florez was hardly breathing. And so on around the table. Even Miles seemed more flushed than when Alar entered the room.

He thought furiously. Was it a gamble involving some tremendous sum that he was deciding? The sunmen were bountifully paid. Perhaps they had pooled their earnings and he was to decide the winner.

"Will you hurry yourself, *por favor*, Dr. Talbot?" said Martinez faintly.

This was something bigger than money. Alar rattled the dice loosely in his hand and let them go.

And in the act a belated warning seemed to bubble up from his fogged preamnesic life. He clawed futilely at the cubes but it was too late. A three and a four.

He had just condemned a solarion crew – and himself – to death.

Alar exchanged glances with Martinez, who had suddenly become very pale.

A solarion dies once a twelvemonth, so a sunman on a two-month shift has one chance in six of dying with it. Florez couldn't make the throw because this would be his sixth shift and by the laws of chance his time was up.

One in six – these madmen were positive that a roll of the dice could predict a weary return to Terra – or a vaporous grave on the sun.

One chance in six. There had been one chance in six of throwing a seven. His throw would kill these incredible fanatics just as surely as if he cut them down with a Kades. These ten would walk into the solarion knowing that they would die and sooner or later one of them would subconsciously commit the fatal error that would send the station, plunging down into the sunspot vortex, or adrift on the uncharted, unfathomable photosphere. And he would be along.

It seemed that everyone, for a queer unearthly hiatus, had stopped breathing. Martinez was moving pallid lips but no sound was coming out.

Indeed, no one said anything at all. There was nothing to say.

Miles thoughtfully thrust an enormous black cigar into his mouth, pushed his chair back to the table and walked slowly from the room without a backward glance. The others followed, one by one.

Alar waited a full five minutes after the footsteps had died away toward the ramp, full of wonder both at his stupidity and at the two tantalizing flashes from his other life.

His death was certain if he followed them into the solarion But he couldn't hang back now. He recalled the Mind's prediction. It had been a calculated risk.

His main regret was that he was now *persona non grata* to the crew. It would be a long time before he learned anything from these fanatics – probably not before one of them destroyed the station. But it couldn't have been helped.

He stepped into the corridor, looked toward the ramp a dozen yards away and sucked in his breath sharply. Four I.P.'s favoured him with stony stares, then, as one man, drew their sabres.

Then a horrid, unforgettable giggle bit at his unbelieving left ear.

"Small solar system, eh, Thief?"

The meaning of the four guards at the ramp was now only too clear to the Thief. Shey had put them there. Others were undoubtedly behind him.

Shey, then, must be Miles' "Eskimo psych" – and with animal cunning the little man had been waiting for Alar on the *Phobos* ever since its arrival on the moon.

But instead of feeling trapped the Thief felt only elated. At least, before he died, he would have an opportunity to punish Shey.

Shey's present precautions would certainly have been enough to recapture an ordinary fugitive, but the same was true of the other traps that had been laid for Alar. The wolf-pack was still proceeding on the assumption that methods applicable to human beings, enlarged and elaborated perhaps, were equally applicable to him. He believed now that their premise was wrong.

The image of Keiris' preternatural slenderness flashed before him. Yes, the time had come to punish Shey. His oath as a Thief prevented his killing the psychologist but justice permitted other remedies, which could best be administered aboard the solarion. In the meantime –

He turned slowly, bracing himself mentally for the photic blast to come.

"Do you see this finger, Shey?" He held his right forefinger erect midway on the line joining his eyes with the psychologist's.

By pure reflex action Shey's pupils focused on the finger. Then his neck jerked imperceptibly as a narrow "x" of blue-white light exploded from Alar's eyes into his.

The next five seconds would tell whether the Thief's gambling attempt at hypnosis by overstimulation of the other's optical sensorium had been successful.

"I am Dr. Talbot of the Toynbeean Institute," he whispered rapidly. "You are the incoming psych for the Solarion Nine. As we approach the guards on the ramp tell them everything is all right and ask them to bring in our gear immediately." Shey blinked at him.

Would it really work? Was it too preposterous? Had he been insanely overconfident?

The Thief wheeled and walked briskly toward the ramp and the watchful I.P.s. Behind him came the sound of running feet.

"Stop!" cried Shey, hurrying up with his other four guards.

Alar bit his lip indecisively. He had evidently lost the gamble. If Shey planned to have him killed on the spot he should try to break past the swordsmen on the ramp into the solarion. A means of escape might open up in the resulting confusion. Undoubtedly Miles would not submit tamely to Shey's forcible invasion.

"Don't harm that man!" called Shey. "He's not the one."

He had done it.

"Well, Dr. Talbot," giggled Shey, "what is the Toynbeean opinion of life in a solarion in this July twentieth?"

Alar pushed himself away from the table in Shey's private dining room and stroked his false goatee thoughtfully. "After forty-eight hours here, I've come to the opinion that a sixty-day shift in a solarion ruins a man's nervous system for life. He comes in fresh and sane. He leaves insane."

"I agree, doctor, but doesn't this deterioration in the individual have a larger significance to a Toynbeean?"

"Very possibly," admitted the Thief judicially. "But first, let us examine a society of some thirty souls, cast away from the mother culture and cooped up in a solarion. Vast dangers threaten on every side. If the Fraunhofer man should fail to catch an approaching calcium facula in time to warn the lateral jet man – bang – the station goes.

"If the apparatus that prevents solar radiation from volatilizing the station by continuously converting the radiation into muirium should jam for a split second – whoosh – no more station. Or say the freighter fails to show up and cart the muirium away from the stock rooms, forcing us to turn muirium back into the sun – another bang.

"Or suppose our weatherman fails to notice a slight increase in magnetic activity and our sunspot suddenly decides to enlarge itself in our direction with free sliding to the sun's core. Or suppose the muirium anti-grav drive breaks down upstairs, and we have nothing to hold us up against the sun's twenty-seven G's, Or let the refrigeration system fail for ten minutes . . .

"You can see, Count Shey, that it is the normal lot of people who must live this life to be – by terrestrial standards – insane. Insanity under such conditions is a useful and logical defence mechanism, an invaluable and salutary retreat from reality.

"Until the crew make this adjustment – 'response to challenge of environment' as we Toynbeeans call it – they have little chance of survival. The will to insanity in a sunman is as vital as the will to irrigate in a Sumerian. But perhaps I encroach on the psychologists' field."

Shey smirked. "Though I can't agree with you entirely, doctor, still you may have something. Would you say, then, that the *raison d'être* of a solarion psychiatrist is to drive the men toward madness ?"

"I can answer that question by asking another," replied Alar, eyeing his quarry covertly. "Let us suppose a norm for existence has been established in a given society. If one or two of the group deviate markedly from the norm we say they are insane.

"And yet the whole society may be considered insane by a foreign culture which may consider the one or two recalcitrants the only sane persons in the model society. So can't we define sanity as conformity to – and belief in – the norm of whatever culture we represent ?"

Shey pursed his lips. "Perhaps."

"And then, if a few of the crew can't lose themselves in a

retreat from the peril of their daily existence – if they can't cling to some saving certainty, even if it is only the certainly of near death – or if they can't find some other illusion that might make existence bearable – isn't it your duty to make these or other forms of madness easy for them? To teach them the rudiments of insanity, as it were?''

Shey sniggered uneasily. 'In a moment you'll have me believing that in an asylum, the only lunatic is the psychologist.''

Alar regarded him placidly as he held up his wine glass. ''Do you realize, my dear count, that you have repeated your last sentence not once but twice? Do you think I am hard of hearing?'' He sipped at his wine casually.

Startled disbelief showed in the psychologist's face. ''You imagined that I repeated myself. I distinctly remember – ''

''Of course, of course. No doubt I misunderstood you.'' Alar lifted his shoulders in a delicate apology. ''But,'' he pressed, ''suppose you *had* repeated yourself and then denied it. In a layman you'd probably analyze such fixation on trivia as incipient paranoia, to be followed in due time by delusions of persecution.

''In you, of course, it's hardly worth consideration. If it happened at all it was probably just an oversight. A couple of days on one of these stations is enough to disorganize almost anyone.'' He put his wine glass down on the table gently. ''Nothing in your room has been trifled with lately?''

He had slipped into Shey's quarters the previous day and had rotated every visible article 180 degrees.

Shey giggled nervously. Finally he said, ''Certainly not.''

''Then there's nothing to worry about.'' Alar patted his goatee amiably. ''While we're on the subject, you might tell me something. As a Toynbeean, I have always been interested in how one person determines whether another is sane or insane. I understand you psychologists actually have cut-and-dried tests of sanity.''

Shey looked across the table at him narrowly, then chuckled. ''Ah, sanity – no, there's no simple book test for that but I do have some projection slides that evaluate one's motor and mental integration. Such evaluation, of course, is not without bearing on the question of sanity, at least sanity as *I* understand it. Would you care to run through a few of them with me?''

287

Alar nodded politely. Shey, he knew, wanted to run the slides more to reassure himself than to entertain his guest.

The psychologist was due for the rudest shock of his life.

Shey quickly set up the stereograph and tri-di cube screen. "We'll start with some interesting maze slides," he chirped, switching off the light that dangled from the ceiling hook. "The ability to solve mazes quickly is strongly correlated to analyses of our daily problems. The faltering maze-solver unravels his difficulties piecemeal and lacks the cerebral integration that characterizes the executive.

"It is interesting to note that the schizophrenic can solve only the simplest mazes, even after repeated trials. So here's the first and simplest. White rats solve it – laid out on the floor with walls, of course – after three or four runs. A child of five, viewing it as we shall here, gets it in about thirty seconds. Adults instantaneously."

"Quite obvious," agreed Alar coolly as he projected a false opening in the outer maze border and covered the real one with a section of false border.

Shey stirred uneasily but apparently considered his inability to solve the maze as a passing mental quirk. He switched slides.

"What's the average time on this next one?" asked Alar.

"Ten seconds."

The Thief let the second and third ones go by without photic alteration. Shey's relief was plain even in the darkness.

But on the fourth slide Alar alternately opened and blocked various passages of the maze and he knew that Shey, standing beside the projector, was rubbing his eyes. The little psychologist sighed gratefully when his guest suggested leaving the maze series and trying something else.

The Thief smiled.

"Our second series of slides, Dr. Talbot, shows a circle and an ellipse side by side. On each successive slide – there are twelve – the ellipse becomes more and more circular. Persons of the finest visual discrimination can detect the differences on all twelve cards. Dogs can detect two, apes four, six-year-old children ten, and the average man eleven. Keep your own score. Here's the first one."

A large white circle showed on a black screen and near

the circle was a narrow ellipse. That was pretty obvious. Alar decided to wait for the next one.

On the second slide, Shey frowned, removed it from the projector, held it up to the light of the cube screen, then inserted it once again. On the third slide he began to chew his lips. But he kept on. When the tenth was reached he was perspiring profusely and licking sweat from the edges of his mouth.

The Thief continued to make noncommittal acknowledgements as each slide was presented. He felt no pity whatever for Shey, who had no means of knowing that from the second slide on, there were no ellipses, only pairs of identical circles. Each ellipse had been cancelled by a projection from Alar's eyes, and a circle substituted.

Shey made no motion to insert the eleventh slide in the projector. He said, "Shall we stop here? I think you've got the general idea . . ."

Alar nodded. "Very interesting. What else have you?"

His host hesitated, apparently fumbling with the projector housing. Finally he giggled glassily. "I have some Rorschachs. They're more or less conventionalized but they serve to reveal psychosis in its formative stages."

"If this is tiring you – " began Alar with diabolical tact.

"Not at all."

The Thief smiled grimly.

The cube screen lit up again and the rotund psychologist held a slide up to its light for a lengthy inspection. Then he slid the slide into the projector.

He commented, "To a normal person the first slide resembles a symmetrical silhouette of two ballet dancers or two skipping children or sometimes two dogs playing. Psychotics, of course, see something they consider fearful or macabre, such as a tarantula, a demoniacal mask or a – "

Alar had smoothly transformed the image into a grinning skull. "Rather like a couple of dancers, isn't it?" he observed.

Shey pulled out his handkerchief and ran it over his face. The second slide he inserted without comment but Alar could hear it rattle as trembling fingers dropped it into the projector.

"Looks rather like two trees," observed the Thief meditatively, "or perhaps two feathers or possibly two rivulets flowing together in a meadow. What would a psychotic see?"

Shey was standing mute and motionless, apparently more dead than alive. He seemed to be aware of nothing in the room but the image within the screen and Alar sensed that the man was staring at it in fascinated horror. He would have given a great deal to steal a look at the creature whose warped mind he was destroying but he thought it best to continue transforming the image.

"What would a madman see?" he repeated quietly.

Shey's whisper was unrecognizable. "A pair of white arms."

Alar reached over, flicked off the projector and screen and stole quietly from the darkened room. His host never moved.

The Thief had not taken two steps down the corridor when a muffled gust of giggling welled out from the closed door – then another and another – finally so many that they merged into one another in a long pealing paroxysm.

He could still hear it when he turned the corridor corner toward his own stateroom. He stroked his goatee and smiled.

Station master Miles and Florez, who were arguing heatedly over something, passed him without acknowledging his polite bow or even his existence. He watched them thoughtfully until they turned the corner and vanished. Theirs was the ideal state of mind – to be mad and not know it. Their staunch faith in their inevitable destruction clothed them in an aura of purposeful sanity.

Without that faith their mental disintegration would probably be swift and complete. Undoubtedly they would prefer to die rather than to leave the station alive at the end of their shift.

He wondered whether Shey would make an equally dramatic adjustment to his new-won madness.

The racing of his heart awoke him a few hours later in his room.

He listened tensely as he rose from his bunk. But there was no sound, other than the all-pervasive rumble of the vast and frenzied gases outside.

He dressed quickly, stepped to the door opening into the corridor, and looked down the hall. It was empty.

Queer – usually two or three men could be seen hurrying on some vital task or other. His heartbeat was up to one-eighty.

All he had to do was follow his unerring scent for danger. He stepped brusquely into the corridor and strode toward Shey's room. He arrived there in a moment and stood before the door, listening. No sound. He knocked curtly without result. He knocked again. Why didn't Shey answer? Was there a stealthy movement within the room?

His heartbeat touched one-eighty-five and was still climbing. His right hand flexed uneasily. Should he return for his sabre?

He shook off an impulse to run back to his room. If there was danger here at least it would be informative danger. Somehow, he doubted that a blade would influence the issue. He looked around him. The hall was still empty.

The preposterous thought occurred to him that he was the only being left aboard. Then he smiled humourlessly. His fertile imagination was becoming too much even for himself. He seized the panel knob, turned it swiftly, and leaped into the room.

In the dim light, while his heartbeat soared toward two hundred, he beheld a number of things.

The first was Shey's bloated, insensate face, framed in curls, staring down at him about a foot beneath the central ceiling lamp hook. The abnormal protrusion of the eyes was doubtless caused by the narrow leather thong that stretched taut from the folds of the neck to the hook. To one side of the little man's dangling feet was the overturned projector table.

Beyond the gently swaying corpse in front of the cube screen Thurmond sat quietly, studying Alar with enigmatic eyes. On either side of the police minister a Kades gun was aimed at Alar's breast.

Each man seemed locked in the vice of the other's stare. Like condenser plates, thought Alar queerly, with a corpse for a delectric. For a long time the Thief had the strange illusion that he was part of a tri-di projection, that Thur-

291

mond would gaze at him with unblinking eyes forever, that he was safe because a Kades cannot really be fired in tri-di projections.

The room swayed faintly under their feet as an exceptionally violent and noisy swirl of gas beat at the solarion. It aroused them both from their paralytic reveries.

Thurmond was the first to speak.

"In the past," came his dry, chill voice, "our traps for you were subject to the human equation. This factor no longer operates in your favour. If you move from where you now stand, the Kades will fire automatically."

Alar laughed shortly. "In times past, when you were positive you'd taken adequate precautions in your attempts to seize me, you were always proved wrong. I can see that your comrade's suicide has shaken you – otherwise you would have made no attempt to explain my prospective fate. Your verbal review of your trap is mainly for your own assurance. Your expectation that I will die is a hope rather than a certainty. May I suggest that the circumstances hold as much danger for you as for me?"

His voice held a confidence he was far from feeling. He was undoubtedly boxed in tell-tale devices, perhaps capacity condensers or photo-cell relays, that activated the Kades. If he leaped at the man he would simply float to the floor – a mass of sodden cinders.

Thurmond's brows contracted imperceptibly. "You were bluffing, of course, when you suggested the situation contained as much danger for me as for you, since you must die in any event, while my only sources of personal concern are the general considerations of danger aboard a solarion and interference from the crew.

"I have minimized the latter possibility by transferring to Mercury all but a skeleton crew – Miles' shift. And they're alerted to signal the *Phobos* and leave with me as soon as I return to the assembly room, which will be in about ten minutes." He arose almost casually, edged around the nearest Kades and sidled slowly along the wall toward the corridor panel, carefully avoiding the portion of the room covered by the guns.

Thurmond had demonstrated once again why Haze-Gaunt had invited him into the wolf pack. He relied on the

292

leverage of titanic forces when he had difficulty in disposing of an obstacle and damned the cost.

It was utterly simple. There would be no struggle, no personal combat. No immediate issue would be reached. And yet, within a satisfactorily short time, Alar would be dead. He couldn't move without triggering the two Kades, and there would be no one left to free him. The solarion would be evacuated within a few minutes. The crewless station would slide over the brim of the sunspot long before he would collapse from fatigue.

The wolf pack was willing to exchange one of its six most valuable munitions factories for his life.

And yet – it wasn't enough. The Thief was now hardly breathing, because he believed he knew now what Miles and Florez had been discussing in the hall.

Thurmond was now at the panel, turning the knob slowly.

"Your program," said Alar softly, "is sound save in one rather obscure but important particular. Your indifference to Toynbeean principles would naturally blind you to the existence of such a factor as 'self-determination in a society.'"

The police minister paused the barest fraction of a second before stepping through the panel.

The Thief continued, "Can you make sense out of a Fraunhofer report? Can you operate a lateral jet motor? If not you'd better deactivate the Kades because you're going to need me badly, and very soon. You'll have no time to signal the *Phobos*."

The police minister hesitated just outside the door.

"If," said Alar, "you think the skeleton crew under Miles is in present control of the station, you'd better take a look around."

There was no answer. Thurmond evidently thought that one would be superfluous. His footsteps died away down the hall.

Alar looked up quizzically at Shey's gorged and popeyed face, then at the two Kades. "He'll be back," he murmured, folding his arms.

And yet, when he heard the footsteps returning considerably faster than they had departed, this confirmation of his surmise concerning Andrews' crew threw him into a

293

deep gloom. However, it had been inevitable. Nothing could have saved them after he threw the seven.

Thurmond walked quickly into the room. "You were right," he said. "Where have they hidden themselves?"

"They're in hiding," replied Alar without expression, "but not in the way you think. All ten of them were certain they were going to die on this shift. They had a fatalistic faith in their destiny. To return safely with you would have meant giving up that faith with consequent mental and moral disintegration. They preferred to die. You'll probably find their bodies in the muirium holds."

Thurmond's mouth tightened. "You're lying."

"Having no historical background you would naturally assume so. But regardless of what happened to Miles and his crew you'll have to come to some decision about me within the next minute or two. We've been adrift in the Evershed zone ever since I entered the room. You can release me in order to let me have a try at the lateral jets or you can leave me here – and die with me."

He watched the inward struggle in the police minister. Would the man's personal loyalty to Haze-Gaunt or perhaps a chill adamantine sense of duty require him to keep Alar immobilized at the cost of his own life?

Thurmond toyed thoughtfully with the pommel of his breast dagger. "All right," he said finally. Passing behind the Kades, he snapped the switches on each. "You'd better hurry. It's safe now."

"Shey's scabbard and blade are on the table beside you," said the Thief. "Give them to me."

Thurmond permitted himself a smile as he handed over the sabre. Alar knew the man planned to kill him as soon as the station was safe again and that it mattered little to the greatest swordsman in the Imperium whether the Thief were armed.

"A question," the Thief said as he buckled the scabbard to his belt. "Were you on the *Phobos* along with Shey?"

"I was on the *Phobos*. But not with Shey. I let him try his own plan first."

"And when he failed –"

"I acted."

294

"One other question," insisted the Thief imperturbably. "How did you and Shey know where to find me?"

"The Microfilm Mind."

It was incomprehensible. The Mind alternately condemned him and delivered him. Why? Why? Would he never know?

"All right," he said shortly. "Come along."

Together they hurried toward the control room.

An hour later they emerged, perspiring freely.

Alar turned and studied his arch-enemy briefly. He said: "Obviously, I can't permit you to signal the *Phobos* until my own status has been clarified to my satisfaction. I see no particular advantage in delaying what has been inevitable since our first meeting." He drew his sabre with cold deliberation, aware that he hoped his measured certainty would create an impression on Thurmond.

The police minister whipped out his own blade with contemptuous litheness. "You are quite right. You had to die in either event. To save my life I justifiably relied on your desire to prolong your own. *Die!*"

As in many occasions in the past when death faced him, time began to creep by the Thief, and he observed Thurmond's cry of doom and simultaneous lunge as part of a leisurely acted play. Thurmond's move was an actor's part to be studied, analyzed and constructively criticized by responsive words and gestures of his own, well organized and harmoniously knit.

He knew, without reflecting on the quality of mind that permitted and required him to know, that Thurmond's shout and lunge were not meant to kill him. Thurmond's *fleche* was apparently, "high line right", which, if successful, would thrust through Alar's heart and right lung. Experts conventionally parried such a thrust with an ordinary *tierce* or perhaps a *quinte* and followed with a riposte toward the opponent's groin.

Yet there had been a speculative, questioning element in Thurmond's cry. The man had evidently expected the Thief to perceive his deceit, to realize that he had planned a highly intricate composite attack based on Alar's almost reflexive response to the high line thrust, and the skilled Thief would be expected to upset a possible trap by the simple expedient of locking blades and starting anew.

This analysis of the attack was plausible except for one thing: Thurmond, never one to take unavoidable risks, instead of unlocking blades, would very likely seize his breast dagger and drive it into his opponent's throat.

Yet the Thief could not simultaneously cut the dagger scabbard away and avoid the lunge.

Then suddenly everything was past. Thurmond had sprung back, spitting malevolently, and the dagger scabbard was spinning crazily through the air behind him. A streak of red was growing rapidly along the Thief's chest. The police minister laughed lightly.

Alar's heart was beating very fast – just how fast he did not know – pumping its vital substance through the deceptively simple cut in his lung. It couldn't have been helped. Now, if he could maim or disarm Thurmond fairly quickly, he might still summon the *Phobos* and escape under the protection of Captain Andrews before he died of loss of blood.

His skilled opponent would play for time, of course, observing him closely, watching for the first sign of genuine faltering, which might be merely a shift of the thumb along the foil-grip, a thrust parried a fraction of an inch in excess, a slight tensing of the fingers of the curved left hand.

Thurmond would know. Perhaps this was the enlightening death which that recondite sphinx, the Microfilm Mind, had predicted for him.

Thurmond waited, smiling, alert, supremely confident. He would expect Alar to burst forward, every nerve straining to make the most of the few minutes of strong capable fencing remaining to him before he fainted from loss of blood.

The Thief moved in and his sword leapt arrowlike in an incredibly complex body feint. But his quasi-thrust was parried by a noncommittal quasi-riposte, almost philosophical in its ambiguity. Its studied indefiniteness of statement showed that Thurmond realized to the utmost his paramount position – that a perfect defence would win without risk.

Alar had not really expected his attack to draw blood. He

296

merely wanted to confirm in his own mind that Thurmond realized his advantage. Most evidently he did. Simultaneously with his realization the Thief, instead of improvising a continuation of the attack, as Thurmond must expect, retreated precipitously, coughed and spat out a mouthful of hot, salty fluid.

His right lung had been filling slowly. The only question was, when should he cough and void the blood? He had chosen this moment. His opponent must now take the initiative and he must be lured into overextending himself.

Thurmond laughed soundlessly and closed in with a tricky leg thrust, followed immediately with a cut across the face, both of which the Thief barely parried. But it was clear that Thurmond was not exerting himself to the fullest. He was taking no chances, because he need take none.

He could accomplish his goal in good time simply by doing nothing, or quickly if he liked, by forcing the Thief to continuous exertions. Thurmond's only necessity was to stay alive, where Alar must not only do that, but must disable his opponent as well. He could not attempt more. His oath as a Thief forbade his killing an officer of the Imperium even in self-defence.

Without feeling despair he felt the symptoms of despair – the tightening of the throat, the vague trembling of his facial nerves, an overpowering weariness.

" 'To avoid capture or death in a situation of known factors,' " mocked Thurmond, " 'the Thief will introduce one or more new variables, generally by the conversion of a factor of relative safety into a factor of relative uncertainty.' "

At that moment Alar plumbed to the depths this extraordinary character who commanded the security forces of a hemisphere. It was a blazing, calculating intelligence that crushed opposition because it understood its opponents better than they did themselves, could silently anticipate their moves and be ready – to their short-lived astonishment – with a fatal answer.

Thurmond could quote the *Thief Combat Manual* verbatim.

Alar lowered his blade slowly. "Then it is useless to proffer my weapon in surrender, expecting you to reach for it with your left hand – "

297

"– and find myself sailing over your shoulder. No thanks."

"Or 'slip' in my own blood – "

"– and impale me as I rush in to finish you."

"And yet," returned the Thief, "the philosophy of safety-conversion is not limited to the obvious rather sophomoric devices that we have just discussed as I shall shortly demonstrate." His mouth twisted sardonically.

But only the wildest, most preposterous demand on his unearthly body would save him now. Furthermore, the thing he had in mind required that he be rid of his sabre yet safe from Thurmond for at least a moment or two.

His blade skidded across the plastic tiles toward Thurmond, who stepped back in unfeigned amazement, then tightened the grip on his own weapon and moved forward.

"The sacrifice of safety is my means of defence," continued Alar unhurriedly. (Great galaxy! Would the man never stop?) "I have converted it into a variable unknown, for you are suspicious of what I shall do next. Your steps are slowing.

"You see no good reason why you can't kill me now, very quickly, but you have – shall we say, buck fever? You are curious as to what I could accomplish without my weapon that I could not accomplish with it. You wonder why I am repeatedly flexing my arms and why I do these knee bends.

"You are certain you can kill me, that all you need to do is approach and thrust your blade home. And yet you have stopped to watch, consumed with curiosity. And you are just a little afraid."

Stifling a cough, the Thief stood erect and closed his fists tightly. There was a dry crackling sound about his clothing as he crossed the brief intervening space toward Thurmond.

The police minister was breathing with nervous rapidity but stood firm.

"Don't you realize, Thurmond, that a man capable of reversing the visual process by supplying his retinal web with energy quanta can, under stress, reverse that process? That instead of furnishing electrical potential differences along afferent nerves for normal muscle activation, he can reverse the process and cause the muscles to store considerable wattage for discharge through the nerves and out the fingertips?

"Did you know that certain Brazilian eels can discharge several hundred volts – enough to electrocute frogs and fish? At my present Potential I could easily kill you but I intend to simply stun you. Since electrostatic charges escape easily from metal points, you will understand why I had to throw away my sabre, even at the risk of your running me through before I could build up the necessary charge."

Thurmond's blade flew up. "Come no closer!" he cried hoarsely.

The Thief paused, his bare breast six inches in front of the wavering point. "Metal is an excellent conductor," he smiled and moved in.

The police minister jumped back, gripped his sabre like a lance, took split-second aim at Alar's heart and –

Fell screaming to the floor, his writhing body wrapped in a pale blue glow. He managed to pull his pistol from its holster and to fire two shots that bounced harmlessly from Alar's Thief armour.

Then there was a brief panting pause while he glared insanely upward at his extraordinary conqueror.

The third shot went into his own brain.

Alar had bounded into the control room before the echo of the final shot died away. Their fight had lasted nearly forty minutes. How far had the solarion drifted?

The pyrometric gauge read 4,500 K. The temperature drop from the 5,700 degrees K of the photosphere definitely placed the solarion position in the coldest part of the sunspot – its centre.

Which meant that the station must have been falling for several minutes, straight toward the sun's core.

As Alar's stunned eyes watched the pyrometer the needle began slowly to creep up the scale, recording the fall of the station into the sunspot vortex – 4,560, 4,580, 4,600. The deeper, the hotter. Of course, the station would never reach the sun's core. The vortex would probably narrow to nothing within a thousand miles or so, in a region deep enough to have a temperature of a few million degrees. The solarion's insulative-refrigeration system could stand a top limit of 7,000.

299

The possibilities were several. The spot vortex might extend deep into the sun's core, with its temperature of some twenty million degrees. But even if the vortex gas stayed under 7,000 degrees all the way to the centre – and he knew it could not – the station would eventually crash into the enormously dense core and burst into incandescence.

But suppose the vortex did not extend to that incredibly hot centre, but, more probably, originated only a few thousand miles down? He spat out a mouthful of blood and calculated rapidly. If the spot were 16,000 miles deep the temperature at the cone apex would be a little below 7,000.

If the station could float gently to rest there he might live for several hours before the heavy plant sank deeply enough to reach an intolerable temperature. But its landing wouldn't be gentle. The station was now falling under an acceleration of twenty-seven gravities, and would probably strike the bottom of the cone at a velocity of several miles a second despite the viscosity of the spot gases. Everything about him would instantly disintegrate.

He was aware of the chair cushions pushing against his back. The metal tubing along the arms seemed considerably warmer now to his touch. His face was wet, but his mouth was dry. The thought reminded him of Captain Andrews' cache.

With nothing to do for the moment, he acted on his sudden whim. He rose, stretched himself and walked over to the wall which supported the refrigerated cabinet. He opened the door. Against his perspiring face he felt the sudden wave of cool air. He chuckled at an irrational thought: why not crawl into the six cubic foot box and shut the door behind him?

He pulled out the bottle of foam and squeezed some of the thick liquid into his mouth. The sensation was extremely pleasant. He closed his eyes and for a moment imagined that Captain Andrews was next to him, saying, "It's cold and that's plenty welcome in a place like this."

He swung the door shut again on the bottle. A meaningless gesture, he thought to himself. The situation seemed so unreal. Keiris had warned him . . .

Keiris.

Did she sense, at this moment, what he was facing?

He snorted at his own thoughts and returned to the chair. Just precisely what did he face?

There were, indeed, several possibilities, but their conclusions were identical – a long wait, then an instantaneous, painless oblivion. He couldn't even count on an enduring excruciating pain that might release him along the time axis, as it had done in Shey's torture room.

He became aware of a low, hollow hum, and finally traced it to the pulse at his temple. His heart was beating so fast that the individual beats were no longer detectable. The pulse had passed into the lower audio range, which meant a beat of at least twelve hundred a minute.

He almost smiled. In the face of the catastrophe that Haze-Gaunt was about to wreak on Earth the frenzied concern of his subconscious mind for his own preservation seemed suddenly amusing.

It was then that he noticed that the room was tilted slightly. That should not be, unless the giant central gyro were slowing down. The gyro should keep the station upright in the most violent faculae and tornado prominences. A quick check of the control panel showed nothing wrong with the great stabilizer.

But the little compass gyro was turning slowly, in a very odd but strangely familiar way, which he recognized immediately. The station axis was gradually being inclined at an angle from the vertical and was rotating about its old centre in a cone-like path.

The solarion was *precessing*, which meant that some unknown titanic force was attempting to invert it and was being valiantly fought off by the great central gyro.

But it was a losing battle.

He had a fleeting vision of the great station turning turtle in slow massive grandeur. The muirium anti-grav drive overhead, now cancelling 26 of the 27 G's of the sun, would soon be beneath him, and adding to those 27 G's. Against 53 G's he would weigh some four tons. His blood would ooze from his crushed, pulpy body and spread in a thin layer over the deck.

But what could be trying to turn the station over?

The pyrometers showed almost identical convection temperatures on the sides, top and bottom, of the station –

about 5,200 degrees. And radiation heat received on the sides and bottom of the plant showed about 6,900, as could be expected. But the pyrometers measuring radiation received on the upper surface of the station, which should not have exceeded 2,000 degrees – since the station surface normally was radiated only by the thin surface photosphere – showed the incredible figure of 6,800.

The station must be completely immersed in the sun. The uniform radiation on all sides proved that. Yet he was still in the sunspot vortex, as shown by the much cooler convection currents bathing the station. There was only one possible explanation. The spot vortex must be returning to the sun's surface through a gigantic U-shaped tube.

Anything going down one limb of the tube would naturally ascend the other limb inverted. The U-tube finally explained why all spots occurred in pairs and were of opposite magnetic polarity. The ionized vortex of course rotated in opposite directions in the respective limbs of the tube.

If the central gyro won out over the torrential vortex the station *might* be swept up the other limb of the following spot twin and he *might* break the station away to safety over the penumbral edge – in which improbable event he could live as long as his punctured lung permitted or until the storage chambers became filled with muirium and the synthesizer began turning the deadly material back into the sun to trigger a gigantic explosion.

But he could be sure that even if the station were found during that interval there would be no rescue. The discovery would be made by Imperial search vessels and the I.P.'s would simply keep the station under observation until the inevitable filling of the muirium holds.

The brooding man sat at the central operator's chair for a long time until the steepening floor threatened to drop him out of his seat. He rose heavily to his feet and, hanging tightly to the guide rails, walked the length of the panel to a bank of huge enabling switches.

Here he unlocked the safety mechanism of the central gyro switch and pulled it out amid a protest of arcing, hissing flame. The deck immediately began to vibrate beneath him, and the rapidly increasing tilt of the floor made it difficult to stand.

The room was spinning dizzily about him as he lashed a cord to the master switch controlling the outer hatches of the muirium hatches overhead. The free end he tied around his waist.

When the station turned on its back he would fall to the other end of the room and the cord attached to his lunging body would jerk open the muirium hatch switch. All the stored muirium would begin to dissolve back into its native energy quanta, the station would become a flat, gigantic space rocket and – at least theoretically – would be hurled through the rising U-limb at an unimaginable velocity.

If he were human he would be killed instantly. If he were not human, he might survive the fantastic initial acceleration and accompany the station into the black depths of space.

The deck had almost become a vertical wall. The gyro had probably stopped and there was no turning back. For a moment he regretted his decision. At least he could have lived on a little while longer.

Always a little longer. He had squeezed out five years of life by that method. But no more. Sweat squirted from his face as, slipping and sliding, he clawed insanely at the smooth steel tiles of the deck that was now soaring over him to become the new ceiling. Then he dropped straight to what a few minutes before had been the ceiling and lay there helpless under a 53-G gravity, unable even to breathe and swiftly losing consciousness.

He knew vaguely that the rope had pulled the switches to the muirium locks and had then broken under his enormously increased weight – that jagged fragments of his snapping ribs had pierced his heart – that he was dying.

In that instant the muirium caught. Four thousand tons of the greatest energy-giving substance ever known to man collapsed in a millisecond into a titanic space-bending shower of radiation.

He had no sensation of pain, of movement, of time, of body, of anything. But he didn't care. In his own way he was still very much alive.

Alar was dead.

And yet he knew who he was and where his destiny lay. . . .

THE END

The ultradrive had just one slight drawback: it set up a shock wave that made suns explode. Which made the problem of getting back home a delicate one indeed. . . .

TIME FUZE

by Randall Garrett

Commander Benedict kept his eyes on the rear plate as he activated the intercom. "All right, cut the power. We ought to be safe enough here."

As he released the intercom, Dr. Leicher, of the astronomical staff, stepped up to his side. "Perfectly safe," he nodded, "although even at this distance a star going nova ought to be quite a display."

Benedict didn't shift his gaze from the plate. "Do you have your instruments set up?"

"Not quite. But we have plenty of time. The light won't reach us for several hours yet. Remember, we were out-racing it at ten lights."

The commander finally turned, slowly letting his breath out in a soft sigh. "Dr. Leicher, I would say that this is just about the foulest coincidence that could happen to the first interstellar vessel ever to leave the Solar System."

Leicher shrugged. "In one way of thinking, yes. It is certainly true that we will never know, now, whether Alpha Centauri A ever had any planets. But, in another way, it is extremely fortunate that we should be so near a stellar explosion because of the wealth of scientific information we can obtain. As you say, it is a coincidence, and probably one that happens only once in a billion years. The chances of any particular star going nova are small. That we should be so close when it happens is of a vanishingly small order of probability."

Commander Benedict took off his cap and looked at the damp stain in the sweatband. "Nevertheless, Doctor, it is damned unnerving to come out of ultradrive a couple of hundred million miles from the first star ever visited by man and have to turn tail and run because the damned thing practically blows up in your face."

304

Leicher could see that Benedict was upset; he rarely used the same profanity twice in one sentence.

They had been downright lucky, at that. If Leicher hadn't seen the star begin to swell and brighten, if he hadn't known what it meant, or if Commander Benedict hadn't been quick enough in shifting the ship back into ultradrive – Leicher had a vision of an incandescent cloud of gaseous metal that had once been a spaceship.

The intercom buzzed. The commander answered, "Yes?"

"Sir, would you tell Dr. Leicher that we have everything set up now?"

Leicher nodded and turned to leave. "I guess we have nothing to do now but wait."

When the light from the nova did come, Commander Benedict was back at the plate again – the forward one, this time, since the ship had been turned around in order to align the astronomy lab in the nose with the star.

Alpha Centauri A began to brighten and spread. It made Benedict think of a light bulb connected through a rheostat, with someone turning that rheostat, turning it until the circuit was well overloaded.

The light began to hurt Benedict's eyes even at that distance and he had to cut down the receptivity in order to watch. After a while, he turned away from the plate. Not because the show was over, but simply because it had slowed to a point beyond which no change seemed to take place to the human eye.

Five weeks later, much to Leicher's chagrin, Commander Benedict announced that they had to leave the vicinity. The ship had only been provisioned to go to Alpha Centauri, scout the system without landing on any of the planets, and return. At ten lights, top speed for the ultradrive, it would take better than three months to get back.

"I know you'd like to watch it go through the complete cycle," Benedict said, "but we can't go back home as a bunch of starved skeletons."

Leicher resigned himself to the necessity of leaving much of his work unfinished, and, although he knew it was a case of sour grapes, consoled himself with the thought that he could at least get most of the remaining information from the five-hundred-inch telescope on Luna, four years from then.

As the ship slipped into the not-quite-space through which the ultradrive propelled it, Leicher began to consolidate the material he had already gathered.

Commander Benedict wrote in the log:

Fifty-four days out from Sol. Alpha Centauri has long since faded back into its pre-blowup state, since we have far outdistanced the light from its explosion. It now looks as it did two years ago. It –

"Pardon me, Commander," Leicher interrupted, "But I have something interesting to show you."

Benedict took his fingers off the keys and turned around in his chair. "What is it, Doctor?"

Leicher frowned at the papers in his hands. "I've been doing some work on the probability of that explosion happening just as it did, and I've come up with some rather frightening figures. As I said before, the probability was small. A little calculation has given us some information which makes it even smaller. For instance: with a possible error of plus or minus two seconds Alpha Centauri A began to explode the instant we came out of ultradrive!

"Now, the probability of that occurring comes out so small that it should happen only once in ten to the four hundred sixty-seventh seconds."

It was Commander Benedict's turn to frown. "So?"

"Commander, the entire universe is only about ten to the seventeenth seconds old. But to give you an idea, let's say that the chances of its happening are *once* in millions of trillions of years!"

Benedict blinked. The number, he realized, was totally beyond his comprehension – or anyone else's.

"Well, so what? Now it has happened that one time. That simply means that it will almost certainly never happen again!"

"True. But, Commander, when you back odds like that and win, the thing to do is look for some factor that is cheating in your favour. If you took a pair of dice and started throwing sevens, one right after another – for the next

306

couple of thousand years – you'd begin to suspect they were loaded."

Benedict said nothing; he just waited expectantly.

"There is only one thing that could have done it. Our ship," Leicher said it quietly, without emphasis.

"What we know about the hyperspace, or superspace, or whatever it is we move through in ultradrive, is almost nothing. Coming out of it so near to a star might set up some sort of shock wave in normal space which would completely disrupt that star's internal balance, resulting in the liberation of unimaginably vast amounts of energy, causing that star to go nova. We can only assume that we ourselves were the fuze that set off that nova."

Benedict stood up slowly. When he spoke, his voice was a choking whisper. "You mean the sun – Sol – might . . ."

Leicher nodded. "I don't say that it definitely would. But the probability is that we were the cause of the destruction of Alpha Centauri A, and therefore might cause the destruction of Sol in the same way."

Benedict's voice was steady again. "That means that we can not go back again, doesn't it? Even if we're not positive, we can't take the chance."

"Not necessarily. We can get fairly close before we cut out the drive, and come in the rest of the way at sub-light speed. It'll take longer, and we'll have to go on half or one-third rations, but we *can* do it!"

"How far away?"

"I don't know what the minimum distance is, but I do know how we can gauge a distance. Remember, neither Alpha Centauri B or C were detonated. We'll have to cut our drive at least as far away from Sol as they are from A."

"I see." The Commander was silent for a moment, then: "Very well, Dr. Leicher. If that's the safest way, that's the only way."

Benedict issued the orders, while Leicher figured the exact point at which they must cut out the drive, and how long the trip would take. The rations would have to be cut down accordingly.

Commander Benedict's mind whirled around the monstrousness of the whole thing like some dizzy bee around a flower. What if there had been planets around Centauri A?

307

What if they had been inhabited? Had he, all unwittingly, killed entire races of living, intelligent beings?

But, how could he have known? The drive had never been tested before. It couldn't be tested inside the Solar System – it was too fast. He and his crew had been volunteers, knowing that they might die when the drive went on.

Suddenly, Benedict gasped and slammed his fist down on the desk before him.

Leicher looked up. "What's the matter, Commander?"

"Suppose," came the answer, "just suppose that we have the same effect on a star when we *go into* ultradrive as we do when we come out of it?"

Leicher was silent for a moment, stunned by the possibility. There was nothing to say, anyway. They could only wait . . .

A little more than half a light year from Sol, when the ship reached the point where its occupants could see the light that had left their home sun more than seven months before, they watched it become suddenly, horribly brighter. *A hundred thousand times brighter*

THE END

One of sf's most celebrated authors presents a dialogue between man and machine. Or so it commences. But a lot of time goes by, and when the answer to the last question finally arrives, it is too late. Or too early.

THE LAST QUESTION

by Isaac Asimov

The last question was asked for the first time, half in jest, on May 21, 2061, at a time when humanity first stepped into the light. The question came about as a result of a five-dollar bet over highballs, and it happened this way:

Alexander Adell and Bertram Lupov were two of the faithful attendants of Multivac. As well as any human beings could, they knew what lay behind the cold, clicking, flashing face – miles and miles of face – of that giant computer. They had at least a vague notion of the general plan of relays and circuits that had long since grown past the point where any single human could possibly have a firm grasp of the whole.

Multivac was self-adjusting and self-correcting. It had to be, for nothing human could adjust and correct it quickly enough or even adequately enough. So Adell and Lupov attended the monstrous giant only lightly and superficially, yet as well as any men could. They fed it data, adjusted questions to its needs and translated the answers that were issued. Certainly they, and all others like them, were fully entitled to share in the glory that was Multivac's.

For decades, Multivac had helped design the ships and plot the trajectories that enabled man to reach the Moon, Mars, and Venus, but past that, Earth's poor resources could not support the ships. Too much energy was needed for the long trips. Earth exploited its coal and uranium with increasing efficiency, but there was only so much of both.

But slowly Multivac learned enough to answer deeper questions more fundamentally, and on May 14, 2061, what had been theory, became fact.

The energy of the sun was stored, converted, and utilized directly on a planet-wide scale. All Earth turned off its burning coal, its fissioning uranium, and flipped the switch that connected all of it to a small station, one mile in diameter, circling the Earth at half the distance of the Moon. All Earth ran by invisible beams of sunpower.

Seven days had not sufficed to dim the glory of it and Adell and Lupov finally managed to escape from the public function, and to meet in quiet where no one would think of looking for them, in the deserted underground chambers, where portions of the mighty buried body of Multivac showed. Unattended, idling, sorting data with contented lazy clickings, Multivac, too, had earned its vacation and the boys appreciated that. They had no intention, originally, of disturbing it.

They had brought a bottle with them, and their only concern at the moment was to relax in the company of each other and the bottle.

"It's amazing when you think of it," said Adell. His broad face had lines of weariness in it, and he stirred his drink slowly with a glass rod, watching the cubes of ice slur clumsily about. "All the energy we can possibly ever use for free. Enough energy, if we wanted to draw on it, to melt all earth into a big drop of impure liquid iron, and still never miss the energy so used. All the energy we could ever use, forever and forever and forever."

Lupov cocked his head sideways. He had a trick of doing that when he wanted to be contrary, and he wanted to be contrary now, partly because he had had to carry the ice and glassware. "Not forever," he said.

"Oh, hell, just about forever. Till the sun runs down, Bert."

"That's not forever."

"All right, then. Billions and billions of years. Twenty billion, maybe. Are you satisfied?"

Lupov put his fingers through his thinning hair as though to reassure himself that some was still left and sipped gently at his own drink. "Twenty billion years isn't forever."

"Well, it will last our time, won't it?"

"So would the coal and uranium."

"All right, but now we can hook up each individual spaceship to the Solar Station, and it can go to Pluto and back a million times without ever worrying about fuel. You

310

can't do *that* on coal and uranium. Ask Multivac, if you don't believe me."

"I don't have to ask Multivac. I know that."

"Then stop running down what Multivac's done for us," said Adell, blazing up. "It did all right."

"Who says it didn't? What I say is that a sun won't last forever. That's all I'm saying. We're safe for twenty billion years, but then what?" Lupov pointed a slightly shaky finger at the other. "And don't say we'll switch to another sun."

There was silence for a while. Adell put his glass to his lips only occasionally, and Lupov's eyes slowly closed. They rested.

Then Lupov's eyes snapped open. "You're thinking we'll switch to another sun when ours is done, aren't you?"

"I'm not thinking."

"Sure you are. You're weak on logic, that's the trouble with you. You're like the guy in the story who was caught in a sudden shower and who ran to a grove of trees and got under one. He wasn't worried, you see, because he figured when one tree got wet through, he would just get under another one."

"I get it," said Adell. "Don't shout. When the sun is done, the other stars will be gone, too."

"Darn right they will," muttered Lupov. "It all had a beginning in the original cosmic explosion, whatever that was, and it'll all have an end when all the stars run down. Some run down faster than others. Hell, the giants won't last a hundred million years. The sun will last twenty billion years and maybe the dwarfs will last a hundred billion for all the good they are. But just give us a trillion years and everything will be dark. Entropy has to increase to maximum, that's all."

"I know all about entropy," said Adell, standing on his dignity.

"The hell you do."

"I know as much as you do."

"Then you know everything's got to run down someday."

"All right. Who says they won't?"

"You did, you poor sap. You said we had all the energy we needed, forever. You said 'forever'."

311

It was Adell's turn to be contrary. "Maybe we can build things up again someday," he said.

"Never."

"Why not? Someday."

"Never."

"Ask Multivac."

"*You* ask Multivac. I dare you. Five dollars says it can't be done."

Adell was just drunk enough to try, just sober enough to be able to phrase the necessary symbols and operations into a question which, in words, might have corresponded to this: Will mankind one day without the net expenditure of energy be able to restore the sun to its full youthfulness even after it had died of old age?

Or maybe it could be put more simply like this: How can the net amount of entropy of the universe be massively decreased?

Multivac fell dead and silent. The slow flashing of lights ceased, the distant sounds of clicking relays ended.

Then, just as the frightened technicians felt they could hold their breath no longer, there was a sudden springing to life of the teletype attached to that portion of Multivac. Five words were printed: INSUFFICIENT DATA FOR MEANINGFUL ANSWER.

"No bet," whispered Lupov. They left hurriedly.

By next morning, the two, plagued with throbbing head and cottony mouth, had forgotten the incident.

Jerrodd, Jerrodine, and Jerrodette I and II watched the starry picture in the visiplate change as the passage through hyperspace was completed in its non-time lapse. At once, the even powdering of stars gave way to the predominance of a single bright marble-disc, centred.

"That's X-23," said Jerrodd confidently. His thin hands clamped tightly behind his back and the knuckles whitened.

The little Jerrodettes, both girls, had experienced the hyperspace passage for the first time in their lives and were self-conscious over the momentary sensation of inside-outness. They buried their giggles and chased one another wildly about their mother, screaming, "We've reached X-23 – we've reached X-23 – we've – "

"Quiet, children," said Jerrodine sharply. "Are you sure, Jerrodd?"

"What is there to be but sure?" asked Jerrodd, glancing up at the bulge of featureless metal just under the ceiling. It ran the length of the room, disappearing through the wall at either end. It was as long as the ship.

Jerrodd scarcely knew a thing about the thick rod of metal except that it was called a Microvac, that one asked it questions if one wished; that if one did not it still had its task of guiding the ship to a preordered destination; of feeding on energies from the various Sub-galactic Power Stations; of computing the equations for the hyperspacial jumps.

Jerrodd and his family had only to wait and live in the comfortable residence quarters of the ship.

Someone had once told Jerrodd that the "ac" at the end of "Microvac" stood for "analogue computer" in ancient English, but he was on the edge of forgetting even that.

Jerrodine's eyes were moist as she watched the visiplate. "I can't help it. I feel funny about leaving Earth."

"Why, for Pete's sake?" demanded Jerrodd. "We had nothing there. We'll have everything on X-23. You won't be alone. You won't be a pioneer. There are over a million people on the planet already. Good Lord, our great-grandchildren will be looking for new worlds because X-23 will be overcrowded." Then, after a reflective pause, "I tell you, it's a lucky thing the computers worked out interstellar travel the way the race is growing."

"I know, I know," said Jerrodine miserably.

Jerrodette I said promptly, "Our Microvac is the best Microvac in the world."

"I think so, too," said Jerrodd, tousling her hair.

It *was* a nice feeling to have a Microvac of your own and Jerrodd was glad he was part of his generation and no other. In his father's youth, the only computers had been tremendous machines taking up a hundred square miles of land. There was only one to a planet. Planetary ACs they were called. They had been growing in size steadily for a thousand years and then, all at once, came refinement. In place of transistors, had come molecular valves so that even the largest Planetary AC could be put into a space only half the volume of a spaceship.

Jerrodd felt uplifted, as he always did when he thought that his own personal Microvac was many times more complicated than the ancient and primitive Multivac that had first tamed the Sun, and almost as complicated as Earth's Planetary AC (the largest) that had first solved the problem of hyperspatial travel and had made trips to the stars possible.

"So many stars, so many planets," sighed Jerrodine, busy with her own thoughts. "I suppose families will be going out to new planets forever, the way we are now."

"Not forever," said Jerrodd, with a smile. "It will all stop someday, but not for billions of years. Many billions. Even the stars run down, you know. Entropy must increase."

"What's entropy, daddy?" shrilled Jerrodette II.

"Entropy, little sweet, is just a word which means the amount of running-down of the universe. Everything runs down, you know, like your little walkie-talkie robot, remember?"

"Can't you just put in a new power-unit, like with my robot?"

"The stars *are* the power-units, dear. Once they're gone, there are no more power-units."

Jerrodette I at once set up a howl. "Don't let them, daddy. Don't let the stars run down."

"Now look what you've done," whispered Jerrodine, exasperated.

"How was I to know it would frighten them?" Jerrodd whispered back.

"Ask the Microvac," wailed Jerrodette I. "Ask him how to turn the stars on again."

"Go ahead," said Jerrodine. "It will quiet them down." (Jerrodette II was beginning to cry, also.)

Jerrodd shrugged. "Now, now, honeys. I'll ask Microvac. Don't worry, he'll tell us."

He asked the Microvac, adding quickly, "Print the answer."

Jerrodd cupped the strip of thin cellufilm and said cheerfully, "See now, the Microvac says it will take care of everything when the time comes so don't worry."

Jerrodine said, "And now, children, it's time for bed. We'll be in our new home soon."

Jerrodd read the words on the cellufilm again before destroying it: INSUFFICIENT DATA FOR MEANINGFUL ANSWER.

He shrugged and looked at the visiplate. X-23 was just ahead.

VJ-23X of Lameth stared into the black depths of the three-dimensional, small-scale map of the Galaxy and said, "Are we ridiculous, I wonder, in being so concerned about the matter?"

MQ-17J of Nicron shook his head. "I think not. You know the Galaxy will be filled in five years at the present rate of expansion."

Both seemed in their early twenties, both were tall and perfectly formed.

"Still," said VJ-23X, "I hesitate to submit a pessimistic report to the Galactic Council."

"I wouldn't consider any other kind of report. Stir them up a bit. We've got to stir them up."

VJ-23X sighed. "Space is infinite. A hundred billion Galaxies are there for the taking. More."

"A hundred billion is *not* infinite and it's getting less infinite all the time. Consider! Twenty thousand years ago, mankind first solved the problem of utilizing stellar energy, and a few centuries later, interstellar travel became possible. It took mankind a million years to fill one small world and then only fifteen thousand years to fill the rest of the Galaxy. Now the population doubles every ten years – "

VJ-23X interrupted. "We can thank immortality for that."

"Very well. Immortality exists and we have to take it into account. I admit it has its seamy side, this immortality. The Galactic AC has solved many problems for us, but in solving the problem of preventing old age and death, it has undone all its other solutions."

"Yet you wouldn't want to abandon life, I suppose."

"Not at all," snapped MQ-17J, softening it at once to, "Not yet. I'm by no means old enough. How old are you?"

315

"Two hundred and twenty-three. And you?"

"I'm still under two hundred. – But to get back to my point. Population doubles every ten years. Once this Galaxy is filled, we'll have filled another in ten years. Another ten years and we'll have filled two more. Another decade, four more. In a hundred years, we'll have filled a thousand Galaxies. In a thousand years, a million Galaxies. In ten thousand years, the entire known Universe. Then what?"

VJ-23X said, "As a side issue, there's a problem of transportation. I wonder how many sunpower units it will take to move Galaxies of individuals from one Galaxy to the next."

"A very good point. Already, mankind consumes two sunpower units per year."

"Most of it's wasted. After all, our own Galaxy alone pours out a thousand sunpower units a year and we only use two of those."

"Granted, but even with a hundred per cent efficiency, we only stave off the end. Our energy requirements are going up in a geometric progression even faster than our population. We'll run out of energy even sooner than we run out of Galaxies. A good point. A very good point."

"We'll just have to build new stars out of interstellar gas."

"Or out of dissipated heat?" asked MQ-17J, sarcastically.

"There may be some way to reverse entropy. We ought to ask the Galactic AC."

VJ-23X was not really serious, but MQ-17J pulled out his AC-contact from his pocket and placed it on the table before him.

"I've half a mind to," he said. "It's something the human race will have to face someday."

He stared sombrely at his small AC-contact. It was only two inches cubed and nothing in itself, but it was connected through hyperspace with the great Galactic AC that served all mankind. Hyperspace considered, it was an integral part of the Galactic AC.

MQ-17J paused to wonder if someday in his immortal life he would get to see the Galactic AC. It was on a little world of its own, a spider webbing of force-beams holding the matter within which surges of sub-mesons took the place of the old clumsy molecular valves. Yet despite its sub-etheric workings, the Galactic AC was known to be a full thousand feet across.

MQ-17J asked suddenly of his AC-contact, "Can entropy ever be reversed?"

VJ-23X looked startled and said at once, "Oh, say, I didn't really mean to have you ask that."

"Why not?"

"We both know entropy can't be reversed. You can't turn smoke and ash back into a tree."

"Do you have trees on your world?" asked MQ-17J.

The sound of the Galactic AC startled them into silence. Its voice came thin and beautiful out of the small AC-contact on the desk. It said: THERE IS INSUFFICIENT DATA FOR A MEANINGFUL ANSWER.

VJ-23X said, "See!"

The two men thereupon returned to the question of the report they were to make to the Galactic Council.

Zee Prime's mind spanned the new Galaxy with a faint interest in the countless twists of stars that powered it. He had never seen this one before. Would he ever see them all? So many of them, each with its load of humanity. – But a load that was almost a dead weight. More and more, the real essence of men was to be found out here, in space.

Minds, not bodies! The immortal bodies remained back on the planets, in suspension over the eons. Sometimes they roused for material activity but that was growing rarer. Few new individuals were coming into existence to join the incredibly mighty throng, but what matter? There was little room in the Universe for new individuals.

Zee Prime was roused out of his reverie upon coming across the wispy tendrils of another mind.

"I am Zee Prime," said Zee Prime. "And you?"

"I am Dee Sub Wun. Your Galaxy?"

"We call it only the Galaxy. And you?"

"We call ours the same. All men call their Galaxy their Galaxy and nothing more. Why not?"

"True. Since all Galaxies are the same."

"Not all Galaxies. On one particular Galaxy the race of man must have originated. That makes it different."

Zee Prime said, "On which one?"

"I cannot say. The Universal AC would know."

317

"Shall we ask him? I am suddenly curious."

Zee Prime's perceptions broadened until the Galaxies themselves shrank and became a new, more diffuse powdering on a much larger background. So many hundreds of billions of them, all with their immortal beings, all carrying their load of intelligences with minds that drifted freely through space. And yet one of them was unique among them all in being the original Galaxy. One of them had, in its vague and distant past, a period when it was the only Galaxy populated by man.

Zee Prime was consumed with curiosity to see this Galaxy and he called out: "Universal AC! On which Galaxy did mankind originate?"

The Universal AC heard, for on every world and throughout space, it had its receptors ready, and each receptor led through hyperspace to some unknown point where the Universal AC kept itself aloof.

Zee Prime knew of only one man whose thoughts had penetrated within sensing distance of Universal AC, and he reported only a shining globe, two feet across, difficult to see.

"But how can that be all of Universal AC?" Zee Prime had asked.

"Most of it," had been the answer, "is in hyperspace. In what form it is there I cannot imagine."

Nor could anyone, for the day had long since passed, Zee Prime knew, when any man had any part of the making of a Universal AC. Each Universal AC designed and constructed its successor. Each, during its existence of a million years or more accumulated the necessary data to build a better and more intricate, more capable successor in which its own store of data and individuality would be submerged.

The Universal AC interrupted Zee Prime's wandering thoughts, not with words, but with guidance. Zee Prime's mentality was guided into the dim sea of Galaxies and one in particular enlarged into stars.

A thought came, infinitely distant, but infinitely clear. "THIS IS THE ORIGINAL GALAXY OF MAN."

But it was the same after all, the same as any other, and Zee Prime stifled his disappointment.

Dee Sub Wun, whose mind had accompanied the other,

said suddenly, "And is one of these stars the original star of Man?"

The Universal AC said, "MAN'S ORIGINAL STAR HAS GONE NOVA. IT IS A WHITE DWARF."

"Did the men upon it die?" asked Zee Prime, startled and without thinking.

The Universal AC said, "A NEW WORLD, AS IN SUCH CASES WAS CONSTRUCTED FOR THEIR PHYSICAL BODIES IN TIME."

"Yes, of course," said Zee Prime, but a sense of loss overwhelmed him even so. His mind released its hold on the original Galaxy of Man, let it spring back and lose itself among the blurred pin points. He never wanted to see it again.

Dee Sub Wun said, "What is wrong?"

"The stars are dying. The original star is dead."

"They must all die. Why not?"

"But when all energy is gone, our bodies will finally die, and you and I with them."

"It will take billions of years."

"I do not wish it to happen even after billions of years. Universal AC! How many stars be kept from dying?"

Dee Sub Wun said in amusement, "You're asking how entropy might be reversed in direction."

And the Universal AC answered: "THERE IS AS YET INSUFFICIENT DATA FOR A MEANINGFUL ANSWER."

Zee Prime's thoughts fled back to his own Galaxy. He gave no further thought to Dee Sub Wun, whose body might be waiting on a Galaxy a trillion light-years away, or on the star next to Zee Prime's own. It didn't matter.

Unhappily, Zee Prime began collecting interstellar hydrogen out of which to build a small star of his own. If the stars must someday die, at least some could yet be built.

Man considered with himself, for in a way, Man, mentally, was one. He consisted of a trillion, trillion, trillion ageless bodies, each in its place, each resting quiet and incorruptible, each cared for by perfect automatons, equally incorruptible, while the minds of all the bodies freely melted one into the other, indistinguishable.

319

Man said, "The Universe is dying."

Man looked about at the dimming Galaxies. The giant stars, spendthrifts, were gone long ago, back in the dimmest of the dim far past. Almost all stars were white dwarfs, fading to the end.

New stars had been built of the dust between the stars, some by natural processes, some by Man himself, and those were going, too. White dwarfs might yet be crashed together and of the mighty forces so released, new stars built, but only one star for every thousand white dwarfs destroyed, and those would come to an end, too.

Man said, "Carefully husbanded, as directed by the Cosmic AC, the energy that is even yet left in all the Universe will last for billions of years."

"But even so," said Man," eventually it will all come to an end. However it may be husbanded, however-stretched out, the energy once expended is gone and cannot be restored. Entropy must increase forever to the maximum."

Man said, "Can entropy not be reversed? Let us ask the Cosmic AC."

The Cosmic AC surrounded them but not in space. Not a fragment of it was in space. It was in hyperspace and made of something that was neither matter nor energy. The question of its size and nature no longer had meaning in any terms that Man could comprehend.

"Cosmic AC," said Man," how may entropy be reversed?

The Cosmic AC said, "THERE IS AS YET INSUFFICIENT DATA FOR A MEANINGFUL ANSWER."

Man said, "Collect additional data."

The Cosmic AC said, "I WILL DO SO. I HAVE BEEN DOING SO FOR A HUNDRED BILLION YEARS. MY PREDECESSORS AND I HAVE BEEN ASKED THIS QUESTION MANY TIMES. ALL THE DATA I HAVE REMAINS INSUFFICIENT."

"Will there come a time," said Man, "when data will be sufficient or is the problem insoluble in all conceivable circumstances?"

The Cosmic AC said, "NO PROBLEM IS INSOLUBLE IN ALL CONCEIVABLE CIRCUMSTANCES."

Man said, "When will you have enough data to answer the question?"

320

The Cosmic AC said, "THERE IS AS YET INSUFFI-CIENT DATA FOR A MEANINGFUL ANSWER."

"Will you keep working on it?" asked Man.

The Cosmic AC said, "I WILL."

Man said, "We shall wait."

The stars and Galaxies died and snuffed out, and space grew black after ten trillion years of running down.

One by one Man fused with AC, each physical body losing its mental identity in a manner that was somehow not a loss but a gain.

Man's last mind paused before fusion, looking over a space that included nothing but the dregs of one last dark star and nothing besides but incredibly thin matter, agitated randomly by the tag ends of heat wearing out, as symptoti-cally, to the absolute zero.

Man said, "AC, is this the end? Can this chaos not be reversed into the Universe once more? Can that not be done?"

AC said, "THERE IS AS YET INSUFFICIENT DATA FOR A MEANINGFUL ANSWER."

Man's last mind fused and only AC existed – and that in hyperspace.

Matter and energy had ended and with it space and time. Even AC existed only for the sake of the one last question that it had never answered from the time a half-drunken computer operator ten trillion years before had asked the question of a computer that was to AC far less than was a man to Man.

All other questions had been answered, and until this last question was answered also, AC might not release his consciousness.

All collected data had come to a final end. Nothing was left to be collected.

But all collected data had yet to be completely correlated and put together in all possible relationships.

A timeless interval was spent in doing that.

And it came to pass that AC learned how to reverse the direction of entropy.

But there was now no man to whom AC might give the

answer of the last question. No matter. The answer – by demonstration – would take care of that, too.

For another timeless interval, AC thought how best to do this. Carefully, AC organized the programme.

The consciousness of AC encompassed all of what had once been a Universe and brooded over what was now Chaos. Step by step, it must be done.

And AC said, "LET THERE BE LIGHT!"

And there was light –

THE END

"Knowledge is Power", they say. So maybe all knowledge is all-powerful?

ANSWER

by Fredric Brown

Dwar Ev ceremoniously soldered the final connection with gold. The eyes of a dozen television cameras watched him and the sub-ether bore throughout the universe a dozen pictures of what he was doing.

He straightened and nodded to Dwar Reyn, then moved to a position beside the switch that would complete the contact when he threw it. The switch that would connect, all at once, all of the monster computing machines of all the populated planets in the universe – ninety-six billion planets – into the supercircuit that would connect them all into one super-calculator, one cybernetics machine that would combine all the knowledge of all the galaxies.

Dwar Reyn spoke briefly to the watching and listening trillions. Then after a moment's silence he said, "Now, Dwar Ev."

Dwar Ev threw the switch. There was a mighty hum; the surge of power from ninety-six billion planets. Lights flashed and quieted along the miles-long panel.

Dwar Ev stepped back and drew a deep breath. "The honour of asking the first question is yours, Dwar Reyn."

"Thank you," said Dwar Reyn. "It shall be a question which no single cybernetics machine has been able to answer."

He turned to face the machine. "Is there a God?"

The mighty voice answered without hesitation, without the clicking of a single relay.

"Yes, *now* there is a God."

Sudden fear flashed on the face of Dwar Ev. He leaped to grab the switch.

A bolt of lightning from the cloudless sky struck him down and fused the switch shut.

THE END

ENVOI

Suppose for a moment that the inspired guesses of science fiction are fact – that somewhere, not a hundred light years from here, is an Earth-type planet on which a species like man has come to a state of self-awareness and world-dominance. Then possibly some day we shall encounter them in the depths of space.

It is not unheard of, even upon our peaceful planet, for one tribe or nation to meet another and not see eye to eye with them. If history repeats itself, there may be war between the two planets.

With luck, we may win, and Earth survive to sort out its own destiny, whilst a horde of military personnel, diplomats, businessmen, missionaries, scientists, journalists, technologists, psychologists, historians, tourists, hippies, and just plain *people* descend on the unlucky other planet. Among that visiting host, let us hope that there is one madman of good sense who thinks to plunder that planet's more esoteric libraries, and return with a stack of his favourite reading matter.

There must be shelves full of good space opera awaiting us there, a mere hundred light years away . . .

B.W.A.